MW01504443

PRAISE FOR THE RAVEN

The most decadent treat for anyone with a sweet tooth for just desserts. The Raven is everything a Medieval suspense ought to be and so much more. Cotten takes her readers on a voyage of vengeance, justice, and healing as her characters fight enemies on two fronts. The darkness around them may even pale in comparison to what lies within their tattered souls.

Hannah Hood Lucero, author of The Sons of Vigilance series

If you didn't think anything could top *The Huntress* or *The Viking*, think again. *The Raven* is an unforgettable roller coaster ride of emotions as we follow Revna on her path of vengeance and self-discovery—which just might lead to a happily ever after as well. Be prepared, because there are plot twists that will have your jaw on the floor and leave your mind blown at Carrie Cotten's storytelling genius! Grab your sword (and maybe some tissues), oh, brave reader, and enter the adventure of a lifetime!

The Raven will sweep you away in a world where the lines of hate and love blur, and the battles aren't only against outside forces, but rather, the battle of one's own demons. This book has everything: Vikings, found family, love, sacrifice, and a beautiful deep, rich faith. Ms. Cotten is a master at weaving together raw emotions and grit while reminding the readers of the hope in the only One who can carry us through life's trials. I highly recommend this book—this series—to everyone, even if it's not your typical genre.

Latisha Sexton, author of In the Midst series

THE RAVEN

CARRIE COTTEN

CARRIE COTTEN
Gripping Christian Fiction

Edited by Sarah Stasik
Formatted by Brianna Goodwin
Paperback ISBN: 9798342801690
Hardcover ISBN:9798342801782
ASIN: B0D3N8B8SV

I sat with my anger long enough until she told me her real name was grief.
C.S. Lewis

For the seekers and searchers. There is nothing earth can offer that will satisfy. It is only found in Jesus Christ. What He offers is complete. Total. Sufficient for every need.

ACKNOWLEDGMENTS

My mind is still unable to comprehend how this series came together. It has been the most exciting, emotional, and educational journey.

First, as always, God gets the gratitude and glory for anything good that comes from this book and series. It is my hope that within the pages and words of my stories, readers are ever pointed toward salvation through faith in Jesus Christ.

There are so many people who helped The Raven take flight! From the beginning, my always ready alpha team; Ashton, Nicole, Kelly, Brianna, and Hannah. Your insight got this story off the ground.

Of course, the extremely talented Jennifer Q. Hunt, without your developmental edits, Revna would have crashed before she even flapped her wings once.

Readers can thank Heather Wood for the extra sparring, which made those scenes just ahhh, chef's kiss!

Thank you to my beta team who helped polish and refine! Heather, Danielle, Myra, and Latisha.

Christine, the Viking expert, is a saint! She endured my endless random questions and guided me accurately through the vague era of 800 AD Scandinavia. I am forever grateful.

And I can't brag enough on my ARC team. These ladies kept me laughing, encouraged, and so excited for this release. Everyone should have a group of supporters like them. The world would be a better place.

Finally, thanks to my hunky husband. All my heroes are born from the best parts of him. He is as patient and faithful as Duncan, as strong and talented as Eowin, and as unwaveringly loyal and protective as Aksel. Our family is blessed to be so loved by a man like Jeffrey Cotten.

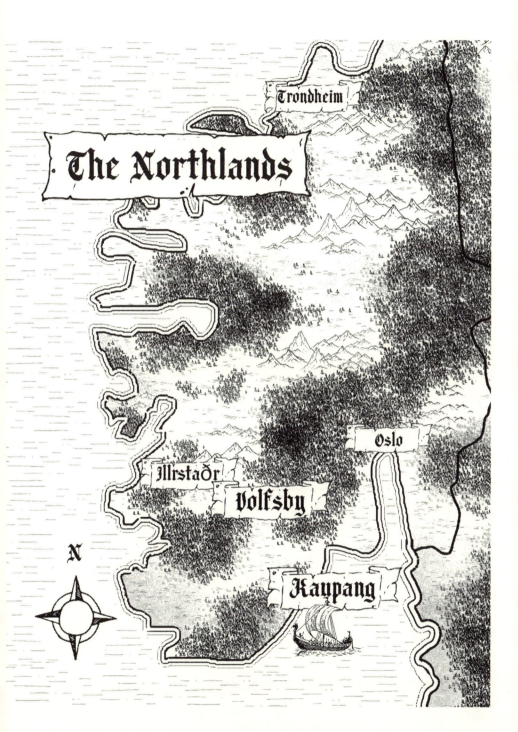

PRONUNCIATION GUIDE

Revna - /Rev-nuh/

Aksel - /Ax-el/

Eira - /Ee-ruh/

Astrid - /A-strid/

Eowin - /Ay·uh·wn/

Cyrene - /Sih-reen/

Ysra - /Yur-sruh/

Isa - /Ee-suh/

Torsten - /Tor-stehn/

Eilidh - /Eh-leed/

Tràigh - /Tʰɾaːj/

An T-aon - /Ahnt-ay-on/

Volfsby - /Vulfs-bee/

Illrstaðr -/Ill-stray-dur/

Kaupang -/Kow-payng/

Trondheim - /Trond-hime/

PROLOGUE

817 AD

Revna

S he stole away to the sea to watch the waves, hoping the other half of her heart would appear on their crests and ride ashore to make hers whole again. A flash of moonlight on the water drew her in as a momentary break in cloud cover released a brilliant sword of white light from the heavens.

But when she reached the shores, that light was gone. There was nothing but a blanket of dull gray fog covering the water.

Up, up, up the sandy dunes she climbed, fingers clawing at the coarse earth. Even though she was just eleven winters, she was skilled at moving silently. Flickering lights in a stone building beckoned her. She knew the chapel would be empty, the holy man long bedded for the night. Mayhap, it was he that left the way lit for lost souls. Mayhap, someone or something else.

Come. Candles winked, teasing her with promises of answers to riddles that kept her awake at night. *Come inside and rest.*

She reached the entrance of the small chapel that sat at the foot of the tower. As she pushed open the oak doors, a gust of wind hit her back. It lifted her midnight hair and swept through the aisles, extinguishing candles in quick succession. All color was vanquished; only darkness remained.

Her foot lingered over the threshold, aching to enter but fearing what lay inside as much as she craved it.

An owl screeched, drawing her gaze to the side. Another beacon of moonlight sliced through the clouds, demanding she follow its path.

It led her to a graveyard. To the home of six headstones.

A delicate limestone marker glowed in the single beam that pierced colorless clouds. She lowered herself to the ground before it, seeking rest. Her bed was lined with needled blades of dead grass atop the mound of a murdered queen's grave. A mother the girl would never know. But that queen never spoke. Not even her ghost was present to whisper comforting words or motherly instruction.

There was nothing carved on the twin markers next to the queen's. The stones were empty, as were the tiny boxes buried beneath. One for her. One for her sister.

Nameless.

As if they never were.

As if she was nothing.

Presumed dead, yet she lived.

"I do not belong there." The girl looked to the tower with its glowing windows. She spoke to the shadows, but she was not afraid. She thought of the enchanted dark forest where another queen waited. "I do not belong there either."

She blinked. The moon was shielded again, leaving nothing illuminated.

I will welcome you. The darkness whispered honey sweet words.

2

Here is where you belong. Safe—in the dark—where nothing is seen. Do what you came to do. I will shield you.

She glared at the silent tower. At the barely flickering light in the window of the king's quarters. The girl felt a tug at her lips. The fool. He slept so high above his subjects, hidden and guarded. As if stone walls and armed men were enough to stop a shadow. To stop her.

He is to blame, said the night. *He needs to pay.*

So she became as the night, donning her cloak of shadows.

Dark.

Silent.

Deadly.

Then she slipped into the tower, easily uncovering a narrow, hidden tunnel. The entrance was exactly as the storyteller described that morning three winters past when she took the girl to the edge of the wood and pointed to the cold stone structure, sharing a tale of the girl's true lineage. How she lived when it was meant for her to die. The day the shadows began to pursue her.

A purpose, the storyteller had said. There was a purpose for her pain and for her life. But the storyteller didn't live long enough to explain. She was taken, as so many others had been taken. The girl was ready to do some taking of her own.

The tunnel—located in a far corner of the church—opened when she pressed a hand flat against loose stone in the back of a hearth. Just as it had in the tale. As if the storyteller meant her to seek it out and enter.

She watched her softened leather boots, their touch on the stone whispers as she wove through cold, hollow halls. The eyes of sentries skimmed over her lithe, unmoving form, mistaking her for a shadow. She tossed stones along a forgotten stair, and the guard's eyes wandered, investigating the noise.

The flicker of candlelight escaping the bottom edge of a large oak door gave her pause, but only for the length of a breath. Then she was through and pasted against the backside before the hinges could groan and the sound of returning footsteps could join the soft hush of a sleeping man's breaths.

His long form stretched over rumpled blankets, one arm lazily draped over his bare chest and the other hooked over his head. The king. Her father. The man who had taken everything from her.

He was vulnerable. Exposed.

In a blink, the girl was a hair's width away, a knife clutched in her small, trembling hand. With a flick of her wrist, the weapon spun, its tip positioned to plunge through flesh and bone—into the organ that certainly must exist to keep him alive but she doubted had any feeling.

She ticked her head to the side, measuring the rise and fall of his chest as air moved in and out of his lungs. Air he had no right to breathe. Not when he'd stolen it from others.

The shine of her blade caught a flicker of flame from the candle on his bedside table, and in a blink, her hand whipped to snuff out the light.

What she needed to do must happen in the dark. It was justice she held in her palm. Righteousness she came to deliver.

She would have to be swift. Rage gave her strength, but she was no fool. She was slight—not yet a woman—and though she'd been trained since she was a bairn, she was not a warrior like the Pictish queen of the woods where she lived. If he woke, he could overpower her in an instant. Stifling a growl, she lowered her dagger.

No. A quick death would not do. His crimes were brutal and lengthy; so should be his end. She would be patient.

He would look into her eyes before he took his final breath. Her face would be the last thing he would see. He would answer for his cruelty and heartlessness. He would dwell in the same darkness he forced upon her.

She was nameless, but he would know her even still. His last words would be that name she was owed. As much as her mouth watered for vengeance and her blood sang for justice, she would wait for that day.

A hearth on the far wall housed the few surviving embers of a dying fire. She snatched the bucket of water from the hearth's side and slowly poured it over the coals, jerking her sharp eyes back to the sleeping king to make sure the hissing didn't wake him.

He slept. Unmoving. Unknowing.

She pressed her hand into cooled ashes mixed with water. Rubbing her fingers together, she created a thick, dark paint.

She raised her hands and sketched a message on the cold stone walls of his chamber.

The girl stepped back, taking in the entirety of her art. It was crisp and black against the gray stones. A perfect warning to haunt his dreams and disturb his slumber for many nights hence.

He shuddered in his sleep, as if he'd received a vision in his dreams. But he did not wake. For this one night, she would allow him rest. The morning sun would usher in the beginning of his torment.

She crept to his bedside again, careful even of the sounds of her breath. A heap of empty mugs, still reeking of staunch ale, littered the floor next to his bed. The girl knew he'd not wake if she were gentle—if her touch was light. With wet ashy paint that still coated her fingers, she traced a matching shape across his forehead. He remained as the dead while she worked.

Her lips pulled back into a wicked grin as she imagined his guards rushing in the next morning, stirred by the sound of his startled cry. She swallowed a bubble of laughter, almost hearing their gasps at the discovery of her masterpiece. First on the chamber wall and then painted across his brow. A great bird with onyx wings spread wide. The symbol of coming death. They would show him a mirror, and he would know how close death had been. That it was waiting.

And she—the nameless one, the raven—with it.

I

REVNA

821 AD: Four years later

"Ye are the one, Revna." *Emerald eyes, silvered with tears, grew wide with a terrible, churning mix of sadness and fear as she pleaded. "It has to be ye."*

Revna shook her head. She wasn't a leader; she stayed in the shadows. That was her place. What the queen was asking...what she was trusting her with, she could not accept.

"Take them over the mountain," Cyrene instructed, as if she knew of Revna's birth, of who her parents truly were. But she couldn't have known. No one knew then. No one living. "'Tis ye who must act in my stead should we fail on the battlefield. 'Tis ye who must love and care fer them."

Revna didn't take them over the mountain. Because she would not let the queen fail. But when she dove into the mob of enemy warriors and came up bloody yet victorious, she met the queen's eyes across the battlefield.

What have ye done? The queen's lips moved with no sound, yet there

7

was deafening anguish. *Revna knew what Cyrene's expression meant. 'Twas ye. Ye who I gave a name. Ye who I loved. 'Twas ye who is the keeper of the storyteller's final tale.*

What have ye done?

Those same green eyes fell on something in the distance. Something that drained the color from Cyrene's already pale face. Wake up. The queen begged, backing away, fading into the shadows.

Wake up. Cyrene's voice was all around, pounding against the shield the darkness had formed.

"Revna. Wake up!"

Revna jerked awake at the sound of heavy footsteps nearing a hatch covering the small cargo space in the hull of the longboat where she was hidden.

Her joints screamed from being cramped in such a small space. She bit back a groan as she pitched herself forward and sprinkled a pinch of herbs over the last bits of dried fish in the nearest storage crate. There was no time to get into the barrel of bread or cask of mead. Dagger gripped tightly in her fist, she flattened herself against the shadowed hull as hinges creaked when the cut planks were lifted.

She couldn't risk leaning closer to see who stood at the opening, but she spied rounded toes of worn boots and leather-clad legs. An arm dusted with light colored hair and decorated with bluish tattooed designs reached into the space, grasping the ropes that secured the wooden crate containing the fish.

The crate vanished and Revna nearly released a sigh of relief, expecting the hatch to close again. But it didn't. She tilted her head a fraction, just enough to view the opening better but still remain in the shadows. A pair of golden eyes settled on her face, and Revna's blood turned to ice. Crouched at the opening, a Viking sailor stared at her.

Neither moved. She forced herself to breathe. He was young, mayhap even as young as she, his beard just beginning to thicken around his chin but trimmed close at his jaws. His head was also shaved close at the sides, and any brown hair not pulled back in braids fell in tangled strings around his shoulders. He tilted his head as she had, just enough to see her better without giving her presence away.

Someone spoke behind him, and he looked over his shoulder. Throat instantly dry, Revna tightened her grip on the dagger. She let the fingers of her other hand roam for the hilt of her sword, ready to draw despite the close quarters.

She should pounce now while she had the chance to attempt escape. But something told her to wait. To be patient.

Her feet tingled from her cramped position, and she doubted her ability to stand should he announce her appearance. Once on deck, her options were few. There was little chance she could best the entire crew, but if she could make it to the edge of the longboat, the sea would offer a swifter death than the men. That ending would be far less violent, at least.

She shifted as much as the space would allow and flexed her aching toes, willing them to give her the strength she needed to flee. The young warrior turned his head sharply toward her, giving her the slightest shake of his head.

A warning? A threat? Revna didn't know. She heard the approach of a second set of footsteps and ice returned to her veins. He looked up at whoever neared, flicked his eyes once more to hers, and then lowered the hatch door, hiding her away.

She froze, unsure what to do. Would he tell the others, rip open the hatch again, drag her to the deck, and mercilessly toss her at their feet? She'd been slowly adding her herbs to their food and drink since they departed. They'd be weakened but not incapacitated. Her only weapons were her dagger, her sword, and the bucket she'd been using to tend to her needs for the week she'd been curled into the small space. It might slow a man down should she chuck the putrid contents but only for a few seconds.

She waited, dagger at the ready, legs alternating stretches to attempt to get her blood flowing again. But he didn't return.

After what seemed like hours, the surge of energy that had jerked her awake and held her rigid during the encounter with the young Viking fled her veins, and she sagged against the hull of the boat, feeling boneless. The effect was similar to that strange rush of power and strength that had overtaken her body during the battle against the army that had attacked Tràigh. The battle that ended with these Norsemen fleeing her home shores and her secretly chasing them. That energizing urgency had vanished completely in the hours after the Viking longboat sailed from Tràigh with her hidden aboard.

Revna inhaled deeply, wishing that urgency had released her before she boarded the longboat, giving her back the use of her mind instead of obeying the intense need for vengeance that tricked her into thinking she was invincible. Then again, she couldn't truly blame that mysterious force; most of her decisions had been powered by fury since she was a lass. Now she was facing the very real consequences of her impulsive actions.

While crafty and skilled with a blade, she was also a girl of fifteen winters. And this longboat was brimming with dozens of grown men. Warriors who'd just been shamed into retreat by the Pictish queen—her queen—and Revna's brother, the king of Tràigh.

Staring at the thin layer of wood separating her from those very warriors, she suddenly felt very foolish. Keeping her eyes on the hatch, she listened for approaching steps.

Night came. Then dawn. The hatch didn't open. Revna ground her teeth against the slow torture of waiting. Her attempt to remain awake and alert made her eyes sting. Despite the twisting in her insides, she ate from the stash of bread she'd pulled out before dosing the rest with her herbs.

At least she'd had the foresight to bring several water skins in addition to her gut-twisting leaves. She'd drained the skins too quickly, though. Now she was exhausted and thirsty. Her traitorous eyes had just dipped closed when she felt the boat slide ashore.

It was night again. The grunts from rowing and barked orders had quieted, overtaken by the sounds of the crew emptying their stomachs over the side. Revna's dry lips pulled back into a cruel grin. Bless Gertrud and her insistence on continuing the lessons on herbs that her mother, Brigid, the storytelling healer, had begun. Revna shook sleep and haunting memories from her mind, swallowing against the thickness in her dry throat. She could not allow regret to overpower readiness. The sound of footsteps pounded and then quieted, as if they'd all disembarked. She let out a long breath. She was safe for the moment, but they would return. The tip of her sword dug into the wood between her feet and Revna rested her forehead against the flat side of the blade, chastising herself for her youthful brashness.

Fool. She was such a fool. In the middle of her self-loathing, the hatch door opened again. She forced herself back into the shadows.

"Girl." A whispered voice beckoned her, curiosity winning over caution because she understood—he was speaking her language. The language of the Vestlands.

Dipping her head, she peered from her hiding spot and recognized his silhouette. It was the young Viking from before. She eased out of the shadows and he did the same, enough that the moonlight bathed his face. His skin was a little greener than it had been before, and darker shadows scooped divots under his amber eyes. His lips and brows lifted, encouraging her forward enough to reach the bulging water skin he held.

"Take it." His whisper was raspy and he shook the offering, glancing over his shoulder as if to ensure no one was approaching. "Fresh. From the streams ashore."

His words carried the heavy accent of his people, but they were clear enough. She snatched the gift and scurried to her hiding place before he could turn his head back toward her. Sniffing the liquid and deciding it was worth the risk, she gulped a mouthful.

"I dunna ken why you are here, but if you want to live, stay hidden. No matter what." He tipped his head, a pointed gaze delivering the seriousness of his warning. "This vessel is cursed."

She lowered the skin. Droplets worked their way down her chin as she stared at him. He stared back until she nodded in agreement. Before he closed the hatch, she found herself doing something completely against her better judgment.

She lifted a hand. He stilled, only moving to cast another glance over his shoulder.

"'Tisn't a curse." Her always hoarse voice was even raspier from the dryness in her throat. She swallowed hard. This was not a good idea. At all. And yet, her mouth moved, tongue over teeth, forming words. "Dunna eat the food or drink the mead."

He tilted his head to the side, his odd colored eyes softening to understanding as she gave a small nod.

"If anyone else but me opens this hatch, hide." A voice from behind had him lowering the hatch and he was gone.

Whatever he said stopped the approaching footsteps. When they turned and moved away, Revna released the breath trapped in her lungs. She was in the dark again—still cramped and nearly suffocated by the smell of urine and unwashed bodies, but a bit of the tension that had threatened to rip through her chest and steal her courage eased.

She was not completely alone. For the first time since she boarded the boat, she slept deeply and without dreams.

When the boat ran ashore the next night in a different place and the crew disembarked, the hatch opened again and the young Viking appeared to extract another poisoned crate of rations.

"Dunna eat it," she reminded him, wondering why he hadn't informed his crew mates of her confession.

He only nodded. Still, he looked weaker, his cheeks sunken. The herb would not kill, but it would steal all strength and inflict enough misery in a man's guts that he would wish for death.

He offered her another skin of fresh water.

"Thank ye," she whispered.

He nodded and moved to close the hatch, but in another irrational moment of impulsivity, Revna raised her hand as she had the night before. "Wait."

He paused.

"How do ye ken my language?"

He glanced around, his movements sharp and tense. He was taking a risk in keeping her secret, and she was risking her own safety by keeping him longer, but she had to know something— anything about this Viking who was nothing like the pure savage plunderers she'd always imagined. He positioned himself so his back was to the shore and let one long leg dangle in the cargo space.

"My father led many voyages across the sea; he said if I learned the language of the Vestmen, I would be a valuable asset to any crew."

He unsheathed a dagger strapped to his waist and Revna tensed. She relaxed when he held it by the blade, showing her the elaborately engraved hilt.

"He gave this to me on my first voyage." He flipped the blade, catching it by the grip. "The carvings tell of the great warriors from Trondheim."

"Trondheim?"

"A settlement in the north. My home."

The blade was sharp—she could tell just by looking at it. Its leather-wrapped grip looked sturdy and worn, as if it had been handled enough to fit perfectly into its bearer's palm. The open mouth of a dragon was engraved into the metal hilt, intricately decorated with scales, loops, and swirls.

"'Tis a good blade. Strong and beautiful," he said.

"Lovely." She meant it too. "Is that where this vessel will land? Yer settlement?"

"Nay," he sighed, brushing his hair out of his face as he looked up at the sky. "Nay, we will land far from there."

He kept his face aimed at the distant stars but let his gaze slide to her. "Do ye mean to allow this boat ashore?"

When she didn't answer, he rolled his head to the side, fully facing her. "I dunna think yer hiding down there because ye aim to be part of the crew. Especially if yer slowly poisoning us, which is quite clever, by the way."

"I had...plans," she finally answered, slightly breathless.

"Had?" He raised a brow.

She lifted a shoulder. "Now I just want the same as ye. To reach the Northlands alive."

He nodded, crossing his arms over his chest and leaning back against the propped up hatch covering.

"Will ye ever return?" She tilted her head, observing him. Measuring his reactions to her questions. "To yer settlement, I mean?"

"I havena been there in many winters. I dunna even ken if my father still lives. I'd like to think he does. That he's heard of his son's many voyages and is proud." A gentle smile tugged at one side of his mouth, revealing a deep dimple in his cheek as he turned the dagger in his fingers.

What would it feel like to have a father who loved her enough to give her such a beautiful gift? Her father had certainly been wealthy enough, but he'd never given her anything. Not even the satisfaction of being the one to take his life after all the evils he'd committed. No, that right was stolen by some short-lived plague. He left her nothing. Not even a name.

"What are ye called?" the young Viking asked, his head cocked to the side, as if reading her thoughts.

She considered lying, unsure if she should reveal her identity, but in truth—she was no one. She was a ghost. Unnamed. Unseen. But Cyrene had called her "Revna."

It felt strange to speak the name Cyrene gave her to this Viking, knowing he'd been in the crowd of warriors that had come with the intention of killing her beloved queen. What had changed for him? She opened her mouth to ask, but he spoke first.

"Revna," he repeated, his brows knotting together. They relaxed as he slid his golden eyes to hers in interest. "Like the bird?"

"Aye." Her dry lips pulled back into a half-grin.

"I am called Rune."

They were silent again and he shifted backwards, making room for the hatch to close.

"Rune."

He stopped. She took a portion of her unpoisoned bread and fish and offered it to him. He stared at her too long. She started to lower her hand when he reached in and accepted her gift, his fingers warm as they brushed hers.

Tucking the rations against his chest, he smiled a fraction in return. He was what she imagined other lasses would call braw, and for the first time in her life, she wanted to be seen.

As he lowered the hatch door, Revna pushed herself out from her hiding place and fully into his view. The hatch only opened a crack, but his golden eyes surveyed her face, taking in every detail. She wondered what he saw. She was not still a lass yet not a woman either. But like Rune, she would have evidence of years in her expression—a weight he also carried in young eyes that had seen too much.

Her heart beat wildly. What was she doing? Even in her crazed, unreasonable movements, she kept one hand behind her back, fingers tightly curled around her dagger. Every second he lingered was a second the crew had to discover her. A second he had to change his mind about helping her. It was also a second she had to breathe cool salty air instead of the stifling, musty stench of the hull. It was a moment to speak to another human being—something she never knew she would miss until she'd spent seven long days in silence.

"What does it mean? Yer name?" she whispered, fighting the urge to close her eyes and bathe in the wisp of fresh air that slipped in from above.

The corner of his mouth lifted again, and as he lowered the hatch the rest of the way, he whispered back, "'Tis a secret."

Revna crouched in her lightless cell, stunned by his answer. What did that mean?

When he returned the next night, he moved hastily, only lingering long enough to trade her water for more portions of the food she'd stowed away. A strange bite of disappointment pinched her heart when he disappeared without a word. She slept peacefully though, nothing but a flitter of sadness wafting through her dreams.

The next day, she could tell the sun was in full display by the golden rays that poured between spaces in the planks above her. Revna wilted in the breezeless space below deck. The stench of sick sailors, salty air, and rotten fish had her gagging more than once, and she pressed her hands hard over her mouth to keep from giving away her presence with a fit of coughing.

One soft sound slipped through her fingers, and she squeezed her stinging eyes closed, willing her throat to swallow any more outbursts. Surely the rush of waves would have covered the noise. Her body rebelled, and when she felt the constriction of her throat, a lonely sea shanty erupted from above, masking her cough.

Other voices joined in, and soon the stifling air was filled with a haunting chorus of song. The deep melody was eerie and slow, but it calmed the panic that had taken hold of her nerves. She nestled into the sacks of grain that had become her makeshift bed. Sweat poured down her forehead and spine, and the heat stole her energy. She just had to hold on a little longer. They had to reach the Northlands soon.

Her people were waiting for rescue. For her.

She listened to the crew's singing, making up her own words to the tune.

Captured and caged. Too long have ye stayed, o'or in the lands of woe. No more shall ye wait, the raven has came, to set ye asail fer home.

Revna nearly laughed aloud at her version. The long days and cramped quarters were certainly going to drive her mad. If only she'd brought herbs that calmed the mind in addition to those that caused cramping and churning stomachs.

A flashing memory of the yellow-haired healer stole two of Revna's heartbeats. Brigid. The soft-spoken storyteller that held knowledge of herbs and history.

It was Brigid that bade her keep her lineage quiet, even from the queen. When Revna was eight winters, the same age Cyrene had been when she became queen to the few Picts who escaped the king's wrath, the storyteller had come to collect her—just her—to help in locating a rare herb for her healing poultices. But they'd not gone to the usual haunts where rich beds of lichen produced colorful and pungent plants. Instead, Brigid had taken her to the edge of The Dorcha, where they could spy the top of the tower of Tràigh peeking over distant hills. She could still see Brigid's strong form silhouetted alongside trees against a brightening sky.

I'm going to tell ye a story, Revna. A story that is only yers to hear. One that will make ye hate me and the world, but it's one ye must hear and one ye must learn to overcome. All our lives depend on it.

The story Brigid told was of a raven haired lass who had the blood of a murderous king flowing in her veins. A lass whose father had brutally slain her mother. He blamed the Picts for her death, and in retribution, sold the ones he didn't slaughter to the Norsemen as slaves. The storyteller said if the queen's Pictish handmaiden hadn't secreted the lass away as a bairn, she would have suffered the same fate as her mother.

Revna asked about the handmaiden who saved her. Eden had been her name. She hoped against hope Eden might yet live and would know her true name. But the storyteller only hung her head. Eden was gone, as were so many others.

But Brigid's tale was not yet finished and had a twist Revna never expected.

The raven haired bairn wasn't the only one the handmaiden swept up in her arms. There had been another princess. A twin sister.

One who was thought dead but who'd disappeared with the Picts who were chained and shipped off to the Northlands.

That was the day Revna's fury took flight and she swore a secret oath that she would make it right.

It seemed that oath would remain unfulfilled. Her half-brother Duncan, the new king, granted mercy instead of justice to the warband of Vikings. They'd negotiated with the king's cousin, William, for a share of the spoils if they helped him sack Tràigh. William was no blood relation to her. He was the nephew of the first queen—of Duncan's mother. Revna's gut twisted at the thought of his betrayal. The sick alliance he'd formed with the Norsemen—a trade of flesh and blood. Still, Duncan let them live.

William might have anticipated Tràigh's alliance with the neighboring kingdom of Nàbaidh, but he hadn't bargained on another union. A secret one between the king of Tràigh and the Pictish queen who was nothing more than a legend of the dark woods. William hadn't expected the skilled Pictish warriors, with their bows and blades, to hold off the enemy armies until Nàbaidh arrived.

He couldn't have guessed those warriors would be filled with an otherworldly strength and speed that kept them alive and fighting long after they should have been felled by simple exhaustion.

And those Norsemen William had bargained with? When their longboat returned to the Northlands, their lives a gift of mercy from the king of Tràigh, they would not expect a plague in the form of a fifteen-year-old Pictish lass they'd unknowingly brought back with them.

That raven-haired lass from Brigid's story would deliver the vengeance the Norsemen were owed. She would fulfill her oath and bring home Cyrene's people, her murdered mother's people. Wrath flowed in her veins, that was true. But if whatever made her father a murderer and enslaver was in her, Revna swore to use it to make wrong things right.

Revna's hand drifted to the small pouch sewn into her vest. Her fingers traced the outline of a folded parchment tucked inside. Brigid's list. The storyteller did her best to record the names of each villager stolen from the fallen Pictish kingdom when Revna was just a bairn. As Revna explored the shape hidden under the softened leather, resting just over her heart, she could picture the tear-drop shaped stains marking the parchment and how Brigid must have wept over their lost people as she scratched their names in indigo ink. How she ached for the ones who had already been forgotten, for the names that no one knew—including Revna's twin sister.

"Revna?" Rune's voice carried a bit of worry. She jolted upright. They were ashore again, and she'd been so lost in her thoughts—so exhausted from the heat—she hadn't heard the scraping of the hatch door.

"Aye?"

A small sigh reached her in the dark, and she dragged herself forward until she could see him. He looked less green and more pink, his eyes the warm honey color she'd first seen.

"You dinna answer, I thought..." He shoved another water skin toward her. "We are close now. We should reach the Northlands tomorrow."

She handed him the last of her rations—the ones she would have eaten herself but kept aside for him.

"Thank ye." Her reply was weak, but thoughts of how she would manage to escape the boat undetected filled her empty belly. Something in her eyes must have betrayed her hunger, because he halved the rations and handed her back a portion.

"Did ye like my song?"

Revna's eyes flicked to Rune's face as she tore off a bite of the crusty bread, finding him with one brow arched and a half grin displaying that deep dimple.

"That was ye?"

He lifted a shoulder. "There was a little bird making quite a bit of noise below deck."

"Ye did that fer me?"

Rune lifted a shoulder again, and his expression grew serious. "When we come ashore, stay hidden. I will make sure I'm the one to unload the supplies."

Revna nodded, relief flooding her veins.

"It shouldn't be too hard, considering I'm one of the few who can still stand."

She flicked her eyes back to his, chewing her bottom lip. Was he angry that she'd poisoned the rest of the crew? Relief turned to suspicion, and she felt her mouth form a hard line.

"Why are ye helping me?"

Rune didn't answer for three breaths, and Revna held hers until he did.

"I've seen enough of death and darkness." Something passed across his expression that told Revna he was speaking truth. "And I was given a second chance at life by the mercy of yer king. Feels only right to return the favor."

She knew what happened to the army of William's men Duncan had trapped in the keep. When Rune and his crew flooded the keep, the sight of those trapped men was meant to send a message that the battle was already over. But she'd heard their screams followed by silence. The men the Norsemen slaughtered were supposed to be their own allies.

Rune stared at his hands, rubbing them together as if trying to wipe them clean. Were his palms stained by the blood of those men? Was helping her his attempt to return from that dark place?

"I..." Rune shook his head as if he couldn't find the words he wanted to say.

Revna nodded. The same darkness still swelled around her, threatening to overtake and drag her into endless depths. It was only the despairing emptiness in Rune's eyes that encouraged her to resist a little longer.

"My father was right. Though I'm but seventeen winters, my gift fer languages led me to join voyages to different lands." He turned his amber eyes on her, his gaze tracing the lines of her face as he offered his arms, showing her the inked designs covering his skin. "To all who see these marks, I am a mighty warrior. We tell stories of powerful gods and we try to please them. We worship ruthlessness, celebrate a glorious death, and fer what? To earn a place in Valhalla only to fight another battle fer another god who cares nothing fer us?"

"Is that what ye believe?" Revna drew closer to him, nearly

touching the leg he let dangle over the edge of the opening in the hull. He gazed down at her with many questions in his eyes; she wished she had answers to give him.

"In my many voyages, there is one story I've heard over and over, from different peoples and tribes. 'Tis the story of a God above all other gods. One that left His kingdom in the stars and came to our lands, walked our soil as one of us, to grant an eternity of peace instead of war."

Was he speaking of *An T-aon*? Surely, he hadn't heard of Cyrene's God.

"Can I tell ye a secret?" His lips twitched, as if he were fighting a smile.

"Like yer name?"

"Aye." The deep chuckle that resonated from his chest sent a chill skating across her skin.

Rune leaned in, bracing his hands on either side of the hatch opening and lowering his torso until her face was bathed with his warm breath.

"I believe in that God." His eyes danced back and forth between hers. "I want that eternity."

Revna found herself wanting it too.

"Is that why yer helping me?" she asked, genuinely desperate for the answer. "Do ye hope to earn that God's favor?"

"I dunna think it's something that can be earned. The stories say 'tis a gift." He held her captive with his searching gaze. Then his lips pulled back into a full grin, displaying two dimples in his cheeks. He playfully brushed the back of his hand under her chin as he sat up straight and pushed himself to his feet.

"Also, I quite like the clever little bird who snuck aboard our boat. I want her to live." His dimples appeared again, but he was gone before she could respond.

Revna settled back into her hiding place, slowly eating the meager rations and humming the tune of Rune's song in her mind, thinking of the secret he'd shared until she fell asleep again.

Her dreams were filled with booming thunder, shouts of dying men, and the coppery smell of blood. Revna awoke with a start to something dripping on her brow from a crevice in the deck above.

It must have stormed in the night. That would explain her terrible dreams and the drops splattering her forehead. Though she must have been more exhausted than she realized to sleep through such a tempest. She wiped at the wetness, but it didn't feel like water. It was thick, and when she drew her hand away, a dark streak painted her palm. It wasn't water. There had been no storm.

Panic seized her insides, muscles tensing at the sounds that reached her from above. Shouts. Cries of pain. The thud of something man-sized dropping on the deck just above her. And the smell.

Fear. Blood. Death.

She closed her eyes and listened. Some kind of battle was raging above. She could hear the clang of metal, shuffle of feet, and grunts of men colliding against each other. The boat was unusually steady, though, as if they'd slowed. That must have meant they were close to a shore.

Rune told her to stay hidden—that he would help her escape. But what if that was his blood dripping through the cracks? What if the one helping her, her friend, was dead?

A plan. She needed a plan. In the chaos, she could slip on deck and grab Rune. They could launch themselves overboard. She was a strong enough swimmer that she could reach the shore if they weren't too far. Surely Rune could swim too. If not, she would drag him with her.

She moved toward the hatch, stretching her legs one at a time and bouncing on the balls of her feet to ensure her body would not fail her when she needed to move swiftly. The crew was still weakened from her trick with the herbs. There was a chance she and Rune could survive. She had to take it.

The sounds from above grew quieter, as if the battle had moved to the other end of the boat. Blade in hand, Revna pushed against the hatch door, easing it open. Something blocked the way, and she was forced to use her shoulder and leverage her weight to urge it upward.

She managed to crack the door enough to fit her head and shoulders through. A heavy obstruction still pushed the wood down against her. Sliding through the opening, she kept low on her belly, noting that the obstruction was the lifeless body of a Viking sailor.

He wasn't the only one. There were bodies everywhere. Revna's stomach lurched and she slapped a hand over her mouth to keep silent. At the front of the boat, a tangle of men grappled with one another. It was a furious mass, and she couldn't tell if there were two sides battling or if it was every man for himself. What had happened?

Keeping her body flat on the deck, Revna pushed herself backward, slithering like a snake over the bloody bodies. She had to reach the edge of the boat.

She scanned the faces of the dead as she crawled over them, searching for Rune. Mayhap he'd already escaped. Mayhap he was in the brawl of men, fighting for his life. She paused, her mind and heart waging their own war. The smart thing to do was to escape while no one would notice, but what if her friend was in trouble?

One man shouted words she didn't understand, but she recognized his gruff voice as the one who barked orders on the ship—the one who had stood beside the leader that Cyrene had taken down with her arrow outside the tower.

He must be the new leader. And he was slaughtering his crew.

As Revna watched, it became clear. Some fought each other, but most of the men fought against him. Revna caught a glimpse of Rune in the fray and let out a relieved breath. He was still alive. For now.

It looked like he was trying to break up two sailors and turn their attention to the leader. To the enemy they could defeat if they'd all work together. She was not the only clever one aboard.

With her help, they would have a better chance. Just when she was pushing herself up, aiming for Rune, his amber eyes landed on hers.

"No," he mouthed, shaking his head before his eyes darted to the edge of the boat, giving her silent instruction.

Still, she hesitated. When he narrowed his eyes, she huffed a breath and pursed her lips as she silently acquiesced. He would rally the men. They'd defeat the leader. Rune would be fine. They'd meet on the shore, and he'd tell her what drove the leader to this madness. She would have a friend in this strange land.

Revna silently rooted for him as she continued her journey across the deck. She tried to keep her eyes on the battle and not look down at the twisted faces of the fallen men so close to hers as she crawled over them.

Breathe in. Breathe out. Keep moving.

Her hand pressed on the chest of one of the sailors, and a gasping breath pushed through his lips. Revna stared with terror as his eyes flew open and his face distorted with pain. She looked up at the battle again. No one noticed her yet. But the sailor began to groan, and Revna slapped a hand over his mouth.

"Shh," she hissed, her hand trembling.

His breath rattled in his lungs and hitched in his throat. Revna lay over him, her face just inches from his. Without lifting her body, she shifted herself until she was beside him. With her free hand, she felt along his body until her hand sank into something warm and wet.

His injury was deep and grave. A slicing wound through his middle that exposed his insides. Revna's stomach revolted and she closed her eyes, forcing her body to remain calm before she met his wild, agonized gaze.

"Shh," she said again, bringing her blade up without taking her eyes off of his. "'Twill be over soon."

She knew he couldn't understand her, and another groan passed through his lips along with a cough and spray of blood that coated her cheeks.

"Shhh," she begged, but he couldn't hear. She could tell from the darting of his eyes that he could no longer see. His end was near, and he was suffering.

Lowering her head, Revna guided her blade upward, direct and sure into his chest where she knew it would pierce his heart. In seconds, his body stilled. Even though it was an act of mercy, it didn't ease the guilt.

"'Tis over," she whispered, eyes burning with salty tears. Running her hand over the man's face to close his eyes for the final time, she said again, "'Tis over now."

Her chest was so tight she thought her own heart had gone still. The dark blood on her blade was a disgusting sight in her eyes. She'd boarded this boat with a craving for that darkness, that blood, but now she only wanted to get as far from it as she could. Fool. What a fool she was.

Limbs shaking, she continued her path to the edge just when the traitorous leader, struck hard with the dull end of a battle ax, spun and his head whipped in her direction. Revna froze. Without hesitation, he came back around with a swing of his own weapon, burying the end in the skull of the crew member who'd been fighting to live.

Then he turned again. Dark, hate-filled eyes came to rest on her. A spark of recognition turned his barred teeth into a lustful grin and Revna's blood to ice. He was going to kill her—or worse.

She'd stood next to Cyrene on the battlefield when the queen fired that single arrow that pierced his leader, and he clearly remembered her. He was going to make her pay for their disgrace. It was over.

"Fly, Little Bird!" Rune's voice bellowed over the rush of waves and grunts of battle.

Her heart kicked into a sprint, pushing a beat against her ears and a streak of pain up the muscles in her throat. She was on her feet, blade in hand.

He took the first step, and Revna matched his movement with her own retreat. In a sheer battle of strength, she would be ended in a second. When she met the dark eyes of the murderer hungering for her blood, she determined it wasn't fear he would see in that split second.

Revna reached inside, seeking the darkness she'd been ready to abandon seconds before. It hummed from the buried pool deep in her gut. A haunting melody. She searched for the string she could tug to unleash its song. There, at the corner of her heart, it waited. When the leader curled his lip, arrogance filling his greedy smile, she yanked that string and let free the rhapsody that constantly thrummed under her skin.

She felt the corner of her mouth peel back into a confident sneer. Before they reached the shore, this murderer would bear her mark and feel the hard side of her blade.

She took two steps toward him, seamlessly unsheathing her sword. A soft song vibrated in her throat. Flipping the blades in her hands, she let loose a cry and rushed the enemy. Before she even reached him, she flicked her dagger through the air. It found purchase in his bicep, drawing a roar of anger and pain. All the while, she sang with the choir of darkness and rage. She snatched a shield from a felled sailor, and before the leader's shout faded, she brought her sword down, aiming for his neck.

He blocked her strike with his uninjured arm, but she spun and sliced the sword's sharp edge across his thigh, bringing him to his knees. She tried to dodge his ax, but he was still too strong, too quick. From his knees, he didn't have the height to put much force behind his blow. It was the only advantage that kept her from being brought to the ground. Her raised shield took the brunt of the hit, but it still vibrated through her bones, nearly shattering them.

The other sailors finally rallied under Rune's direction, and the leader fought a battle on two sides. Revna jabbed, ducked, and parried. Sailors dropped under the force of his ax until only Rune, one other sailor, and Revna were left.

"Look out!" Rune shouted.

She jumped back, barely missing a blow that sent her tripping over fallen men. The leader turned and aimed for Rune, his blade just missing Rune's chest. The blow would have split him in two.

They were tiring, but the leader looked as if he were just reaching his stride. He must have had his own stash of food and mead. He wasn't the least bit winded or green as he brought down the final crew member.

She and Rune were left. They were going to lose. As Revna surveyed the deck, littered with bodies, she saw the faces of her own people instead. She felt the pain of their deaths, the ache of loss for those who had been taken, and she drank it all in. She let it fuel the darkness that begged to be embraced—the want that demanded to be eased.

A coat of red hazed her vision. Revna launched herself at the crew leader. She spun and ducked, swinging her sword with merciless rage. She saw nothing but her prey, and she was the ruthless hunter. In a blind fury, she moved like the wind, untouchable and every-where. She was one with her blade as it sliced through the air. The leader met her with force, and she was lost to the battle between them, never letting him land a blow. She saw nothing else, heard nothing else.

The second she saw her opening, she drove her blade forward, her full weight behind it. But at the last moment, the leader spun and she flew past him, and her blade drove into the chest of the man she didn't see behind him.

Into Rune. His golden eyes went wide as her sword sunk in before she could stop herself.

"Nay!" she screamed, grabbing him as he fell. His weight pulled her down with him. "Rune."

What have ye done? She thought he'd said it, but the voice came from inside of her.

He lifted his arm, pointing to something behind her as a shadow fell over the both of them. Fury, grief, and vengeance still swirling in her, she grabbed the closest weapon she could find and turned, burying a short blade in the crew leader's thigh nearly in the same spot as her first slice.

He bellowed in pain, dropped his hatchet, and stumbled backwards. Revna rose and marched toward him, snatching the weapon he'd abandoned. The crew leader's eyes widened a fraction, and Revna relished the fear that consumed him. He reached the edge of the boat, scanning the deck as he realized he was unarmed. He could still block her blow if she tried to outmatch him. Instead, she lifted the hatchet over her head with both hands and sent it flying. It met the hard wood of the ship's side in the exact place where his chest had been. But he was gone. He'd launched himself over the side into the water.

"Nay!" She slammed into the side just in time to see the waves swallow him whole.

She screamed in rage and jerked the ax free from the edge of the boat, hurling it into the water. He shouldn't get to flee. He shouldn't get to steal her revenge—just as the plague took the life of her father. Not again.

"Revna." Rune's rasped words seeped through her fury.

She raced back to where he lay. He'd pulled out her blade, and she pressed her hands to the gushing wound in his chest.

"Rune," she croaked, her throat near to closing out words altogether. "Ye dunna get to die. Ye hear me!"

"I hear ye, my raven," he said, covering her hands with his.

"Why? Why did he do it?" Revna frantically searched the area close to them for anything that could help Rune—and for some answer as to why the crew leader would have attacked his own crew. *Please dunna let it be the herbs that drove him mad, please dunna let it be my fault.*

"Dishonor." Rune let go of her hand, his arm falling limp at his side. "He would be outlawed fer returning in defeat."

"So he killed his crew?" Salty tears burned her eyes, and she blinked them away, spotting the torn tunic of a nearby sailor. She ripped the fabric from the man's body and balled it up over Rune's wound.

"If he was the only one left, his would be the only story." Rune gasped in pain, and his body tensed.

"He's not the only one left." She turned hard eyes on Rune, willing her words to keep him breathing.

When his eyes fluttered closed, she shook him until he opened them again. "Ye are left, Rune. Ye can tell the story. Ye tell them what a coward he was. 'Tis yer duty."

"Aye." Rune's breath rattled in his lungs, blood trickling from his colorless lips.

"Ye tell them!" Revna's chest was too tight; she couldn't breathe.

"Clever little bird." Rune's golden eyes found hers, a soft smile on his lips and that blasted dimple denting his cheek. He lifted a shaking, cold hand to her cheek. "Find the light. Meet me in eternity."

"Rune."

He was still looking at her, but he no longer saw her.

"Rune."

He didn't see anything. He was gone.

And she'd killed him. The one who had tried to help her. Her friend.

When he'd spoken of eternity the day before, for a brief bright moment, Revna had believed there could be a future for her that was something other than dark and lonely. She should never have dared to hope.

She felt something hard against her skin and looked down at her blood-covered hands. Rune's dagger. The beautifully crafted gift from his father. He'd pressed it into her palm.

Revna shook him, but he did not breathe. She slammed her fists on his chest, but he did not wake. She screamed for him to live. But he did not listen. She knelt at his side and pleaded with him to speak again. But he did not answer.

"I'm sorry." Her words were a strangled whisper as she curled her hands into this torn tunic. "I'm so sorry."

Revna looked down at the red stains spreading across her clothes. *What have I done?*

She balled the fist of the hand that had taken Rune's life and pressed it to her breast. There, just over her heart, beneath the bloodied fabric of her tunic, was a mark on her skin. It had appeared the day Brigid had shared her final story—the day Revna began to plan this very mission.

She thought it was a sign that mayhap the God that Brigid worshiped truly was real. But then, hours later, Cyrene stumbled into the village bleeding from a wound to her ribs with a story of how Brigid was taken by the sea. Revna saw through the lie. Brigid hadn't been to the sea. Brigid had never left the place where she'd told Revna the story. The place that was exposed to the tower where the murderous king lived and where his murderous soldiers patrolled. The king had taken from her yet again. After that day, Revna turned her back on hope from anyone but herself.

Still, the mark remained.

"Why?" she croaked, clawing at the symbol that burned as if it were branded on her very heart. She stared at the cloudless sky. "Why am I marked?"

The sea and sky were silent.

"Why?" she screamed. For the first time since she was a bairn, hot tears seared her cheeks and dripped from her chin. She collapsed on Rune's unmoving chest, pressing her forehead to his. "There is no light, Rune. Not fer me."

When the screech of seagulls pierced the quiet, she pushed herself to her feet. The shore was in sight, and the longboat coursed toward the water despite having no crew. The rippling sound of fabric drew her eyes upward. She didn't know much about sailing, but she knew that boats lowered their sails when coming ashore.

Her body moved as if powered by sheer muscle memory. She picked up a short blade and moved to the ropes that were still pulled taut by the massive sail. She hacked until they snapped, diving out of the way when the mass of fabric fell into a heavy heap where she'd been standing.

Flipping the sword in her hands again, she cut a section of the sail free, carrying it to where Rune lay. She didn't know their language or how to write their symbols, but she could still send a message.

SOAKED WITH SEA WATER, Revna watched from a rocky outcropping as the people gathered on the shore saw her message. Mothers gathered children in their arms and raced inland as the flaming ghost ship plowed ashore, a torn strip of white canvas bearing her mark and flying on the mast where the sail had been.

A raven. Wings spread wide. Painted in blood.

2

AKSEL

825 AD: four years later

The burn of strong mead barreled down his throat as he slammed the mug onto the wooden table and beckoned a servant for another. The maid who'd clung to him all afternoon had long since drunk her fill and was softly snoring as she lay, torso draped over the table, yellow hair tangled, and drool darkening the sleeve of her tunic.

It was the second night of the spring festival of Ostara, and the Chieftain had ordered the mead hall to be opened early. Rumors of the god Odin's ire had blazed to life again. It was just as it had been four harvests past. From Kaupang to Sarpsborg to Oslo, longhouses, barns, and great halls turned to ash. Slaves missing, bloody handprints the only thing remaining. And the symbol. Always the symbol. Painted in black on the side of a freeman's home or even a Chieftain's longhouse—the symbol of a raven.

In a bold move, Chieftain Tollak did not cancel the festivities but chose to endorse extra celebrations in an attempt to show the people of Kaupang had nothing to fear under his protection. Unlike the Jarl before him, the one who could not prevent Odin's wrath, Tollak was determined to prove his right to rule such a large settlement after having been Chieftain of a much smaller one.

The ravens had not visited Kaupang since he won the position. They were safe; the Chieftain swore it.

"Aksel," Guntar Liefsen collapsed into the space beside him, mead sloshing from his overfilled mug. Guntar pressed his shoulder to Aksel's, his ruddy face only inches away and bloodshot eyes clearly trying and failing to focus on any target. "Did you speak with the Chieftain about a truce with Ellerton?"

Aksel's hand flew to his side before he could stop himself. His ribs were still bruised from his attempt to bring the matter before his father. But before Aksel spoke of the meeting, Guntar continued, words interrupted by hiccups but making perfect sense.

"We have long been enemies, but we have goods they need from trading with the foreign ships, and they have the fields we need for grain." Aksel made no attempt to hide a grimace when Guntar shoved his elbow into Aksel's side, but the other man appeared not to notice. "It is the alliance we need to survive."

Aksel had known what would happen; it was always the same. But Guntar had looked at him with such hope that Aksel took the risk. It was a good plan. A smart strategy that would provide exactly the outcome Guntar had suggested. But a truce with the long-time rival and neighboring settlement of Ellerton would require Chieftain Tollak to spare an ounce of humility, and the mere suggestion had thrown him into a fit of rage.

"Trust your Chieftain, Guntar." Head lowered, Aksel repeated the words his father had spat into his own face. "He will keep Kaupang thriving."

"If we do nothing, there will not be enough this harvest, especially if the settlement continues to grow as it is."

"It is not wise to question the Chieftain." The words felt bitter in

Aksel's mouth, but it was the only answer he had. It was a warning that might spare Guntar's life if he would heed it.

Despite the amount of mead Guntar had consumed, evident from the sweet smell that seeped from his pores, the man leveled a disgusted look at Aksel.

"What are you good for?" The question landed on Aksel's cheek with a spray of saliva before Guntar pushed himself from the bench and stumbled over to a group of men huddled at another table.

Aksel didn't look, but he could feel their eyes on him. Their own glares of disappointment crept over his shoulders and sank into his aching chest.

"What indeed?" Aksel's muttered remark was swallowed by the sound of his empty mug slamming against the table.

Aksel stayed plastered to his spot on that roughhewn wooden bench, knowing Guntar's ire would fade with each round. It wasn't long before he was back at Aksel's table, a limp arm draped over his shoulders and a loud, slurred song in his ear.

Well into the evening, and well into his tenth mug, Aksel's head was swimming. His tongue was thick in his mouth, and his face heated to near flames. As the conversation around him faded into incomprehensible murmuring, his own voice grew louder, joining with the other townspeople in songs led by the group of skalds that arrived that morning with colorful costumes and instruments. Tomorrow, Guntar and the rest of the villagers would go back to asking for his help and glaring with disappointment when he could not deliver, but tonight he was simply one of them.

The table where he sat lurched forward, and Aksel turned to see the terrified face of a servant girl who'd been shoved against it. A burly man with ruddy cheeks and glazed eyes held her from behind, his meaty hands fumbling with the strings of her apron. He'd apparently had more mead than Aksel, if that was possible. Giving up on the apron, the man's hands roughly groped the girl's body, and the men surrounding them only laughed at her struggles.

"Ivar!" Aksel called.

Ivar lifted half closed eyes from where he was scraping his beard across the girl's neck. "I already have plans for that one."

Ivar sneered with more vitriol than he would have dared had he been sober. Aksel might not have sway with his father, but he was still the Chieftain's son. He'd still been trained by the best warriors. His skills were well known and evidenced by the blue inked designs scrolling up his forearms.

Realizing their friend's mistake, Ivar's companions pulled him away as he unleashed every unsavory word in his vocabulary. By the time they'd dragged him through the hall, he'd toppled several chairs, upended one rotund mead server and released a guttural belch that very nearly had his friends abandoning him to the offended crowd of burly drinkers near the door.

To save Ivar's hide, and perhaps also his own, Aksel reached into his coin pouch and tossed several bits of silver on the table.

"Buy him some bread to ease the sting." Aksel's words came slowly, and he laughed at their heaviness. Then he loosely waved to the grumbling men glaring at Ivar with violence in their eyes. "And another round for my patient friends!"

Someone shoved the girl into Aksel's lap, and he felt the breath shoot out of his lungs at the same time he felt her petite frame turn to stone.

"Please...I..." she trembled in his arms. She was far too young to be reveling with these men, but Aksel's mind was too fuzzy to think of how she might have ended up here. Drawing upon the last remaining bits of sobriety, he formed a plan.

"Take a message to the ale master, girl," Aksel said loud enough for those around him to hear, then he lowered his voice, finishing his slurred message in a volume only she could hear. "Go. Make haste to your home, and do not return until after the festival is over."

She stared at him with wide eyes as if it were some kind of test she would fail if she obeyed. He jostled her on his knee, jerking his head toward the open door. "Go."

Without a word, she raced for the door and disappeared into the night.

He sloshed back another mug and attempted to lift his hand to signal the servant that was pouring mugfuls as fast as his arms could lift pitchers, but Aksel's arm felt as though a hundred battle axes were strapped to his wrist. Then the packed earth floor was at his back, knocking the breath from his lungs.

Through gasps, he laughed, his arms flailing too much for anyone to help him up. The music picked up pace; people rose to dance and boots slammed into the ground around his head, one colliding with his temple so hard it sent stars across his already blurred vision.

An overly joyous reveler kicked him in the jaw, and blood filled his mouth. Then he was flying. No. Not flying. Someone had yanked him up off the ground. And that someone growled in his ear.

"What beast...oh, hellllo Rendellll." Aksel chuckled to himself at the way he'd drawn out his brother-in-law's name.

Rendel did not share in his amusement. He only flung Aksel's arm over his shoulders and looped a tattooed arm around Aksel's waist, swearing and grumbling at Aksel, "Use your worthless legs!"

Aksel scrambled to get his feet under him, but he could no more control his limbs than his laughter, causing Rendel to increase his swearing.

Eira's husband was no small man, but he struggled under Aksel's long frame. If there had been any concern over his growth when he was a small, sickly child, it certainly disappeared in adolescence when Aksel had grown to tower over even his father.

"You could at least try to stand," Rendel grunted.

"And deny you the glory of this rescue?" Aksel was little help as he accepted the kisses and hugs of all the brash maidens who called his name and begged him to stay longer. Even in his drunkenness, he knew the want and praise was more for the coin in his pouch than true affection. Still, to be wanted, for whatever reason, was a temptation he could not resist.

"Mead for all!" When Aksel reached into his purse and tossed a handful of coins in his wake, a cheer chased him out the door, which had been propped open most of the evening.

Rendel and Aksel tumbled outside into the spring evening; though warm, the air was not as steamy as it was inside.

His brother-in-law growled again, throwing his arms up and releasing his charge. Aksel bent, hands braced on his knees, emptying his stomach onto the packed-earth path leading to the mead hall.

"I swear, if you were anyone else, Aksel!" Rendel's insults were drowned by more retching.

Weakened but still laughing, Aksel's hands slipped, and he went down, barely avoiding planting his face in the dirt by landing on one knee. He ran the back of his hand across his mouth, wincing at the forgotten split in his lip.

"Come." Rendel tried to lift him, but jumped back as Aksel threw out an arm, blindly swiping at the empty space around him.

"Leave me."

He was slightly aware of townspeople coming and going from the mead hall, more embarrassed for them to see Rendel fawning over him than to witness his inebriated state.

"Get up!" Rendel tried again to lift him, but without Aksel's cooperation, he couldn't raise him more than a few inches off the ground.

Aksel snorted at Rendel's order. It was the fact that Aksel refused to stay down that infuriated his father so much. But that was all the power he had against the Chieftain. He would always get back up.

"Eira will have my head if you drink yourself to death."

The mention of his sister erupted a flare of loneliness in his chest. Their home had been so cold, so empty, in the two winters since she'd moved out and into Rendel's.

"I said leave me!" The force with which he resisted made him lose his balance, and he landed on his backside in the dirt. Eira was his baby sister, but she'd fretted over him since she was old enough to lift her finger and order him about. Now she was gone. "Eira did."

As soon as the words left Aksel's mouth, Rendel's face was inches from his. Unapologetic rage burned in the Viking's eyes as he drew Aksel closer with a hand fisted in his tunic. "You will not make her feel guilty. She owes you nothing."

Aksel met Rendel's glare with one of his own. Of course she didn't, but that didn't make her absence any less painful. She was promised to Rendel two winters before their handfasting, and Aksel knew she convinced Rendel to wait so she might stay with her brother just a little longer.

"Why are you here, Rendel?" Aksel turned his face away from his brother-in-law, slouching back against the wall when Rendel released him.

"Because I cannot say no to that woman, and she cannot see you for the *dunga* you are." Rendel blew out a breath. "She is too good for you."

"She is too good for you too."

"At least I know it." Rendel aimed for Aksel again.

Aksel lifted his hand, stopping his approach. "I said leave me. Just tell Eira what she wants to hear."

Rendel stepped back, glaring at Aksel for a moment. "Fine."

Aksel looked up with half-closed eyes to find a blurred Rendel scowling, his arms crossed over his broad chest. "When Odin's ravens find you out here and pick your bones clean, I'll be happy to step into the place of Tollak's shameful son."

"Don't you have a boat to sail or something?" Aksel pushed himself backward on his palms until his back collided with the rough, splinter-covered outer wall of the mead hall. He laughed through a cough as he narrowed his eyes at the bluish markings swirling up Rendel's muscular forearms. Aksel's tattoos might boast of battle skill, but Rendel's were the coveted signs of voyages. Inked tales of all his successes. "A village to plunder to add to your renown?"

He joked, but a chill skated across his skin at Rendel's threat. Everyone knew of Huginn and Muninn, Odin's ravens sent to report back to the god the level of his people's faithfulness.

"Kaupang is safe from the ravens." Aksel breathed, and then added a little extra bite to his next words. "Have you not heard? The Chieftain has declared it so."

"Sandefjord was struck just two days past." Rendel nodded when Aksel rolled his head to the side, looking up at him. This was not news; everyone had already heard. "They made offerings. Slaves and livestock still disappeared. Homes and stables still burned. Kaupang will suffer the same. Perhaps the spoiled son of a rich man will be enough of a sacrifice this time."

"They will not come here. The offerings made last night—"

"Were not enough." Rendel's cold words offered Aksel a split second of sobriety.

When Aksel didn't reply, Rendel continued.

"If you would pay the least bit of attention, you would have heard already. Galdvyn's slaves were gone just this morn."

That was news, but Rendel's taunting smirk heated Aksel's blood, and he retaliated with a lazy smile across his numb lips.

"They could have simply run off. Galdvyn is a feckless rake."

Rendel ignored Aksels' insults.

"He searched the woods when he discovered they were missing. They found him stumbling and wild-eyed in his own fields, his clothes missing and his skin streaked with blood and ash." Rendel shook his head, looking to the sky as if asking the stars for strength. "They say he soiled himself from fear. He was talking out of his head of a raven in human form, winged death itself, cloaked in shadow atop a midnight steed."

Aksel pictured Galdvyn's round, ruddy face alight with terror as he poured out his story while trying to hide the stench of his cowardice. When a snorted laugh burst from his lips, Rendel looked at him as if Aksel suffered the same delirium as Galdvyn.

"I am too quick for Odin's ravens. But you..." He rolled the *r* of

Rendel's name on his tongue. "Rrrrendel, mighty wolf-shield of Kaupang... you would make a fine offering." Another laugh sputtered from his lips at Rendel's frown.

"Indeed I might. To save my people, to protect what's mine, I would gladly march to the offering stone. What have you given? Nothing but disgrace to your family and your people."

When Aksel's smile disappeared, Rendel called him a vulgar name and turned back toward the mead hall as a stumbling group of revelers poured out. He caught the door before it could slam into Aksel and waited for the group to clear before he took a step.

Rendel shot a teasing sneer over his shoulder when he caught sight of something that was blocked from Aksel's view by the open mead hall door.

"This really is your own fault." Rendel scoffed as Aksel gazed up at him, confused. Rendel held the door and bent to whisper, "Your father is here."

It was Rendel's turn to laugh at Aksel's clumsy attempt to scramble to his feet.

Even drunk on mead, Aksel was quick. Before the door closed again, exposing him to the approaching Chieftain, he managed to drag himself around the corner into the shadows.

His father never came to the second night of Ostera. According to him, it was only for "the drunks and those who wish to rob them."

Ah! Aksel was such a fool. That was before Odin's ravens. Of course his father would come. He would need to be seen and make a toast to Odin and Freya. He would need to do what was necessary to ward off the curse. To keep his settlement from burning. Though Aksel doubted his father held true belief in such things. He had always been too busy worshiping himself.

But after the news of Galdvyn's missing servants, the Chieftain would make a show of his presence. Even in his third winter as Chieftain, he was considered newly named and there were still those who would oppose him. Those who didn't trust his ability to protect them. Rightly so, it would seem, if the curse returned.

Panic swelled in Aksel's chest. If slaves were truly disappearing, he needed to get home. He tried to push himself up to his feet, but his knees gave out halfway and he landed hard on his backside again.

Even though he could barely keep a lucid thought for more than a few seconds, Aksel knew his father would be furious with his drunken display. The Jarl would add *foolish* and *undisciplined* to the list of Aksel's many faults. Any hope of securing a spot on the next raiding voyage would be snuffed out. Again.

He dragged his fingers through his sweat-soaked hair, dusting his reddish-brown locks with gravel and dirt from his hands. Trying to force sense into his brain, he knocked the back of his head against the hard wooden wall behind him.

He figured his father meant for him to die when he sent him as a twelve year old boy to train amongst the savage warriors. That was Aksel's greatest offense against his father. He simply would not die. Not in the sickness that weakened him as a child, not amongst the warriors, and not now, no matter how much mead he drank. He just kept getting back up.

Even though he eventually bested all those savage trainers, it only seemed to stoke the flames of his father's ire against him. It had been nearly fourteen winters and he'd still not been allowed to join a voyage. It had become clear he'd never leave Kaupang.

He would live and die in the stuffy longhouse. There would be no ink on his skin depicting his successes on the seas. He would spend his days among the same faces, hearing the same stories and walking the same paths, knowing their troubles and fears better than anyone but being powerless to help them.

His parents didn't even think him worthy enough to seek a bride for their wayward son. Rendel and Eira would carry on the line. They would bless the clan with their offspring.

Rendel was right. It really was his fault. That morning, Tollak had ordered him to make sure everything was prepared for the second night of the feast. It was a demeaning assignment meant for a servant, not the son of a Jarl, and yet—Aksel had failed at that too. It took just one settler, begging him to stay, and he'd drowned himself in mead and dug into the baskets of bread that were supposed to be kept back for the morrow's feast. Odin's feast.

Trapped in the lure of the settler's affections, he'd consumed two full loaves himself, tricking his body into thinking he could in turn consume more mead.

He dragged himself further into the shadows, near the backside of the mead hall where full barrels of sweet smelling drink were stored. At least there he wouldn't be easily seen by someone passing by. It was quieter, but still he could hear muffled echoes of the revelry inside. Boisterous sounds of celebration continued in his absence, despite the people's claims that all joy left with him. Invisible, purposeless, useless. All the names his father had for him swirled in his mind, blurring his vision and reminding him why he'd sought reprieve in mugs of the sweet golden liquid in the first place.

His head fell onto arms he'd draped over his knees, and he groaned at the nausea that swept through his stomach. He'd planned to replace the bread before the feast, keeping his failure hidden while earning the Jarl favor with the townspeople who'd cheered his name when Aksel began tossing loaves to outstretched hands.

Rendel would surely relay his condition to the Chieftain. His father would yell; his mother would simply sigh and stare at nothing as she always did. He wasn't the son she'd hoped for either. They had Rendel though. The great wolf-shield of Kaupang.

The son of a wealthy freeman with many voyages and victories under his belt looked more like Chieftain Tollak than Aksel did. Muscular and dark-haired, Rendel was not as tall as Aksel but broader. If it weren't for Aksel's mother's auburn waves, so similar to his, he'd have sworn he didn't belong to them at all. When he'd said such one night, his mother had blanched and turned away—not that she ever did much else. He didn't speak of it again; he'd only succeeded in pushing her further away.

He should be preparing an explanation for when he faced his

father; he should get home, but his plans only drowned in the mead-filled bog of his mind. A heaviness had already sealed his eyes closed, and he felt the world tilt before rolling waves of silence and darkness carried him off to oblivion.

3

REVNA

T he man slumped against the wall of the bustling mead hall didn't move. Revna, flicking her sharp eyes in each direction, took one step. A midnight black mare matched her steps. Revna's breath was warm against the black linen mask stretched over her nose and mouth. She stroked her hand down the soft nose of her horse, whispering a command for the animal to stay still and silent. Sgail was smart, easily trained, and—once rescued from her master's cruel hand—as grateful for Revna's company as Revna was for hers. Always awkward with people, Revna felt a kinship with animals, particularly horses.

Assured by Sgail's quiet snort that the beast would remain in place, Revna raised the dark hood of her cloak over her head and took another step, keeping her weight on her toes. Her fingers danced along the opening of the leather pouch at her side, ready to make use of its contents if necessary. She'd tweaked the recipe slightly after the last batch sent the settler racing through the fields naked. She'd had a good laugh, but she wanted people terrified of the woods—not entertained. Entertainment led to curiosity, and curiosity led to trouble.

Sounds of music and revelry had drawn her close, and the now-unconscious man's interaction with the hulking dark-haired Norseman even closer. At least, she thought he was unconscious. He looked more dead than alive.

She crept close enough to see his chest rise and fall again. He was dressed differently from the rest of the villagers. Better. She had been too far to hear everything, but from what she could interpret from their conversation, she thought his name was Aksel and he was the Chieftain's son. Even if she had translated incorrectly, she'd seen him toss a handful of silver over his shoulder as he was dragged from the mead hall. It was the only reason she'd approached.

Mayhap he still carried enough coin to do her some good, as she certainly wasn't looking for what the old woman in Sandefjord suggested.

Lingering in that small settlement might have been a mistake, but after visiting its bustling market, she'd spied an old woman who never left her stool in the shadow-kissed corner between two merchant stalls. Curiosity got the better of her, and Revna approached the milky-eyed old woman. Like Revna, she seemed to be a person who knew things others did not. Also like Revna, the woman was invisible, passed by and ignored, though she never reached out or begged. She simply...waited.

The woman seemed to sense her approach though Revna didn't speak. Without a word, Revna offered a loaf of crusty bread she'd purchased. The woman's nostrils flared, and when she stretched a weathered hand, Revna didn't recoil but allowed the woman's leathery fingers to wrap around hers.

"Take it, Móðir." Revna spoke as few words as possible in the Norse language. "Tell me, is there a settlement near that is home to many slaves from the Vestlands?"

At the sound of her voice, the woman stilled, narrowing unseeing eyes.

When Revna moved to withdraw, her fingers tightened. Again,

Revna didn't jerk away. She allowed the woman to pull her down to a crouch. Allowed soft, wrinkled fingers to explore her face.

When she answered, it was Revna's turn to freeze, because she spoke in Revna's native tongue.

"I've heard that sound before—the tone of yer words. From the Vest, ye are. Before I was brought here, I lived in another settlement. Kaupang has what ye seek. A prince waits fer ye there, lass."

"I dunna seek a prince. I seek boats and passage to...distant lands."

"Kaupang has what ye seek," she said again.

Revna had been to Kaupang before, when she first landed in the Northlands. It was nothing more than a small trading post then. She almost dismissed the old woman's words.

But when the crone wrapped the spindly fingers of one hand around her wrist and touched her cheek with her other, the heat that blazed from the mark on Revna's chest nearly knocked her off her feet.

"Kaupang has what ye seek," the old woman repeated her eerie chant.

Even when Revna jerked free, stumbling back and slipping unseen through the crowd, the fire on her skin remained. It was only satiated when she crossed the border into Kaupang. While there was little to be found in the port settlement four winters ago, Kaupang had changed drastically.

She quickly learned that a new Chieftain had taken over and the borders were nearly bursting. She'd have never known that without the chance encounter with the strange old woman.

Sometimes things come by chance, Revna. But sometimes they do not. And sometimes memories of Brigid's cryptic words snuck up and assaulted her without warning or permission. With a shake of her head, Revna brought her mind back to the present and focused on the man at her feet.

Was this the old woman's prince? Revna gave him a soft kick. He didn't move or even groan. She stepped between his long outstretched legs, bending slightly to see him better in the dim light.

He looked like any other Norseman: pale skin, reddish brown hair, thick beard, inked designs wrapping his muscled forearms. He wasn't quite as brawny as most of them, but he was nearly as tall as Eowin.

Revna huffed at the thought of the king's captain—her brother's captain. Her jaw ached with the force with which she clenched her teeth, and she forced herself to release that tension.

Fighting back guilt over leaving without explanation was a daily battle. But Cyrene was the queen of two kingdoms now. She was guarded; she was safe. Astrid would make certain of that.

The queen's captain only looked fair—her moon-white hair and pale skin made her impossible to ignore, especially paired with her distinctly Norse features. But she was no dainty beauty. She was fierce and deadly accurate with a bow, but instead of the savageness usually displayed by the people of her homeland, the Viking-born captain demonstrated relentless protection of the queen. Like Revna.

Except Astrid hadn't abandoned Cyrene without a word. Astrid hadn't boarded a ship and disappeared over the horizon, leaving her queen wondering what had happened to her. That's why Revna needed to stay the course and not let anything—or anyone—distract her. *I'll bring them all back.*

She'd made a promise, and she intended to keep it. She wouldn't leave them to suffer. Even if it cost her life and her heart, she would bring them home.

Revna twisted her head, stretching the tense muscles in her neck before she dropped to a crouch before the unconscious man. She searched the pouch at his waist, finding it empty but for a lonely coin.

"Hmm," she growled, tucking the coin in her own pouch. "Not much of a prince."

His head lolled to the side, and a tangled curtain of hair fell across his face. Her hand instantly dove for her other pouch. Herbs crushed to a fine powder coated her fingers, but she didn't withdraw her hand. Instead, she poked at his shoulder.

He didn't stir.

She shoved him once, and then again, harder. Still, he didn't respond. Confident he wasn't going to wake, she wiped her hand clean on her trousers and roughly gripped his chin, turning his face to view him clearly.

From the way the old woman in the market had pressed her hand to Revna's heart when she spoke of the prince, she must have thought him to be quite the prize. Revna scanned his face again, brushing back his hair. It was more auburn than brown now that she looked closely. Whoever had gushed about his good looks to the old woman had greatly exaggerated. Well. Maybe not *greatly*. He wasn't too bad. For a Viking.

Then again, the old woman was clearly out of her mind, droning on about handsome trolls as Revna left her.

She didn't bother with gentleness as she released him. His head made a soft thud when it collided with the wall, eliciting an unconscious groan. Still, he didn't move. Sighing, she pushed herself up and glared at him.

"What a waste." She crossed her arms, mentally running through her options.

With half the men of Kaupang gathered in the mead hall, she'd have a better chance of getting close to their slaves and possibly locating some of her people.

She glanced down at the man again and had a sudden flash of inspiration. She felt the corner of her mouth pull up in a wicked grin. Sliding her satchel from her shoulders, she withdrew a wax pouch of charcoal paint made with oil and gathered ashes from the celebratory bonfire the settlers of Kaupang had burned the night before.

Painting her raven right above the sleeping head of the Chieftain's son might send a strong message.

The old woman had been wise to send her here, even if she didn't know the true reason. There were ships arriving daily, and from the

48

looks of their sailors, their homelands were varied. All it would take was a vessel sailing close enough to Scotland's coast and a bit of coin, and the trade ships would make a small detour. As soon as she gathered enough coin, she could send another gift of her own back to Tràigh. With the freed Picts she'd collected on the way to Kaupang, this would make the fourth vessel she'd loaded with rescued Picts in as many winters.

This was the largest settlement she'd visited so far, and scouting such a broad area without raising suspicion when slaves began disappearing was more than troublesome. If there was only a way to collect all her people and enough coin to send them home at once.

She looked again to Aksel, tempted to use an herb that would force him awake and demand to know where his father kept his riches. A surge in the noise from inside the hall urged her to abandon that idea and make haste with a more reasonable task. She'd have to settle for him being a pawn instead of a prize.

She dipped her fingers into the chalky black paste and began adding art across the rough logs of the mead hall. Something about that paint emboldened her, as if the Norsemen's fear was embedded in the gray ash. With great sweeping strokes, an image appeared. Ash from their burning villages would provide the paint for her symbols, and their coin would pay the passage for her people to return home. All that was taken would be restored.

Teeth grinding with passion, heart pounding with fury, she guided her hands over the logs, creating the vast wings of the raven. The shadowed side of the angled mead hall was hidden, but not so much that someone couldn't stumble upon her—especially if that someone had drunk too much mead and needed a private place to relieve himself. So she worked quickly.

Stopping only to pull splinters from her fingers and jerk the cloth mask down from her face for a few breaths of cool air, she was nearly finished when the lump of a man at her feet groaned and rolled over. Revna had planted her feet on either side of him, needing to get as close as possible to the wall to trace the bird's head. She didn't have time to untangle her feet from beneath him, and the weight of his limp body pulled her down. She swallowed a yelp as she was brought to the ground.

The breath whooshed out of her lungs at the impact, and a blinding flash of white light filled her vision as the back of her head bounced off the hard ground. Something firm clamped on her ankle, and she was hauled across the rough ground, her fingers flying toward the leather pouch at her hip. But her head was swimming, her fingers were covered in paint, and she fumbled with the flap.

When she blinked herself into reality, her breath halted again. Aksel was staring down at her, two shaking arms braced on either side of her head. Her face was uncovered. Her identity revealed. She scolded herself for not blowing powder into his lungs from the start.

Never let them get their hands on you. That was the number one warrior rule, ingrained in her mind from the moment she first stepped into the sparring ring at six winters old. That this near unconscious Viking didn't even have to try and got past her defenses, that he'd been one of the few people to ever catch her off guard, lit a fire in her belly.

There's always a move to be made. That was another rule, and the one she had to use now that she was pinned beneath his very warm, very close frame.

When she scrambled for her pouch, his large hand clamped down on her wrist, holding it immobile. Mayhap he wasn't as inebriated as he let on. He was even closer, still holding himself over her with one muscular arm—not that she noticed or cared one bit for his muscles.

She'd never been so close to a man—to a person—and when her eyes met his, that fire in her stomach spread. Rage. That's what it was, most certainly, because he made her vulnerable.

She should fight him off. The grip of a dagger was within her reach, but there was no violence in his glassy blue eyes and his mouth pulled to the side in a half grin. Revna froze, waiting as he peeled his fingers from her wrist and slowly placed his hand beside her head again.

"Are you Huginn or Muninn?"

She wasn't familiar with those names, and with the added difficulty of his slurred speech, she wasn't sure what he'd asked—though something about the words reminded her of one of Astrid's stories she'd heard in passing. For once, she wished she'd made time for Astrid's tales. She also wished her fingers weren't coated in ashy paint so she could reach the powder in her pouch that would send the prince's eyes rolling back in his head and his mind reeling with ghostly visions.

Those very eyes cleared for a split second. He tilted his head to the side, braced himself on one arm again, and lifted his free hand to brush a strand of hair away from her face, tucking it behind her ear. The warm tips of his fingers barely touched her skin, and yet her heart slammed against the bony cage holding it inside her body. What was wrong with her?

Mayhap his fingers were coated in his own poisoned herbs, because she couldn't move. Everything was motionless. Her limbs. The breath in her lungs. Even the heart in her chest had gone still. She'd never been touched like that before, not with such... tenderness.

"You are very beautiful, Little Bird."

She understood that clearly enough. *Little Bird.* Revna hissed, locking up beneath him. Then she noticed how his arms shook.

Oh, no. He was about to collapse. She'd die right there under his weight. A black handprint decorated his chest as she pushed him off with a groan. Luckily, he didn't resist and was unconscious again before she'd raised herself to her knees beside him. His eyes were closed, but he'd seen her. He'd touched her.

Clever little bird. Meet me in eternity.

The memory of Rune's final words had her eyes stinging. Aksel had called her the same name. Her fingers traced the path his had taken along her cheek. Realizing what she was doing, she jerked her hand away from her face. There was definitely something wrong with her and it was obviously his fault.

"What do I do with ye now, prince?" Revna growled to herself, knowing he couldn't hear her. She rolled him until he was flat on his back.

The powder would keep him subdued. It would also torture his mind with shadowy, terrifying images. She'd never hesitated to use it before, but for some reason, the thought of blowing it into this man's face—seeing his eyes widen and fixed with terror—kept her clean hand from reaching across her body to the pouch.

She'd watched since the doors of the mead hall were opened. He was the worst sort of man. Nothing but the spoiled son of a wealthy Chieftain used to getting everything he wanted. A drunk who was latched to a different woman every few minutes. Though they were mostly latched to him—and she didn't see him grope them like the rest of the Norsemen did—he hadn't earned any respect from her.

Except for the strange instance of the young maid who'd been pawed at by another man and then shoved into Aksel's lap after whatever words they'd exchanged. From where she watched, she couldn't understand what he said, but the girl had fled the mead hall, unharmed, seconds later.

She considered propping him up just beneath the drawing of her raven and adding talons that appeared to reach for him. She didn't know much of what these Vikings believed, but her handprint on his chest might mark him as cursed. She smiled at the thought.

"It would serve ye right." She gave his leg a soft kick and an insult in her native tongue. "*Cladhaire.*"

He was everything she despised about her enemy. Ungrateful, entitled, and lazy. His food and clothes came at the expense of her enslaved people. His world was built on their backs. And he didn't care about any of them. He only cared about drink and pleasure. Except for the maid he'd helped. And the teasing, warm look in his eyes...the softness of his touch.

Why did those wretched thoughts keep coming to her mind? Had

Aksel played a trick on her? Was her half-serious theory true, and his fingertips *were* coated with mind-altering herbs?

Before she knew it, Rune's blade was in her hand, fingers burning as she gripped it tightly. Better than the drawing would be the dagger buried in his chest. That would certainly make a statement. When his body was discovered, she could fashion herself wings from wax and feathers, ride through town on Sgail's back, and walk straight onto any available ship with no resistance, all of her people in tow. Her preparations had sent the whispers and tales of the raven ahead of her wherever she went. One dead Chieftain's son could solidify that lore into enough terror she could simply take what she needed and leave.

He could usher in that new era. One sacrifice for the good of many? Worse things had been done. She flipped the blade, knelt beside him, and brought it swiftly toward his chest.

What have ye done?

The tip of her knife was a hair's breadth from piercing Aksel's flesh, but her hand froze at the echo of Cyrene's voice and the memory of Rune's colorless face. The shame and regret gutted her still. She ground her teeth and squeezed the grip, trying to force it forward. This was the best move. The smart choice.

But there was a force more powerful than reason—more powerful than whatever good she thought might come from his death. That force urged her to choose life, even that of an enemy.

The cries of the Viking families when that death vessel slid into the rocky sand erupted in a deafening roar in her mind. She could still taste the burn of the black smoke as it billowed in the sky. Still see the groups huddled on the shore, watching as the boat crumbled apart in flames. Had Rune's family heard of his fate? Would they ever know how bravely he'd fought? How he'd helped a stowaway even though it would gain him no glory? How he'd been her friend?

"*Cladhaire,*" she spat at Aksel again, curling her lip in disgust. Whatever pagan magic permeated the air in this settlement, she was

53

certain this handsome Viking had conjured it—making her mind spin and her thoughts roam without purpose.

"'Tis true. I am a rogue."

His words sent the dagger clattering from her hand to the ground. Revna snatched it from the dirt, freezing as she aimed it at his heart again. She understood him clearly. She understood because he spoke her language.

"What?" Her whole body trembled, and she suddenly felt exposed, as if all her clothes had been stripped from her body.

Before she could move, Aksel grabbed her shoulders, drawing himself close enough that their noses almost touched.

Aksel's eyelids fluttered, a painful grimace twisting his lips. Again he spoke in her language. "Am I the reason ye were sent?"

She felt the tug of her brows moving together. How was he doing this? How did he know her language?

"Did I anger the gods?"

She was too shocked to answer. His eyes swept over her, no fear in his gaze—only a deep, sober sadness as he rasped, "I dunna belong here."

He slumped against the wall again as Revna stumbled back at the desperation in his weak voice. At the way his words latched onto something in her own heart and wouldn't let go.

She looked down at the dagger still in her hand and cursed the red that coated the blade. He'd driven her blade into his own body when he'd jerked himself close to her. "Ye idiot."

When she pressed her fingers to the dark spot on his shoulder and pulled them away red, she swore again.

The noise from inside the mead hall quieted. A singular deep voice, muffled through the wall but still powerful, began to speak. Revna pushed the cloth up over her face again.

She didn't know much of their celebrations or how long they lasted, but something in her gut told her she should hurry. She took one step in the direction she'd come, prepared to dart throughout the settlement and get on with what she'd planned. But she stopped, looking back at Aksel over her shoulder. The Chieftain's son. The bleeding prince of Kaupang that had stabbed himself on her blade.

"Idiot."

It wasn't a terrible wound. He would survive. Wouldn't he?

But he'd seen her face. Though there was a chance no one would believe him or he wouldn't even remember when he woke up, that wound wasn't something they could say he imagined. And there was more than just her life at risk.

Her fingers twitched toward her blade again, but a greasy, sickening feeling coiled in her stomach. She clenched her fists, growling at the man whose vices might have nearly ruined everything.

She cocked her head to the side. Would he be missed if he was suddenly gone? Maybe he could prove to be worth something after all.

"Idiot," she hissed again.

She moved to his head and crouched, sliding her arms under his and clasping her hands together around his chest. It took three grunting yanks and all her strength to get him far enough into the shadows that he wouldn't be immediately spotted if someone came around the side of the building. He was not hidden by any means, though. Her mind raced, searching her surroundings for a way to transport him. The thickest part of the woods where she made her camp was on the other side of the small farm behind the mead hall. Too far to drag him, and she certainly couldn't haul him onto Sgail's back. She could barely move him another inch.

For the moment, she just needed to get him out of sight before a mead hall full of drunk Vikings came pouring out.

She almost caught herself praying to *An T-aon*, but it didn't settle in her heart. What right did she have to ask anything of Cyrene's God when she hadn't even acknowledged His existence? As sweat trickled down her spine, she found herself sincerely wishing Him to be real, wishing she had someone to ask for help. Her limbs were nearly out of strength, and she really could use assistance.

No. She was on her own. As she'd always been. Tears of frustration stung her eyes as she scanned the shadows. There.

A small structure, just steps away. Pushing air out through her teeth, she jerked and lunged until she'd hauled Aksel behind the crumbling lean-to. Breathless, she collapsed against its one standing side, his head and shoulders landing in her lap.

Her aching arms fell on his chest as she gasped for air. He looked wiry, but his arms weren't the only muscular part of him. No wonder he was so heavy.

She pulled back the fabric of his tunic, dabbing her fingers around his wound. There was quite a bit of blood, but it didn't look too deep.

Just because he had made such a nuisance of himself, she gave him an extra hard prod, eliciting a groan from his chest. If she wasn't willing to permanently silence him, she would have to keep him somewhere he couldn't cause trouble, and she'd have to take care of that wound. At least until she was done with her business in Kaupang. Then she would...well, she'd decide what to do with him later.

Revna pushed sweat-slicked wisps of hair from her face. Tonight, she needed to get him deep enough into the woods where she could keep him quiet when he came out of his drunken stupor and realized she'd stabbed him.

"Ye stabbed yerself." She poked him, but he didn't respond.

She pushed against his shoulders, freeing her legs from his weight. Darting along the shadowed side of the mead hall, she clicked her tongue until Sgail silently worked her way over. Taking care to cover her and Sgail's tracks, she returned to the unconscious Norseman.

She crouched at his side, lightly patting his cheek. Mayhap she could get him to climb on Sgail's back himself.

"Aksel." It felt strange to say his name. He didn't respond. She patted his cheek harder. "Prince."

Still, nothing. Even though she was confident he wouldn't wake, quick work around his hands and feet with a bit of rope she kept in her satchel made sure he wouldn't go anywhere.

"If he moves, trample him, Sgail." Revna patted the horse's neck before slipping off into the darkness.

Shadows worked as cover while she kept low and explored the backside of the farm nearest the mead hall. She swiped a drying cloak and tunic from a line strung between the longhouse and nearby tree. A large hide was stretched near their smokehouse, in its final stages of tanning. She quickly loosened the ropes holding it in place and left it by the tree to collect on her way out.

With the warming weather, most of the villagers kept their doors propped open to let in fresh air, and she easily slid into the darkened longhouse. Glowing embers rested in the hearth, and strips of fish smoked on racks above. Before she helped herself to a few of the filets, she investigated a mound nearest the door. A woman and her two young children slept on a mat stuffed with straw. She looked from the woman to the hearth. She'd picked up chatter from settlers on her way to Kaupang. Too many people. Too little food.

Tightly packed longhouses and the daily arrival of ships at the port were evidence that the rumors were true. The settlement was rapidly growing—so much that fear the autumn harvest wouldn't be enough to feed everyone made the air thick with tension. Revna slid two small potatoes and a handful of carrots for Sgail into the folds of her vest but left the fish. It would only turn to mush if she tried to transport it very far. She did lift her eyes to the high ceiling and decided they could probably spare a few short lengths of meat that were drying in the rafters.

Swinging effortlessly along the beams, she almost felt like she was home in the high branches of the redwoods and pines. She froze as one of the boards creaked under her weight, but neither the woman nor her children stirred. Before slipping back through the door, she paused and pushed Aksel's silver coin under the bundle of fabric the woman was using for a pillow.

As she'd suspected, Aksel hadn't moved; in fact, he was softly snoring. Revna rolled her eyes and sucked in a deep breath before she untied and lugged him toward the deer skin she'd helped herself to. It would still take some effort, but she could roll him onto the skin, and, with the help of Sgail, drag him into the woods.

Getting him onto the pelt was no easy task. Her mask didn't last more than a few minutes before it was pulled down around her neck again. She might have been ashamed at the curses she muttered under her breath had there been anyone conscious to hear her.

An T-aon will always hear ye. Brigid's guiding words slipped uninvited into her mind, and Revna grumbled an apology to the diamond-speckled sky. If everything Brigid and Cyrene said was true, if any being would understand her level of frustration and desperation in trying to free people from slavery, it would be *An T-aon* made flesh.

The holy man had called him The Christ. According to Alistair, The Christ had suffered all manner of trials without transgression. Her language alone had ruined any semblance of righteousness in her. This reminder only frustrated Revna further, but she channeled that exasperation into her muscles, and with a groan, she hauled Aksel far enough onto the pelt that he wouldn't slip off with a few bumps.

"I should just tie a rope around yer neck and let Sgail drag ye." She'd collapsed on his chest after a final grunt-fueled push. At least she did it without swearing.

Revna bit back the curses again as Sgail resisted the discomfort of Revna's ropes snaking around her chest and under her girth.

"I ken, Sgail. He is a lump, but we shall bear the burden together, aye?"

Sgail snorted in response, cutting what looked like a glare at the Norsemen now strapped to her. When the horse took her first step, Aksel slid off the pelt a bit.

Revna ground her teeth, glaring at the sliver of night sky she could see through the canopy as she marched to where he lay. She'd have to haul him higher onto the pelt, and her strength was almost gone.

"I *am* trying," she said to the sparkling black, unsure to whom she was speaking. Mayhap *An T-aon*, mayhap no one. "It would have been a lot easier to leave him wi' my dagger in his chest."

She waited, catching her breath for another minute, and then rolled her eyes at herself. What was she expecting? Some supernatural pat on the back for not murdering the Chieftain's son?

"He tried to murder himself," she reminded the sky and herself as she aimed a finger at the sleeping lump. She poked him one more time for good measure. "Idiot."

Hooking her arms under his, she took a deep breath and jerked his body as hard as she could, letting him drop with a thump when he was in place. Aksel groaned as the jolt banged his head on the ground. Revna braced her hands on her knees, panting as she tried to catch her breath again.

"I'll hear nothing from ye, Prince. I dunna have to do this, ye ken. I could still let ye live and just carve yer tongue out to keep ye quiet." She raised her brows, considering the idea for half a breath before she glared at her cargo again.

As if the heavens answered her threat, her foot caught on a hidden root at her first step toward Sgail. She flew forward, her forehead meeting the unforgiving bark of a nearby tree. Another jutting root slammed into her ribs, causing her to suck in a sharp breath and release it with a groan.

Unable to hold back, she dabbed her fingers over the stinging spot, cursing again when they came back slick and red. She stomped her foot against the earth like a child throwing a tantrum and pushed herself to her feet. She'd never felt so clumsy.

"Ye better be worth it, Prince." Ignoring the cut and her screaming ribs, she hauled herself onto Sgail's back and forged on until she reached the small clearing she'd scouted earlier. She dumped Aksel onto the rough ground. The ropes she'd used to secure the pelt to Sgail were repurposed to secure him to the trunk of a mid-sized pine. Her head was pounding by the time she finished.

She added the extra protection of a length of fabric forced between his teeth and tied at the back of his head before checking his wound again. It had stopped bleeding and would need to be cleaned, but keeping her presence a secret was a more immediate need. She grabbed her satchel and hurried to retrace their path, covering her tracks. On the ride, she'd picked spots to plant some deterring traps should they be followed, but she couldn't find it in herself to stop and set them. That would be tomorrow's task.

Aksel's unexpected presence cost her, and more than just her plans. She was exhausted, her head and side ached, and she was too close to letting her frustration muddle her concentration.

Focus, Revna. Deep inhales and slow releases temporarily cleared her mind.

She slipped along shadows to the mead hall, filling one of her water skins with the amber colored drink from a cask that still remained outside. The hall was still bustling with activity and showed no signs of quieting soon. The rest of the settlement had grown eerily quiet except for the lone song of a pair of Norsemen who stumbled along the path between huts, their arms draped over each other's shoulders. The melody followed her deep into the woods and rang in her ears as she stumbled into the clearing, nearly dead on her feet.

She unrolled the mat she'd stashed with her supplies, then took a long swig from a water skin she'd filled earlier in a stream before pausing to stare at the snoring Norseman. She blew an annoyed breath through her nose and pushed herself to her feet with a groan, snatching her satchel on the way.

She planted her feet on either side of his legs, talking herself into what she was about to do instead of simply giving in to her weariness and dealing with him in the morning. If he lived.

"'Tis just a scratch," she murmured. While it was true that she didn't believe the injury to be life threatening, her bothersome brain kept conjuring images of Rune's face as the life left his body.

Tugging the gag free from Aksel's mouth, she poured half the water down his throat. Clamping her hand over his mouth, she tilted his head and forced him to swallow. She didn't have much compassion for a man who'd drowned himself in mead, but she also didn't envy him the headache he'd have in the morning. She certainly didn't want to hear him moaning about it.

He coughed but swallowed, and before she could get the fabric back between his teeth, he mumbled, "Thank ye, Little Bird."

She stilled, uncomfortable with the familiarity he assumed. He tried to open his eyes, and she couldn't imagine the amount of mead he must have consumed to keep him unable to control himself for so long.

"Ye willna be thanking me in a minute."

Without warning, she pulled aside his tunic, exposing his wound. She doused it with cold water before scrubbing it with a clean bit of fabric. He sucked a breath through his teeth. She gave no warning before splashing the wound with mead.

She shoved the gag back in his mouth to stifle his groan and met his blazing blue eyes with a fierce look of her own.

"Thank ye," he ground out through the fabric.

Ah. A challenge it was to be then? She quite liked a challenge. "Aye. Well...dunna get used to it. I'm most likely to kill ye before the mornin'."

He closed his eyes but, to her surprise, his chest vibrated with a soft chuckle. She stepped to his side, dug out small pouches of herbs from her satchel, and packed his wound with ones that would stay a fever and aid in healing. "I dunna ken why I'm even doing this."

He seemed to be dozing again, which prompted her to prod him a little more forcefully than necessary. When he grunted against the pain, she mumbled, "Ye deserved that."

He hummed a low laugh. He clearly knew her language well. His

61

eyes fluttered open, lazily drifting over her face. Even in the dark, they were as blue as the sky. His smile faded, and he said something she couldn't understand. She only paused a breath before removing the gag.

"Yer hurt." He shifted, as if trying to move his arms, but he gave up when they didn't budge.

She didn't know if it was the alcohol or arrogance that kept him from being afraid. She didn't get a chance to ask. His eyes closed again, his breaths deep, and she shook her head, envious of his ability to slip so easily into sleep. Of course, she might do the same if she'd consumed as much mead as he had.

She slipped the gag back into his mouth, and as soon as she lowered herself onto her mat, warning pangs of hunger cramped across her middle. Her need for sleep won, and she folded her arms under her head, keeping a watchful eye on her captive until she couldn't hold her eyes open any longer.

4

AKSEL

Someone was pounding on the inside of his skull with a dull battle ax. When he tried to open his eyes, it was as if the sun dropped from the sky and hovered directly in his face. He attempted to raise his hand to shield his eyes from the light, but his arms wouldn't move. In fact, he could barely feel them. Did he still have arms? Nausea swirled in his stomach, along with...

His groans were absorbed by something soft and scratchy against his lips. Oh gods, had his tongue swollen to fill his mouth? What was happening? He was suffocating and...and he was going to be sick.

Panic raced up his spine in icy streaks at the same time heat burned his skin. His stomach lurched, warning him it was about to expel everything he'd ever consumed.

"Oh," a voice said. "Oh no. Hold on."

His mouth was suddenly free, and not a second too soon as he gagged and retched on ground that was now close to his face.

He desperately wanted to push himself up, but his hands were still missing. No. There was a tingle where his fingers should be and something rubbing raw on his wrists. The same was true for his toes and ankles.

Small, warm hands pushed against his shoulders, lifting him until he was sitting up.

Flashes of memory assaulted his mind. A mug of mead in his hand; the grinning face of a busty village maiden so close to his; Rendel's grim, disapproving scowl; a sharp pain in his shoulder; and then darkness and ravens swirling around him, increasing in number until they blotted out the stars. Finally, he saw a beautiful young face. The longing in her too-blue eyes was so deep. Mirroring the emptiness in his own chest, it stole his breath even in this muddled memory.

Was it all a dream? He almost believed it was, save for the very real pain in his shoulder.

Odin's curse.

Was he...did they take him to the hall of Hel?

Something soft was pressed against his lips, and cool water poured into his mouth. He accepted the gift, taking a long drink. Was there cold water in the hall of Hel?

"Was it worth it?" a raspy voice asked.

He blinked until the world came into focus. The hands on his shoulders belonged to a girl...or a woman, rather. He couldn't tell her age. Her face filled his vision, and his gaze darted over her, taking in each feature rather than the whole.

Warm olive skin—the color of wildflower honey at the end of summer. A shallow cut at her hairline. He didn't like that. Wisps of black hair, so dark it had hints of blue. Those fine hairs had worked free from lines of braids at the sides of her skull. They danced in the breeze. He wanted to smooth them back from her face with the fingers he couldn't find. Instead, he found her eyes, so striking against her tanned skin and dark hair. They were the color of a cloudless sky. Hers was the face from his dream. Or memory—or imagination.

Nothing that beautiful would exist in the hall of Hel, but there was no way he could have made it to Valhalla.

"Aksel?" she said his name, her voice soft and hoarse.

Aksel. That wasn't his name. No. Yes it was. He was Aksel, that's right.

"Am I dead?"

Her dark brows turned down, matching her lips, which seemed to be in a permanent frown.

"Yer lucky, that's what ye are." She helped him sit back against a tree, pulling his bound feet around in front of him. Why were his feet bound? And where were his hands? "Though ye should be dead, considering how much mead ye drank."

Her accent was strange, and his mind worked hard to make sense of her words. He understood them, but they didn't sound right. Maybe he was dreaming. Maybe it was a bad batch of mead. He let his head fall back against the rough bark of the tree as she dug for something in a small leather satchel.

"Where are your wings?" He could barely hold his head up straight; it felt like it was full of water and wind. "And yer steed?"

The wings he might have imagined, but she definitely had a horse.

The woman cut her eyes up but didn't raise her head. Her expression hinted that she didn't understand his question—or maybe that he was a fool to ask. He didn't trust his memory, and maybe the flicker of image in his mind was not real. But he could see her clearly, hovering over him, her sky-blue eyes narrowed and disapproving, charcoal wings spread wide and rising up behind her.

"You stabbed me." He remembered the burn of the blade and looked down at his shoulder. A patch of sticky herbs coated his skin.

She watched as he attempted to examine his wound. "Ye stabbed yerself."

When he looked up, she flicked her gaze to his shoulder as if to confirm the truth in her words. She was at his side again, sitting on her heels with forearms casually resting on her knees, watching him in a way that made him think she could see straight into his mind.

"Which do ye want?" She held out a small potato and a strip of dried meat. There were scars marking her palms. He didn't let her know that he noticed and shook his head, swallowing another attack of nausea. He couldn't imagine ever eating again.

Behind her, he risked a glance at the bright sky. The sun was at its highest peak; he'd not slept so long in months.

A hint of pain flicked across her face as she lowered herself to the ground, her hand instinctively hovering over her ribs.

He was met with a scowl when she noticed him watching, and she didn't touch her side again. Instead she sat, one leg tucked under her, her arm hanging over the bent knee of her other. She ripped off a bite of the meat and let her eyes rake over him before she bobbed her chin up.

"How do ye understand me?" she asked, tossing the food in her mouth.

A fresh chorus of pain began in his brain, and he closed his eyes, giving his head a slight shake. "I do not know what you mean, Little Bird."

Little Bird. He'd called her that before. Why?

"Can ye not tell that I amna speaking yer language?" she said. "How much mead did ye have to drink?"

He opened one eye, watching her as she chewed the meat and buried the potato in a nearby bed of coals he hadn't noticed before. Courtesy of the mead, or lack thereof now, his eyes watered too much to open them both at the same time.

A screech from high on a branch drew his attention, and a shape as black as night swooped to the ground next to the woman. A raven. Despite the sting, Aksel did open both eyes then, gazing in wonder as the bird hopped close, snatching a crumb from the ground.

Was Rendel speaking truth after all? Odin's spies, Huginn and Muninn, memory and thought, had never taken human form, but did that mean they couldn't? Was she Huginn and this bird Muninn? Memory made mortal and thought still in animal form?

Was the language she spoke the language of the gods? No. He

knew it from somewhere else. The truth was, he didn't remember. There were a good many memories from his childhood that were lost. That might be courtesy of the mead or the childhood sickness that nearly stole his life. His father always said there was something wrong with him.

No matter how hard he trained with the warriors, no matter how he'd tried to please his father, it was never enough. He didn't measure up.

"Prince." The woman nudged his bound foot, bringing him back to the present. "How do ye ken the Vestland tongue?"

He tried to force his mind to find the answer to her question. He concentrated on the sound of her words, the way her mouth moved to form them. Then he remembered. Vestland.

"A servant. In my father's house." Ethni spoke like her, though she hadn't used her native tongue in many years—not since she learned his fluently. "She taught me."

Prince. He didn't like that word. His father was no king, even though as Chieftain of Kaupang, he might as well have been. And this mysterious woman didn't seem to like his answer either. She frowned at him and let a low hum rumble under her breath.

Maybe she would tire of him quickly and put him out of his misery. Rendel might have been right. Mayhap he had been trying to drink himself to death. He felt but two steps away from Hel's hall right now.

She poked the embers of her flameless fire and cast her gaze at him suspiciously. "Last night ye said ye dinna belong here. What did ye mean?"

So, she was intent on torture. Fine. He could endure torture. He'd survived warband training. How much worse could this small woman do?

Another flash of memory crossed his mind. It was more of a feeling than an image. A lostness. A deep longing for something... somewhere else. He closed his eyes again, willing that terrible emptiness to fade away.

"I do not remember that." He shook his head, immediately regretting the movement.

"Hmm." She didn't pry but only hummed again. The sound hinted that she didn't believe him.

The tingling in his fingers was uncomfortable, and he moved, trying to find a position where it didn't hurt as much. Every time he shifted, his shoulder protested in pain. Why was he bound?

"You can untie me. I will not try to escape."

She didn't answer, but her brow furrowed again.

"I promise."

"I dunna..." she shook her head. "I amna used to yer language yet."

"I understand you but..." He searched his brain for memories of learning her language but found none. He could understand her but couldn't answer back. When he lifted his shoulder, he winced, reminded of the injury. "I am sorry, I do not know how to speak your language."

Sorry? He was apologizing to the person who stabbed him and now had him tied to a tree. He wiggled his fingers, realizing they were bound behind his back. Very well. She had him tied *near* a tree.

She seemed to comprehend his apology, but it didn't make her happy. "Doesna mead usually encourage one to forget instead of remember? Ye truly are a strange one, Prince."

At the second mention of the amber colored drink, his tongue started to tingle. He was certain it was the mead that led to his capture, yet he already craved it again. Maybe his father was right. The childhood sickness stole whatever sense he'd had and left him empty-headed. He tapped the back of that empty head against the tree. The best he could do was silently endure the discomfort in his limbs and shoulder until his tiny captor gave him instructions or stated his fate.

Discomfort roused him, and he shook his head, stomaching another wave of nausea. He must have drifted off again. He decided if the woman was one of Odin's ravens, she definitely must be

Huginn. She had mercy on him and remained silent, letting him sleep.

When he blinked her into focus again, she was fishing the potato from the coals. She used a bit of water from her water skin to clean it before tossing it back and forth in her palms until it cooled. The raven was still there, hopping about and pecking at fallen leaves. She stared at the bird as she nibbled her food, occasionally tossing bits that it captured with its beak. Aksel wondered if they were having a conversation. If they were deciding what to do with him.

"Do ye ken the people of this settlement well?" she finally asked, still staring at the bird.

"Ehh..." he searched for a simple way to answer so that she might understand. "Yes. Most," he added a nod.

When they'd first come to Kaupang, and out of what Aksel assumed was desperation, his father trusted him to ensure business around the settlement ran smoothly while he was away on voyages. That was until Kaupang was discovered by traders and grew from a few dozen to nearly two hundred almost overnight. Then noblemen were hired to handle the business of running and protecting Kaupang, and Aksel was left with little else to do than sit at the villager's tables and hear troubles he no longer had power to ease. To refuse their company and drink seemed too great an insult. Requests for his presence at their tables became greater, as did their concerns. Most of those woes revolved around the very noblemen his father had hired to care for the people. Not one of them was honest.

Aksel flinched, remembering the consequences of trying to tell his father what he had discovered. Whatever trust he'd earned with his father in those early years was snuffed by Tollak's desire for coin and power.

The human raven pulled her full bottom lip between her teeth and cut blue eyes up at him. It was strange they were blue. He would imagine they would have been black, like those of the bird at her feet. "What about the slaves...the, um, thralls? Do ye ken their names?"

69

The thralls? Why was she asking...oh, yes. It was slaves that had disappeared from Sarpsborg, Sandefjord, and even Kaupang several winters past.

"Prince." Every time she called him that, a shudder shook his bones. It wasn't a compliment. It was a crisp reminder of who he was supposed to be but wasn't, and somehow he thought she knew it.

"Each slave brought into Kaupang is recorded." The way her eyes bored into him while he spoke made him feel as though he were confessing a terrible crime, especially since it was his father's list. He cleared his throat before he finished. "For the tithes owed to the Chieftain."

She didn't speak for a minute. He assumed she was translating in her head.

"Yer saying there is a record of all their names?" Her hand fluttered to her chest, lingering just above her heart. She understood more than she let on at first. Or maybe she just didn't realize how much she could comprehend.

"Yes."

"Every slave in Kaupang?"

"Yes."

"Ye can read those records?"

He hesitated. Should he be so quick to reveal everything about himself? He couldn't think of a reason why his answer would doom him; if anything, it would be an asset to keep him alive. "I am one of the few who understand runes."

She tossed the last bite of her meager meal to the bird, who greedily accepted before returning to his perch on a low branch of a nearby pine. That's when he noticed she was not dressed as most women—she was clad in black. Head to toe. The tunic she wore under a patched-together worn leather vest was the color of the darkest sky. And her trousers must have been made from the skins of a black wolf, even then—they were dyed darker. A cloak of onyx was clipped at her neck, flowing nearly to the ground behind her. It was as obsidian as the sky without stars or moon or clouds. She was night itself, able to become one with the shadows.

She slapped her hands together and stood, pacing a few steps before turning to him again. "Do ye ken where this list is kept?"

"Yes." His eyes trailed down her slender frame. What could she possibly want with those strips of rune-carved bark?

"Ye will tell me where it is." She straightened, hands on her hips.

He didn't respond. She raised her brows, her hand moving ever so slightly to the dagger sheathed at her waist. She meant to retrieve those records herself. Panic seized him, twisting his already rolling insides further.

"I will bring it to you." He tried to keep his voice level, his expression calm.

Her sudden, sharp laugh made him jump, and his stomach cramped again.

"No one will question me. You will not have to travel into the settlement and risk being discovered."

Those dark brows dipped over her narrowed eyes. "Ye will tell me where it is, or I will tear apart this settlement until I find it myself." Then she leaned forward, her face just inches from his. "Starting with your father's house."

That was not an empty threat. He was trapped. Either he sent her to the one place she could not go, or she would go there on her own to punish him. His already pounding heart sped up. Maybe he could break free, race ahead, and beat her to his father's house. He knew every inch of these woods, he could...no. He had a faint memory of how he had arrived in this prison of a clearing. She had a horse. A steed as dark as she was. There was no avoiding it, unless...

"You do not need those records."

She straightened in a jerky motion, her jaw set hard and lips pursed. "Very well. Ye have made your choice."

She turned on her heel as if to make good on her threat.

"No," he called, the force of his words burning his raw throat. "I mean, you do not need the records because I was the one who carved them. I have the list." He rolled his eyes up, as if looking at his own mind. "In here."

She didn't respond and took another step.

"I will tell you everything you want to know, you do not need to go to the Chieftain's—" Idiot. He was an idiot.

She turned then, a half-grin tugging at her beautifully cruel mouth. Of course he would give her what she wanted; she'd known that all along. That last step was only to ensure he knew it too.

She stood over him, one of her feet planted on either side of his bound legs, her sharp eyes crawling over his face. His head was still swimming. His father was right. He was a fool—a blasted, cursed fool.

She pelted him with questions then.

How many thralls were in Kaupang? What would all the settlers be doing the last night of the festivities? Was there a ceremonial offering site? Where was it? Did his father have a warband? How large? How well trained?

She fired them off one after another, seeming to struggle only slightly with translating his answers. He resolved to give her what she wanted. Maybe she wouldn't go to his home if he kept her happy. Nothing he'd told her so far would lead her there.

"Will your father's warband be patrolling the settlement tonight or taking part in the merriment?"

"Merriment, most likely," he answered without thinking.

"What is so important in your father's longhouse?"

"Eth…" He stopped himself, snapping his mouth shut.

Aksel closed his eyes, searching his muddied thoughts for some answer that would keep her from going there. Anything he settled on would only either give him away as a liar or send her rushing in with her daggers flying. The truth. That was the only way out.

"The thralls. They are innocent." He looked up at her, letting her see the honesty in his words. "Take what you want, whatever you want, but please, do not hurt them. They will not try to stop you. I know they will not."

Her lip curled, as if he'd just said the most disgusting thing. To her, he probably had. Any of his countrymen would think him daft for caring about captured servants. And if she was the one they spoke of, she'd made a name for herself slaughtering slaves all across the country, leaving nothing of them behind but smears of blood.

Maybe he was daft. He was also disgusted with himself. He'd guessed who she was from the beginning but sat there marveling at her beauty and mystery. Despite his ability to barely move without retching, he'd not done anything to try and free himself, to get away and go for help. Now because his mind was so liquified with mead, he didn't have the foresight to curb his words, and he'd doomed two more souls.

"Please." He squeezed his eyes closed. He couldn't watch her walk away, not when he knew where she would go and what she would do.

"You do not have a mother?"

She was still there, but he didn't open his eyes. He couldn't stand to bear whatever judgment she would heap on his head. Why hadn't he said he worried for his mother? That would have been much more believable than his strange concern for a few slaves. And why *didn't* he name his mother? He was not only a terrible human but a terrible son as well.

"I do. She will be wherever my father is." That was the truth.

There was nothing but condemning silence. Then water was forced down his throat again. There was a strange taste to it—some subtle, earthy hint.

Poison, most likely. He didn't even struggle but let her pour it into his stomach. He could only hope it was fast acting. She didn't speak again, and he kept his eyes closed like a coward. When he finally found the courage to peel his lids open, they felt like sand scraping across his eyes.

She was gone. Now, the only two people in this cursed settlement who cared whether he lived or died would be gone too, and he had sent the raven right to them.

5

REVNA

T he Chieftain's longhouse was larger than all the others. His stable and slave quarters were separate buildings and seemed utterly empty.

Hmm. The prince told the truth.

Ceremony. Woods. Offering. The words she'd collected from Aksel's explanation told her she could expect most of the village to be gathered elsewhere tonight.

She normally wouldn't risk daylight visits to the settlement, but Kaupang was so large and full of foreigners that it was easy to pass through unnoticed. She'd waited as long as she could, but she had much to do and needed to hear the village news before the settlers left the market. From whispered gossip she picked up near the port, no one had discovered Aksel's absence yet. Or if they had, it wasn't unusual. It must have been common for him to sleep off his drunken stupor somewhere that wasn't his home.

What could be so bad in his life that he needed to drown himself in mead and live so carelessly no one would think anything of it if he didn't return?

She found herself frowning in disappointment. Then her mind

74

snapped to attention as she slipped through the door to the Jarl's home.

The decadence and finery turned her stomach. She suddenly didn't care about Aksel's troubles. Not with the cloth-covered chairs, glass jars, and bowls filled to the brim with still-warm bread blatantly mocking the poverty of the rest of Kaupang.

She snatched a handful of crusty rolls and shoved them in the satchel strapped across her torso.

She'd seen the conditions of the slave quarters all across Kaupang during her inspection of the town days before. Most were barely allowed a fur to sleep on and cracked pottery to warm thin broth for their meals, yet this family lived in such luxury. Aksel lived in such luxury.

It would serve the Chieftain right if she left his son gutted on the ceremonial stone Aksel had told her about. She desperately wanted to make the Chieftain pay for all her people to be returned home, but even then, no amount of coin could excuse his treatment of the ones who baked his bread, washed his fine tunics, farmed his land, and carved the elegant arms of those cloth-covered chairs.

He didn't even care for his own people. The few farms dotting the countryside were not nearly enough to produce enough food for such a large population. She'd witnessed some thugs claiming to be in the Chieftain's warband roughing up a man in the market until he gave them the coin he'd earned for the day. From the way things looked, Kaupang would soon collapse on itself and the Chieftain would have no people to rule. It couldn't happen soon enough for Revna.

She ground her teeth and worked her way through the open area surrounding the hearth, loading her bag with potatoes, carrots, and wax-coated linens full of dried fish and meats. There was so much, the Chieftain would never notice any missing.

The abundance in his home compared to the utter sparsity in the others she'd seen had her fingers itching to leave him the surprise of a completely empty longhouse. Or better yet, a steaming pile of ash.

She couldn't do that until she'd found whatever Aksel was

protecting, because she knew it couldn't have been what he actually named. She scanned the room.

In the corner was a chest. Lifting the lid, she fished through the contents, looking for anything of value. On top, she found stacks of birch bark marked with runes. One of those might have been the list Aksel said he carved, but they were too bulky and too numerous to shove into her satchel.

There was a leather pouch of silver coins and beaded belts, which she did slip into her satchel. Beneath a stack of fine linens was a small ornate box filled with jewelry.

It was more than most freemen had but nothing a person would be so panicked to keep secret. "What are ye hiding, Prince?"

Unlike most of the longhouses belonging to the commoners, the Jarl's home had walls separating private bedroom areas. Revna peeked through the curtain-covered doors of each until she found the area she assumed to be Aksel's.

There were a few carved bits of bark on the short table next to his mattress and, of course, empty mugs still reeking of mead. A clean tunic and pair of trousers lay over the back of a chair. She snatched the clothes and a woven blanket from his bed. It was strange being in his room. It smelled like him. Not only the smell of barley from the mead, but of pine and smoke and fresh mint. Aksel's smell. She frowned at that recognition. She didn't want to know him; he wouldn't be around much longer, even if she let him live.

She'd left him sleeping under the influence of the mixture she'd added to his water. It lightened burdens and gave a sense of tranquility, but it wouldn't affect him once it wore off. Still, she hesitated in giving him something that might ensnare him like his taste for mead. He was clearly enslaved to the drink, and she was fundamentally opposed to any kind of slavery.

She kicked at the chair. Why did she care about the drunken son of the Chieftain? Why did she keep hearing his plaintive tone when he said he didn't belong here? He had plucked a string in her heart that wouldn't stop reverberating. She frowned at that too.

She stepped toward a table that held rune-carved bark. A thin, curved blade lay next to one, shavings littering the table's surface. He'd been carving his own symbols on one piece. She picked it up. There was only one symbol, carved over and over in different sizes and slightly varying forms. It didn't look anything like the runes she'd seen before, not that she could understand what they meant.

She squinted and tilted her head. It looked like...almost like...a thump from outside sent a sword of ice slicing through her veins, and she shoved Aksel's clothes, a blank birch bark slate, and his carving tool in her now bulging bag and draped the blanket over the top as she made herself one with the shadows.

The sound of muffled voices reached her through the walls. Her first thought was that Aksel had escaped and sent the Chieftain's men to find her. She glanced at the roof. There was an opening high above the rafters. It was small, but she thought she could fit through it. She peeked through the small space between the curtain and wall.

She released a soundless breath when she saw two servants moving about the longhouse common area. One worked lighting torches and stoking the fire. The other was chopping vegetables and pouring broth into a cauldron. Revna moved back along the wall and rolled her eyes. They wouldn't be leaving any time soon.

"What do ye think of the rumors?"

Revna's ears perked at the sound of her own tongue, and she whipped her head around again, peering at the two women. Or rather, one woman and one girl no more than ten winters, if that. It was the younger one who spoke.

"They say thralls are disappearing. Not even bodies left behind. Only blood. They say it is the work of Odin—a curse, but..." The little girl chopping the vegetables shrugged. "I dunna ken what to think."

"Aye. Neither do I." The woman near the hearth stilled, a sadness drawing her mouth into a frown. "I ken it 'tisn't Odin though."

These women were Picts—at least the older one was. She was grown now, but she would have been young when she was taken. Though they shared language with the rest of their Scottish countrymen, there were a few words distinct to their Pictish heritage, and Revna was certain these were some of her people. She could rescue them now. They would not spend one more minute as slaves.

She still didn't think Aksel was telling the truth about his real aversion to her going to his home, but because of it, these two women would be saved.

Ye've earned yerself another day on earth, Prince.

She would have to get them to trust her. She'd done it before. First in Sarpsborg, where Rune's boat had slid into shore bearing her bloodied flag. It had taken her a month, but she'd found six of her people in that small port settlement. She closed her eyes, still able to see the billowing smoke that had blackened the morning sky in the seaside village. While the people were watching the smoke and attempting to save their burning barns and great hall, they were not watching six escaped slaves board a small merchant ship from the Dutch colonies.

By some act of fate, the Dutch vessel had missed Kaupang and ended up in Sarpsborg just as she'd freed the last of her people. They would have all been caught and most likely killed had she not gotten them aboard that very night. It had taken every piece of silver she had—and a few threats—to convince the captain to make a stop in the Vestlands, but it had been the start she'd needed.

Sarpsborg had paid dearly for its part in her people's captivity. It might have also paid for her fury at not being able to find the cowardly crew leader responsible for Rune's death.

She'd since become less dramatic but still made sure every settlement she visited felt the presence of the raven. When she'd visited Kaupang four winters before, she'd left her mark. This time would be no different.

Revna stepped from the shadows and the women froze. The younger one at the table still held her knife; it trembled in her small fist.

"Dunna fear." Revna held up her hands. "I am here to bring ye home."

They didn't move. They didn't even look at each other. Revna launched into the speech that had brought tears to nearly everyone she'd told.

"Queen Derelei's daughter survived. Cyrene is queen, and our people are safe. The war with Tràigh has ended. There is a new king. There is peace. I have come to bring ye home."

The older woman at the hearth released a cry, and her hand flew to her mouth to cover it.

"Are there others of our people here? In Kaupang?" Revna asked.

"Aye. But I dunna ken how many." The older woman moved to the side of the child. They had different coloring but similar features. "Alpia, did ye hear? Cyrene lives."

Alpia. Revna didn't recognize the name, and she knew the names of all who were taken. At least, all who Brigid had recorded. But Alpia was too young to have been taken with the Picts originally. She could have learned of their history from the older woman, or she was a child of Tràigh and had been taken in the Viking raid before Cyrene had married Duncan—one winter before Revna had left the Vestlands.

Alpia only stared at Revna, the knife still in her hand but her knuckles pink instead of white. She flicked her eyes to the older woman, who had stilled as she looked at Revna.

"Ye look..." the woman said, her hand fluttering to her pale throat. "I thought ye to be—"

"Fiona?" Revna answered. It wasn't the first time someone had thought her the ghost of the dead queen of Tràigh.

"Aye," the woman breathed.

"She was my mother." Revna prepared herself for the shock that always followed her admission and for the disappointment that, thus far, always came after her next question. "My sister was also taken. She would have been just a bairn. Less than a month old. Do ye ken what happened to her?"

"Nay." The woman seemed to regain her senses and shook her head. "Nay, I'm sorry. Everything was so..." She wiped the soot from her hands and smoothed the worn fabric of her dress. "I am Ethni, and this is my daughter, Alpia."

Ethni. She knew that name. It was also what Aksel had started to say before he caught himself. Revna's eyes drifted to Alpia, then back to Ethni. She would have been about Revna's age when Alpia was born.

"Daughter," Revna repeated, studying the girl. Her hair and eyes were brown, much darker than Ethni's. "Is yer husband here too? Is he one of us?"

The glance Alpia shot Ethni was so slight it might have been overlooked but for Revna's sharp eye.

"Aye. He works wi' the animals." Ethni answered quickly, a casual smile lifting her lips. It was rehearsed. She didn't meet her daughter's eye. She was lying.

Alarm prickled Revna's skin, and she settled back on her heels, her eyes covering every corner of the longhouse. Her satchel was swung around her back, and Revna had a dagger at the ready, but she did not draw it. Doubtless Ethni had suffered any number of unknown evils; there could have been countless reasons for her deception. Revna softened her tone. "Why do ye lie?"

Ethni attempted a look of innocent surprise as she subtly placed herself in front of Alpia. "I dunna lie. She is my daughter."

Revna remained alert, ready. Something was wrong. It was Alpia who stepped forward, skirting her mother as Ethni reached for her. Revna admired the little girl's boldness; if they'd been back in The Dorcha, she'd have brought her straight to Astrid to be trained as a warrior. Mayhap she'd send word for Astrid to do just that.

"Ye are truly here to rescue us?" Alpia asked, a fire igniting her brown eyes.

"Aye." Revna flicked her gaze between the two women.

Alpia looked over her shoulder at Ethni. "She looks like the queen in yer stories?"

"Aye," Ethni's breathless answer came with a nod.

"She doesna lie." Alpia turned to face Revna again, squaring her shoulders. "I am her daughter."

"Alpia, nay." Ethni reached for her daughter, her face colorless and filled with terror.

"And to anyone who asks, Conall is my father." Alpia stood at her tallest, which was barely to Revna's shoulders. "That is all we can say."

Conall was not a name she knew either. Revna read the shock and shame on Ethni's face, the deep pain and fear behind both. She measured the dip of her head as she glanced down at her wringing hands. Then she examined Alpia, who reached back and took her mother's hand. The lives of these two women balanced on people believing this lie about a man named Conall. He was clearly not her father though, which meant...

Revna's first thoughts were rage directed at Aksel, but she didn't believe he could be Alpia's father. It could have been anyone in the Chieftain's household—any of his warband, a fellow nobleman, the Chieftain himself.

Alpia stood before her, chin high. A brave little warrior.

Revna offered her an approving nod and spoke as if the child were just that—a warrior and her equal. "The man who sired me isna one I care to think about either. He wasna my *father*. He doesna determine what I make of myself."

Alpia's brows lifted, her lips curving into a determined smile.

"He doesna matter now. What matters is that ye are going home." Revna flipped her dagger, sheathing it in her next breath. "We must go."

Revna started toward the door and turned when she didn't hear the women following her.

Some of the first had also been reluctant to follow her. Some had outright refused, even though they wanted nothing more than freedom. The fear of what happened to those who escaped and were caught was too great; they had to fear something else more to take that risk, and Revna would bear the burden of being that thing if it meant they gained their freedom. She never hurt anyone, and they all ended up on a vessel home.

Revna didn't hold their fear against them, but if they didn't return with her, they were a danger to those who did. She wouldn't allow that.

"I ken ye are scared. Ye have heard the rumors. Ye ken of those slaves who were never seen again. 'Tisn't because they were killed or caught." Revna approached the ladies, taking one of each of their hands in hers. "'Tis because they were freed."

Tears dripped down Ethni's face. She nodded in encouragement.

"Come wi' me. I've not lost one of our people yet, and neither of ye will be the first."

Ethni moved to follow her, but Alpia remained frozen at her station at the table.

"Alpia, come." Ethni tugged on the girl's arm, but the child remained in place.

"Aksel." Alpia looked toward the room from where Revna had come. "He dinna return. What if he's..."

Alpia didn't finish and Revna didn't answer, unsure if Alpia was worried about the Jarl's son because she cared or because she was afraid of him. He might not be her father, but that didn't mean he wasn't a danger to her.

Revna's face flamed and she drew even closer to the mother and daughter. Ethni's eyes widened and she leaned away.

"Did he hurt ye?" Ice edged Revna's words.

"Nay." Ethni's hand went to her throat. Her eyes flew to the ground, and a blush of bright red painted her cheeks. "Not Aksel. He is good to us."

Not Aksel. But someone else. Revna saw it plain as day when Alpia finally let her teary gaze meet Revna's again.

"Is he..." Ethni's throat moved as she swallowed hard. "Did ye —"

"Nay." Revna started, finally realizing what Ethni was asking. How could she explain the man she'd left tied up at the clearing.

82

Were it not for the herbs she'd added to his water, he'd most likely be gone when she returned. "He's...helping me."

It was a lie. Half of one, anyway. It wasn't the first Revna told and certainly wouldn't be the last. She'd found such things were sometimes necessary to get people to put one foot in front of the other. She'd heard Brigid tell a dying woman that everything would be well. She'd heard Cyrene give a brave speech to her warriors when Revna could smell the fear seeping from her every pore. In battle, be it against an illness, an army, or a captor—truth and lies fell behind blurred lines.

"Really?" It was Alpia who spoke, her lips drawing back in surprise.

She was beginning to think Aksel might have been telling the truth after all. These two were the treasure he was protecting. Mayhap he'd bought himself more than just one night of life.

"Aye." Revna nodded, squaring her jaw to add to her look of sincerity.

Ethni whispered something to her daughter that didn't make sense to Revna. "I told ye."

She saw Alpia's remaining hesitation and took the blade from the young woman's hand. "I will make sure they dunna come looking fer ye."

When Revna dragged the blade of the knife across her own palm, Alpia covered a yelp with her hand. Ethni grabbed Alpia's shoulders and pulled them both back as Revna's blood coated the knife and table where the half-cut vegetables lay waiting.

When a noticeable amount had pooled, Revna coated her hand, stamping a bloody handprint on the table. Alpia stared at the pool of red now dripping onto the dirt floor.

"Is that how ye freed them all?" Alpia didn't look away from the blood. "Ye bled fer all of them?"

"Nay. I usually carry rabbit's blood fer the markings, but I wasna expecting the good fortune of finding ye both here. Our display will just be a bit less gory than usual." Revna moved about the common room, turning over chairs and baskets, placing bloody handprints as she went. She considered the chest for a moment before turning it on its side and scattering the contents across the floor.

Ethni moved to the hearth and picked up a loose stone. She used Alpia's knife and made a small cut in her own palm, painting the stone red. She even ran her fingers through her hair, tugging hard. She placed the loosed strands on the sticky crimson coating.

When Revna stopped to watch, Ethni positioned the stone where it was sure to be seen and looked between Revna and the wide-eyed Alpia. "I'm not the first to bleed fer freedom."

Revna nodded in approval and bobbed her head toward the door that faced the back side of the longhouse. The sun had just begun to set, and it was still too bright for Revna's comfort.

When they followed her out, she held out her arm, silently ordering them to keep close to the shadowed walls. The Jarl and his wife would be at the ceremonial fire, and the Jarl's guards as well, but she didn't want to take any chances. She moved to the edge of the house, scanning the yard, relieved to find it empty.

"Follow me." Revna kept her eyes on the open space. When she didn't hear them agree, she looked over her shoulder to find Alpia tugging on Ethni's sleeve and Ethni nodding as if she knew what the girl was asking.

"Conall." Ethni inched up beside Revna, pointing over Revna's shoulder toward a small building on the far side of the Jarl's property. "He will be wi' the animals."

Revna hesitated. Ethni answered her unasked question with a hand on Revna's arm.

"He isna from our village, but he is from our homeland. He deserves to go home too." Tears welled in her blue eyes. "He took care of us."

"We must take him." Alpia was behind Ethni, gripping the woman's arms, her fear palpable.

Revna measured the distance in her mind, plotting a route that would keep them hidden. By herself, she could cover it quickly, but the three of them...

"He is strong." Ethni's voice pleaded. "He can help. He can fight."

Even though she could see that this Conall was special to Ethni, Revna considered leaving him behind. But with the Jarl's son as her captive, she could use a man who could easily overpower Aksel should he try to fight or escape. Then she wouldn't have to keep lacing his water with her subduing herb.

Revna told the women to follow her as she darted across the land, skittering from boulder to tree until she came to the backside of the stable.

Ethni slipped in and brought Conall to where Revna and Alpia waited. He was about the same age as Ethni, and just like his wife, would have been barely more than a lad when he was taken. He might not have been from Tràigh, but he bore the features of their people. High cheekbones, defined jaw.

His beard was short, his dark blonde hair was shaggy and his eyes were a deep blue. Revna only paused for a blink at the jagged scar that ran across his face, its pink mark stretching above his eye and below. He was lucky to still have the use of the eye.

"Just listen." Ethni's hand rested on the shoulder of his too-small tunic.

Conall's suspicion rolled off him in waves, but he was clearly not going to allow Ethni to go without him. Arms crossed, he listened to Revna's well-rehearsed speech. He was not as affected by the mention of the surviving Pictish queen, but he was willing to go with Revna. He was even willing to use one of the Chieftain's hens and create a scene that spoke of violence and death.

They collected the sacrificial hen's pale feathers, replacing them with midnight black ones from Revna's satchel. A symbol that she knew left quite an impression on those who discovered it.

She knew the time would come for thralls to simply vanish. She'd give up the effort to make their owners think they'd met some horrific end then. But until she knew how many of her people were scattered through the village, she'd stick with what she knew worked. Even terrified of The Raven, some Norsemen went in search of their missing property. Revna had plenty of tricks to dissuade them from pursuing further than the tree line.

"Keep that bird. She'll make a fine dinner fer tonight." Revna nodded to the limp animal in Conall's hand.

When Conall's hungry gaze drifted to the livestock, a chill crept across Revna's skin at the flash of bloodlust she saw in his eyes.

"Time is short." Her tone was clipped, snapping him out of whatever dark thoughts had taken over. He'd probably watched the Chieftain's family eat their fill of meat every night while he, Ethni, and Alpia survived on scraps.

When Conall lowered that furious look on her, Revna had to turn away. It carried too much pain and rage and threatened to slice through a taut string inside her own heart that she couldn't let break again.

She could only imagine what scars Conall bore beneath his clothes—what even deeper and hidden ones were carved beneath his skin. If he asked, if he persisted, she would let him take whatever price was due for his suffering.

Ethni turned desperate, hope-filled eyes to the man who had been a lad forced into slavery yet still chose to protect her. Alpia looked to him too. Their lives rested on his shoulders. A wife and a daughter that wasn't his but he'd claimed anyway. All of them at the mercy of men who didn't care if they lived or died. Who could tear them from each other at any second. It should not be.

This farm should burn. All of Kaupang should burn for its part in such pain. She snatched the torch from where it rested and offered it to Conall.

"I will follow ye." Conall looked down at Ethni, letting her slide her hand down his arm and thread her fingers through his. Then he glanced at Alpia, who stood at his other side, her small hands clutching his sleeve. He closed his eyes for a moment, and when he opened them again, the pain remained but his rage was gone. "I will fight fer freedom, but I will not become ruthless and savage like them. There will be a time fer flames, but not tonight."

Revna nodded, lost for words. He deserved his revenge; they all did. And she could see in his eyes he wanted it, but whatever well he drew from inside was deep enough to douse the embers of hate.

She had no such well. The fire in her chest didn't fade until they'd breached the tree line. The tension in Revna's shoulders released slightly as she set her traps, but her mind raced to find a way to understand the mercy Conall possessed and to explain Aksel's current state of captivity. She could simply confess that she'd lied. They were already willing to leave with her, their false demise already laid out. But she knew from experience that the fear of the first few days could be consuming. The captor they knew was less terrifying than the unknown. And if they suspected the Chieftain would come looking for his kidnapped son, there would be no convincing them to stay. They might even go so far as to earn his good favor by turning her over. Fear and despair made even the best people do the worst of things.

It was Conall who finally solved the problem for her. Quickening his steps, he came to Revna's side and whispered his question after looking over his shoulder to make sure Ethni and Alpia couldn't hear.

"They said the Jarl's son is helping ye. I ken that canna be true."

"He is." Revna cast a glance at Ethni and Alpia, who walked arm in arm, faces pale but hopeful. "Just not willingly."

"Ethni is a dreamer—she will believe anything. She was here before me, but she helped raise the lad. She wants to believe he cares about her." Conall's brows drew together. He opened his mouth as if to speak but closed it again. Revna waited, allowing him time to work out whatever plan was brewing in his mind. "I dunna ken yer plans. There is but one way for us to return home, and passage on the trade ships canna be light. Unless, yer queen sent ye with baskets of coin—"

"I have always found a way," Revna snapped, unsure of what Conall was getting at.

"I am only saying that any Chieftain would pay handsomely fer his only son to be returned, should he learn he'd been...detained." Conall gave her a pointed look.

"I thought ye had no interest in their savage ways."

"I'mna suggesting ye harm him, but ye could make truth from yer lie. He could be helpful."

Revna didn't answer, and Conall fell back in step with the women, Ethni's adoring smile causing him to send a warning look at Revna. *Ye better not lead us to our deaths* it seemed to say.

Conall's ransom plan wasn't a bad idea. It didn't solve the problem of what to do with Aksel once her mission in Kaupang was finished, but it could certainly speed up the plans she'd already put in place. The drunken prince had seen her face, and the longer she kept him around, the quicker he would realize her purpose in Kaupang. There would be no chance of quietly returning him home.

She cast a look at Conall over her shoulder. His fingers threaded through Ethni's again, and he gave her a nod that told her he knew the same. Conall already drew his boundaries. It would ultimately be left to her to decide how to deal with their captive. An uneasiness settled over her stomach until even the thought of the fresh bread in her satchel made her sick.

Since she'd spotted the waiting families on the shores of Sarpsborg, since she'd swam to the rocky shore and heard the wailing carried to her hiding spot by the waves, the heat of her rage had begun to fade. Rune's lifeless eyes haunted her dreams more often than not. Since then, it wasn't a painless feat to fight or to take a life, even in defense of her own. It hurt, and she'd done what was necessary to avoid it. She had the scars to prove it. She clenched her fist, the cuts aching under a bandage she'd quickly wrapped around her sliced palm. She didn't relish the pain; she didn't find relief in shedding her own blood. It was simply what was necessary to spare her enemies' lives while saving her people's.

Aksel was another unavoidable stone in her path. One way or another, she would have to make a decision regarding his fate. If it came down to rescuing the rest of her people or letting him go, she would choose them. She had to.

When they neared a stream they'd have to cross, she handed two empty water skins to Ethni and beckoned Conall to her side with a wave of her arm. "I need yer help."

He nodded, crossing his arms over his thick chest and leaning down to listen to her quiet instructions.

6

AKSEL

His lungs burned with every wet cough. Each inhale was rattling and painful—not that he could do anything other than hack away at the weight that had settled in his chest. The breaths he could manage didn't give him enough air.

If the panic didn't kill him, the pounding in his head would. Stomach cramping from the effort of breathing, he wrapped his arms around his middle and begged for it to end. Though his skin burned, chills racked his body and made his teeth clack together so hard he thought they would shatter.

The world pitched from side to side, tossing him about as if he were a child's toy. He was aboard a ship of death, aimed for the halls of Hel. Shrieks of fear and cries of agony filled the air. Lost. They were all lost.

Aksel jerked awake with a gasp. His lungs were open and his throat sore but functioning. The hammering in his head remained, but it was bearable. It was a dream. Just a dream.

Why could he still hear the shrieking? He turned one eye up to the darkening sky. An eagle soared over the canopy of trees, screeching a haunting call. He sighed, squeezing his eyes closed.

His stomach still cramped, demanding food, while his mouth

watered for something liquid, honey sweet, and laden with the promise of forgetfulness. His skin alternated between flashes of heat and bone-rattling chills. He should be free of his restraints already, yet he sat at the base of the tree where he'd been dragged by an intriguing villain. His feet were bound at his ankles, and one of his wrists was tied to the tree behind him. He was still there. Bound. Useless. A failure.

A heaviness settled in his chest—an unease like he was being watched—and he opened his eyes. A shadow shifted at the edge of the clearing. The little killer stood, leaning casually against a tree, her arms crossed.

"Yer awake," she said, as if they were friends. As if she hadn't just ripped away the only good thing in his life. Was that blood splattered on her face?

A growl crept up his throat, one he knew she could hear, but she didn't move or even flinch. Her ocean eyes raked over him, as if she could see through his skin into the depths of his soul. A flash of unbidden desire to allow her full access to the deepest parts of him had his head spinning before he reigned in his wayward thoughts and reminded himself that she was the enemy.

It was the mead. It was still affecting his mind.

"What have ye done?" In the moments when he'd managed to drag himself from whatever herb-induced stupor she'd put him under, he had worked the gag from his mouth. It hung, damp and uncomfortable around his neck.

That dream had also worked something loose in his mind—a knowledge long buried freeing his tongue from whatever restraints time had placed on it—and he remembered how to speak her language.

He kept his free hand hidden behind him, hoping she was bold enough to approach. Her impressive knot tying skills aside, she was a plague upon his settlement, and if he could stop her before she did more damage, he would.

"I did what I came to do." She tilted her head, still gazing at him with those too-blue eyes, not mentioning his newly acquired language skills.

Bile rose in his throat, but he swallowed it down. If he hadn't been weakened by his overindulgence in mead, her herbs wouldn't have kept him down for more than a few minutes. He'd have gotten himself free and run straight to the ceremony, alerting his father of what evil had come to Kaupang. In such a public setting, he'd have no choice but to listen.

"Are they dead?" He closed his eyes. There was no need to lie to himself. He wouldn't have gone to the ceremony; he would have gone straight to the longhouse. To Ethni and Alpia. A move that might have saved them, but one his father would have criticized.

"Would it pain ye if they were?" Her voice was so calm.

His lids flew open. Why was she looking at him like that? Like his life depended on the answer he would give.

What did it matter now? She was the raven. The one who swept through settlements and left them weeping with ash and blood. Ethni and Alpia were dead. They were the only ones, besides Eira, to ever see him as anything other than a mistake, a disappointment. Eira was gone, starting a new life with Rendel. Now Ethni and Alpia were gone too.

"What did ye do?" He trembled but continued working the remaining knot keeping him tethered, daring her to come closer. Did they suffer? Were they afraid? Did they call for him, look for him to save them?

He couldn't bring himself to ask those questions, uncertain if his heart would keep beating should the woman answer.

She took one step. *Keep coming, Little Bird. Just a little closer. I'll pluck those feathers; you will never fly again.*

"I dunna answer to ye." Fury seeped into every word, but her breathing was controlled.

Part of him ached to get his hands on her and wring out every secret she hid, but another part—a thin rebellious vein that pulsed with fascination—wanted to follow this exotic creature to the ends of the earth.

She opened her mouth to say something else, but her eyes snapped up and her head jerked. She stared at something in the darkness behind her.

She spun, daggers he hadn't seen before suddenly in her hands. Letting her satchel fall to the ground, she bent her knees, arms loose at her sides, battle ready. He was about to ask what was coming when a sound reached his ears that had a thousand tiny needles prickling his scalp.

A growl seeped from the shadows, deeper and much more menacing than the one he'd uttered. The snap of a twig coated his skin with ice. She took one step back and then another.

Her movements were matched by what crept from the darkness. A massive gray wolf, mouth open, teeth bared. It wasn't alone. Another, larger, animal with russet fur prowled from the woods to her left. Her head swiveled, watching both. He didn't move or even breathe.

The gray wolf lowered itself, inching closer, its lips quivering over razor sharp fangs. Low growls rolled across the ground, working their way into Aksel's bones and making them ache with fear and dreadful anticipation.

But it was the russet wolf that pounced, catching the little bird off guard. In the split second it took for the wolf's paws to leave the ground, the woman shifted, tucking her small body into a tight ball and rolling out of the path of attack. She came up on her feet flicking her dagger. The russet wolf yelped as the blade found purchase. The animal slid across the ground, landing in a motionless heap.

Aksel jerked at the ropes, desperately fighting to free his other hand as she readied herself for the gray wolf's attack. His feet were tied at the ankles and he kicked his legs, trying to loosen those bonds. Her second dagger was pinched between her fingers, ready to fly.

He saw the third wolf only a split second before a blur of brown flew through the air at her back, pushing her to the ground on her stomach. He didn't have time to give a warning. If she was killed before he was free, he was as good as dead too.

The gray wolf joined the attack, and as Aksel scrambled to get free, all he could see was a horrible mix of brown and gray fur and her black hair. He hated her for what she'd done to Ethni and Alpia, but he had no desire to watch anyone be devoured. He certainly had no desire to be devoured himself.

"Aksel!" He found her face as she grappled with the gray beast. Her foot shot out, landing a blow against the brown one's nose, sending it jumping back with a yelp. He expected her to cry for help, but a flash of silver flew through the air, and a dagger landed between his legs—too close to a part of his body that he was not prepared to lose.

Was she truly threatening him right now? But when he found her eyes again, her hands were on the gray wolf's face, pulling its jaws apart as it attempted to close saliva-coated fangs on her neck. She only bared her teeth at Aksel and growled one word.

"Run."

Aksel didn't waste time questioning her order. He grabbed the dagger with his free hand and, with a swift slice, freed his feet and other hand. He pushed himself up and raced away from the clearing. All he could think of was getting back to his home and finding Ethni and Alpia. Maybe he could do something—maybe they would still be breathing. The wolves would take care of the raven that had been spreading terror across the Northlands. He could lead his father to what was left of her in the morning.

That was the smart thing to do. The best thing. He heard an angry cry of pain, and his feet stopped moving. His body turned back. She was still down, pushing herself across the ground on her back, somehow avoiding the snapping jowls of the brown wolf while shoving her elbow into the snout of the gray one. And she had another dagger in her hand.

When she saw him coming, a flash of anger narrowed her eyes. "Run, ye idiot!"

Ignoring her insult, Aksel palmed the dagger she'd chucked at him and leapt onto the gray wolf's back, driving the blade to the hilt into its neck. The animal shook him to the ground, but Aksel kept his hold on the knife. As he avoided the wolf's snapping fangs, Aksel twisted the blade, dragging it across its neck. He blinked as a spray of blood coated his face. His limbs felt useless; his lungs aching for breath. But he left the animal twitching as he rolled over and got back up.

He was on his knees as the woman scrambled back, just missing the deadly swipe of the brown wolf's sharp claws. Her back met the rough bark of a tree and she was trapped, the brown wolf on her before he could get to his feet.

"No," he shouted, launching himself at the animal. But when he buried the blood-slicked dagger into its side, the wolf was already still.

He plunged his fingers into its coarse fur, dragging its body away from her. She sat against the tree, chest heaving with heavy breaths, blood soaking her face and neck. Her hands lay limp at her sides, but she was alive.

When he looked down at the brown beast that twitched at his feet, he saw her third dagger sticking out of its chest. He reached down and jerked it free.

"What did ye do to the women from my father's house?" Their near-death experience with the animals hadn't sated his rage; it only served to incite it. But he didn't turn the blades on her—not yet.

"Why didn't ye run?" Breathless, she let her head fall back against the tree, as if she was too tired to hold it up.

"Answer me." His response to her incredulous question came with a presentation of the two blades he possessed. He was doubly armed, she had nothing, and she was questioning him?

She laughed—Laughed!—before turning those blazing blue eyes on him, a half-smile pulling at her lips. "I have another."

He saw it then, another blade in her right hand. Where was she getting these weapons? Her left arm still lay at her side, unmoving. She had to know he could best her, especially if she was injured, yet she only closed her eyes as if he was nothing but a figment of her imagination.

He could walk away. He could run home and discover the answer to his questions himself. He was half sure she wouldn't stop him. It was the other half that kept him standing over her. The half that was certain she could send the blade in her hand into his heart through his back before he could get three steps away.

"What did ye do?" He punched out each word, the tip of one blade aimed at her throat.

"I will tell ye," she said, her voice huskier than normal, and opened her eyes again. "But answer me first. Why did ye come back?"

He ground his teeth together and dropped to the ground, pinning her with a knee on either side of her legs. Gods, she was frustrating. She raised her dagger, too slowly, and he snatched her wrist with one hand. With his other hand, he held a blade to her blood covered throat, ignoring the tugging in his gut to make sure the thick red coating wasn't hers—ignoring his fascination at her fearlessness.

He was twice her size—twice as armed—yet she watched his face with mere curiosity, and it was she who asked the question burning on his own lips.

"Why?" It was nothing more than a whisper, and he knew she was asking for much more than a simple explanation of his actions.

"Because if ye hurt them, no one gets to kill ye but me." He flicked his eyes between hers, and he could see that she understood there was so much more to his answer than he was able to say. He pressed the blade harder against her neck. She raised her chin but never took her eyes from his.

"Dunna worry, Prince," she spoke through clenched teeth, a jump of her brow striking a fire in his stomach. "Yer slaves are alive."

He wasn't surprised. Why wasn't he? And why did it seem like an insult when she called them *his* slaves? His eyes dashed to her throat as she swallowed hard again.

"Now, I need yer help," she said.

"I just saved yer life, isna that enough?" He was almost unable to catch the laugh that burst from his lips. When something pricked his ribs, he dropped his gaze to her injured arm. Though blood dripped from her hand, she held yet another blade. It was aimed directly at his heart.

"I told ye. I have another." Her threat caressed his skin. He worked to suppress the shiver that both chilled and heated his blood.

"Ye can either help me and live through the night, or I can end ye now." She cocked her head, her mouth quirking up in a vicious smile.

Something passed across her eyes, and though he knew she was telling the truth, he did not believe she would kill him. He was almost disappointed. Not that he truly wanted to die, but there was something about the violence she emanated that connected with a gaping hole inside him. He knew it was destructive and dark, but he longed to reach out and touch that invisible hair-thin string that seemed to be the only thing holding her back. He imagined wrapping it around his wrist and reeling her in just to see what would happen when her fury mixed with his.

He couldn't help the curious tip of his lips. There was a hardness about her. He'd seen the same in his father and the trained men who formed the Chieftain's war band. It was a stone strength that only touched men who had seen battle and death at their own hands. She wore that darkness like a cloak. But there was something else too, a tiny flicker of...something. It intrigued him. He would allow her all the threats she wanted, but she wouldn't end his life. Not tonight anyway.

Raising one brow, she tipped her head to confirm that he agreed to her terms.

"As ye wish, Little Bird."

She withdrew her knife, but not before a slight flick of her wrist nicked him. When he reached under his tunic to touch the spot, there was blood on his fingers. He nearly scoffed that she could have killed him, but the taunting smile told him that move was very much intentional.

If she'd wanted him dead, he would be.

"I want the list of slaves."

He felt his brows furrow, and her eyes flicked upward, interpreting his expression.

"All the ones in Kaupang," she added.

"Why?" It was his turn for answers.

She glared at him, speaking through her clenched teeth, punching out each word as he had minutes before. "My business is my own. I need the names."

"The slaves in my father's house, ye said they were alive, but did ye harm them? Did ye speak to them?" This little bird needed to start singing.

"Tell me the names," she challenged.

He stared, marveling at her audacity, or arrogance maybe, that she cared nothing for the blade he still held at her throat. She only lifted her chin in defiance, daring him to try to cut her. She kept her injured hand in her lap. The other still dangled from where he held her wrist. He imagined she had some plan, some hidden trick that would have him begging for mercy if he even attempted to draw blood.

"Fine." He pushed off of her, noticing how she sagged against the tree as if every bit of strength had left her body.

The sudden burst of energy from the fight with the wolves had finally run out of him, too, and his limbs felt as if rocks had been strapped to his wrists and ankles.

"Every name," she warned, her face pale.

Something in him couldn't help the urge to challenge her, and he cast a look over his shoulder to the satchel she had abandoned when the wolves approached. He swiped the bag from the ground by its strap and opened the flap.

"There are no names in there, Prince." Her tone was teasing.

"If ye dunna stop that bleeding, ye'll not be conscious to hear them." He pulled a bundle of cloth from the bag, hesitating when he recognized it as one of his own tunics. She had been in his home—in his room. He couldn't meet her eyes as he asked, "Ye swear they are unharmed?"

"Aye." Her answer was strained, and he did look then. She was peeling back the dark sleeve of her tunic, exposing a long bloodied gash along her arm.

He searched further in her bag and found another strip of linen, tossing it to her along with the water skin that had been tied to her satchel. She caught it and raised it to her lips but froze when he pulled his torn, bloodied tunic over his head.

He pressed his lips together, hiding his smirk as her eyes widened. Moving slower than was necessary, he pulled on his clean tunic, relishing the deep red that blossomed on her cheeks and the way her throat moved as she swallowed. This little bird wasn't as unshakeable as she appeared. With a blink, she was back to glaring at him, and he couldn't help the chuckle that bubbled in his chest at her murmured insults.

After watching her take a long drink, wash her wound, and tear the linen in strips with her teeth, he grew anxious as she struggled to properly wrap her forearm. He marched across the clearing, sidestepping the wolves' bodies, and dropped to his knees at her side, ignoring her daggering look.

When he reached for her, she jerked away, but he caught her wrist and held her arm still.

"Dunna be stubborn. Do ye really think those three were the only ones in their pack?" He tipped his head toward the animals, wrapping her arm as he talked. "We need to get moving, and ye, Little Bird, are going to tell me exactly what happened when ye visited my home."

"After——"

"I ken, I ken. After I give ye the names." When he'd finished securing the bandage, he looked her over, feeling his brows furrow at the sheen of sweat across her forehead. "Are ye injured anywhere else?"

She shook her head but her hand fluttered, as if subconsciously, to her shoulder. That's when he noticed a ring of dark stains against her black tunic.

"Ye've been bitten." He pulled her tunic aside, acknowledging that she clenched her teeth but didn't stop him. He scanned the punctures along her shoulder. "It isna deep. But it broke the skin. Ye'll need to clean yer shoulder well."

"I ken what to do. 'Tisn't the first run in I've had wi' wild animals." She held his gaze as he lifted her tunic back in place.

"I believe ye." He gripped her uninjured hand, pulling her to her feet, fully aware of how she bit back the pain. "We need to get away from here before their friends come sniffing around."

She pushed past him and snatched the satchel from where he'd left it. "This way," she said, heading east.

"Away from Kaupang?" He caught her in two long strides.

"The names," she demanded.

"Very well." He straightened, slowing his pace to keep step with her.

She pulled something out of her vest, unfolding it and tilting it so it was illuminated by the remaining daylight. It was something his people didn't use, but he somehow knew it was called a parchment. Over her shoulder, he spied inked markings in neat rows across its surface, but he couldn't make them out.

Visualizing a list in his mind, he began to speak. She scanned her parchment as he talked. He named every slave in Kaupang, only skipping over the names of the ones owned by his father.

Whatever this little raven's endgame was, he was leaving Ethni and Alpia out of it, and by relation, Conall. When he finished, he heard her release a long breath, as if she'd been holding it. Her parchment had disappeared—he assumed back in its place near her heart.

There was a new expression that passed over her face then. He

100

was used to the hard glare of anger or annoyance, but this was... almost sad.

"Is there someone yer looking for?" As soon as the words were out of his mouth, that stone expression was back and he snapped his lips shut.

"'Tis all? Yer certain?" She cast wide eyes at Aksel.

"I recalled every name."

When she narrowed her eyes, he raised his hand. "I swear it."

There was something in that gaze. He wasn't lying. He had recalled every name, just not aloud.

"Have ye ever seen anyone in Kaupang that looked like me?"

"Ye mean tiny and murderous?" He tilted his head to the side, watching every detail of her expression, wishing he could read the thoughts swirling in her mind. "Nay."

That same sad look lowered her brows. Even injured, her steps made no sound as she walked. She truly was a shadow. They were not following a trail, but she seemed to know exactly where she was going, even so much as to make a sharp step to the side of a dark pile of brush, guiding him with a hand on his arm. She was moving slowly and kept her injured arm pressed close across her stomach.

"If I needed to send a message to the Chieftain, how would I do that?"

"Are yer ravens not message enough?" Aksel peered down at her.

"So, ye ken who I am?" Those shadows she could have melded with seemed to swirl around her ankles, snaking up her calves.

"Ye are the one terrorizing the settlements, ridding freemen and Chieftains of their thralls."

"Are ye not afraid?"

Aksel lifted a shoulder, moving a branch for her to duck under. "I suppose I should be. But I have never been known to do what is wise."

She raised a brow, seeming to agree with his self-assessment but still expecting an answer.

"The message would have to come from someone the Chieftain

trusted. He is a suspicious man. It would have to be something he couldna' ignore." Aksel watched her as he talked, taking in her response. "Ye promised to tell me of the slaves from my father's house."

"I promised nothing."

He opened his mouth to argue but remembered her exact words. She hadn't promised to tell him. *Clever, Little Bird. Very clever.*

"Ye ken runes. Would he be able to read a message?" She ducked under another low hanging branch, lifting it as she passed and waiting for him before she let go.

"As I said before, few Norsemen ken how to interpret runes. He would have someone read it fer him."

"Are there others besides ye in Kaupang that have the knowledge?"

"Aye, a few."

"Hmm." She pulled her bottom lip lightly between her teeth, as if she were formulating a plan.

"Please tell me what happened to them." When he stopped, she did the same.

He knew he could overpower her; she was practically dead on her feet. What he doubted was whether he could get hands on her, even in her exhaustion and pain. She clearly knew her way around these woods, and though he did too, the way she'd avoided the brush made him think she'd laid traps. She also possessed an unknown but seemingly endless supply of weapons.

"I told ye they were unharmed, and I meant it."

He ground his teeth as she swayed on her feet, finally growling, "Ye need water."

She scoffed but took a long swig from her water skin. When she started walking again, he followed. He could bide his time, wait for her to let her guard down, and then make his move. She was only one woman. She had to sleep at some point. If she truly was the raven so feared by his people, he would be quite the hero bringing her before the Chieftain. It might be the act worthy enough to earn his father's respect. At the thought, he was ready to pounce.

But knowing she hadn't harmed Ethni and Alpia had him admitting there was another part of him that was undeniably intrigued by this violent little bird. He might follow her into whatever dark place she was going just to see what happened. Even if it earned him no glory. Even if he never saw his family again. Even if that darkness swallowed him whole. He was already halfway buried anyway.

She turned her head, only partly looking at him. "Do ye want to live?"

He nearly laughed. "Do I really have to answer that?"

"Well, from the way ye chose not to save yer own life wi' the wolves, and the way ye were guzzling mead, it doesna really seem like it."

"Fine, yes I want to live." He sped up then, fascinated by her questions. Something was churning in her mind and she seemed almost...hesitant...to ask it of him.

"Ye want to ken about the slaves from yer household?"

"I have said as much, more than once. Do ye desire that I should beg?"

"First, ye lied to me, and I want to ken why."

He kept himself moving, but every muscle was taut as he attempted to school his expression, aiming for bored. "How is it that I have lied?"

"There are names ye dinna say."

Aksel held back his breath. She had definitely spoken to them.

"Why?" She stopped then, whirling on him, almost stumbling. Still, she was relentless. He towered over her, but she stepped closer, having to tilt her chin up so that her piercing blue eyes locked onto his. "Why did ye lie?"

She'd been asking this same question over and over. Why? Why did he want her to stay away from his home, why did he skip Ethni, Alpia, and Conall's names, why did he save her from the wolves? He somehow knew there was an answer she was looking for, and he felt as though it wasn't because she despised the slaves.

Once again, the best answer was the truth.

He released his trapped breath. "I dinna give ye three names. Names of servants—"

"Ye mean slaves."

"Very well, slaves in my father's house. I dinna name them because I dinna want harm to come to them. They are special to me."

She smashed her lips together, lightly rubbing her injured arm before she blew a short breath and started walking again. Aksei slapped his hands against his legs in frustration. "Where are we going?"

'If ye want to see yer slaves, ye'll come wi' me and not make trouble." She didn't stop walking.

"Wait," he was at her side, even a step ahead to see her face. "What do ye mean? Did ye take them?"

She only glanced at him before focusing on the woods ahead.

"What have ye done?" His stomach cramped, but he ignored it.

"If ye want to live, if ye want to see them, I have conditions."

He was distracted by the sudden wave of nausea brought on by an abundance of energy and a lack of food and mead. "State your terms."

"I'll let ye remain unbound, but there will be eyes on ye. Day and night. Not one second will ye be left to yerself. So dunna even think about running." She pulled that trick where she had a dagger one second and not the next. It was meant to threaten him, but it only heated his blood with fascination.

"What if I need to—"

She slowed, spearing him with a look. At least it wasn't a blade. "Even then."

He still didn't understand the motivations of this woman, still didn't know what she'd done with Ethni, Alpia, and Conall, but he couldn't curb his curiosity about her. Somewhere deep inside, he truly believed she hadn't harmed them and that she never would. It was dangerous and exhilarating to push her, to see just how far she'd let him go. Maybe he had been lying. Maybe he didn't want to live, because he couldn't help himself and pushed aside his discomfort to goad her. "Ye will watch me?"

She raised one brow, leaning against the trunk of a birch and taking a drink from her water skin. "Do ye have a problem wi' that?"

"Nay." He matched her expression but clenched his teeth to keep from grinning when the vein in her neck began to pulse. She was... gods, whatever she was, whoever she was, it was magnificent. Vikings were no strangers to strong warrior women. Tales of the valkyrie had spanned his childhood, but she was more than a warrior. She was driven by something more than the want for glory, something far more powerful. Something that kept her walking when he could tell her body was screaming at her to fall to the ground.

Aksel watched her every move: the way her fingers drummed a silent melody on her leg, the little expressions she let slip past the stone exterior, and how quickly she brought her emotions under control when she caught him staring. He mentally cataloged all her tells, storing the knowledge for when he'd need it most. She moved like a person who'd lived a thousand lifetimes, but she couldn't be more than...

"How old are ye?"

She jerked, a blade resting atop her knuckles from where she'd let it dance over her fingers.

"I'm only curious."

"Twenty on my next turn."

Nineteen? Most in his settlement were handfasted by twelve or thirteen. Twenty found most with their third or fourth child. He let his eyes skim her face. It was her eyes that made her seem more than her years.

"And ye?" Her question surprised him.

"Twenty-five."

She looked like she wanted to ask him something else, but

instead, she wagged the knife at him, holding it loosely between her thumb and forefinger. He noticed her gaze dip to his hands. Was she looking for a handfasting band? Did she wonder if he had a wife? He figured she knew he didn't, but she wouldn't know why.

"As long as ye are useful, ye live," she said.

"Ye dunna need to keep reminding me."

She took another drink, her fingers trembling slightly as she capped the water skin before offering it to him.

"But, very well," he said, accepting her gift. "I agree."

"Ye dunna even ken what I'm asking ye to do." The dagger remained a silent threat between them. That was fine. She could keep her weapon if it made her feel safe. He'd find out the true purpose of this raven, ensure Ethni and Alpia were not in danger, and, when the moment was right, he'd deliver a message to his father himself. One that said he was not the useless son the Chieftain claimed.

"Does it really matter?" Aksel's tone was light. "My choices are to agree or die, am I understanding correctly?"

She didn't answer. She only ticked her jaw to the side in what appeared to be irritation at his lack of fear. She swung her satchel around to the front, lifted the flap, and reached in. A blank flat of birch bark was thrust toward him, followed by his carving tool.

"Ye'll carve a message to yer father. Ye'll be returned if he delivers the amount I request."

"So, I am to be ransomed." He didn't know why, but her words stung. What else did he expect? He was the son of the Chieftain, and she was a clever little thief.

"Ye can tell yerself 'tis fer a good cause." She offered a sarcastic smile.

"I am certain it is." He squared his jaw, turning his eyes forward, staring at the black woods ahead of them with the birch bark and knife at his side. She did the same. "Tell me, Little Bird, how will ye prove ye have his son? Will you send one of my fingers wi' yer messenger? An ear, mayhap?"

Her blade stilled, and she cut a quick glance his way. He almost felt her eyes sliding from that ear down his arm to those very fingers. "Not a bad idea."

He wouldn't give her the satisfaction of looking appalled. "Then I have my own request."

She pursed her lips, head cocked to the side. "I dunna think ye are in the position to—"

"'Tis but a small thing." He pinched the fingers of his free hand together, leaving a fraction of space between them.

She raised her brows and waved a hand, as if to invite him to continue.

"Yer name." When she met him with that unwavering stone stare, he shrugged. "I will find out sooner or later." When she still didn't answer, he added, "I have to call ye something."

In truth, he wanted the name of the one who would most likely be his end.

He decided to stop begging and meet her stare for stare. When she rolled her eyes and released an exasperated sigh, he controlled the smile that attempted to break across his lips.

She pointed to the stump of a sawed-off tree in a bright patch of moonlight, motioning for him to sit.

"Carve the message," she hesitated, and his face heated, suddenly riveted by the possibility of knowing her name. She cleared her throat and continued, "I am called Revna."

7

REVNA

er shoulder screamed from the wolf's bite, and her arm pulsed with pain from the gash the gray one dug with its claws. More than once as they hiked through the woods, she felt the world tip sideways and her vision blackened.

She refused to fall. Just as she had on the boat that carried her to the Northlands, she willed herself to stay conscious—to keep moving. Rune. It was his face that made her yell for Aksel to run, even if it meant her destruction.

Now, Aksel was waiting for her to lead. She stared at the bark he'd carved, her head swimming with symbols she didn't know how to interpret.

He could have written anything. Her name, where she'd kept him, her weaknesses, the fact that she was human and not some immortal bird sent by the gods of his people.

She'd been a fool to tell him her name, weak to keep him alive when the smart thing to do would have been to bury him some place he'd never be found.

Except for Rune and the way he'd ruined her easy, dark vengeance by giving her a taste of light. Even four winters later, his amber eyes were still bright in her memory, his last whispered request tugging at her heart. *Meet me in eternity.*

If only she could.

She squeezed her eyes closed, fighting the swell of emotion that held her heart with a grip so firm she thought it wouldn't allow the next beat. A deep, painful breath kept her on her feet, and sheer willpower kept her expression placid instead of twisted in agony. She had to be strong, cunning, and fierce. Aksel could not know the depths of uncertainty and grief that swirled constantly inside of her.

But he had those eyes. Those keen, observant eyes like Duncan's captain, Eowin. Always watching and noticing.

The way he looked at her twisted her insides. It confused her and made her blood feel like fire in her veins. His blasted blue eyes and the way he wasn't afraid of her at all—she didn't know what to do with these strange feelings. Every taunting smirk had her hands flexing with the need to drive her fist straight into his handsome face.

She pressed the heel of her palm against her chest where the lion-shaped mark pulsed. The wolf's fang had just missed it, and had Aksel pulled her tunic any lower to examine the bite, he'd have seen. In that moment, despite her disdain, she might have let him. Just to have another living person verify it was really there.

She curled her lip. No. She was shadow and night. Not meant to be seen. She stuffed the bark in her satchel, plans of a ransom becoming less and less appealing. It really was too dangerous.

Mayhap one of the others could read the message Aksel had carved and ensure it wouldn't get them all run through by Viking blades. Or worse.

She could tie him back up and leave him while she confirmed. Yes, that was a good plan. He couldn't be trusted to see the ones Revna was protecting. Not yet.

His observant eyes couldn't witness their little hidden make-shift village. She wasn't ready for his reaction to tent-like shelters, smoldering campfires, and former slaves with skills they'd used to build their master's households now put to use keeping themselves alive until they were sent home.

A wave of nausea swept through her, blackness clouding her vision until she had no choice but to reach for the nearest tree to keep herself upright.

"Revna?" Aksel's voice sounded far away—barely audible over the pounding in her ears.

Seconds away from unconsciousness, she fumbled for her bag. The rope—she needed to tie him up, needed to—where were her herbs? She had to weaken him. He would leave; he would bring his father. *Stay awake, stay in control.*

"They'll die." Her lips moved, but no sound came out.

"Revna."

She was on the ground. Hands were on her face, brushing back her hair, and water was being poured into her mouth. She gagged as her throat resisted. He had saved her before when he wanted information, but now that he knew she'd not harmed his slaves, he would leave. He knew who she was...he...

"I have Ethni and Alpia." Her voice wasn't more than a rasping whisper.

He launched himself to his feet, sparks igniting in his blue eyes before he turned and took three steps away.

He couldn't leave. She couldn't let him. Working by muscle memory alone, she sent a dagger flying. It landed in the trunk of the tree, inches from his face. He didn't even blink. In fact, he took a step toward her, fury fanning sparks in his eyes to blazing flames

"I have another," she croaked, holding up her hand as a warning against his approach. She tried and failed to push herself up. *Stay awake, Revna.*

"Where are they?" he ground through clenched teeth.

She groaned at pain radiating from her shoulder and blinked back fog that coated her vision. "Safe. They came wi' me because they wanted to."

He didn't respond, but for the first time, he didn't bear that half-amused smirk. He looked as pale as she felt.

"They're helping me." She paused, choosing her words carefully. "And I'm helping them."

He jerked the dagger from the tree and dropped to his haunches in front of her, never taking his eyes from hers as if keeping her gaze was the only thing holding her hand from sending a blade into his skull.

She'd faced more terrifying villains than him. And she wasn't lying. She did have another dagger. Several, in fact. He didn't need to know she couldn't move her arms to retrieve them.

"Take me to them." Tucking the dagger between his teeth, he hooked his hands under her arms and hauled her to her feet. His hands remained under her arms, steadying her.

As her vision blackened again, she grasped his forearms. "I was... I am."

He bent, his arm moving to sweep her legs out from under her.

"Nay." She weakly pushed him away, panic heating her skin. When he stopped and looked at her again, his mouth was so close to hers that his breath fanned her face. She put what force she had remaining behind her words. "I willna be carried."

"Ye can barely stand."

"I willna be carried." She was adamant, one hand curling into a fist against his chest.

He was still so close, and her eyes slid to his jaw, watching as the muscle feathered under his bearded skin with the clench of his teeth. He tipped his head, capturing her gaze. "If ye die before we reach them, I'll hunt ye down in the Hals of Hel and make yer afterlife miserable."

"I'd rather that than be carried." She felt the twitch of her lips as a sly grin tugged at the corner of her mouth. "Besides, yer already insufferable; wouldna be much different."

With a growl, he straightened, placing his hands low on his hips and shaking his head. Revna let her head fall back against the trunk of the tree for three heartbeats before pushing herself forward.

He was right, she could barely stand. She needed rest, food, and herbs—mayhap a needle and thread to sew up the gash on her arm. All of which waited at the encampment where they were headed. Aksel's arm snaked around her waist, and he daggered her with a look that promised she would end up in his arms if she complained about his assistance.

She huffed in agreement. Before they took one step, she touched his arm, drawing his gaze to hers.

"Ye need to ken they are under the impression that ye are helping me. Willingly." She found it difficult to meet his eyes. There had never been a need to explain her actions before. Lives were at stake, and she did what was necessary to save them. But confessing to Aksel twisted her insides.

His expression was drawn. "Why would they think that?"

"Because I told them such." After a beat of silence, she continued, "They worried fer ye."

He released a breathy laugh and shook his head. "Mother hens."

Revna tilted her head to watch his expression, not understanding this Viking's connection to Ethni and Alpia. Aksel relaxed slightly, adjusting his grip on her. "Which way?"

Revna nodded to the east, and Aksel aimed them in that direction —mostly carrying her but keeping quiet about her willingness to let him.

"I ken it willna make sense to ye, but Alpia is like a little sister to me and Ethni..." Aksel's eyes roved over the ground, as if the right words were mixed amongst the fallen leaves. "I became very sick when I was a child. My parents sent everyone away. All the family, all their servants and slaves, even my younger sister. Everyone but Ethni. She was only a few winters older, but she stayed by my side. Every minute. Even when my mother..."

His voice trailed off again, and Revna didn't shake him from his thoughts. She had many mothers in the village. Women who cared for her and loved her as their own, but still, she had always longed to know Fiona. The one who had given birth to her.

And there was Cyrene. Cyrene was... she didn't have the words to describe her. She wasn't a mother. Sister wasn't strong enough. Friend seemed irreverent.

Cyrene was her queen. When Revna was a lost little girl, trailed by nightmares and so much angst she didn't know what to do with herself, Cyrene made her a scout. She gave her purpose; a way to use the shadows for the good of her people instead of a place to hide from them.

"I ken what it is to ache fer something lost." Again, she found herself revealing inner thoughts to this stranger, and even more surprising, the weight in her chest reached for him.

Her mother would have loved her had she lived, but his...his was alive, and from the way his brows drew together over his blue eyes, she knew the woman was farther from him than Fiona was from her.

Revna almost hated herself for it, but for their own good, she had to exploit his feelings for Ethni and Alpia.

"If I dunna return to them, they'll be found, and ye ken what will happen. When we do reach them, if ye dunna want them to suffer watching ye die, I suggest ye put on a convincing show."

She nearly flinched at the glare he shot her. "Bold words for a woman currently at my mercy."

"Ye truly think I was ever at yer mercy?" She didn't bother to show him the blade she'd palmed when he wasn't looking.

"Nay." He tightened his grip on her waist. "I'm certain ye have something pointy aimed at some vital part of me."

"Yer wiser than ye look, Prince."

She'd never failed to do the hard things. To take the low road or even threaten vulnerable people if it meant completing her mission. When she was young and living in the dark woods, it was how she kept food and supplies coming into her hidden village from a kingdom that wasn't supposed to know they existed. It was what got Tràigh's healer to follow her when Duncan was dying in the queen's hut and what convinced Duncan's holy man to breach the border of The Dorcha when those woods were said to be cursed by trolls and fang-toothed fairies. She'd never failed to do what needed to be done at the expense of her own conscience; it was why Cyrene sent her and no one else on those errands. It was why she boarded that longboat nearly four winters ago.

But for the first time, she couldn't brush aside what settled in her stomach. Where once it was a comforting dark covering to hide her violent deeds, it now felt like bubbling tar. Once it coated her insides, she'd not be able to scrape it off, even with the sharpest blade.

"I will do my part," he breathed his reply.

"Good." She jerked her head, prompting him to turn slightly north. This wretched son of her enemy would not deter her, no matter what foreign feelings he caused inside of her. She'd remain alert and prepared, never taking her eyes from him.

Her gaze trailed over his form, taking in every detail. She loathed the vulnerableness of her condition and the fact that she was irrevocably dependent on him. Her throat dried, an uncomfortable thirst creeping up her neck, and the realization of why she felt so agitated made her grind her teeth.

It was more than being injured and needing his support to take each step. It was more than the knowledge that this Viking, this owner of her people, was the only thing holding her up.

Before the wolves attacked, she knew Aksel was almost free from his bonds. She knew they were going to fight, and she had been nearly salivating for that battle. She wanted it. She desired the burn of her muscles and the rush of adrenaline that preceded the promise of death. She wanted the sweat-soaked victory.

Even though the wolves had sated that hunger, it had already returned. But there was something else brewing below the surface of her angst—a different kind of irritation. She didn't know what she wanted more—for him to be exactly as she expected or for him to be just the opposite. Mayhap, it was a longing for something truly surprising that settled like a hard stone in her gut.

"The word rune, what does it mean?" The question had been burning against her lips from the second she'd seen his carvings.

"A secret."

She shook her head, desperately wanting to push him away and walk on her own as she grumbled under her breath. "Why will no one just answer me?"

He laughed softly. "It means *a secret*, Little Bird."

"Oh." Something ached in her heart. A pair of kind amber eyes flashed in her mind above a set of dimples that flanked a friendly smile. Rune hadn't been teasing. What might have happened if she'd not been so blinded by rage? Would it be Rune at her side instead of Aksel?

She was silent after that, but when a dull ache began to form behind her eyes from the constant attention she paid his every move, she released a soft growl. "There is something else ye need to ken."

He didn't ask about her cryptic comment but kept moving in the direction she'd indicated.

"Ye'll see more than Ethni and Alpia when we arrive."

She felt his hauntingly intense gaze on her skin. "Conall is also there."

He hissed, and she jerked to face him. He only shook his head. "He hates me."

"Does he have reason to?"

Aksel took a deep breath. "I suspect..." He shook his head again, helping Revna step over a fallen log. "When I was twelve, my father sent me to train with his warband. It was...unexpected. I did not return for three harvests. Not until I was a man."

Revna waited for him to continue.

"Before I left, Ethni hardly spoke to Conall. When I returned, they were handfasted and Alpia was two months old."

"Why would that make him hate ye? A lot can change in three winters." She already had her own suspicions but was curious about Aksel's perspective.

"My father never allowed his slaves to wed. He claimed it

fostered a sense of rebellion. I learned what Conall had to endure to earn the right to Ethni's hand. It was..." Aksel's fingers tightened around her waist. "I dunna ken how he survived it."

"He must truly love her." Revna eyed him, searching his expression.

"Aye," was all Aksel offered before drawing in a deep breath. "So, I understand why he would despise the son of the man who caused him such pain."

Revna let her eyes drift to the tattooed arm Aksel had wrapped around her. "Is that where ye earned these marks? From yer days of training?"

She felt the muscle in his arm flex, as if he'd forgotten the lines of blue decorating his skin. He only hummed an affirmation.

When he spoke again, Revna wasn't sure he was talking to her.

"I hated my father for what he did while I was away."

Revna met his explanation with an accusing tone. "And what would ye have done had ye been there?"

Aksel stopped, causing Revna to do the same. She managed to stay on her feet when he released her. There was fury and something else in his expression. Shame?

He pressed his finger to his chest, brows inching toward his hairline. "What could I do? I was fifteen, and he is the Chieftain."

She blew a breath through her nose. "I was fifteen when I stepped foot on these shores. Yer never too young to do the right thing."

"Is that what yer doing?" His brows tipped together, and a wave of crimson crept up his neck. "The right thing?"

Of course it was. She started to lift her hand to her heart, but pain in her shoulder halted her movement. She was fulfilling her vow, taking back what was stolen, but before she could find the right words to respond, the snap of a twig garnered both their attention.

"Aksel?" Alpia's bell-like voice reached them through the trees.

Revna had wanted another few seconds to prepare him for what he would see, but Alpia was beyond the bounds of the clearing. The bundle of sticks in her arms that explained her presence dropped to the ground, and she raced toward them. Ethni and Conall appeared seconds later, having heard Alpia's call.

The girl flew into his arms and he curled her into his strong chest, leaving Revna swaying on her feet. The look of joy on Alpia's face renewed the unease creeping along Revna's bones. Ethni's worried expression relaxed into a soft smile, and she reached for Aksel. He allowed her to pull his head down and place a kiss on his forehead.

Conall leveled a knowing look at Revna, flicking his eyes to the exchange as if to warn her to tread carefully.

She couldn't tread carefully, though. She could hardly tread at all. It was all she could do to give instructions to Conall to guard Aksel and not to answer any of the questions the Chieftain's son would surely ask. Then she stumbled into the woods alone. She needed to clean her wounds, but more than that, she needed to get as far away as possible from the strange connection between Aksel and the slave women.

She knew they cared for him, but the way he held Alpia as if he loved her. How could they be held against their will—how could they have suffered so much—and still care for him like that? Especially Ethni, after what had been done to her by his people—by someone in his own house?

She didn't know what to make of Aksel. He was crazed with worry when he thought they were in danger. He was willing to do anything to keep her from going to his home where he knew they would be. She couldn't get the image of little Alpia in his arms out of her mind. He'd held her so tightly. He was a Viking, and Vikings were the enemy.

And how could he, a savage Norseman, connect with people so deeply—his own slaves for that matter—when she'd spent her entire life with someone as loving as Cyrene and was still without that ability?

But Aksel had helped the maid at the mead hall, and he'd saved her life in the wolf attack. He'd agreed to whatever demands she'd made if only she promised that Ethni and Alpia were safe. And he was the only person she'd met in the last four years, besides Rune, who didn't look at her with fear in his eyes.

Is that what yer doing?

Aksel's question consumed her. She took a seat on the flat part of a lichen-covered rock jutting into the stream outside their camp. Why did it vex her so much?

Her people were captives. Nearly twenty years they'd been enslaved. Any means she used to rescue them was acceptable. Wasn't it? Their captors deserved whatever vengeance came upon them. Didn't they? She wasn't taking their lives, after all. Burned homes and stables could be rebuilt.

The years stolen from her people could never be bought back.

She took her time cleaning her shoulder and used herbs from her satchel to concoct a poultice to press into the puncture wounds. There were more herbs waiting at the clearing, but these would do for now.

She cleaned her forearm next. It would definitely need sewing if she wanted to ensure it wouldn't fester. For now, she rinsed the linen she'd used to bind it and wrapped it again. By the time she finished, she'd decided the answer to her questions was yes. She was doing the right thing.

Aksel was a mystery, but the rest of his countrymen were as savage and brutal as she'd been taught. Even Astrid had said such, and she was born in these lands. Revna pushed aside the nagging doubt and filled her mind with images of each stolen Pict and villager of Tràigh when they heard the words they'd been dreaming of since they'd been taken: "Yer going home."

That was all that mattered. For that look of relief, she could use Aksel to fund their voyage home. And when she was done with him, for her people, she could do unthinkable things. She could give whatever she had to give and take whatever she had to take. In an attempt to quell the irritating discomfort, Revna rubbed her fist

against the place on her chest where the lion-shaped mark burned—
as if it disagreed with her decisions.

When the sensation didn't fade, she added a dab of clove poultice to it too.

Collapsing at the base of a redwood, she waited for the herbs to
take effect. The clove worked quickly, dulling the pain and letting her
take deep restful breaths. She couldn't feel the juniper and elder-
berry working, but she trusted they would stave off any festering and
quicken her healing.

Thank ye, Brigid. The storytelling healer had been gone for over a
decade, but her lessons lived on, saving Revna more than once over
the years. Revna refused to let her mind drift to the mark on her
chest or Brigid's final lesson. It had not been one of herbs and remedies but of history and warning.

That mark was obviously a mistake. It was meant for someone
else. But Brigid's words had most certainly been meant for her, and
Revna couldn't dwell on all the ways she'd failed to do what Brigid
requested. There was no changing the past.

There was only what was in front of her, and that was the group
of people in the clearing to whom she'd made a promise. A promise
she intended to keep, no matter what. She allowed herself a half
hour of solitude before laboring through the woods to the clearing
and the Viking she'd been forced to trust.

8

AKSEL

When Revna returned, Ethni abandoned her attempts to force a third helping of venison stew on Aksel. Instead, she turned her attention to the mysterious shadow-kissed woman who was looking at everything but him.

Using a dried branch of oak and one of the knives he'd collected from Revna, Aksel carved the slivers of kindling Ethni said they would need for the next morning's fire. He was surprised Revna allowed him to keep the weapons. She either had a death wish or she realized Ethni and Alpia's presence was enough to keep him from doing anything but what she ordered. Apparently, she didn't consider him to be more than a mangy dog because, according to Conall, her orders for him were to sit and stay. Her orders to Conall were not to answer any of his questions. And he certainly had questions.

He couldn't keep his eyes from traveling across the clearing. They weren't but a half-day's journey from Kaupang, but a well-run miniature settlement had been established in the clearing.

A small structure built from sturdy branches, flats of canvas, and woven ropes had been built over the fire. It was high enough to avoid catching ablaze but low enough to disperse the smoke so it would dissipate into the air before reaching the treetops, keeping their presence hidden.

Ropes, crisscrossed between trees, created a loose boundary and held everything from drying clothes to drying meats. Somehow, they'd gathered plentiful baskets of onions, carrots, and potatoes. In any other place, the forest would have been abuzz with the noise of such a thriving population, but here the volume didn't rise above a soft whisper. Even the birds silenced their chirps and calls, as if they were part of the conspiracy to conceal this wayward group.

They were all slaves. He hadn't been told as much, but their features were foreign—more like Ethni's and Conall's than his people—and they spoke in the Vestland language. There was a crackling air of urgency that kept Aksel alert, but the people moved confidently with broad smiles. As if they were unaware of the danger that lurked just on the outside of these woods. As if they were protected by some other-worldly shield.

That thought drew his attention to Revna, who stood on the outer edge and surveyed her kingdom. Her blue eyes worked their way across the clearing and back again, as if she were counting every face, numbering and assessing every article of clothing and each bite of food.

Her hands were clean, cheeks less pale, and movements more certain. As he cast a glance over the people again, he found he was not the only one watching her. Everyone was. Their gazes didn't linger, their expressions a strange mix of admiration and avoidance. From the slight dip of every head that noticed her subtle presence, he knew for certain she was their queen.

He felt a small quirk of his lips; he understood quite well, only the avoidance part was quickly being replaced with a fascination that made him desire to know all her secrets.

How she'd managed to gather this many slaves and cross the

countryside without being followed or captured was one of the biggest mysteries he wanted to unravel. Then again, he had a vague memory of Rendel recounting how Galdvyn had been found naked and crazed after going after his missing slaves, spouting a story about a human raven on a midnight steed. He was certain it was no coincidence there was a solid black horse loosely lashed to a tree on the other side of the clearing. It might have been a trick of the moon light, but he felt the animal looked at him with the same disapproval as its owner.

Revna moved to the horse's side, slowly stroking her hand down its silky neck. The mare lowered her head, wrapping Revna in what looked like an embrace after Revna whispered in her ears and peppered her long nose with soft kisses.

He kept his head low, flicking his eyes up at her as she was approached by a woman with a babe in arms. He stifled a laugh when the feared raven stiffened as the woman deposited her child in Revna's arms. She could face a pack of blood-thirsty wolves without blinking, but a tiny babe filled her with obvious terror.

After a few seconds, Revna's shoulders relaxed. Aksel felt his chest tighten at the way she tenderly ran the back of her finger over the babe's rounded cheek and more so at the way the child's mother wiped tears from her own face.

Revna handed the babe back and made her way through the clearing. Aksel attempted to keep his eyes on his work, but when she volunteered her arm to Ethni and allowed the woman to sew up her wound, he found himself overly interested. Revna never flinched. She never once looked away, either, but kept her eyes on Ethni's steady fingers as she worked. If he could bottle even a drop of that grit, he could make himself king of the entire Northlands peddling it to warriors who desired enough bravery to earn their way into Valhalla.

Once mended, even Revna was no match for Ethni's persistence, and she reluctantly accepted a double helping of steaming stew. When she finished her meal, she stood silently near the fire, rubbing her hands together as if they were still coated with the wolves' blood and she itched to wash them clean.

Ethni, with Alpia as shadow, busied herself tending to others. Aksel counted ten slaves in the clearing, not including Ethni, Alpia, and Conall. Ten more souls for Ethni to gather under her mother hen wings.

Alpia was young, but she was a replica of her mother in every way but appearance. She, too, was unable to resist caring for someone who needed it. He let his gaze bob from one face to the other. One was missing. Conall.

The man could barely stand to look at Aksel. Revna's condemning question from earlier left him wondering if Conall would ask the same. Would he have intervened against his father? In truth, he didn't know.

But he suspected Conall had done just that for Ethni. Aksel found Alpia in the crowd, and, as if she sensed him watching her, her sparkling grin flashed, her dark brown eyes dancing in the firelight. Eyes so different from the blues of Conall and Ethni. Eyes the same color as his father's.

Aksel knew why his father changed his mind about slaves hand-fasting while he was gone. He even knew why the Chieftain wouldn't want anyone knowing about a child sired with a slave—most likely having to do more with Aksel's mother than his father's shame. What he didn't know was why Conall had given so much for Ethni and Alpia. He owed them nothing; they were little more than strangers then.

Because Ethni was owned by his father, by their laws, Alpia was too. He'd never seen the Chieftain approach Ethni after Alpia was born. And he didn't have the chance to tell Revna, but he had tried to intervene when his mother was unusually cruel. It seemed a trivial and insignificant act, though, especially after meeting the mighty little bird who was sweeping across his homeland with her para-lyzing terror.

Masters and slaves. It had always been the way of things, but feeling the unspoken blame from Conall, the sadness from Ethni, the judgment from Revna—it churned unpleasant irritation in his stomach. It was a feeling of wrongness, as if his eyes had been closed for many years and were now being pried open.

"Thank ye."

Aksel jumped; having been lost in his thoughts, he hadn't noticed when Revna materialized at his side and lowered herself to the ground, sitting cross-legged. She was a shadow, something that slipped silently through the night. A ghostly little bird.

He nearly asked her to repeat what she'd said, but as he stared at her, the words finally made sense in his ears. He felt his brows furrow as he asked, "For what?"

"Ye could have let the wolves have their way. Ye could have run, but ye came back."

He watched his hands, focusing on the blade sliding smoothly through the soft wood. "Ye could have taken back yer blades."

When she didn't answer, he kept his chin low but looked up at her from beneath his lashes. Her gaze met his for too long before she lifted a shoulder in a casual shrug, sniffing as she said, "I have another."

He pulled his bottom lip between his teeth to control his smile and stroked the blade through the wood several more times before adding the strips of kindling to his growing pile.

"Mayhap we both have a dangerous relationship wi' fate. A need to walk the edge to see how close we can get wi'out falling."

"Mayhap." Her answer was low, as if she might agree.

But he knew she was in complete control. She knew just how near to death she could dance. But him helping her without being threatened seemed to rattle her.

"I willna ask ye why. And I dunna care if ye regret it now." Her words were tight, her voice more raspy than usual. "I just...thank ye."

He offered a tight smile which broadened into a more genuine one when Ethni approached, bearing another helping of stew for them both.

Aksel forced himself to accept his portion, willing to risk the nausea just to keep the smile on the woman's face.

"'Tis good to see yer appetite has returned. I dunna ken where it went." To his horror, Ethni turned to Revna. "When he was a lad, there was not enough food in all of Kaupang to fill his belly."

Aksel didn't know how to interpret the lift of Revna's lips, her constant frown lessening a bit before it returned almost as quickly. She stood abruptly, muttering something about refilling water skins, and disappeared into the shadows of the forest again. A hint of amusement warmed his skin, for as fearless as she seemed to be, she was quick to run from anything that made her uncomfortable.

He didn't have that luxury. Ethni and Revna both knew exactly where his appetite had gone. Revna wouldn't have known it had been gone for nearly three winters, but she was certainly aware it had been buried under a barrel for a while. Still, neither of them judged or accused him, and he almost wished they would.

"What do ye think of Revna?" Ethni settled beside him, urging a few more bites into his mouth as she talked.

"I dunna ken enough about her to think anything." It was a partial lie. He had definitely formed an opinion. That woman was a volatile weapon, something deadly held back with the thinnest of strings. Of that he was certain. What he didn't know was if it was a blessing or a curse.

"Ye remembered our language quite well." She gestured to the rest of the group.

"How could I forget? 'Tis all ye spoke to me when I was young." Aksel watched Ethni's face, curious as to why she watched him so intently. Did she think he would betray her—that he would do anything other than ensure her safety?

"Revna says yer helping her, but I have a feeling she isna one to give many choices when she wants something."

Aksel lowered his brows at Ethni. He could lie, but she would know. She nodded, a forgiving smile stretching her lips.

"It doesna matter." She touched his shoulder as she stood, and he gazed up at her. "I'm just glad yer wi' us. I could never leave ye behind."

There was an edge to her tone that made him wonder if there was something she wasn't saying. He wanted to ask, but Conall returned, scowling and impatiently waiting for Aksel to get on his feet.

Once Aksel had been humiliatingly escorted deeper into the woods to tend to his needs, the stableman returned him to their camp and took up his guarding position by leaning against a tree, arms folded over his chest.

Ethni worked her way through the group again, making sure everyone was fed and comfortable.

Revna didn't return until the fire burned so low it was nothing but orange embers. Even then, she kept her distance while everyone settled in for the night. He listened as Alpia and Ethni whispered prayers to their God. It wasn't the first time he'd heard them pray. Their words were always of gratitude, which he couldn't understand. Their God had not freed them from their situation, yet they praised Him. Never once had he heard them bargain or offer anything for His help. It was only ever thanksgiving.

His people's offerings were always made out of fear. They were bargains, begging for more rain, a good harvest, a safe return from a voyage. Never had he seen an offering of praise when requests were not met.

While Alpia and Ethni's heads were turned together, their hands folded, he felt a strange stillness settle over the camp. He swung his gaze to find Revna watching them with the same curiosity—as if she had the same questions.

What was her relationship to these people? She didn't look like them with her tanned skin and black hair. He looked more like a Vestman than she did. Maybe she was hired by some benevolent

Vestman king who finally saw fit to send a warrior to retrieve his people? Whoever she was, they loved her. Although, he suspected she didn't see it.

Maybe in gratitude for him saving her she'd answer his questions. Movement near the fire caught his eye. Conall had finally abandoned his post and moved to Ethni's side.

After a soft brush of her hand down Conall's arm, Ethni turned to where Alpia was curled by the coals and worked her way under their shared blanket. She lifted her head, finding Aksel's eyes. He nodded, letting her know he was well.

"Mother hen," he chuckled under his breath, flicking his eyes over the sleeping bodies until his gaze settled on Revna. She must have exchanged watch posts with Conall.

Since she'd not bound his hands or feet again, nor had she dragged him into the woods or put a knife in his heart, he assumed he had done enough to prove himself worthy of living through the night.

He couldn't understand why she didn't simply end him, other than the possibility of using him for ransom. Once he'd carved her message, she didn't need him alive to carry out her plans. Not that he was disappointed in her choice—he simply couldn't begin to guess what Revna's endgame was.

Settling back against what he'd claimed as his tree, Aksel let his eyes wander over the mysterious woman who sat on the opposite side of the clearing—the only other person awake. She turned her folded parchment between her fingers as her eyes danced over every sleeping form, counting. The permanent frown on her full lips lessened slightly upon her final inspection.

His gaze drifted to her hands. She traded her parchment for one of her daggers. The blade danced over her knuckles as she moved her fingers. When the blade suddenly stilled, he snapped his eyes to her face, finding her narrowed glare centered on him.

He felt more exposed under her stare than when Conall had watched him relieve himself in the woods, and for the first time all day, a sharp slice of pain slowly worked its way across his stomach. He regretted every bite of stew and knew it wouldn't be long until his stomach freed itself of his dinner.

He'd fought off sporadic bouts of sweat and chills since she'd led him to the clearing, and for Ethni's sake, he'd managed to keep his discomfort hidden. He'd ignored it as long as he could, the work of carving kindling staving off thoughts of the growing starvation in his belly. It was an emptiness made worse by food. But with Revna's eyes looking right through him, that gaping hole inside tore open, and all his weaknesses floated to the surface, including his undeniable need for a stiff mug—or ten—of mead.

Her eyes darted to his forehead, and he couldn't help the movement of his hand as it shot to his brow to hide the coating of sweat he could feel forming. For years, he'd tried to fool himself into thinking he was visiting the settlers' homes to keep up with the business for his father, but the dryness of his tongue and burning ache in his throat told the truth. They would laugh at all his jokes, lie about his accomplishments, and pretend to be happy to see him. They filled his mug, over and over, and, most importantly, they made him feel like he belonged at their tables.

He'd stumble home and fall into bed where sweet, dreamless sleep claimed him before guilt and worthlessness could haunt his nights.

Revna was stealthy, but he knew even if he begged and offered her the wealth of his father's hoards, she would not steal into the settlement and bring him a cask of mead. Plus, she had probably already obtained the wealth of his father's hoards despite the ransom she demanded.

No, she was intent on setting those pale eyes on him, prying out every one of his weaknesses and setting them at his feet to keep him company during what was sure to be a sleepless night. Maybe she *was* a messenger from Odin sent to exact a cruel punishment on him for whatever wrongs the god deemed he'd done.

Her eyes drifted to his throat as he attempted to swallow, but since he'd been assaulted by the first thought of a drink, every drop of moisture had evaporated from his body. His eyes watered and stung with the effort of blinking and breathing.

His heart picked up pace, trembles seizing his fingers, and he closed his eyes, unable to bear the weight of her stare. A dull ache began behind his eyes and quickly grew into a more intense pain. His legs were drawn to his chest, and he barely had enough strength to wrap his arms around them before his head thumped heavily onto his knees.

His dinner churned in his stomach. Revna had seen him sick before; he remembered that much from their first hours together, but he desperately wanted to keep from doing that again, especially in front of all these people. His retching was sure to wake them.

This was going to be a very, very long night.

Something nudged his shoulder and he lifted his head, blurred vision taking in the shape of Revna's water skin.

She said nothing as he raised a shaking hand and accepted the gift, downing nearly every drop before wiping the back of his hand across his mouth.

She didn't say anything. She didn't scowl or look at him as if he should do better. Be better. She simply handed him a few minty-smelling leaves and jerked her head toward the woods.

"Walk wi' me." Her whispered order might as well have been a gift of gold, and he cast a quick glance to the sleeping women before rising and following her into the darkness.

"Yer meant to chew those." She dipped her eyes to the leaves in his hand.

She led him a short distance to a stream and had the decency to turn her back when he knelt and emptied his stomach onto the thick grass away from the water's edge.

When he'd caught his breath and rinsed his mouth with the icy water, she crouched by his side, filling her water skin again. She was so quiet. And he was so exposed. His insides still cramped and chastised him for filling them with food instead of mead. Placing the leaves on his tongue, he slowly moved his jaw, a burst of cool spice soothing his tumbling stomach. His legs still felt boneless, and he wasn't sure he could stand if he needed to.

He might need to run, though, after he revealed the thought plaguing him since Revna requested he carve the message to his father. She would probably kill him when she found out the truth, but what did it matter if it was now or in a few days?

"He will not pay."

She swung her gaze his way. "Why not?"

He pushed himself up from all fours until he was on his knees in front of her. Even though she stood, the top of his head came nearly to her shoulders. She didn't back away; she also wasn't surprised at his announcement.

"I amna the son he would ransom."

Her blue eyes rounded. "He has another son?"

Aksel lifted his hand, tapping his temple. "In his mind, he has another son."

She stared at him, revealing nothing about her thoughts through her expression.

"Why do ye tell me this?"

"Fer Ethni and Alpia." He sat back on his heels, wiping the back of his hand across his sweat-soaked forehead. "I willna risk their lives on whatever plan ye have fer me. It willna work."

She only looked at him. Gods, what he wouldn't give to see inside her mind—to be party to whatever schemes were swirling inside her lovely head.

She was beautiful in the way a thunderstorm was beautiful. It was something one would step outside the safety of their home to witness—a vibrant, terrifying power that demanded attention.

It was a strange time for him to notice that about her, but once she realized he was telling the truth, he'd probably be dead. He might as well have the last thing he saw be something pleasant.

"He willna pay the ransom, but he will search fer me, if fer nothing else than appearances. And he cares nothing fer gods and spirits. Yer tricks willna work on him. He only cares fer his position and keeping it. If you're discovered, they're all dead. All of them. And ye too." He added the last part for emphasis, but as he watched her face, he knew it was the lives of the others—not her own— that would move her.

"What are ye asking me to do, Prince?"

What indeed? Something had been brewing in the back of his mind since she announced that Ethni and Alpia were with her, and it had started to bubble over when he'd seen them in an embrace with Conall earlier.

Conall's arm was draped over Alpia's shoulder, his other tenderly around Ethni's waist. Ethni had looked up at Conall with a softness in her eyes, her shoulders relaxed. She smiled before rising up on her toes and placing a kiss on Conall's cheek. He'd never seen them look that way, and Aksel realized all the smiles Ethni offered him over the years had been forced. They had all been for his sake and not because of her own happiness.

When she saw him as he approached in the woods, the grin she unleashed nearly brought him to his knees. He'd felt as filthy as the mead hall floor and as useless as a Chieftain's son who would never voyage the seas.

He'd had his entire life to make something of himself. To become a son that his father would have trusted to join him on voyages or to hold a position of importance in the settlement. And even if his parents never saw fit to secure a marriage union, he could have taken a wife of his own, and he could have taken Ethni and Alpia with him. There were so many things he could have done for them.

Revna still hadn't revealed her plans, but from the way she had taken care of these people—from the way they all had the same sharp features and coloring—he knew they were all from Ethni's homeland. Maybe she was freeing them, or maybe she was lying and only pretending to help them with secret plans to sell them to some unknown Chieftain. But one thing he knew for certain: if they remained on these shores, they would never be safe. If he were to die, he at least wanted his last act to be one of bravery.

"There are boats and ships in Kaupang," he said. "I ken a way to sneak them aboard. Passage could be purchased. Ye could send them home."

He waited, watching. Studying the way her fingers opened and closed in a fist—the way her lips parted and snapped shut again as if every part of her was working up to what she wanted to say. She stepped around him and pushed up her sleeves, scooping palmfuls of cool water that she splashed on her face before shaking the remaining droplets from her hands. Those wet hands rested on her hips; she stared at the flowing water before facing him again.

"It would cost a great deal." Her blue eyes were dark in the moonlight, but there was a spark there. "Fer all of these, and the rest I will collect from Kaupang."

Of the slave names he'd recited, at least ten were also on her list. He'd moved close enough to read them from her parchment over her shoulder without letting her know he could. He'd needed to know what her weaknesses were and was surprised to find education was not one of them.

So far, her only weaknesses seemed to be asking for help and sticking around when she was uncomfortable.

"'Tis over twenty people." With a groan, he pushed himself to his feet, rubbing his palms along the soft leather of his trousers to clean them.

"They all go." It wasn't a request or explanation. It was a solid, set-in-stone fact. "I just..." for the first time, she faltered. "I dunna have the coin fer their passage."

She faced him, her apparent resistance to requesting anything of him making her fidget.

"I can get it, but 'twill take time," she admitted.

He had no doubt she could sweep through Kaupang and rid every freeman of their entire purse in one night, but the morning would bring alarm, and all those people in her clearing would never make it onto a boat. If she was also collecting slaves—there would definitely be an uproar.

Any disturbance would alert his father's warband. They'd be watching the docks with such care that none would escape. His father might even shut down the ports. Oslo, another port settlement, was a few day's journey. But it was not nearly as large, not nearly as easy to mix in escaping slaves with traders, fisherman, and adventurers from many lands. Only Norse boats sailed in and out of Oslo. Any Norseman who suspected what they were doing wouldn't allow it, not for any amount of coin.

Kaupang was the only option for that large of a group.

"What will ye do? When they've gone home?" He'd seen her parchment. Though some names had a mark beside them, there were many more names than those in the clearing or in Kaupang.

"I have more work to do here."

When he mentioned passage, she didn't ask how much coin would be required. He was certain it was because she already knew.

"I can help ye."

She snapped her eyes to his, that spark flaring to flame.

"I ken this settlement, and I ken the people. I ken the ones who work on the docks, I ken the merchants in the square. I can secure passage. And I can get ye the coin ye need."

Again, she locked her gaze on his, staring for much too long. He was a heartbeat away from opening his mouth to beg her to let him do this one thing that would make his miserable life worth something to someone.

"I ken why you want to help Ethni and Alpia." She cocked her head to the side, looking every bit like the raven she was said to be. "They clearly love ye, but why the others? What are they to ye?"

Aksel let the breath from his lungs and tipped his head back, scanning the inky purple sky. He scrubbed rough hands over his face before answering. "If they are Ethni's people, she willna leave without them. She will be the last to board as it is. The only way fer her to live is to escape these shores."

He knew when he lowered his eyes that he'd meet her pene-trating stare. But he was surprised to find something other than suspicion and a promise of violence. She looked confused and angry. He was trying to help, so why was she angry? Besides the fact that she always looked a little furious. More than a little, if he was truth-ful. More like the gods had dealt her some great wrong, and she wouldn't rest until it was righted or the gods themselves were all dust. Maybe both.

"How will ye get the coin and passage?"

Revna was of a singular mind. He'd suspected she would want more details of his plan.

"Did ye choose the raven as yer symbol fer a reason?"

"It is a symbol of death where I come from. I wanted the men who stole and hurt my people to ken what waited for them should they come after my people again." That flame flared again in her eyes. Of course it meant death. He almost chuckled.

"So violent." Aksel pushed his breath out through his lips, feeling the tug of a smile as he let his eyes wander over her face. He clenched his fists at his sides to keep his fingers from brushing over the soft-ness of her cheek.

She scoffed and speared him with a glare as if she could feel his intentions. He knew she hated when he reveled in her threats instead of cowering, and he was beginning to crave the satisfaction of that power—maybe even as much as he craved a drink.

"Ye may not have realized it, but that symbol is yer key. Ye've already set in motion everything ye need."

"But ye said yer father cares nothing fer folklore and spirits."

"He doesna, 'tis true, but the rest of Kaupang does. He pretends to honor the gods fer the sake of his position."

Revna pulled her bottom lip between her teeth, holding it there as she considered his words. Finally, she nodded to a large flat rock just a few steps away.

He easily sat on its raised surface, but Revna had to hoist herself up. When he offered his hand, the look she gave him made him snatch it back before he lost it.

She settled onto the rock, crossing her ankles and leaning back on her palms. "I'm listening, but," she aimed a finger at him, "if I suspect yer even thinking of betraying me, I'll—"

Aksel pushed her hand down. "I ken, I ken. Ye will kill me before the morning."

9

REVNA

Revna's fingers skimmed her cheeks, completing the last marks of her disguise with oily black paint. She'd opted for winged streaks across her eyes and one long stripe that began at the center of her bottom lip and stretched down her neck to disappear under the V of her tunic. It had taken them most of the day, but Aksel's plan was laid out and, now that the sun was setting again, underway. She had to admit, it was as dangerous as it was clever, and she was slightly annoyed she didn't think of it herself.

Conall, who had come up behind her with surprising stealth, didn't flinch at her appearance.

"We ar'na the only ones to have discovered this particular corner of the woods." The hair on the back of her neck raised with his too-calm statement. When she tilted her head in question, he continued. "Last harvest, a freeman was outlawed by the lawspeaker fer attempting to steal from the Chieftain. I believe I found him as I was setting the last of the traps."

Revna's hand moved to her side, her fingers dancing over the hilt of her dagger. "Will he be a problem?"

"Not unless his bones rise up and assemble themselves into a ghostly warrior."

"Here, ye'll need this," she said, offering him the mixture. "Being outlawed is a death sentence?"

He accepted the bowl-shaped stone filled with charcoal paint. "Outlawers are marked wi' the Chieftain's brand across the forehead so any villager will ken of the sentence. Even if they ar'na killed on sight, none are allowed to take them in. Few survive."

Conall's words were nearly a whisper by the end of his explanation. Revna's gaze drifted in the direction he'd come, as if she would see the mysterious skeleton of the man who died outcast and alone.

In the four winters she'd dwelled in the Northlands, this was the first she'd heard of this particular punishment. She'd been alone most of that time, so being outlawed sounded preferable to some of the more gruesome ways Vikings dealt out justice. If her purpose for being in the Northlands was ever discovered, she knew she'd be on the receiving end of such torture, but she'd decided the second she stepped foot on the northern shores, her people were worth the risk.

When she looked back at Conall, he was staring at the shiny black mixture.

"Do ye need help?"

"Nay." He dipped two fingers in and drew black lines down one side of his face, starting at his hairline. "I just dunna enjoy looking like a Viking."

"Better than looking like yer bony friend." Revna jerked her head toward the shadows before leaving him to finish his disguise. She marched toward the clearing.

When the eyes of the freed slaves widened and they released sputtered gasps, she had to remind herself of her appearance. Her eyes passed over their shocked expressions, seeking out one particular set of blue eyes.

Aksel was leaning against the wide trunk of a redwood, arms crossed over his chest. He rubbed a wicked half-smile from his lips when she approached.

"Terrifying," was all he said.

And she knew she was. Even Ethni curled Alpia closer when she first saw Revna's painted face. Upon a second glance, Ethni raised her brows. "Ye look just like a warrior."

"Gather what ye can," she instructed the group. "Ye'll be sailing fer yer homeland the dawn after next."

Sighs and soft exclamations of joy spread throughout the clearing. Everyone celebrated with embraces and clasping hands. Revna's heart beat a little quicker at their excitement.

The soft touch of a hand on her shoulder had her turning to meet the wide eyes of a young woman called Fotla. She'd been captured in the Viking raid on Tràigh a few months before Cyrene and Duncan's wedding. Cyrene had secretly brought her warriors to defend the village after they'd learned of the first raid, but many had already been lost. Including Fotla, who had witnessed her parent's deaths as they tried to save her.

If it weren't for another citizen of Tràigh, Revna would have never found her. She wouldn't have answered Revna's questions, for she hadn't spoken a word since the night she was taken.

Young Fotla's tear-filled eyes skimmed over Revna's face, a flash of terror fading as her gaze settled on Revna's eyes. With a shaking hand, Fotla touched her lips and then Revna's shoulder.

"I ken," Revna whispered, squeezing the woman's arm. "I ken."

Her appearance was forgotten as every member of the group began to gather meager possessions. All but Aksel. He stood still, looking at her as if she were a fascinating thing to be examined and treasured, like an ancient weapon found after centuries of being buried. Even with her back turned, she felt the weight of his stare. Skin about to crawl right off her bones, she spun, ready to smash her palm into his nose, and collided with his broad chest.

"Ye...what..." She jumped back, disentangling herself from his arms as he caught her shoulders. "Idi—"

"Yer route is mapped." Aksel smirked, cutting off her stuttered insult and jerking his head as if he hadn't just turned her spine to stone. When he moved away from the clearing and she remained an awkward statue, he bunched his brows and called over his shoulder. "Ye coming?"

If he heard the growl curling up from her throat, he didn't let on.

"Ye coming?" Revna mocked under her breath.

She was forced to follow him to a make-shift table where he'd created a rudimentary map with sticks and pebbles.

"The ones marked are the farms where ye'll find the slaves yer looking fer." He stepped aside, allowing Revna space to examine his work.

"Ye truly ken all the slaves in Kaupang?"

Aksel reached up, rubbing his hand along the back of his neck. "Aye. I have spent much time among the farmers. They get rather chatty once they...get to ken ye. One of the few things my father appreciates about me is my ability to learn secrets."

He looked almost sheepish, and Revna didn't understand until his tongue ran across his dry lips. Mead. Mead loosened the lips of the farmers until they shared everything about their households with the charming Chieftain's son, including the names and number of slaves they might not want to pay tithes for.

"What does their trust in ye cost them?" Suspicion weighed her words.

"Just a bit of coin." Aksel didn't meet her eyes when he added, "I ken what secrets are safe to share."

She nearly asked how he'd benefited from keeping such secrets, but something told her he hadn't gained anything at all. Instead, she asked, "What has that discretion cost ye?"

She set her gaze on the side of his face, willing him to meet her eyes. He wouldn't.

"Nothing I amna prepared to pay." Aksel narrowed his eyes at some bauble on his map and shifted its position until he was satisfied. With a deep inhale, the tension seemed to lift from his shoulders. "I dinna realize the reason fer his sudden interest in my relationship wi' the settlers at first. But I should have. My father gives nothing wi'out expecting something in return."

His eyes scanned her face, as if expecting—needing—her to shame him for his ignorance, but Revna had plenty of shame of her own and found herself unable to let him wallow.

"I dunna care how ye learned this knowledge, just that yer willing to share it." Her tone was light, but Aksel's gaze bore down on her shoulders until she had to physically shrug it off and pretend to study the map.

She glanced to where Ethni and a few other women were mixing a larger portion of charcoal paint. As soon as the sun set, Revna and Conall would take their pouches of paint and follow Aksel's route through the settlement, leaving masterpieces on barns and longhouses where Aksel identified farms holding her people as slaves. There were at least ten spread across the settlement. It would be a long, dangerous night.

Aksel's breath caressed her neck as he leaned in, looking at the map over her shoulder. "It would be quicker if I went wi' ye. I ken my way around every corner of this settlement."

He straightened as Revna turned, staring down at her. She'd never counted her lack of height as a weakness, as her small size let her squeeze into places where larger bodies would never fit. It had saved her life more than once. But under Aksel's intense stare, she suddenly wished for a miraculous growth spurt, if only to be eye level with him.

"Even disguised, ye canna be seen, Aksel. We canna risk it. Besides, yer doing enough." Her eyes lowered to his chest with her last statement and his hand drifted to his sternum.

"Aye, better get on wi' that as soon as ye return. It takes...time."

"Are ye certain 'tis necessary?" Revna couldn't meet his eyes, thinking of the second part of the plan Aksel had formed.

"Ye asked what would force the Chieftain to listen. This will." Aksel stretched out one arm, revealing the tattoos running along his corded forearms. "'Tis nothing I havena experienced before."

Revna took his wrist, examining the bluish designs as she ran her fingers over his skin. "I am skilled wi' the blade and wi' paint, but I've never carved artwork on a person before."

She flicked her eyes up when he laughed. "Ye'll hardly be carving, *Little Bird*. 'Tis only a tiny prick and then the slightly uncomfortable process of smearing ink into my skin."

"Slightly uncomfortable?" She raised a brow, swatting his hand away when he reached to tap her nose with his finger.

"'Tis where yer herbs come in." He wiggled his fingers, as if casting a spell. "Ye promised to make it painless."

"I said it would dull the pain, Prince, not eliminate it."

He laughed again, rubbing his hand over his chest as if she'd already begun. "Ahh, dunna worry, Revna. I promise not to shed a tear."

When the sun was fully set and Revna was settled atop Sgail's muscled back, Aksel handed up her midnight cloak.

"Ye ken the way?" He stroked his hand along Sgail's neck as Revna fastened the heavy fabric over her shoulders and lifted the hood.

"Aye." She resisted the urge to kick the mare into a run when Aksel's hands brushed over her leg, tightening the leather cords that held her many pouches in place. "Aksel, all is in place."

"There is much at stake, Little Bird." He squeezed her calf in what seemed like a warning. "Dunna get caught."

"Did Conall take kindly to the same warning?" She shifted her weight, a soft dig of her heel causing Sgail to step to the side, out of Aksel's reach.

"I dunna worry about Conall being cautious. He kens what he stands to lose."

"And I dunna?" Whatever nerves had tightened Revna's muscles were forgotten at Aksel's insinuation.

"'Tisn't what ye will lose, but me." He folded his arms, cocking his head to the side.

She mirrored his expression. "And what is that, Prince?"

Aksel stepped close, grabbing Sgail's reins quicker than Revna could jerk them away. The jump of his brow and half-smile on his lips made Revna grateful for the darkness that hid her flaming cheeks.

"I already told ye. No one gets to kill ye but me."

Before she could respond, Aksel landed a firm pat on Sgail's rump, sending her trotting into the night.

IT WAS WELL after dawn the next day before Revna was fed and rested enough to follow Aksel away from the camp with Ethni's bone-carved needle and indigo ink.

"Sgail seemed to have enjoyed her tour of Kaupang." Aksel spoke from her side as they trudged through the woods.

Revna looked up at him, her brain taking seconds too long to translate the sounds he made into words even though he spoke her language.

"She's been itching fer a run. Last night was good fer her." Aksel's teasing had loosened her anxious nerves the night before, but the tension had returned as soon as she woke. "And no one stole yer right to murder me."

Aksel hummed softly, "Aye, good thing."

With Sgail's racing steps, Revna was able to visit seven farms. Conall visited the other three. They took nothing but left behind a sign at each location. A raven, black as night, with wings spread wide. A warning to the marked farms that Aksel said would be more ominous than setting the buildings ablaze.

They would assume Odin was watching and that he was displeased. Word would spread of those symbols, and the Chieftain would be looking for a way to calm the growing panic.

In a few minutes, she'd draw another symbol—another warning. The dread had her stomach tied in knots as tightly as she assumed the stomachs of those farmers were tied this morning.

"This is far enough and the stream is nearby." He shook out the pelt he'd been carrying and laid it on the ground before dropping to his knees.

When Revna stood frozen before him, he lifted his chin, watching her intently. "I'm certain Conall would—"

"Nay." Revna lowered herself to the pelt beside him, hunting through her satchel for tools. "I will do it. He is already doing enough."

Aksel was silent despite the sweat Revna knew he would see forming on her forehead. He reached behind his head and tugged off his tunic in a swift motion before lying back, exposing his bare chest for the second time since she'd met him. She didn't flush this time. She only surveyed her canvas.

When Aksel winced at the first prick of her bone-carved needle, she nearly lost her nerve. But when she pulled back, he snatched her wrist, jerking her close so quickly that her free arm shot out to the ground next to his head to break her fall.

Her lungs locked down the breath she'd inhaled as his blue eyes met her, their noses nearly touching.

"I want Ethni and Alpia on that boat." Teeth clenched, his words were harsh and growled. "Now do it or I'll do it myself."

Each second she remained hovering over him, her heart thudded harder against her ribs. His grip was firm, but his thumb grazed over her knuckles and his expression softened.

"Breathe, Little Bird," he whispered, his breath fanning her face and his lips twisting into the smirk she'd learned was all his own. "Ye've stabbed me before; ye can do it again."

His teasing unlocked the hold of her lungs, and she shoved off of him, coming to her knees at his side. Heat coated her cheeks, not only at his chiding but at the way her skin tingled where he'd stroked her hand. He grunted with a laugh as she landed a soft jab against his side.

"I keep telling ye, ye stabbed yerself." Revna didn't hesitate again as she aimed the tip of the needle at his skin and went to work on her design, letting her lips form their own sly smile. "Besides, I've seen yer carvings. If ye do it, it'll resemble a malnourished elk and our plans will all be fer naught."

Aksel didn't flinch but drew his bare arms up behind his head as if he were relaxing under the warmth of the summer sun. "Ye wound me, Little Bird." He didn't speak again after letting his eyes drift lazily closed.

She forced an extra dose of clove infused tincture down his throat before rubbing the ink into his raw skin. There was no possibility it was painless, but Aksel kept his eyes closed, his face expressionless as she worked.

When she finished, he allowed her to clasp his hand, hauling him up. He gazed down at his chest, now marked with the elaborate tattoo.

"Yer quite the artist." Aksel gingerly tapped the edges of her design. "This could never be mistaken fer a starving deer."

"Malnourished elk," she corrected, watching his face for any sign of discomfort. She knew he must be hurting, but he hid it effortlessly. "Pay attention."

"Now comes the real pain." Aksel raised his brows and pressed his lips together as he pushed himself to his feet. "Where is Conall?"

IO

AKSEL

Dust flew up from the ground and filled his nose and lungs as he collapsed at the edge of the market.

"What is this?" A boot met his side and Aksel groaned. A shadow blocked the sun, and he felt strong hands turning him over. "Who are...Aksel?"

He couldn't place the voice, his mind still drawing sounds out too long and too low.

"Eira, it is Aksel." More hands touched him then, sliding under his shoulders to cradle his head in someone's lap. Eira. He knew Eira.

"Aksel? You are alive! Oh, gods, Rendel, he is bleeding." A woman gasped. Cold fingers danced over his raw skin. "His chest! Is that...he is marked."

"He needs water," the man said quietly before calling out, "Get the Chieftain! Someone find Chieftain Tollak; his son has been found."

Rendel. Eira. Their voices broke through the swirling mass of noise in his mind. The soft edge of a water skin was pressed to his lips and Aksel accepted the cool drink, choking as it poured too quickly down his throat. He groaned as his ribs screamed with each cough.

"He must have been captured. Look at him, he is half alive." It was Rendel's voice. Rendel. The brother-in-law who was now growling at him. "I warned you, Aksel."

"What are you talking about?" It was Eira.

"Nothing," Rendel grumbled.

A fleeting moment of clarity had him flailing. Eira was here. Why was she near the ports? She was about to deliver her babe. Had something happened?

But he couldn't ask, his lungs could barely squeeze out a breath. This had all been his idea, and he tried to remind himself of that as he replayed Conall's well-placed strikes, which had most definitely cracked a rib and quite possibly broken his nose. Revna's herbs had dulled the pain while she completed her part, but once they wore off, the tattooed skin of his chest was blazed with fire. That was also his idea. Maybe his father was right; there had to be something wrong with his mind for him to consider torturing himself like this, even if he knew his plan would work.

He'd added to his ailments by demanding Revna dose him with the same herbs that had driven Galdvyn mad. Her narrowed glare flickered in his mind.

"Ye won't be able to deliver the message with that potion in ye."

"Dilute it then. If my father suspects this is anything less than genuine, all this truly will be fer naught. He will already be suspicious." They entered into a battle of glares, which he won, surprisingly.

"Fine," she grumbled as she used her wooden pestle to grind a mixture of herbs into a powder that she blew straight into his face without warning.

If this was the diluted version, he couldn't imagine what Galdvyn had endured. As he'd stumbled through the woods, the trees came to life, reaching for him with gnarled fingers. The leather of his pants felt like a thousand ants crawling on his skin. If Revna and Conall hadn't had hold of him, he might have stripped

146

off his clothes too and run naked through the settlement just to escape.

The thought sent him into a fit of laughter that seized him with pain and sent him curling in on himself.

"Aksel? What is happening? Rendel, what is wrong with him?" Eira's panicked voice filled him with the desire to hold her, but his rebellious limbs wouldn't move where he commanded them. "Help him!"

"Eira, stay calm. He just needs…" Rendel's voice trailed off as his large hands came down on Aksel's arms, holding him still.

"Do not hurt him." Eira's tears were warm on Aksel's face, and he fished through his thoughts to catch the ones that reminded him why he was there and what he was supposed to be doing.

Shapes and flashes of nightmarish images pummeled his mind. More voices joined Eira and Rendel's, ones he thought were familiar but couldn't name.

"He is marked! He bears Odin's raven. Just like the farms."

"Do not touch him, he is cursed."

"Hold your tongue, Ragnar," Rendel barked, silencing the mutters.

Human-like figures hovered, their faces warped and flickering under the influence of Revna's herbs. She was a genius; he acknowledged that, even through the panic. Fierce but small, she recognized her weaknesses and played to her strengths. Her herb mixture, which she assured him would wear off in an hour, left anyone pursuing her with nothing but horrid memories and a terrifying story that would keep others from entering the woods.

They're people, she'd held his face in her hands when the herbs began to take effect, *they are only people, not monsters. Ye must keep telling yerself that. Ye must deliver the message.*

They were people. He could remember that. His lips began to move, and he tripped over his words, uttering jumbled up sounds.

"Did you hear?" Eira leaned in, listening to his ragged words. "Quiet! He is speaking."

147

More figures gathered until he was completely shadowed and surrounded by curious, frightened whispers.

"What did he say?" someone asked.

"Something about birds and an offering," she said. "I could not hear it all."

"He comes. The Chieftain comes."

The pressure of the crowd was replaced by the weight of a judging stare accompanying the thump of familiar boots. Eira's arms tightened around him.

"Who did this?" his father's voice boomed in Aksel's ears. "Who did this to my son?"

Was that...concern?

"We do not know. We found him like this." Rendel's voice was strong, but there was caution in his tone.

Eira's soft hands brushed back Aksel's sweat-soaked hair as she spoke. "He must have come from the woods, Faðir."

Tollak was there. Tollak must hear the message. Aksel forced sounds through his lips.

"What is he saying?" Tollak demanded, making Eira jump.

"Tell him, Aksel," she whispered, stroking his cheeks and forehead.

"The ravens," Aksel groaned. "They have come."

Whispers and murmurs traveled across the gathered crowd, names of marked farmers slipping between the townspeople. He repeated his message, hoping he could pull his thoughts together enough to get it right.

"Make an offering tonight at the ceremonial stone when the moon is at its highest. Every..." A cough seized his throat and his arm shot to his side, holding the place where his ribs ached. "Each marked villager must go...everyone in the household."

"How is it you came to be here? Why did the ravens release you?" His father spoke, still an imposing shadow over him.

Tell the truth as much as possible. Revna's instructions broke through the thinning fog in his mind. *Ye'll get trapped in lies.*

148

"I was going to be killed, but when it was discovered I was the son of the Chieftain, I was sent with a message instead. If we do not obey, there will be only ashes left in Kaupang."

Chaos erupted amongst the gathered crowd. Aksel tried to decipher one voice from another, but they were still all deep and rolling like thunder.

"Did you hear?"

"An offering?"

"We will do it, will we not?"

"We must, you have heard what has become of other settlements."

"Burned! They were burned to the ground."

"How do we know he is telling the truth?"

"He is the same as Galdvyn, look at his eyes."

"Do you not also see the mark of Odin on him? It is inked on his flesh."

"Anyone could have done that. He could have done it to himself. You know he is a dru—"

"Enough!" His father silenced the crowd with a word. It was a minute before he spoke again. "We will obey Odin's command. Spread the word. Not only the farmers who were marked, but all settlers will give an offering tonight. If anyone is unable to make the journey, they will send a double portion. No further harm shall come to Kaupang."

Hands darted under Aksel's arms, dragging him to his feet. "Where are you taking him?" Eira's cries were drowned by the growing murmurs from the crowd. "He is hurt."

"I am taking him home, Dóttir." Tollak's voice was gentle, words spoken with a tone he only used with Eira.

"I will go with him."

"No." Tollak's response was quick and harsh, making Eira flinch. Aksel jerked against the hold of his father's men but stilled when Rendel stepped up to her side, the aggression slight but obvious, even to Aksel's blurred vision. Tollak blinked once before his expression softened as he touched Eira's shoulder. "Stay with your husband, Dóttir. I will send for you tomorrow."

"But, I—"

"Eira," Aksel rasped. His words drew her wide eyes to his, some panic brewing there as her gaze bounced between his and their father's. He forced a smile across his dry lips. "It is well. Listen to Faðir."

"Come, Eira. There is not much time." Rendel kept his eyes on the Chieftain, but his grip on her waist was gentle, tenderly urging her away even as she reached for Aksel.

Aksel didn't understand what Rendel meant, but it didn't matter as long as Eira was safe. The Chieftain's men jostled him for a better grip on his limp form, sending his aching ribs into a fiery rage.

"Tomorrow!" Eira called, urgently reminding her father of his promise.

Loud enough for the crowd to hear, Tollak ordered, "Bring my son home."

Aksel tried to focus on his father's face—to discern the strange tone in his voice—but the herbs were still working through his blood, confusing his thoughts. The sounds of the marketplace quieted as he was hauled away. His mind started to clear when he was half-way home, and his feet finally caught the ground beneath him, easing some of the strain on his ribs.

He still worked to blink the world into focus and noticed they'd veered off the path leading to the Chieftain's home. Aksel shook his head, trying to clear the remaining fog from his mind when he was shoved through a darkened doorway and once again landed in the dirt.

When he pushed himself up on his forearms, it was the smell that told him where he was. The mead hall. During the day, when there were no celebrations or festivals, this building was dark and empty. Aksel's stomach twisted. It was a safe assumption his father didn't bring him here to celebrate.

"Get him up." His father leaned against a table, arms crossed over his broad chest. Inked records of his many voyages and battles scrolled along his bare forearms. Brutal victories that brought Tollak fame and wealth. Journeys that had Kaupang teeming with captured slaves, quickly lifting him to the position of Chieftain after the previous Jarl crumbled under the shame of the raven's curse. If only he knew it was his actions, and not Aksel's, that brought the raven back to Kaupang.

Aksel was hauled to his feet again, finally able to make out the faces of the men holding him. They were two of his father's warband. He didn't know their names, but from their scowls, they didn't care to know his either.

"Light the fire." The Chieftain jerked his head to the side, and one of the men released Aksel, marching toward the raised pit in the center of the mead hall.

"Are you determined to ruin me?" The Chieftain's dark eyes settled mercilessly on Aksel.

"Faðir?" He worked to keep his composure, though his already racing heart sped up even faster.

Tollak stepped toward Aksel, gripping his chin with a bone-breaking hold.

"Marked by Odin's ravens?" Tollak tilted his head, his eyes nearly black with rage. "We both know that is not true."

"I do not know what you mean." He really wanted to ask if his father meant to call off the offering. If he didn't keep his word, none of this would matter.

"Rendel left you outside the mead hall and now days later, you arrive in this...state." His father raked his eyes down Aksel's form. "With a message from Odin."

It wasn't a question, and Aksel felt the slice of icy warning race up his spine. A fleeting thought of self-preservation pressed to the front of all others. He could confess. He could lead his father straight to Revna. He could still keep Ethni and Alpia safe. Tollak would believe the slaves were stolen for profit rather than being rescued—who would rescue slaves?

That look of disdain in his father's eye would turn to pride. Kaupang would be the settlement that ended the raven's reign of terror. It wasn't the first time in the last two days he'd entertained the idea, and it also wasn't the first time he'd been nearly driven to his knees in shame.

Revna, a palm-sized land-dwelling hurricane, had come alone across the sea, barely more than a child, with nothing but a list of names and a determination to hunt down every single one. Not only had she survived—she'd succeeded so far. And he, son of the most powerful Chieftain in the North, who had been given everything, was contemplating selling her out for the slim hope of his father's approval.

"Yes." He steadied himself, even as he watched his father's warrior shove an iron brand into the flames. Whatever Tollak needed to assume of him, he would allow as long as it meant his and Revna's plan worked. That Ethni and Alpia were safe and free. "Yes. Faðir, that is what happened."

"Tell me, *son*." The word was a curse. "Were you too weak to avoid capture, or did you seek it out? How long did you wait before announcing I was your father to save yourself?"

He had been too weak, but that truth would lead to more questions he couldn't answer without the risk of revealing some bit of information that might send Tollak's warband storming into the woods.

"Who is truly behind this?" Tollak was close, his sneer making Aksel's knees tremble.

"I...it is as I said." Aksel readied himself. He'd seen that look in his father's eye before. This would not end without pain. *Stick to the truth.* "The raven has come."

Tollak stepped close enough that Aksel smelled the reek of day-old mead on his breath. "However it happened, you left yourself vulnerable. You were a coward, and now I have to pay the price."

Aksel held in a groan of pain as the warrior holding him twisted his arm behind his back and his father took the shredded edges of his tunic and ripped them apart, exposing his tattooed chest.

"Odin will get his offering," Tollak spat in Aksel's face. "But I require one of my own. And I will have answers."

Aksel ground his teeth, his nerves frayed and buzzing at what was to come. Revna wasn't there to see, but he'd promised her he wouldn't shed a tear, and he meant to keep his word even as his eyes involuntarily widened at the sight of the warrior approaching with the glowing red-tipped brand.

II

REVNA

"Everyone is in place?" Revna asked from her perch in the middle branches of a redwood just inside the tree line edging the settlement of Kaupang. Given her shorter stature, she wasn't as skilled a climber as Astrid and Cyrene, but she was still able to scramble up a decent number of branches without much trouble. From that height, she could see several of the farms edging Kaupang's borders.

Conall, face freshly blackened with kohl, leaned against the trunk below, his arms crossed casually over his chest. Their mission the night before had been successful. He'd impressed her with his ability to blend into the shadows almost as well as she could.

"Aye." Conall flexed his hand, his knuckles red and raw from his part in making Aksel appear to be an escaped captive of Odin's ruthless spies.

Revna watched from above, unable to see Conall's expression from this angle in the dark. Aksel had been the one to ask Conall to do it, joking secretly to Revna that it would probably be a dream come true for the man. But Conall hadn't smiled or gloated while delivering the blows, the weakest of which had split Aksel's lip and

154

blackened his eye. It had been quick but brutal. They'd gone far from the clearing so there was no risk of Ethni or Alpia witnessing the violence, but Revna forced herself to watch, feeling Aksel's pain as her own. It was only right, since it was for her people, that she not turn away. Conall had been even more sullen than usual since.

"It had to be done, Conall." Revna slipped down to the ground without a sound. "Aksel kens his father."

Conall dropped his hand at her words, crossing his arms over his chest again. "So do I."

His reply was so dark, Revna couldn't help the shiver that raced through her body. Her people were safe here in the woods, but Aksel was in the hands of the Chieftain. Surely, he would believe his son. Aksel said his father wouldn't pay a ransom, but the Chieftain couldn't balk at the demand for an offering—not when the message was so publicly delivered.

They didn't dare risk venturing close enough to watch, but they'd helped Aksel to the edge of the wood before leaving him to travel the rest of the way on his own. They wouldn't know until the moon was at its highest if the Chieftain would heed Aksel's message.

In the hours since Aksel had stumbled over the hill separating them from the market, she and Conall had returned to the clearing, ensured everyone was ready, and made their way to this particular spot, Sgail trotting silently behind them. Now they waited to see if Aksel's complicated plan would be their salvation or their ruin.

She felt a rush of panic. Thoughts of everything that could go wrong locked her muscles.

"Tell me we can trust him, Conall."

She felt Conall's heavy stare before he sucked in a deep breath and watched the empty hillside with her. "For all his faults, the Norseman loves Ethni and Alpia. He willna do anything to put them in danger."

His words were meant to relieve her anxiety, but Aksel being out of her sight, not knowing what he was doing or what was happening to him, had her insides twisted in painful knots. What if Aksel decided protecting Ethni and Alpia meant giving up everyone else?

"I will say," Conall's soft statement pulled her from her thoughts. "I am surprised by his willingness to suffer fer them."

His words were few, but Conall's admission spoke, if not complete retraction of the disdain he'd held for the Chieftain's son, at least the beginning of it.

He shifted again, his tone lighter. "I will not be sad to watch this place burn."

Revna agreed. Most of the freemen of Kaupang were the worst sort. Their slaves lived in squalor and endured such mistreatment that Revna had added her own bit of mischief to the plan. She was surprised Conall hadn't objected, but he saw the necessity in it.

Aksel had looked a bit green when she shared her suggestion with Conall and three more of her countrymen who would carry it out. But when she raised a brow and asked him if he took issue with her decision, he only glanced at Ethni where she tended to an older woman and shook his head.

"Nay," he'd said. "It will ensure their attention is diverted. 'Tis a good plan."

Of course it was. So was his part. Mayhap he was smarter than she thought. His idea was ingenious and would get her people home in a tenth of the time as her efforts alone. If it worked. If everyone did what they were supposed to do. Aksel most of all.

"They are coming." Conall pushed off the tree, pointing to the path leading into the woods.

Silhouetted figures moved through the night, slowly making their way from their farms to the distant woods. She breathed a sigh of relief. "It worked. He did it."

Conall's expression remained hard, but he nodded. "I will see ye at the meeting place."

She tossed one more look toward Conall before pulling herself onto Sgail's back and raising her hood over her head.

"May *An T-aon* be wi' ye," he whispered before darting into the darkness.

Revna hesitated, struck still by his blessing. When she realized her fingers were rubbing the spot on her chest where the mistake of a mark burned, she huffed and wrapped her hand around Sgail's leather reins.

She'd not heard Conall mention Cyrene's God until then. She'd assumed he was far too reasonable to believe in such fairy tales. Although, she was putting a lot of faith in the stories Aksel shared of twin ravens belonging to the Norse god, Odin. And in the settlers' fear of true retribution by that god.

The settlers were moving to the clearing. Everyone in the household would be attending the offerings—everyone except the nameless slaves. It worked. Just like Aksel had said.

"Well done, Prince," Revna muttered to herself before she rode in the opposite direction as Conall.

He and three other Vestmen would collect the slaves from the farms they marked the night before, and she would visit the rest of the farms. It took three minutes for Sgail to carry her to the first and less than that to convince the slaves to follow her.

"We've been praying fer ye to come fer us," a woman said, clinging to a second woman Revna knew was her sister. "When we saw the signs, we prayed it meant our suffering was over. *An T-aon* has answered our prayers."

Revna accepted her embrace and then sent her safely to the tree line. She tossed a lit torch into a pile of dry hay just inside the door of the empty barn—her mischievous part of the plan.

When Revna checked again, the women had disappeared into the blackness, armed with pouches of hallucination-inducing herbs and Revna's directions of how to reach the others and avoid her traps. They shouldn't encounter anyone in the woods, but a single breath of those herbs would buy them enough time to escape if they did.

"Just dunna inhale even one fleck," Revna had warned, holding the women's gazes to ensure they understood. "We will not be able to risk returning for ye."

All across the settlement, slaves were gathered, torches tossed, and smoke began to fill the black night sky. They'd planned their rescue carefully, choosing the farthest farms first so the smoke from their fires wouldn't be seen right away.

"Hurry," Revna whispered to her final group.

She accompanied the last of the freed slaves to the meeting place, dismounting as she spied a group of women clustered around something, Ethni kneeling in the middle of them.

"What is—Conall! What happened?" Revna dropped to her knees next to Conall, whose skin was blackened by more than just kohl. His arm was being wrapped by Ethni.

"I lit a barn and didn't realize someone was still inside. I went back, and a weak beam collapsed on me." His voice shook and his face was pale.

"He'll live," Ethni said, her tone sharper than Revna had heard before. "This foolish man almost got himself killed over a chicken."

Revna shot a questioning look to Conall, who traced the back of his uninjured hand along Ethni's cheek. "In my defense, it sounded like a bairn."

Revna laughed softly. "Did ye at least save the chicken?"

Conall nodded toward one of the women circling them. She held a clucking orange hen in her arms and grinned.

"She is called *cearc fortunach*."

"Lucky biddy? Aptly named." Revna laughed, running her hand over the bird's soft feathers. "Have the others returned? Did ye get to all the farms?"

"All but one." Conall hissed the name of the farmer as Ethni, less than gently, tugged on a strip of linen she'd tied around his arm to hold it in place. He made to push himself up, but Revna nodded in agreement as Ethni shoved him back to the ground.

"We're almost out of time. Get them all to the boats. Send Aengus and Cian to the ceremony stone to collect the offering once it's clear. I'll go to the last farm and meet ye at the docks." Revna pushed herself to her feet, preparing to race back to the settlement with Sgail. But when she scanned the clearing again, she froze and turned to Ethni, who still knelt by her husband.

"Where is he?"

A strange look passed over Ethni's face, something akin to dread. She only shook her head before whispering, "He has not returned."

Revna felt her face flame, and she cut her eyes to Conall, who looked green for an entirely different reason. Aksel was supposed to slip away from the ceremony once the smoke was spotted and meet them there. He planned to go with Ethni and Alpia to the docks and then disappear. It was the only answer for him after this night— after what he'd done and seen.

I cannot return to this life, Little Bird. Something has to give.

His words echoed in her mind. There were only three reasons Aksel wouldn't have returned. He'd escaped the ceremony and Kaupang already, he'd betrayed them, or he was dead.

Of the last two, she wasn't entirely sure which was worse. She'd seen the people marching for the clearing; surely if he'd betrayed her, they wouldn't still be gathering. Her heart began to pulse a hammering beat. He wouldn't betray them. He wouldn't.

But he might have needed the extra time to escape Kaupang. Once his father realized he'd been tricked, there was no distance Aksel could run that the Chieftain wouldn't follow for revenge. And he was hurt, he'd be moving slowly.

"Conall, where did ye say ye saw those bones?"

"Near the pool under the waterfall. Why?"

The farm Conall didn't reach was on the farthest edge of the settlement from where the rest of the people were gathered. With Sgail's speed, she could carry out her new plan and make it to the farm before the owners returned.

It was a risk to take the time to help Aksel, but without him, not one of her people would have been escaping that night, much less all of them. If he was alive, she could keep him that way for the price of a few extra minutes. She had time.

It was Ethni's certain nod that solidified Revna's resolve.

"I have need of our skinny friend." She nudged Sgail into a run in the direction of the waterfall, muttering a threat under her breath. "Ye better not be dead, Prince."

12

ASKEL

Aksel's parents had left just before the moon was at its highest. He'd pretended to be asleep when he heard his mother's soft footsteps next to his bed. She didn't wake him, and he needed her not to for this to work. Still, some part of him desperately wanted her to. Just to ask if he was well—to say she didn't approve of what Tollak had done.

He almost held his breath so she would be forced to touch him. But there was too much at stake, so he let his breaths come naturally. A sigh was the most he was given before he heard her leave again.

He had memories of a smile, of tender touches, of hummed songs and combing his fingers through fiery red hair. Gods, he had loved her hair, even long after she pulled away from his reaching fingers. It was like touchable flames when it caught the sun. He even had memories of the heavy, guiding weight of a father's hand on his shoulder, strong arms swinging him through the sky. He could almost believe he'd been adored by his parents before he got sick. He could almost feel it.

But at his first memory of waking up in the longhouse after a raging fever had finally broken, those memories ended. Then, when Alpia was born, his mother retreated into herself completely. She was nothing more than a spirit floating about the longhouse. A beautiful adornment on his father's arm.

Eira was still a light in his parent's eyes. In truth, his sister saved them all. Her little round face and dark head bobbed through the longhouse, planting tiny seeds of happiness that blossomed as soon as they landed. He missed her, too, so much it hurt. He even tried to despise Rendel for stealing away what little bit of brightness they had. But Rendel was good. He was strong, and he worshiped the ground Eira walked on. She deserved a love like that.

His only peace that night was that Rendel's house was not one of the marked ones. He sighed. There was much to do before dawn, before the other light in his life sailed away. And then he would go... somewhere. Anywhere but here.

Even though he'd tried not to move since he collapsed onto the straw stuffed mattress, the slightest whisper of a cold breeze across his skin had him grinding his teeth. There had been the appearance of genuine concern etched in Tollak's dark eyes when Aksel had been found in the marketplace. But an appearance was all it was.

He'd obviously mistaken his father's annoyance and rage for care. He could still see the fury in Tollak's eyes, reflecting the glowing end of the brand wielded by one of his men.

Aksel held his breath as he sat up and pulled on a clean tunic. He hissed as the fabric brushed the raised red lines on his chest.

When the Chieftain's men dumped him inside the longhouse, he'd fought the urge to fill his mug with the mead waiting on the table in the other room. His chest was pulsing with pain, and the thought of the slightest bit of relief had his mouth both dry as sand and watering for the taste. But Revna was counting on him. Waiting for him. No. Not Revna. Ethni and Alpia were the ones he couldn't disappoint. He was supposed to be in the clearing already. He had promised to be with them until the end.

162

He knew it was his obvious love for them that had earned Revna's trust. Her knowledge that he was telling the truth when he warned her of what would happen should they be caught. Which is why he needed to act like a man, push aside the pain, and get on his blasted feet.

He attempted to stand, but the searing pain across his chest was too much, and he lingered on the bed until a wave of nausea passed. He just needed one more minute.

This plan had many moving parts—ones that had to fall in place at exactly the right moment. That hinged on his people behaving exactly as he expected. He knew very few were as devoted to the gods as they let on, but when faced with losing their property or lives, their fear seemed to usher in stronger faith.

Even now, they were bringing offerings, praying to the gods that their homes be left untouched. Those prayers would go unanswered. Not with what Revna had added to the plan.

He had to admit, it did solve the problem of how to quickly draw a large group of people away from the ceremony site and back to their homes while also keeping them distracted from the port. Their offerings would be left behind for Revna's people to collect.

He knew his father hadn't developed a sudden devotion to the gods and could only imagine that Tollak had meant to do the very same thing. But the Chieftain wouldn't have counted on the fires. By the time he snuck back to the ceremonial clearing, his bounty would be gone and the slaves would be safely beyond the horizon.

Yes. Revna was definitely brilliant. Violent. But brilliant.

He finally pushed himself to his feet, his skin burning and screaming at every stretch and turn. It wasn't as bad as it could have been. His father had a single brand placed on the middle of his chest, centered in the raven design. When Aksel kept to his story instead of revealing Revna's identity, his father ordered his man to trace with fire the lines of Revna's tattoo. Even still, that was better than wearing the mark permanently on his forehead.

"Yer not dead." Revna's always-hoarse voice startled him, sending a fiery burst of pain across his torso.

Her shadow lingered at the edge of his room. Unmoving. She'd been suspicious of him since the moment they met, but the accusation in her voice now was far weightier than ever before. A wise man would have run, no matter what pain he was in, at the coldness of her tone.

His father had already proved beyond any doubt that Aksel was anything but wise.

"You sound disappointed." He ground out the answer in his native tongue. He couldn't even think to translate into her language. His entire body was pulsing with fire, and he squeezed his eyes closed.

"Why are ye still here?" She sounded close. He heard the soft clatter of something being dropped to the floor. "What happened?"

"I was...delayed." While his father was searing a permanent mark on his still tender flesh, he'd had bouts of every emotion that existed, including anger at the little raven that stood before him now.

When his eyes flew open, hers were searching his room, as if she were looking for something. Empty mugs of mead, most likely. But then they grazed over his entire form, stopping on the bit of flesh visible under the unlaced cut in his tunic. Her eyes flicked back to his in an instant, a flame turning their sky blue to a blazing cobalt.

When she reached for the hem of his tunic, he snatched her wrist, his grip firmer than he could control. She didn't flinch or jerk away.

"Let me see." Her voice was calm, her breaths steady. Much more level than his.

"You should go." He couldn't let go of her wrist. The thought of anything touching his skin made his hand tremble.

"We have time." Revna's voice was soft, the menacing threat directed elsewhere. "Let me see."

At the tick of her chin, he knew she wouldn't accept anything other than obedience, and he held his breath as she lifted the fabric. He couldn't bring himself to release her wrist though, as if he needed to retain some morsel of control. Even moving his head hurt, so he only lowered his eyes, watching her expression harden as she viewed the additional art his father had added to his body.

Revna was as still as he was, her fingers holding his tunic up and away from his skin. She raised her blue eyes to his, torturously slow, locking his gaze into an inescapable cage.

"Who did this to you?" Her tone was dark.

He'd recognized the tone in her voice when she first appeared in his room, before she suspected that something was wrong. She thought he'd betrayed her—that he would have abandoned Ethni and Alpia. Then she thought he'd given in and succumbed to the drink. He couldn't rightly blame her, but still, he didn't much feel like sharing the details of his torture at the moment.

"We need to go," Aksel said through his teeth.

"Who?" she demanded.

He met her piercing stare with one of his own. Biting back a groan, he leaned in until he felt her give an inch.

"Tollak."

She blinked. White-hot fire flashed in her eyes for an instant before her expression morphed into something violent and grave. "Does this mean he dinna believe ye?"

"No." Aksel couldn't manage more than a few words at a time, but he felt his grip on her wrist loosen just enough that he could distinguish the racing beat of her pulse against his fingers.

"There willna be a warband waiting at the docks in a few hours?" Whatever distance she'd given before, she took back with the threat she let drive her question.

He would have asked the same questions if he thought there was even a chance she would have risked Ethni or Alpia's lives, even under duress. Still, her distrust stung almost as much as the burns on his skin.

"No." The gravel in his voice relayed his irritation, and her eyes dipped again to the wounds on his chest. "I would never put them —"

"I ken." Her gaze dropped for a moment before she met his eyes again with a compassion so deep it made the muscles in his stomach clench. "Why? Why would a father do such a thing?"

A father, she said. Not his father. As his brain worked to form an answer, another lonelier part of him wanted to ask what pain had darkened her past. And a strange possessive part wanted to take that pain away.

"I made him look weak, cost him the trust of the settlers by appearing in the market like that. As if he could not protect his own house." Aksel rubbed his thumb across the soft skin of her wrist when her slender throat moved as she swallowed. It wasn't to soothe her. He needed the sensation. He needed something delicate and beautiful to battle the ugliness of which he spoke.

"Ye should sit," she said.

"I feel better standing."

He knew the look that turned her lips into a frown. It was guilt. But whatever shame she bore for his situation, he owned an equal share. She had taken him to the woods, but his father was right. He'd left himself exposed and incapacitated outside the mead hall.

"Hold this." She flicked her eyes to the hem of his tunic. When he hesitated, she lifted her other hand, peeling his fingers off her wrist and pushing the linen into his palm, keeping his tunic raised and off his raw skin.

When she fully saw his chest, he waited for an inquisition. He waited for disgust at the sight of the Chieftain's brand, marking him an outlawer. But neither came.

Had she been born of the Northlands, she would have turned at the first sight, leaving him to whatever mercy his father might decide to show. Her Vestland heritage must have clouded her under-standing of the severity of that brand.

She shifted her satchel from her shoulders to bring it around front, not once taking her eyes off his. Her hand dipped into the bag, removing a small linen-wrapped bundle. She dropped her satchel and motioned for him to give her his free hand.

When he opened his mouth to protest, she speared him with a sharp look and said again, "We have time."

"Very well." His throat was dry, his reply crackling.

She placed the bundle in his palm and unwrapped it, revealing a greenish brown glob. She smeared a bit on her fingers and hesitated as her hand hovered over his skin.

"Ye willna be a bairn about it?" she asked, completely serious.

"Never." Whatever was in that mixture, nothing could possibly make his pain worse.

He flinched at her first touch. The ointment was too cool against his tender skin and he jerked back, but her other hand caught his arm and held him in place. "Ye promised not to cry."

A grunt snaked its way up his throat and his gaze centered on hers. "Do you see any tears?"

Her only answer was the lift of one brow. She continued spreading the ointment over the blazing planes of his chest.

"Ye should try to breathe before you topple over. 'Tisn't built into our plan fer ye to crush me tonight."

Aksel couldn't help but release his held breath then, groaning against the laugh that tightened the skin across his chest.

"That was cruel, Little Bird." He was finally able to speak her language again.

Her deft fingers moved over the shape burned into his skin. He watched her, observing the way her dark head tilted to the side as she gingerly covered his wounds with her healing salve. She flicked her eyes to his once, a spark of amusement flashing behind the bright blue.

"Did ye keep yer word then too?" When his brows furrowed, she reached for the pouch in his hand, scooping up another generous portion on her fingers. "No tears?"

"Not a one." He felt the lift of one side of his mouth.

"Well done, Prince." Her lips mirrored his, a devilish smirk tugging her mouth. "Mayhap, I will let ye live 'till the morrow."

He intentionally inhaled and released another breath, finding it easier. As was the next breath. And the next. The herbs she'd applied had an almost instant numbing effect, and when she took the bundle from his palm, he was so grateful he didn't think before wrapping both hands around the back of her neck and lowering his forehead to hers.

"Thank ye."

She didn't respond. Didn't move.

"I can only imagine the dark places ye've been to come up wi' this plan, Aksel. I admit, I dinna think ye'd go through wi' it as it was. If I'd of ken what yer father would do, I would have found another way." Her voice was soft, some of the harder edges melting as they stood there, enclosed in a private world where she'd promised they had minutes to spare.

"There was no other way. Not before we ran out of time." He trembled as the herbs soaked into his wounds, easing the burn and soothing his screaming nerves.

"I ken what it is to want to undo wrong things so badly that ye'd...ye'd destroy yerself and yer soul to do it." Her confession was so soft his ears strained to hear it.

Is that what he was doing? Not just saving Ethni and Alpia because he needed them but because it was the right thing to do? Aksel reached down and lifted her hand, stroking his thumb along the scars on her palms and then up to her arm, lightly tracing the jagged lines the wolf had carved into her honey-brown skin. Ethni had whispered the story of her and Alpia's rescue, how Revna had used her own blood to create the illusion of a struggle. He expected Revna to pull away. But she didn't. In that sacred moment, she let him see her scars. Evidence that she would, indeed, carve her own heart from her chest if it meant freedom for the captive.

And she'd come looking for him. As if he were one of her own.

He lifted her hand and moved it toward his own chest. She pulled back, but he tugged it close anyway, pressing her fingers to his heated skin, directly above the outline of a raven with spread wings, now both tattooed and seared on his body.

"I was not always this man. I dinna always see the wrongs, but I do now. I want to right them too. Ye and me. We are the same."

It had only been two days, but somehow she'd managed to grant him vision after a lifetime of blindness. She'd swept in as this swirling cloud of violence and wrath that cleaved his world open from the center, exposing filthiness within. That's what made him willing to endure any amount of pain to keep their plan secret. It was the realization that Ethni, the woman who had loved him more than his own mother, wasn't a servant. She wasn't a hired hand. She was a slave. A prisoner. And he'd done nothing to help her. Nothing to set her free. He'd simply accepted it was the way things were. He'd chosen not to see.

But he could see now.

"I canna go back to the way things were." He'd said it before, but now his heart sped up again as he reached for Revna, his fingers sliding to the back of her neck, diving into her hair, as his thumbs rested on her jaw. Her hands covered his, and the two of them stood there. Together. Simply existing just for a few more stolen seconds.

They'd never discussed exactly what would happen to him once that ship set sail at dawn, just that he couldn't return home. He was certain she first meant to tie up any loose ends that might endanger her mission, including him. If she meant to stay on these shores, he would be a great liability. Now, having watched her, how she battled back the darkness inside, he was certain she would let him live. But though it was hidden, he did bear the outlaw mark. Once his father discovered the offering was stolen, barns were burned, and slaves missing, that mark would be the least of his worries. His father would want more of a payment than pain. He'd be out for blood.

He couldn't stay in Kaupang, and he couldn't board the boat with

Ethni, for he wasn't of the Vestlands. He would be an outsider all his days, a dark shadow over Ethni's life.

"Take me wi' ye," he breathed his request and felt Revna exhale in what sounded like relief. Her head was pressed to his still, and he felt her nod.

"I have a plan, but now we do have to go," she said too soon for his liking, somehow having sensed when her herbs had their full effect. "Our time has run out."

He straightened, noting the numbness across his chest. "Does it have to do with that strange sack ye hauled in here?"

Revna lifted the bag and opened it for him to see. "Aksel, meet yer new self."

Wrinkling his nose at the sight of the pile of bones she presented, he shook his head. "Do I want to ken where ye got those?"

"Most likely not." She stepped past him, dumping the contents of the bag on his bed and hurriedly arranging them into a person-like shape. "They'll char in the fire and to anyone's knowledge, Aksel Tollaksen will be dead."

Finishing her placement, she turned to face him.

"Ye mean to burn it then," he said, grazing his eyes over the space that had never been a home.

"Aye." Her answer was determined, unapologetic. She stooped to lift her satchel back to her shoulders. "Do ye object?"

He peered down at her, knowing the same certainty hardened his look. "Nay."

"Can ye get to the docks on yer own? Conall was hurt. I need to visit the last farm after I take care of this."

She hooked her thumbs under the straps of her satchel, waiting for him to agree.

"Ye go on to the farm, I will finish things here."

"I..." she looked as if she were about to argue but snapped her lips shut before watching him intently for a moment. "Are ye certain?" she finally asked.

"If Ethni doesna get to do it herself, it should be me."

She squeezed his arm once before aiming for the curtain, stopping to glance back at the bones lying on his bed.

"Whatever he did to deserve his miserable end, he can at least do some good now." She offered him a sympathetic smile.

He nodded and she was gone. Seconds later, he moved through the common area of his home to the far end door. Outside, he collected an armful of dried branches from the stack not yet cut for firewood, being careful not to let them brush against his chest. It took him far too long, but even though Revna's miracle herbs had done their job, he wasn't willing to risk agitating his burn to the point where he couldn't make it to the docks in time. Ethni wouldn't leave if she wasn't sure he would be all right.

He dumped the branches near the hearth and took a final look at the longhouse. There was nothing he would miss about it. He picked up a clay mug off the table. It still held a few abandoned sips of mead, as if someone might come back for it. The toppled chairs and look of violence Ethni told him they'd created had all been righted. Aksel wondered if his father had cleaned up the mess himself since his slaves were gone. He wondered if Tollak had even shed a single tear for Alpia, for the daughter he never claimed.

No one had ever confessed that she belonged to him, but there was no denying those dark eyes or the way his mother couldn't bring herself to look at the girl. Aksel shook his head. He'd known. For so long, he'd known what his father had done.

He kept Alpia close, far from his father's harsh hand, but he had never once tried to convince Tollak to free them. Never once suggested that letting them go might ease his mother's suffering or even attempted to get his mother to whisper that idea in his father's ear. For all the Chieftain's faults, he did care for Aksel's mother. He cared too much. He would have done anything she asked. Aksel stilled, heat creeping out from his chest up his neck to his face.

The mug in his hand shattered under the force of his grip, jagged bits of pottery scattering at his feet. Never had he seen his father even look at another woman. Not once. There was only one reason he would have sired a child with Ethni.

His concern over the wound on his chest vanished as his boot met the wooden leg of the table. It flew against the wall, falling into a heap of useless planks. His hands found his hair, fingers curling into the strands until the roots screamed.

How could she?

He'd heard them speak of how surprised they were when his mother learned of her second pregnancy. How they declared Eira a true miracle blessing from the gods. Because after him, his mother could bear no more children. That was no secret. But a Chieftain with only one heir was a sign of weakness. Maybe even a cause for challenge.

Aksel had to brace himself with both hands on the stone wall of the hearth, a bitter taste of bile burning up his throat and into his mouth. He slammed his fist against the rocks and kicked a pitcher of water that waited next to the fire. The water's dark stain coated the packed earth floor, creeping closer to the dying fire.

He thought it would be more difficult, but Aksel had no reservations in snatching one of the longer branches from the stack of firewood and shoving it into the fading flames. When the end caught, he looked for the best fuel. In the corner, a layer of straw covered the mound of sand where they buried potatoes to preserve them through the winter months. Flames devoured the dry straw and licked up the walls.

Aksel turned and touched his torch to the curtain that hung between the common room and sleeping areas, giving a nod to the outlawed man who would be mistaken for him when the ash settled. Before the smoke filled his lungs and sent him in search of fresh air, he touched the flame to anything else that would quickly catch.

Once outside, he wondered if Revna's herbs had seeped into every part of his body, because he felt nothing as his home was consumed by fire. That wasn't entirely true. He felt the always present thirst in the back of his throat that only a stout mug of sweet mead could appease.

His eyes swept over the orange flames flickering from every crack. The panicked whinny of a horse jerked his gaze to the stables. That didn't seem right. His parents would have taken the horses to the ceremony. With the strain of Revna's presence, his mother might not have found herself able to keep herself astride her own horse; perhaps she rode with his father. He wasn't the only one in his house fond of the drink.

Any night before this, Aksel would have felt a sense of longing at the thought of his mother. Not tonight. He was content to watch this place where Ethni was taken against her will, where she was used and cast aside, burn until it was a pile of ash.

The heat had just begun to reach his skin when he froze and a wave of ice skated up his spine. Something moved inside the longhouse.

Aksel was running before he could think, holding his hand in front of his face to shield his eyes. He tried to call out, but his lungs filled with smoke, choking him before he crouched to get below it.

He moved slowly forward, becoming increasingly afraid that his mind was playing tricks on him and there would be two sets of remains found in the morning. His foot met something soft and he was on his knees, feeling around with his hands.

The lump that he discovered groaned, and when he blinked through burning, tear-blurred eyes, he saw the owner of the whimper.

"Móðir!" Aksel coughed and gagged as he leaned over her, checking for injuries. Even above the overwhelming smell of smoke, his mother reeked of mead.

His anger flared as hot as the fire surrounding him, but he couldn't leave her. He slammed his fist onto the unforgiving dirt floor. Streaks of pain shot up his arm.

With a growl, he slipped his arms under her. Her limp body scraped against the burns on his chest, sending flares of agony through him even with the help of Revna's herbs. Less than a minute later, he stumbled through the door and collapsed on the ground, crawling with his mother in his arms until they were a safe distance from his burning home. He lowered his head to her shoulder as he dragged in ragged, painful breaths.

Forcing himself to swallow even though his tongue was so dry and gritty that it stuck to the roof of his mouth, he lifted his head, looking at his mother's face.

"Why?" His question was little more than a strangled groan. "Why did you do it?"

For the first time since he was a boy, Aksel felt the sting of tears welling in his eyes as he brushed back her sweat-soaked hair. It was still the bright color that was several shades lighter than his. Her eyes fluttered open. Her chin began to quiver when her glazed gaze scanned his face.

"Who are you?" Her words were slurred, much the same as his had been when Revna first stumbled upon him outside the mead hall.

"It is Aksel, Móðir. I am here. All is well. Just go back to sleep." There was no use demanding answers from her in this state. She didn't even recognize him.

"No." His mother moaned, her face contorting into a pained grimace, and she curled into a ball, hugging herself as he tried to keep her calm. "No, Aksel is gone. My boy is gone."

Tears slipped down her cheeks as she sobbed. He soothed and shushed her, hoping she would simply slip off to sleep again and forget she ever saw him. She must have seen the bones. She must have come in while he'd gone out to collect the wood. How could he have not checked the longhouse again? What was she doing there by herself? He wanted to ask her all those things, but there was still so much at stake. Revna was waiting for him.

"I am sorry." His voice was hoarse, and it hurt his throat to talk. "I wish I could have been the son you wanted. I wish you would not have needed another child enough to—"

She turned her face to him, eyes barely open, and lifted a slender hand to his cheek. He froze. It was the first time she'd touched him since...he couldn't remember. "You were a good son, too."

"Sleep, Móðir." He held her face, pressing his forehead to hers before pushing himself up to his knees.

He didn't worry that she'd seen him. She wouldn't remember any of this in the morning. She never did.

Black smoke rose in billowing puffs to the sky, blocking out the moon. Matching dark clouds would be rising all over the settlement, soon to be seen by the settlers at the ceremony, sending them racing back to their farms. If they weren't already.

"Who are y..." Her voice trailed off as she slipped back to sleep. He kept his hand on her shoulder, searching for a place he could leave her so it would look like she stumbled out on her own.

"Eira." His mother's cry had him shushing her again. "Tell Eira to come, I have to tell her about Aksel."

"Eira is well, Móðir. She is at home with Rendel."

"No!" She swatted his hand away, trying and failing to get up. "Eira is with Amah. Tollak sent Rendel on a voyage. He left this morning."

So that's what Rendel meant by not having much time. And father, how could he send Rendel away knowing Eira was about to have her babe?

"Rendel did not want her alone. She was not at the clearing, she stayed..." she broke into a fit of coughing. "She stayed in the home of Sten."

Sten's farm was one of those marked on his map. One Revna would have visited tonight. Revna didn't know who Eira was. She wouldn't know Eira was only visiting Rendel's sister and her husband. If Eira tried to stop her...oh gods. Maybe it wasn't too late. Stens farm was the farthest from the clearing; maybe it was the one Revna had been headed to.

Aksel hauled his mother farther away from the house and pulled himself onto the horse in the stable. He didn't pause to say farewell.

He'd already given her the only parting gift he had by dragging her from the flames.

His chest felt like it was splitting open, but he ignored the pain and the blood that soaked through his tunic as he tore through the woods. His sister was innocent, but if she stood between Revna and her people—he couldn't think about what would happen. He could only keep riding toward his sister.

13

AKSEL

He nearly fell from his ride when he saw the smoke rising over the trees. He was too late.

Eira! Despite the pain of his ruined chest and broken ribs stealing his breath, he nudged the mare toward Sten's farm.

Please let her be safe. He cried out to all the gods he'd ever heard of, even the one Ethni called *An T-aon*. *Please let her live.*

Orange flames were already lapping their searing tongues through the doors of the stables when he breached the tree line, slipped from the horse's back, and gave her a pat with instructions to return home. Without turning to see if she obeyed, he hurdled across the narrow patch of tall grass leading to the farm.

What if Eira had gone into the stables? What if the fire spread to the longhouse and she was trapped inside? His throat nearly closed at the thought, and tears burned behind his eyes. How could he bring that news back to Ethni? She couldn't bear it. She would never forgive him if she knew it was his plan that was the cause of Eira's death. And her babe.

No, please no. He begged anyone who would listen, his mind focusing on Ethni's God. *For Ethni, please. I beg you.*

But as he stumbled further down the dirt path, grunting in agony, his eyes fell upon chestnut hair whipping against the night wind.

"Eira!" His voice was little more than a croak. She didn't turn, but he felt a pressure lift from his lungs. She was alive.

When he crossed the last few steps, his breaths stopped again. Eira wasn't alone. Revna, a dagger in each hand, faced his sister.

"No," Aksel rasped, pushing beyond the pain to reach them. In the few steps it took to cross the field, he saw Eira's arms raised, a bow poised awkwardly to the side to allow room for her swollen belly with an arrow notched on the shelf.

It was aimed at Revna, who had her own arms spread, shielding the trembling family of slaves behind her. The cry of the enslaved mother's babe cut through the night, soaring over the growing roar of the fire consuming the stables.

Aksel dove toward them, managing to stay on his feet as he placed himself between the two women, using his arms as a shield.

Eira's stern expression turned to confusion as she took in his face, but she didn't lower her bow. "Aksel?"

"Ye ken this woman?" Revna growled from behind him.

He turned to the side, hands still raised, one palm facing Revna, the other Eira.

"She is my sister."

Revna's gaze darted to Eira, a look of surprise passing over her face before she narrowed her brows.

"What is going on, Aksel?" Eira breathed heavily, her arms shaking from the weight of her bow.

"Go." He turned to Revna, leveling a look that had her dark brows jumping over her piercing blue eyes. "I will take care of this."

Revna stepped close, peering at Eira over his shoulder and lowering her voice to a whisper. "She saw."

He clenched his jaw, giving emphasis to each word. "I will handle it."

"Aksel?" Eira's voice was high, panicked.

He whipped his head toward her, holding up a hand and answering her in their native tongue. "Put the bow down, Eira."

"Who is she? What is happening?" Eira's eyes were wide, her gaze darting toward the burning stable and the slaves behind Revna. "Is she going to kill them?"

"No." Aksel's hand went to his side when a sharp spear of pain raced across his middle.

"Did she hurt you?" Eira was trembling, tears brimming around her dark eyes. Then when he bent, groaning at the fiery pain blazing across his chest, Eira screamed. "Aksel!"

He felt Revna tense, felt the anxiousness and urgency rolling off her, and his hand flew out again, stopping Eira's approach. He felt the same urgency. The smoke from the other farms would have gained the attention of the villagers at the ceremony by now. They would be racing back to their farms, finding their stables in flames, their slaves gone. Though this farm was the farthest from the clearing, well hidden by a thick grove of trees, Sten would be coming soon. Hand braced on his knees, he peered up at Revna, speaking in her language.

"Take them and go."

"I canna leave ye here. Yer supposed to be dead. She's seen me, she kens...If she goes to the Chieftain—"

When Aksel saw her fingers tighten around her daggers, his own hands were on her shoulders, holding her in place.

"I willna let ye hurt her," he growled, his face in hers.

But she was not afraid. He couldn't place the expression she wore when she jerked her shoulders, tearing herself from his grip. A movement from behind had them both turning their attention to Eira, who had her bow raised again.

"Drop it, Eira!" Aksel's tone was sharp, his heart racing as he whipped his head back to face Revna without waiting to see if Eira obeyed his command.

"Ye think I would harm a woman wi' child?" Clearly unbothered by Eira's threat, Revna was only focused on Aksel. Her lips turned down, she shook her head as if he'd slapped her.

His eyes dipped to the blades in her hands and hers followed. She lifted her arms, daggers laying flat in her palms as if offering them to him.

"Do ye think I consider one life more sacred than another?" Revna only closed her fingers around one dagger to sweep her hand behind her, gesturing to the people still huddling together, the babe now quieted by its mother. "That her babe was any less important than this one?"

"Then what were ye going to do wi' her?" The truth was, he didn't know what she thought or felt about his people. She was a mystery, seemingly intent on making herself the most frightening thing to ever visit the Northlands but also willing to give her life and blood for her people. She was from the Vestlands; they were enemies. Enemies fought, they killed, and they enslaved each other. That was just the way of things.

"I..." Revna's look hardened, her jaw tight. "She will have to go on the boat too."

"What?" He straightened.

"There's no other way. She saw. She canna stay. If she doesna go, these will be the last bound for their homeland." Her hand moved to her vest, fingers pressing against the leather. "There are more. And we must go now."

His eyes danced between hers. They needed more time, but there was none. She was right; Eira now knew the truth of the raven. But he would not force this upon her. He would not steal his sister's future from her.

"I have given too much not to finish what I started." Revna folded her arms over her chest. "Ye can bring yer sister or I will."

"Have I not earned a say?" Aksel felt his face flame. "Have I not paid enough fer ye to trust me even a little?"

Revna's eyes fell on his bloodied shirt, but there was determination when she met his gaze again. "Ye bring her or I will."

"Nay, Revna." He raised his voice. "I willna allow this. Ye will give her the same chance ye gave me."

Revna's lips parted in preparation for an argument, but he threw his arm out over her shoulder, finger pointing in the direction of the port.

"Take them and go. I will handle it."

Her jaw clenched, followed by her fists, but she spun on her heels and ushered her people toward the safety of the trees. Just before vanishing into the shadows, she looked over her shoulder at him.

"Dunna tarry, Prince. And dunna die. No one gets to kill ye but me."

He couldn't help the breathy laugh that blew from his lips when she repeated his own words back to him. But all humor faded when he turned to face his wide-eyed sister.

"You tell me what is going on right this minute, Aksel Tollaksen."

All the things he'd planned to say evaporated from his brain. How could he explain that he was questioning everything he'd ever known? That he was beginning to think the way their people had always lived was wrong? That he was even questioning their gods?

"I do not have much time, Eira. And I am sorry to do this, but you have to make a choice."

"What choice?" Her bow had been lowered since he'd barked the order, but she still clutched it as she curled her arms protectively over her belly.

"You can never speak of what you saw here tonight, including my presence." Aksel watched her, trying to guess what she was thinking.

"Or?" She took a step backward as he sucked in a deep breath.

"You can come with me and sail for the Vestlands tonight."

"I do not understand. Why? You..." Her brows furrowed, eyes

dipping again to his tunic. "You were not bleeding like that when you left the market. If it was not her, did *he* hurt you?"

There was no question as to which "he" she meant. He'd served as a barrier between Ethni and Alpia and his mother while Eira had always been the barrier between him and his father.

"It does not matter. I cannot give you any answers but this: a wrong has been done. I am helping to right it."

She turned to the stables, and then looked to the place where Revna had disappeared before her eyes returned to him. "The slaves. She is the one taking them."

"Yes." He couldn't help it. He was giving her all the answers he'd just said he could not. But the look in Eira's eye was not that of disdain; it was a slowly unraveling understanding.

"But they are not dead."

"No."

"That is the wrong you are righting." It wasn't a question. "Sending them to their homeland."

"Yes," he scrubbed his hands over his face before continuing. "Please, Eira. If you want to remain here, you cannot speak of what you know. You cannot reveal that you saw me or anyone else tonight, no matter what you hear come dawn. You cannot even hint that anything is other than it appears."

He expected her to scoff or refuse, but she tipped her chin down to stare at her stomach.

"Before, I would have argued. But now—" She caressed her belly. "I cannot imagine the pain of losing this child, and I have not even met him yet."

Eira's eyes were wet with tears when she looked at him again.

"I cannot imagine him being taken from me to some strange land. I cannot imagine Rendel ever hurting him as Faðir hurt you. Something has changed because of this babe, and I...I understand why you would do what you are doing. But, you have always been different. Better."

He was stunned at her admission. Both at her feelings about

what he was doing and that she had come to some strange conclusion that he was anything but a wretch.

"Tell me Ethni is truly with you. And Alpia. Tell me they are alive." Eira dropped the bow as her hand flew to her mouth, smothering a sob. "When you disappeared, and I heard of the scene at Faðir's house, I thought they were dead. I thought you were—"

"They are safe." He couldn't let her continue to suffer.

"Oh thank the gods." Eira tipped her head to the sky.

Not gods. One God. He was beginning to believe just one God had a hand in this.

"So, you will not speak of this?" Aksel knew he needed to leave— that every second he lingered meant danger for everyone—but walking away from Eira was harder than he thought it would be.

"I will not."

Aksel moved toward her, rubbing his hands along her arms, warming her as she shivered in the cool night air. "I knew you would listen."

She eyed him with a tilt of her head. "You have always had a kind heart, Bróðir. That is not something our people value as a strength, but I think it makes you the strongest of us all."

She leaned into him, resting her cheek against his shoulder, careful not to touch his chest. He folded his arm around her, pressing his lips into her soft hair.

"I should have done something long before this, Eira. I should have listened to the churn in my gut that told me it was wrong."

She tilted her head up, meeting his eyes. "The past cannot be changed, only the steps you take next. But I meant it; you have always been different, Aksel. At least, ever since I can remember. Maybe it was your sickness. Maybe it changed you. Changed everyone, but you for the better."

When he offered her a soft smile, she turned her head again, nestling back against him.

"What will Rendel do when he returns?"

Eira stiffened and pushed herself upright at his question. "He will do nothing. Because he will not know."

"What about when he brings home his own slaves? I will not have you putting yourself in danger trying to defy him."

She shook her head, clenching her thin shawl tighter around her shoulders. "Rendel is a good man. He would never hurt me. He will give me whatever I ask, even if he does not understand. I will tell him what he needs to know, and in time," she gazed down at her belly again. "I know he will understand as I do."

Aksel crushed his sister to his side again, his heart clenching at the small sniff he heard. He was out of time.

"I will not see you again, will I?" Eira's question was so loaded with pain and sorrow, he had to grind his teeth to bear it.

"I do not know."

"If there is a way to live in peace, to live with what our people... what *we* have done to the mothers of stolen children, you will find it, will you not? You will come tell me?" Her voice broke with soft sobs.

His throat was almost too tight to answer, but he managed to croak a soft, "Yes."

"Tell them...tell Ethni and Alpia that I wish them freedom and happiness."

"I will." His promise filled him with purpose, a feeling so new he almost didn't recognize it.

It had taken him too long to see what his sister conveyed with a few simple words, but now he understood with clarity. He understood why Revna had burned her way across the country. There was a message that needed to be delivered. A truth he shouldn't have been surprised his brilliant sister interpreted right away. Something she would teach to her children and her husband.

There has been a great wrong. It must be made right. One has come to set the captives free.

"I do not want to leave you, but I must." He stroked his hand down her soft brown hair. His eyes scanned the dark woods at the sound of distant shouts. Eira turned toward the woods too. "Where will you go?"

"I will go meet Sten and Amah. I will keep them away for as long as I can and tell them all that I saw was a flash of black wings." Eira wiped at her glistening cheeks with the frayed end of her wrap and gave him one last long look. "I love you, my bróðir."

Then she walked toward the woods. Away from him.

"Aksel," she stopped, rushing back and picking up his hand, speaking with rushed words. "I do not have words for what Faðir has done. His heart is as cold as stone. You are nothing like him. And I know you do not remember a time when Móðir was not also cold and distant. I do not either. But she told me stories. She told me when you were born, you were the smallest babe. She doted on you; bathed you with kisses and would not let anyone else hold you for more than a minute. Not even Faðir."

She opened her mouth and closed it again, as if deciding against what she was going to say. After a quick glance over her shoulder, she spoke again. "I do not know what happened to her when you were so sick. When I was older, she told me she knew then that you were going to die, that the gods were going to take you from her because you were so lovely. And when you lived..." she shook her head. "She said she could not believe it. As if the son she loved had truly died. I even saw her sneaking off to the graves. Mourning over a small mound that must have been someone else's child."

Eira squeezed his hand. "I think that fear of losing you broke something inside of her, Aksel. She became confused. Sometimes she would say your eyes were as green as the summer grass, sometimes as blue as the sky."

Aksel could only clench his teeth, his throat too tight to swallow. The shouts were getting louder and he needed to go, but he could not bring himself to leave until he'd heard what Eira wanted to say. He did not tell her he knew just how broken their mother was. Eira didn't need to live with the knowledge of what had truly happened to Ethni. He would bear that alone.

185

"I know in her way, she did love you. But her confusion is her trouble, Aksel. Her burden to bear and her joy to miss out on. It has nothing to do with you, and I am sorry that I did not tell you sooner."

She was in his arms again, and after one crushing embrace when he ignored his pain, he pressed his lips to her forehead and released her. "I am sorry, Eira, I have to leave. I love you."

She nodded and hurried to the woods. When she was swallowed by the shadow of the trees, he snatched the longbow she'd discarded and tossed it into the glowing flames of the stable as he passed, not caring one bit about the blazing wound that set his chest on fire.

He pointed himself in the direction of Kaupang's port, and as he pursued the raven-haired woman who had ripped his world apart, he did not look back.

14

REVNA

S oft waves lapped the wooden docks and licked the curved sides of the ship that bobbed on the water. Her people were on board. Even the luckiest hen that ever lived. Everyone except Ethni, Alpia, and Conall.

As she expected, Ethni refused to climb the boarding plank without Aksel. Revna and the ones she'd gathered from the last farm had arrived nearly half an hour before. Aengus and Cian had arrived with the stolen offering. Passage was paid. The plan was complete. Yet there was still no sign of Aksel.

Ethni paced, slapping away Conall's hands as he urgently pleaded with her to board.

The sky was already turning from obsidian to indigo, and the air was thick with the smell of smoke. The settlers would have all returned to their farms, would still be working to douse flames and just beginning to realize their offering was given in vain. The Chieftain might have already sent his men back to the ceremonial stone, finding it empty of the riches the people had sacrificed.

Revna clenched and unclenched her fists. She should have stayed. How could she have left him? He was hurt; when her herbs wore off, he would have slowed down. Revna had lingered long enough to see that Eira would not ruin their plans, if for no other reason than she loved her brother, but what if things had gone wrong after that?

What if the Chieftain had sent men to check on Eira and found Aksel? He was strong, but he couldn't fight off a warband. And he couldn't hold out forever if his father wanted answers. He wouldn't last one minute if the Chieftain leveraged his sister against him. And after the cruel punishment he'd inflicted on Aksel already, she had no doubt the vile leader would do just that.

He loved his sister; that was clearer than the stars dotting the sky. His insistent arguments that Revna give her a chance, his certainty that Eira would listen and be sympathetic to their cause, had been rolling around in her stomach since she'd stormed from the last farm.

What of her lost twin? When Revna found her, would they instantly know each other? Would they look upon each other as Aksel and Eira did? And if Duncan, her brother, were here, would he fight to give her a chance as Aksel did for Eira?

Did the new King of Tràigh even know she was his sister? She'd almost told Cyrene when Duncan ended up in their woods, bleeding and near death, and they realized who he was. She'd almost told the secret again when she saw the queen softening toward him. When Cyrene announced her plans to marry him, the conflicting emotions nearly sent Revna into a wild rage. Cyrene had quite literally wrestled her to the ground. Again, the truth had been there on the tip of her tongue.

Now she was thousands of miles from her queen and facing the very real possibility that she might never see her again. She wasn't even sure Cyrene would *want* to see her again after she blatantly disobeyed the order to remain with the villagers and joined the battle instead. A waiting Viking longboat had been the perfect excuse not to face her when the fighting had ended.

"Ethni," Revna spoke so quietly, Ethni stilled her pacing and flicked a look that sent Conall to the ship's boarding plank, Alpia at his side. "I need ye to do something fer me."

"Anything." Ethni took her hands, and Revna didn't pull away.

"I need ye to give a message to the king and queen of Tràigh." Revna felt the burn of salt water behind her eyes, but blinked until her vision was clear. "I need ye to tell them I am Fiona's daughter. That Duncan still has family. And that I am sorry I left wi'out a word."

Ethni blinked, her lips parting as a soft gasp slid through. "They dunna ken who ye are?"

Revna lifted a shoulder, her eyes dropping to closely examine the toe of her boot. "I dunna ken, truly. But the king has lived so long believing all of his blood kin were dead. He should ken that isna so."

"Revna, why will ye not tell them yerself?" Ethni squeezed her hands, forcing Revna to meet her eyes. "Why will ye not come wi' us?"

"I canna." Revna shook her head. "There are too many still here, waiting. I canna go home until they do. I'm going to find Aksel. I'm staying."

"No need to find me, Little Bird. I'm here." A deep baritone had Revna whirling, unable to hide her relief at the sight of Aksel limping toward them. "And if ye stay, I stay."

Ethni beat her to him, and he hushed her cry when she saw his condition. He hushed her again when Ethni turned an accusatory glare on both Revna and Conall.

"Dunna blame them, Ethni. This wasna by their hands." He held her shoulders, forcing her eyes to his and offering a soft smile. "Most of it, anyway."

"There's so much blood." Ethni, still trapped by Aksel's hands, sobbed. "Oh, Aksel. He dinna…I am so sorry."

"Never mind, I need to see ye board this ship. I need to ken ye'll be free." He turned her toward the ship. "It will all fade when yer safe."

Ethni pulled herself from his grasp. "Ye have to come, too."

"I agree." Revna stepped to Ethni's side. "An outlawer bought yer freedom. Take it."

"Do I not get a say in my own fate?" Aksel raised a brow as he continued to shuffle both women closer to the ship.

"Nay." Revna crossed her arms, planting her feet and refusing to be moved.

When Aksel wordlessly threatened to carry her aboard, forcing her to leave with him, her warning glare and shift to a battle stance halted his efforts.

Aksel's hands found his hips, his blue eyes narrowing on hers even as a slight smile tugged at his lips. "Are we going to stand here and argue as the sun rises and this dock floods wi' Vikings?"

"Get on the ship, Aksel."

Conall was tugging on Ethni's arm, urging her to do the same.

"Nay." Aksel and Ethni answered as one.

"Aksel, dunna make me force ye."

He snorted. Actually snorted at her. Revna felt her cheeks flame. When her hand went to her side, aiming for the pouch she always kept on her hip, his hand shot out, gripping her wrist.

"The only way I'm leaving ye behind is if I'm dead, and ye already promised me I'd get to live 'till morning." His words were for no one but her and he jerked her close, his lips brushing her ear as he whispered. "Ye'll not go back on yer word now, will ye, m'lady?"

They stood toe to toe. He was so near, and she immediately regretted lifting her chin to meet his too-close stare. Did his eyes just dip to her lips, and why did that thought make her want to shrink away? She didn't cower for anyone.

"For someone who has made freedom her life's mission, ye dunna seem to care much fer mine." His voice was low, the sound flooding over her with a challenge that turned her blood to fire. "What of my choice, Little Bird?"

"I have always been alone, always worked alone." She bit back the curse she wanted to hurl at him for making her stumble over her words. "I dunna need yer help."

"Well, too bad. Ye've got it." His hand was still on her wrist, his eyes still holding her hostage.

"Ye've got mine too." Ethni was at his side.

"Now look what ye've done." Revna jerked her hand free, knowing she was only able to because he let her. "Ethni, ye canna —"

"Dunna tell me what I can and canna do. I've had my every move decided fer me fer nearly twenty years. If I now have the freedom to choose, then I will do it." Her blue eyes blazed, and she held out her arm for Alpia, who was already on her way to her mother's side. "These are my people, too; do I not deserve the chance to help them?"

"Aye, but—" Revna was drowning, and she looked to Conall for help.

Ethni did too, aiming a finger that warned him against interfering. Conall, smart man that he was, kept silent as Ethni spoke to him. "If yer allowed to suffer fer me, then I am allowed to take risks fer them." Then she worked her gaze back to Revna. "If ye dunna accept our help, I'm going to assume yer doing all of this fer yer own glory and not fer the good of our people."

Revna felt her mouth drop open. That wasn't at all why she was doing this, and she said as much.

"Then why, Revna?" Ethni wasn't letting up on her inquisition. "Is it penance? Have ye done some great wrong yer trying to make up fer? Because there is only one path to forgiveness, and it is paved wi' stones too heavy for any human to lift."

The mark on Revna's chest blazed to life when Ethni started her tirade, as if her words were a flintstone, and Revna stumbled back. The woman didn't stop; she matched Revna's retreat with a step of her own.

"*An T-aon* is the only one who can grant forgiveness. He is the one who earned it wi' His death on the cross. Any attempts we make are foolish, worthless efforts."

"Nay," was all Revna could say. Even Aksel lowered a sympathetic look, clearly having been on the receiving end of one of Ethni's truth-filled lectures more than once.

"Tell me why." Ethni advanced again, and for the first time in her life, Revna felt completely outmatched.

"I dunna ken." Her voice was meek, heart slamming against her ribs.

"Well, until ye figure it out, ye've gained yerself a small army."

"I work alone." Revna's arguments were growing repetitive and weak.

"Ye may have intended to come to this land and remain a ghost. Ye freed them from their chains but left them slaves to fear. Ye are the messenger from their home. If ye are cold and distant; what keeps them from thinking that is what waits fer them on the shores of their homeland? They've had enough of darkness, Revna. Ye clearly need our help."

Ethni's words sliced through all of Revna's plans, the solid pattern she'd kept to for four long winters. Before Revna could respond, Ethni grabbed her arms, directing a pointed stare at her that might as well have wrapped her in a steel cage.

"If ye hear nothing else, hear this. Ye canna lead anyone to the light if ye dwell in darkness yerself."

As if the matter was settled, Ethni turned to Alpia, resting her hands on the girl's shoulders. "Ye've lived more in yer young years than most do in a lifetime. Yer brave and smart. Ye deserve to make yer own choice. Our people will welcome ye if ye want to go on ahead and start a new life in Tràigh."

Alpia searched her mother's eyes, the weight and privilege of her decision turning her mouth into a small frown. Ethni didn't rush her, even though the sky was lightening by the second.

"I want to stay wi' ye." Alpia turned her large brown eyes to Revna. "Wi' all of ye."

Revna couldn't swallow around the lump that formed in her throat. She looked to Conall. Surely, he would put his foot down and drag his family onto the waiting ship. But the traitor only lifted a shoulder before slipping his arm around Ethni.

"I go where she goes," he said.

Revna threw her hands in the air and marched aboard the ship to speak with the captain.

"I canna believe this," she muttered half an hour later as she stood in a hidden spot on the docks, watching the sails of the ship grow smaller in the distance, flanked by the army Ethni had formed.

"Believe it, Little Bird." She felt Aksel's warm presence at her back. "Yer stuck wi' us."

"Well, I hope ye've got another plan, because we have about five minutes before this place will be swarming with people who want to kill us. Especially ye." She stopped short of shoving her finger into Aksel's wounded chest.

"Why me?" He feigned offense, but his smirk had returned.

"Because ye, Prince, are already supposed to be dead."

He laughed, slinging his arm around her shoulders and pointing to a slip of a space between two buildings. "Lucky fer ye, I am a ghost who is familiar wi' every secret place in this settlement."

With Ethni, Alpia, and Conall following close behind, Revna trailed Aksel through all the hidden paths of Kaupang until they were safely back in the woods and nearly halfway to another settlement.

"'Tis helpful to have a spirit such as I, is it not?" Aksel's tone was light, but he was starting to slow, his injuries clearly causing much discomfort.

"Fer now." Revna began to look for a safe place to make camp. "But I wouldna get too comfortable. I'm still considering killing ye in yer sleep just to rid myself of yer incessant whining."

"It will have to be another night, remember?" He laughed again, wincing as his hand flew to his ribs. "Besides, ye ken ye love having me around, Little Bird."

Revna found herself unable to respond, disturbed by the fact that he might be right.

15

REVNA

825 AD: four months later

Five summers in the Norselands and still, Revna was amazed. The woods were glowing with brilliant greens and splashes of yellow and white from blossoming flowers. The chilled spring winds had been enveloped by warmth, and the days were at their longest. Revna stretched to let her bare arms soak up the golden rays. Her normally olive skin had paled in the winter months, leaving her with a slight sickly sheen that was finally fading. She needed the light. The sun felt like honey on her skin, coating her arms and almost driving away the slithering unease that was a constant source of irritation.

It was a never-ending worry that death waited around each corner, which had her training every second they were not rescuing slaves. She'd never considered herself a teacher, but Astrid wasn't there to lead, and just because Revna could defend herself didn't mean she would always be able to protect the ones who depended on her.

They'd called themselves her army, so an army they would be. Ethni had been the most surprising of her students, with a strength and speed that didn't seem natural for her thin frame and meek personality. Conall and Aksel proved to be decent opponents when it came to sparring, but they still failed to successfully predict her own sneak attacks. As for Alpia, Revna felt like the girl would have made a fine warrior under Astrid's command. Her increasing skill with the longbow promised she might yet outshine even the queen's captain.

Revna found Ethni basking in the sun as she had been minutes before, but when she started gathering blades and arrows for their daily training, Ethni shook her head.

"Not today, Revna." Ethni kept her eyes closed, a smile pulling back her lips. "Today we rest."

When Revna didn't respond, Ethni cracked open one eye. "Ye ken rest is just as important as training fer keeping yerself ready and alert." She leaned back on her palms, closing her eyes again. "Besides, Conall and Aksel have gone to fetch supper, so ye have no one to spar wi'."

"Ye dunna give yerself enough credit; yer as formidable a sparring partner as either of them." Revna laid down the weapons, though the thought of skipping a day frayed the ends of her nerves.

Revna and Conall had just returned from Oslo. In the months since the raven had set Kaupang ablaze, they'd heard rumors that chaos reigned and Aksel's father was unable to regain control. Many of the trading ships moved on to the next closest port, offering a safe harbor for Revna and Conall to sneak five more souls aboard a foreign ship while Aksel watched over Ethni and Alpia in their make-shift camp.

It had taken them nearly ten days to reach Oslo and return, but now they were all together—everyone able to breathe easier again. Her little army would enjoy a few slow, warm days before heading further north.

Why she couldn't simply enjoy a single battle-free day without her fingers searching for the cold hilts of her daggers had Revna gritting her teeth. When Ethni turned her back, Revna plucked Rune's dagger from the pile and tucked it into the leather belt at her waist.

It had been days since they'd seen another soul, but she still found herself prowling the woods at night, eyes examining every shadow, almost as if she were hoping for danger.

She sucked in a breath and closed her eyes, determined to force herself to be at peace. Finally, Aksel and Conall returned from a hunt, both wearing wide, proud grins. They carried three rabbits they'd trapped. Conall aimed for Ethni, who used a scrap of linen to clean a smear of dirt from his cheek. Aksel looked at Revna, rolling his eyes when Conall leaned close and whispered something that had Ethni's face flaming bright red.

When Aksel bent to lay their dinner over the stone he used for skinning, his loose tunic fell away from his skin, revealing the pink scar atop the inked blue lines on his chest. From the moment she'd seen what his father had done, Revna felt pangs of guilt so sharp she winced every time she thought of it. Even though he was completely healed, she turned her face away.

When her eyes found his face again, Aksel was staring at her, his brows inching together. Abandoning the rabbits, he marched over and grabbed her hand, hauling her into the trees.

He didn't stop until they were well out of sight and earshot of the others. She opened her mouth to slam him with some sarcastic remark when he shocked her into silence by reaching behind his head and removing his tunic.

"Why do ye insist on constantly baring yer chest?" Her tone was light, but her eyes immediately went to the ground and she turned, aiming for the clearing. "If yer trying to impress me, dunna bother, I—"

"Look at me," he demanded, grasping her arm and then her chin when she tried to turn away again. "Look, Revna."

When she finally did, she kept her eyes on his, jaw squared and

THE RAVEN

teeth clenched. Huffing, he released her.

"This—" He ran his hand across the raven shaped mark and his father's brand in the center. "I would bear it a thousand times if it meant I would get to see what I witnessed this morning."

She held his gaze, waiting for him to share this blessed sight that was worth so much pain.

"I saw Alpia. She had discovered a single patch of sunshine, and she had her arms out as she spun. She wasna afraid. She wasna worried about who would see her or scold her. She was just spinning and spinning, and Ethni..." He closed his eyes; the silvery glisten that shone in them was gone when he opened them again, but his voice was tight. "She smiled. I tried to remember if I'd ever seen her smile before, and I couldn't. Not like that. Not wi' such... freedom."

Revna released the breath in her lungs as if someone had shoved an elbow in her gut.

"So, dunna look at this mark as something to be ashamed of. I wear it with pride. I wear it knowing what it stands fer and what it has purchased." He picked up her hand, his thumb stroking over the marks that scarred her skin. "Just as these have purchased many lives. They stand fer the battle we have fought fer others' freedom. I wouldna take that from ye. Dunna take it from me."

Revna held his gaze for a minute before letting her eyes drift lower. She controlled their movement, keeping their descent slow as she followed the strong line of his neck and muscled curves of his shoulders. Finally, swallowing hard, she took in the expanse of his bare chest. He didn't move, didn't touch her; he simply stood, allowing her to take however long she needed before she could accept his explanation.

Her fingers drifted up, as if to touch him, but they trembled until she folded them into a fist. When she started to lower her hand, he caught it swiftly.

"Am I making ye nervous, Little Bird?"

She inwardly cursed him for that stomach-tumbling half-smile

197

and how he held her small hand in his even when she tugged to be released. "Not nervous, just nauseous."

The low rumbling chuckle that vibrated in his chest tightened the already coiled muscles in her middle.

"Just, breathe," he whispered as his thumb worked its way beneath her curled fingers, urging them open. He pressed her splayed hand to his skin, holding it there for three heartbeats before he let go, allowing her to decide if she would remove it.

She felt the weight of his gaze as she lightly dragged her fingers over the raised lines on his skin, concentrating on her breaths to keep from allowing her cowardly legs to carry her back to the clearing.

When she traced the outstretched wings over his ribs, she felt him inhale a controlled breath and hold it. He didn't release it until she lifted her hand.

"Where did this one come from?" She brushed her thumb over a puckered white line on his bicep.

He tore his gaze from hers to peer at the scar, his brows drawing slightly together. "I dunna remember. Most likely from my days of training wi' my fa—the Chieftain's warband."

She felt the tug of a smile as she pressed one finger to the small scar on his shoulder. "And this one? Yer proud of it too?"

When her eyes met his again, she felt her cheeks warm at the sparkle that danced behind their deep blue.

"Aye," he said, tilting his head to the side. "'Tis not every man that can say he survived getting stabbed by Odin's raven."

She raised a brow. "Ye stabbed yerself."

"Ye keep saying that." He slid his tunic back over his head. "I recall differently."

"Anything ye recall from that night is most definitely clouded by the amount of mead ye consumed." She noticed he shortened his stride to keep with her as they walked back to the clearing.

"Ye keep saying that too."

She shook her head and glanced one last time at the place on his chest where his tunic now covered his scars, promising herself that she would never again think of those marks as anything other than utterly beautiful.

"Ye shielded me."

He lifted his eyes, confusion etched in his expression.

"The night we left Kaupang. When ye stepped between yer sister and me. Ye were afraid I would hurt her, but ye shielded me." She watched as he worked out what she was saying.

He dragged his bottom lip through his teeth before answering. "I ken ye were angry wi' me fer suggesting that, but somewhere inside...I ken ye wouldna."

"And ye dinna have the same faith in her?"

Aksel lifted a shoulder. "I dunna remember thinking about it. I just acted."

Revna hummed a soft reply, feeling slightly dissatisfied. She wasn't sure what question she was truly asking, or what she wanted his answer to be. Now she was uncomfortable with the way he was watching her, so she quickened her steps, speaking over her shoulder.

"Just to be clear, I dunna need shielding."

He followed, close at her heels, a deep chuckle raising the hair on her arms. "Of course not, Little Bird." He leaned close, his breath heating her neck. "And I have never made ye nervous."

Whatever humor he meant to claim from his trick was forced from his body by her elbow to his gut. She laughed as he searched for his missing breath.

"Nauseous, Prince. Nauseous. Pay attention."

When they reached the edge of the clearing, she tossed him two empty water skins hanging from a branch and sent him in the direction of a nearby stream. He walked backwards, holding her gaze with a teasing grin as Alpia ran up to Revna. Alpia raised a stiff animal skin mat smeared with lumps of oily-black paste.

"How is this?" The girl chirped.

Revna gathered a small amount on her finger and smeared it on a clean area of the mat. "'Tis a bit thick still." She offered a smile. "But the color is perfect."

"Mama said I should test my war paint skills on ye." Alpia lifted her palette, hopeful eyes dancing.

Revna looked across the clearing. Conall stood behind Ethni, his arms snaked around her waist and his chin resting on her shoulder. Ethni had her hands clasped together as if in prayer, and they both mouthed silent pleas. Revna pressed her lips together to quell the smile threatening to give away their secret plan.

Ethni looked so different. Despite sleeping in make-shift shelters or sometimes on the hard ground for months at a time, there was color on her cheeks and meat on her bones. Alpia had grown too, filling out her clothes so much they'd had to acquire new dresses for her. Conall had gained weight as well, nearly rivaling Aksel's size without the height. But it was more than their size that had changed. Aksel was right; they were genuinely happy.

There had been very few days in the four months since they'd left Kaupang that there was not some urgent matter. Some danger to be wary of, some growing group of freed people to care for. This was one of those rare times. Ethni and Conall deserved every second alone they could steal.

"Come, Alpia," Revna said, tossing a wink over her shoulder and her arm over Alpia's. "Let's walk down to the stream and see if we canna get it the right consistency."

Aksel wasn't there when they arrived but found them not long after, and Revna couldn't help the laugh that burst from her lips at the blush of red that stained his cheeks, bright even beneath his beard.

"Stumble upon something unexpected in the woods, did ye?"

He ran his tongue across his bottom lip as he closed his eyes and shook his head. "I came to beg ye to burn my eyes from my skull."

Revna laughed again. A full, hearty laugh that started in her stomach and raced up her throat. She had to wrap her arms around her middle when she doubled over, and soon Aksel had joined in. His deep chuckle draped over her shoulders, warming her even more than the sun. For a moment, she found that peace she had been searching for earlier.

Revna, finally catching her breath, sank onto the soft soil of the riverbank and leaned against the smooth side of a stone. She let her eyes drift closed as Alpia painted fearsome designs on her face.

"What do ye think, Aksel?" Alpia asked.

"One look will strike fear into the hearts of our enemies."

Revna kept her eyes closed but felt the pull of her lips as they drifted up into a smile when he continued.

"They'll drop their weapons wi'out us having to speak a word."

His mention of weapons had her fingers moving across her body, landing on the hilt of Rune's dagger. Her hand drifted to the place on her vest where she could feel the lump of folded parchment. Once Ethni found out about it, she'd insisted they all memorize it. Revna still kept it near her heart, but every name was tucked inside their minds. And their list was shrinking.

"Yer next, Aksel. I will make ye look like a warrior too." She heard Alpia shift, moving closer to him.

Enjoying the feel of the sun-warmed stone at her back, Revna let her wandering thoughts drown out Aksel and Alpia's soft conversation. She thought back over the months since they'd carried out the plan that left him with that mark on his chest.

Word had spread, just as Aksel predicted. At the first marking of the raven in new settlements, offerings appeared. Revna let them believe themselves blessed by the gods when only their slaves disappeared instead of their stables and homes. Aksel had suggested letting him leave a new message instead.

One has come to set the captives free. The true reason for the raven.

Something was changing across the land. The more of her people they found, the more stories they heard about Norsemen who had once been cruel and unforgiving suddenly looking at their captives with a strange reverence. Even kindness. It was as if the freemen were suddenly afraid of harming those chosen by the gods.

Maybe they *were* chosen. Maybe it was by the God Cyrene worshiped.

Revna scoffed at herself. She didn't believe in any of that. But the mark on her own chest seemed to disagree and tingled uncomfortably.

She hadn't had to spill another drop of her blood since Kaupang. The rumors had taken that burden from her. She lifted her head and looked at her arms, brushing her palm across her scarred skin.

Aksel was right. Her scars were valuable. A reminder of a cost paid. Of lives redeemed.

He bore our stripes. That's what it says in the Word. Brigid's voice echoed from somewhere forgotten in her mind, from one of her many stories. It was one of the few Revna had actually stayed by the fire to listen to. At least for a while.

She never found use for the fairy tales and didn't understand why the young ones would linger long after dark, seeming to hang on to each word as if it were a rope saving them from dropping into a bottomless pit. She was more interested in skirting the edges of the training ring. Mirroring the warrior's movements. Or sitting at the feet of the metal-maiden, the carver, or the healer. Learning useful things; things she could see and touch and feel.

But that story. It almost forced her to remain. The tale of the God who turned himself mortal and walked the earth as a humble and unknown king. Revna expected a great battle—for the king to don his crown and drive out his enemies. But he didn't. He was meek. He healed with his touch, even with his words. Then he allowed his enemies to beat and torture him. Allowed them to drive nails into his hands and feet and display him on a cross, his dignity stripped away as his life drained from his body.

The God-man died. Revna had been so angry at that injustice, she stormed away before hearing the rest. What else could there have been? He was dead.

"Revna." The warning in Aksel's voice had her on instant alert.

He was already on his feet. "Alpia, go back to the clearing. Call fer Conall."

Revna moved to his side, scanning the woods for whatever had alarmed him. "What do ye see?"

"I heard something."

Before the words were fully out of his mouth, a distant scream shot through the woods. Aksel dropped his gaze on her.

"I heard it too." A faint drumming sparked to life in Revna's mind. There was a relief in her breathed reply that didn't belong, and she refused to meet his eye again in case he noticed. Of course he would. He was always noticing.

Alpia was gathering her paint. Revna tugged on the sleeve of the girl's dress. "Leave it. Go find yer parents. Call out for them when you get near. Tell them to stay there wi' ye."

The terror-filled screech reached them again, and Revna abandoned all worry of Alpia stumbling onto her mother and adoptive father in some compromising state. She just wanted her safe. "Go, Alpia. Now."

Aksel already had his short blade drawn as he crossed the stream in one long stride. It took Revna some carefully placed steps, but she managed to get to the other side without soaking her boots.

"We are only scouting," Revna breathed. It was as much a reminder to him as to herself. They didn't need to risk a public skirmish that would make their presence known.

She angled herself closer to Aksel so she could press her own boots into the footprints he made. If they were tracked, it would appear there was only one of them. Hiding their true number had saved them more than once. At least their faces were already painted, just in case they did meet enemies.

Aksel kept his steps surprisingly light for his size, a trick she had taught him in their months together. She kept her own weight on her toes, and they moved soundlessly through the woods until they neared the edge where trees grew more sparsely and shadows lightened.

"Wagon." Aksel tipped his chin up, directing her eyes to a horse-drawn cart. It was unmanned.

A soft sob had them both searching the small clearing. The thud of that drum in her brain grew louder, more urgent, and her warrior training had her senses sharpened, ready.

"There," Revna breathed against Aksel's neck as she moved from one side of him to the other.

A small, cloak-covered lump trembled on the ground; a feminine groan seeped from underneath. Revna scanned the woods and the dirt path beyond. The woman seemed to be alone, but something twisted in Revna's gut, warning her not to drop her guard.

Aksel tensed, preparing to move. Revna's hand shot out, gripping his shoulder. "Wait," she whispered. "Something is wrong."

They waited, but no one else appeared.

"I'm going." Aksel's warning came as he was already inching toward the clearing.

Dagger between her teeth, Revna slipped around to grasp the low branches of a tree, hauling herself up until she could see almost fully into the back of the wagon. It was littered with toppled stick cages that housed softly clucking chickens, a few barrels of mead, and crates of straw, which she assumed was packing for vegetables. She didn't see another person.

Aksel crept closer, continually scanning the clearing with each step. Revna gripped the branch, its rough bark scraping against her palms. That growing rhythm inside her mind was booming now, heaving a heavy weight against some invisible door she'd kept locked and barred.

Aksel reached the woman, and Revna held her breath when he crouched and stretched out his hand. He touched her shoulder, speaking softly. There was a beat of silence as she lifted her head.

Then the air was shattered with a scream that sent him retreating so quickly he stumbled, landing on his backside.

Revna was on the ground in her next breath, dagger palmed and feet carrying her toward the screeching woman, who had scooted back awkwardly until she collided with the trunk of the nearest tree.

Aksel's hands were in front of him, his tone pleading. "Shh, we mean you no harm."

This was a trap, and this girl was the bait. Her screams were the signal. In time with that now deafening boom, the warning pulsed over and over in Revna's mind. A trap. A trap. She was only steps away, blade ready to silence the woman's wails.

"Revna, no!" Aksel pushed himself to his feet and dove for her, wrapping his arms around her until her hands were pinned to her side.

"This is a trap. She's bait," Revna said aloud the mantra that acted as a key. The door in her mind swung open and a rush of icy flames surged through her chest. She was rage and fury and death. Just as she had been on the longboat that brought her to these shores, when evil had come in the form of a cowardly crew leader. When Rune met that misplaced rage—when she was consumed.

It wasn't right. It wasn't fair.

Her vision was clouded with a familiar red sheen that easily slid into place as if it had been waiting to be released. Aksel stumbled under the force of her determination to silence the threat. A trap. It was a trap. She could barely feel his arms locked around her, his strained breaths on her neck as he begged her to stop.

She could only see the danger in front of them. She could only see a swarm of faceless Vikings pouring from the trees, her blade and Aksel's glinting against the sun as they tried and failed to fend them off. He would go down first, a slice through his heart or neck. She would feel the warmth of his blood as it splattered her face, and she flinched as if it was actually happening.

The press of their hands, the sting of their blades, it was all so very real. As was the sound of Ethni and Alpia's cries as they would be dragged to the clearing. Alpia would no longer freely spin, and Ethni's smile would turn to a grimace of fear. The villain hoard would hold her down as they drove their blades into Revna's sides.

And then, as her life drained from her body, she would see Conall's wild blue eyes as he threw himself in front of his wife and daughter, as they were forced to their knees. They would watch him die. They would look to her, and with their last breaths, they would ask why she didn't stop this. Why she didn't save them?

"'Tis a trap," Revna seethed again, the horrors of what she knew to be coming heating her skin and forcing Aksel to haul her off her feet to keep her from breaking free.

"Revna, stop." Aksel began backing them out of the clearing, Revna's feet sought purchase on the ground to take her to the woman who would be the end of them all.

"'Tis a trap," she said again. Panic, fear, and an unquenchable desire to wield her blade were driving her mad.

"Then let's go. We can leave." There would be no distance Aksel could carry her that her rage would not stretch. They had come too far. Ethni and Alpia and Conall—they'd given too much. She would not allow this. Aksel's grip slipped, and she was free. His shouts were devoured by the drumming in her skull as she crossed the few steps between herself and the one who would bring them to ruin.

Palming her dagger, she drew back her arm, and the woman flung her hands, tied together with rope, up to defend herself. As Revna brought down her hand, the hood of the woman's cloak fell back and the sight of her hair tumbling free stopped Revna's attack as if she'd been frozen solid.

She didn't move. Didn't breathe. Didn't blink. Then she was slammed to the ground, a large hand wrenching the blade from her aching fingers. Aksel held her down, his knee on her chest, but she didn't fight.

The fight was gone. The rage nothing but a smoldering ember that glowed from under the door that had been slammed shut at the new vision that filled her mind. A true vision.

"Let me go." Revna was clawing at Aksel's arms, peeling his fingers off her skin. "I willna hurt her."

With a hand to his chest, she shoved him away and crawled, her nails digging into the musty ground until she reached the cowering woman.

With trembling fingers, she reached out and touched the woman's bound hands that were still raised, shielding her face. The woman jerked, and Revna pulled back.

Her throat burned, heart so shattered it pulsed shards of glass through her veins. Revna couldn't take her eyes off the woman and the hair that spilled over her shoulders. It was tangled and matted, caked with dirt and spots of dried blood. But under the filth, she could see the color. Moon-white.

"Astrid?"

16

REVNA

"Is it...how did ye...who did this?" A flare of the rage returned, but not toward the woman before her.

The woman slowly lowered her hands, her wrists raw and bleeding under the bonds.

When she took in the features staring back at her, Revna's next breath was a mix of relief and disappointment. It wasn't Astrid. She was much too young. Hardly a woman at all. But she looked so much like the captain it made her angry. What right did this girl have to wear a face so similar to Astrid's?

Those achingly familiar ice-blue eyes widened when they met Revna's. If this girl was bait, she had paid the price to make her deception effective. Her face was covered in bruises, old and new. Her slender nose was slightly crooked in the middle as if it had been broken and remained unset. Her skin was smeared with dirt, cut only by the tracks of tears that had long since dried.

"W-what did you say?" The girl's voice was hoarse, ragged from screams and sobs.

When Revna released her, the girl grabbed her arm with both

hands, her freezing fingers digging into Revna's flesh with surprising strength. "What name did you say?"

"Astrid," Revna repeated, her heart having chosen a pace that threatened to cleave through the sinews of her chest.

"How do you know my sister?" The girl's grip tightened even more. She shifted, pushing herself to her knees. Her next words tumbled out with such speed, Revna could hardly decipher them. "Is she here? Did she come?"

Revna opened her mouth to answer when those ice-blue eyes widened and her gaze shot to something over Revna's shoulder.

Revna pushed the girl behind her and came around in time to hear the whack of a wooden staff being slammed against the side of Aksel's head. Just as she drew Rune's dagger from her belt, the same staff crashed against the back of her hand. The knife flew from her fingers, lodging grip side up in the soft ground. Revna snatched her stinging hand to her chest, narrowing a furious glare at her attacker.

"The gods have smiled upon me." A staggering man dragged a wanton gaze over Revna. "Two for the price of one."

Aksel lay motionless on the ground, a trickle of blood rolling across his face from a wound on his temple. The sound that came from Revna's mouth was nothing that could be interpreted as human. She leapt for the man, hands extended like claws aiming for his throat.

Surprised, he swung the staff again but stumbled over Aksel, who was now groaning and trying to open his eyes. Revna ducked under the staff and drove her shoulder into his middle, taking them both to the ground. She was nearly knocked sideways by the strong stench of mead before his elbow met her cheek. Pain blazed across her face, and she tasted the coppery tang of blood in her mouth.

His lucky strike didn't slow her down though; it only blazed to life her simmering rage. Fury burst through the closed door in her mind, and despite the possible broken bones in her hand, the man's stick was torn from his fingers and wielded by Revna before he could lower his arm.

Legs tangled, they rolled. He howled when he attempted another strike and Revna blocked it with the hard middle section of the staff. From the corner of her eye, she could see Aksel trying to get to his feet, but they slipped from under him and he went to his knees. The girl was still by the tree. She wasn't running. Why wasn't she running?

The man released a string of curses insulting Revna's ancestry and managed to get his hands on her arms, pulling her too close for her to use the staff with any amount of force. He slammed her against the ground, sending stars across her vision, and her grip loosened enough to drop the staff. Since she was already dazed, she brought herself forward and drove her forehead into his nose.

That finally broke his hold, and she maintained enough wits to scramble out from under him. The world tilted one way and then the other as she rolled across the ground. She saw the wagon, a spilled barrel of mead underneath, and a person-shaped absence in the stain of dark ale seeping into the dirt.

She pushed herself up to her knees, sending her foot into the man's groin as he cursed her for the injury to his nose. He toppled over and Revna nearly did too.

As her vision cleared, she saw the girl frantically working loose ropes tied around her ankles that Revna hadn't noticed before.

Aksel hadn't managed to get to his feet but was clawing his way toward Revna, refusing to stay down.

"Help her." Revna's order stopped him. She wiped the back of her hand across her mouth, a streak of red painting her skin. "He's mine."

Both Rune's dagger and the staff lay within reach, but something vicious and ugly reared its head inside her chest. She picked up the staff.

The man held his hand to his nose, blood pouring out between his fingers. He turned vengeful mismatched eyes on her. One light, one dark. He lowered his hand, red coating his lips and the teeth he bared in a taunting smile. She tilted her head to the side, narrowing her eyes on his vile expression. Before he could stand, she was moving.

Anger pushed her past any hesitation. She shoved the dull end of the staff into his side, driving him to the ground. It wasn't sharp enough to pierce his skin, but it stole the breath from his lungs and, from the snap she heard, broke at least one rib.

Just before she brought the hard upper end of the wood down on his skull, his eyes widened, and she knew he'd seen what truly stood over him. Fear replaced his fury, and she drank it in. It coated her lips and tongue like the warm spiced wine of her people, trickling down her throat and filling her belly with fire.

She saw herself reflected in his eyes, both colors taking in the beast that had come to collect on the debts of his vileness. She saw her lips draw back, a wicked grin slicing across her face. She saw her arms moving, Seconds later, the staff lay discarded on the ground, and her fists met the flesh of his face, pain from her injured hand only fueling her assault.

Aksel's arms came around her. With a cry of frustration, she jerked against his hold before she went limp in his arms. Her muscles had given out already, her body moving by sheer will alone.

"Stop," he breathed. "Revna, stop."

His chest heaved against her back, his breaths coming in short bursts against her hair. She stared at the bloody mess she'd made of her attacker, unable to tear her eyes away. His chest still moved, and he rolled to the side, his arms curling in. It seemed too much of a gift to leave him with his life. Her uninjured hand reached toward the ground, tightening around the slick surface of the staff. Aksel must have sensed her intentions; he lifted her with one arm, turning her away from the groaning man. He slid one hand to grip hers, coaxing her fingers to release the staff.

"Let it go, Little Bird." She felt his forehead against the back of her head, his soft words bringing her back to the light from the dark place she'd gone. "'Tis over. 'Tis over now."

She'd said those same words once, to a dying man who lay

amongst a boatful of other dying men. Her rage then had cost Rune his life, and if Aksel hadn't stopped her, even though the man at her feet wasn't innocent, she would have killed him too.

Both Aksel's arms came around her, the pressure of his hold releasing the rest of her fury until it seeped into the ground at her feet. The beat of his heart against her back took possession of hers until it joined in the same rhythm.

"Breathe," he coaxed, his voice deep and rumbling against her spine. "Breathe wi' me."

So she did, even as she watched her attacker grow still, his consciousness slipping away. His chest moved. He lived. With Aksel's warmth wrapped around her, she finally felt relieved.

"When I saw ye on the ground, fer a moment, I thought ye were dead." Her confession was quiet, not truly meant for him to hear.

"I'm alive. I'm here wi' ye."

At his confirmation, she threaded her fingers through his, pulling his arms tighter around herself and pushing away the images of Rune's lifeless face. Aksel was alive. He was breathing and talking.

"Someone is coming," a scratchy voice warned.

Aksel turned, taking Revna with him. She lifted her eyes to the girl. Still by the tree, her hands and feet were freed, her thin cloak pulled tightly around her. She looked at Aksel, and then at the ground, as if she were afraid to let Revna catch her eyes.

The drum of hoofbeats and the clatter of wagon wheels sounded in the distance. The girl looked over her shoulder and whipped her head back, terror seizing her expression. Still, she looked only to Aksel.

"They are with him. T-they are outlawers. He only stopped to wait." She glanced at the wagon, and then the woods. Revna could see her dilemma. Try and take the wagon to escape and risk being overpowered by whomever was coming, or take to the woods and risk getting lost or overtaken by whatever wildlife roamed the night. Or stay and face whatever consequences would come when the man dragged himself to his feet or his friends arrived.

"He will talk." Revna turned in Aksel's arms, facing him, her hands fisting the fabric of his tunic. "He'll tell them what he saw. They'll follow us."

The caravan of men crested the hill, and Revna lunged for her dagger that still lay upright in the trampled grass. The men would be on them in seconds.

"There isna time, we have to go." Aksel wrapped his hand around Revna's waist, hauling her back to him. He looked up at the girl, speaking in his native tongue. "Come with us. We can help you."

She hesitated for half a second before racing across the clearing. Aksel shoved Revna gently toward the woods even as she protested. "My dagger."

"Take her," he said, his hands on her shoulders. "I will get it."

With one last glance at Rune's dagger, she was off. The girl followed on her heels. Revna hauled her behind a wide tree and then hid behind the one next to it, scanning the woods both for pursuers and Aksel. It was dangerous to delay, but the girl's breaths were wheezy, her legs trembling. Revna couldn't imagine how long it had been since she slept or ate.

"What are you called?"

"He called me *Stjarna. M-mi Stjarna.*"

The world seemed to slow and then still as Revna centered her gaze on the girl's. Held against her will, clearly abused, and forced to answer to a name that was not her own. My *star.* It took all of Revna's strength not to go back to the clearing and finish what she'd started. To call her something so intimate and yet treat her so ruthlessly.

"That is not your name. That is not who you are." The girl seemed to calm at Revna's words. "Who are you?"

"Isa." Her voice was small when she spoke her true name, as if it were a secret. "I am Isa."

Revna flicked her eyes from the woods behind them to Isa, who, despite her weakness, seemed ready to bolt on her own at any second.

"If she is truly the same Astrid, I know your sister. She would want you to come with us. She would want you to live." Revna extended a hand.

Isa stared at Revna's offering. It might have been a snake, ready to strike.

Revna met Isa's eyes. "You are safe with me, Isa." She extended her hand further, and Isa took it, but with a flinch as if it hurt. When Revna loosened her grip, Isa tightened hers in silent rebellion against her fear—or perhaps the horrors she experienced.

"You are a warrior like Astrid. I see it." Revna glanced over her shoulder again, seeing only the movement of branches and leaves. She looked back to Isa and pulled her close, making sure Isa saw the promise in her eyes. "Whatever else he took from you, he cannot have that."

Revna didn't let her gaze linger on the tears that sprang to Isa's eyes, and she didn't let go of her hand as they raced through the woods. They didn't stop once. When Isa tripped over a hidden branch, she hid her cry under her hand and Revna hauled her up before she hit the ground. Isa wasn't the only one struggling to keep moving. The fight with Isa's attacker had stolen most of Revna's strength. Her head pounded, her hand ached, and her heart raced so wildly her breaths thinned. Still she pushed on. She promised Isa she was safe, and she would keep her word.

The sun was at its crest when they reached the clearing. Revna collapsed, breathless, into Ethni's waiting arms. "This—" she gasped for air. "This is Isa. She needs food and—and care fer her wounds."

Ethni nodded and looked to Alpia, who wrapped an arm around Isa and led her farther into the clearing and out of sight.

"Were you followed?" Conall appeared at Ethni's side, sword in hand.

Revna shook her head, trying to catch her breath. "Nay."

"Where is Aksel?" Ethni held Revna at arm's length, searching her face and then the woods over her shoulder. Ethni's eyes dipped to the hand Revna curled against her chest. "What happened?"

Before Revna could answer, Aksel appeared. Revna felt the rush of relief swell and fade quickly when she saw his tunic was ripped, fully baring his scarred chest. His hands were shaking and...they were covered in blood.

"Aksel?" Ethni moved toward him.

He took one step and stumbled. Conall caught him before he hit the ground, helping him stay on his feet. Ethni rushed forward, but Revna reached him first.

"What happened? What's wrong?" Her hand ran over his face and shoulders, searching for injuries.

"I thought I had more time," he groaned.

"What?" His words stunned her, freezing her hand where they'd reached under his shredded tunic to check his ribs.

"He was unconscious and I had a few seconds. I was going to leave a message."

"You idiot." Revna reached up and gripped a handful of his hair, bringing his forehead to hers. "You bonnie idiot."

"He got yer dagger, we fought, and my tunic tore. When he saw the tattoo and scar, he knew who I was."

"What? Are ye certain?" Revna lifted her head, searching his eyes, begging him to say no.

"Aye." His gaze was as intense as she felt hers was, as needy. "He called me a ghost. He kens."

"I have to go back." Revna shifted, but Aksel caught her by the arm.

"I have yer dagger."

"'Tisn't the weapon," she said as he reached to his waistband, blood already dried on his fingers. "If he kens who ye are, it might get back to yer father."

"'Tis no matter." Aksel's voice was weak, his breath ragged.

Revna looked up at Ethni, who turned to Conall and touched his shoulder. "Go fetch the skins. Aksel needs water."

Conall nodded, ensuring Aksel was steady before he walked away.

"Is he dead?" Revna breathed.

"He was breathing when I left him," Aksel wheezed.

How was he so calm? Someone knew he lived—knew who he was. All her fears were coming to life before her eyes. If his father found out, he would assume it was Aksel who stole the offerings and aided in the disappearance of the slaves. He would hunt him to the ends of the earth.

Ethni seemed to be in agreement as she ran her hands through her hair, "I dunna think yer taking this seriously enough, Aksel. If this man is breathing, he can be a problem fer us."

"Ye ken Tollak willna entertain such stories. If he has announced my death, it will only make him look inept to find me alive. 'Tis in his best interest I remain a ghost."

"Still..." Revna's heart wouldn't slow, her panic barely contained.

"I'm telling ye, Revna." Aksel grimaced in pain, but continued, "Tollak will take care of any 'problem' fer us. He willna risk any more scandal on my behalf. Besides, I doubt that man would even make it to Kaupang. If he was in the presence of outlawers, he is no better off than if he were one himself. And I made certain he willna be able to tell anyone anything ever again." He released his hold on Revna and his soiled hands moved to his throat.

"Ye id——"

"Idiot, I ken." Aksel's eyes closed as a smile drifted across his lips. "Call me bonnie again."

Revna drew her hand back, prepared to shove him. But Aksel slumped forward onto her shoulder, and her hands instinctively went around him.

"Aksel!" Her voice was strained as she tried not to let Aksel's weight crush her. Conall was already returning, and Revna called for him.

Tossing the water skins to Ethni, Conall hauled Aksel off of Revna. She looked down at her fingers, finding them coated with sticky red. Her heart nearly crawled out of her throat. Aksel groaned as Conall laid him on the ground. His body was limp, his jaw slack and breaths shallow.

"Aksel?" Ethni pressed her hand to his chest. She looked up at Revna, terror filling her blue eyes before she rolled him into her arms, revealing the back of his tunic soaked through with his blood.

17

AKSEL

S he'd stabbed him again. That was his first thought when his brain crashed to consciousness with such force it sent him shooting upright. Why was she always stabbing him?

His sudden move sent the earth careening, and if it hadn't been for hands grasping his arms, his face would have met the ground with no chance of him slowing his fall.

His second thought was of how much a staunch mug of mead would ease that combination of both dull and searing pain.

"Easy there, Prince."

His Little Bird's always hoarse voice was close, and he blinked her into focus. Her form was shadowed. It was night. Or else his eyes were still adjusting.

"Why are ye frowning at me? I just saved ye from smashing yer princely face."

He tried to speak, but his throat was so dry the words stuck to his mouth as if he'd taken a spoonful of honey. As he gulped down the water she offered, he became acutely aware of the throbbing pain across his ribs in the back.

"Ye stabbed me," he said when the water washed away enough of the dryness in his mouth.

"I did no such thing." Revna removed her hands from his arms, but he tipped again and his weight had her grunting to hold him up. "I have half a mind to let ye flop over like the fish ye are."

"I thought ye said I was a prince. And what else..." he let his eyes drift to the dark canopy of leaves above them, silhouetted against a moonlit sky. "Oh, aye, I am bonnie."

"Idiot." She did let go then, and he stuck out his hand to brace himself. "A bonnie idiot is what I said. And if ye remember that, then ye remember I dinna stab ye. It was the man in the clearing who ye wouldna let me end."

Aksel sucked in a breath through his teeth when he attempted to scoot himself back and a searing flare of pain cut across his back.

"I was trying to help ye."

"Help me?" She laughed, but it wasn't a true laugh. Not like the one she blessed him with at the creek before they'd heard...

"How is she?" He scrubbed his hands over his face, wondering how long he'd been out. "Has she said anything?"

"She's not said much, but when Ethni and I helped her change into clean clothes..." Revna shook her head. "Aksel, ye canna imagine..."

Revna's words felt like a cord had been looped around his insides and jerked tight. He shifted against the tree until he found a position where his wound didn't hurt as much and looked over his shoulder. The girl, who looked even younger than Revna, sat on a fur near the fire. Ethni used a bone comb on her freshly washed hair. Even though a cloak draped her shoulders, he could tell her clothes hung loose on a far-too-thin frame. But there was color on her cheeks and her face worked through a myriad of expressions, as if she couldn't settle on one or as if she'd only worn a frown for so long that her muscles couldn't remember how to do anything else. She looked tired, as if she was expending all her energy to simply exist.

"It should not be." Aksel still looked at the girl, and when Revna didn't answer, he turned to face her. The flames behind her blue eyes were proof enough that she agreed. Her fury was obvious, but still— it was nothing compared to what he'd seen in the clearing. She had been...he shook the thought from his head. He never wanted to see her like that again.

Revna, who'd been on her knees, shifted to tuck one leg beneath herself and the other knee up under her chin. As she wrapped her arms around her bent leg, Aksel noticed one of her hands was wrapped in linens.

He wiggled his fingers, urging her to place her injured hand in his offered palm. When she did, he gently ran his fingers over the wrappings.

"He did this?" There was a growl in his tone. He kept his head down but flicked his eyes to hers. "Broken?"

She lifted a shoulder, as if it were nothing. "Just bruised."

He slid his hand up her arm, silently asking her to scoot closer so he could lightly grip her chin and examine her bruised face. Heat climbed his neck as his thumb barely grazed her swollen lip.

"I could go back and silence him all over again."

"'Tis nothing, compared to—" She shook her head then pulled her lips back into an awkward, broad grin. "At least I still have all my teeth."

Her attempt to lighten the dark moment fell flat, as did her smile when she realized it.

"I canna imagine what would have happened if we hadna heard her screams," Aksel said.

"Isa said she dinna scream."

"Of course she did; we both heard it." Aksel looked at the girl again before searching Revna's drawn expression. He felt his brows furrow. "Isa? That is her name?"

Revna finally looked at him again. "She said she never gave him the satisfaction. That the first time she ever opened her mouth was when she saw ye."

"I..." Aksel blinked, taking in her words. "I dunna ken if I should be offended by that or not."

With her uninjured hand, Revna reached for a flake of bark beside her that served as a tray and offered Aksel a handful of berries before tossing back her own.

"I wanted to scream the first time I saw ye too, so take it as ye will," she said with a mouthful of fruit.

"Because I am so bonnie?" His playful shove was a little more forceful than he intended, and he had to wrap his hand around her arm to keep her from falling over. The act earned him another bite of pain.

"Ow," he laughed, immediately regretting that too.

"Because I wanted to cry out to *An T-aon* and ask how He could create such a hideous creature." Revna righted herself and pushed his hand away.

"I thought ye dinna believe in Ethni's God?"

Whatever merriment they shared slipped away, and Revna only shrugged again. They sat in silence for so long, Aksel felt himself starting to drift off.

"Where I'm from, my homeland, I mean, I serve a queen." Revna's quiet comment had him alert again.

"Aye, ye've mentioned her." He helped himself to another handful of berries.

"The captain of her warriors is from here." Revna lifted her eyes, scanning the surrounding woods.

Aksel froze mid-chew. "Are ye saying the leader of the Vestland queen's warband is a Viking?"

"Aye." Revna flicked her gaze to Isa. "And Isa claims to be her sister."

He nearly choked on the news, groaning again at the painful stretch of his skin over his wound.

Revna crawled behind him, lifting his tunic to inspect his back. "'Tis barely more than a scratch, I dunna ken why yer acting like such a bairn. Ye feigned dying and then slept until nightfall."

221

"He nearly gutted me," Aksel said, finally able to swallow the berries. He wiped the back of his hand across his mouth, his skin coming away stained purple.

"Ye just lost a little blood. Which, again, wouldna have happened if ye'd let me end him like he deserved." Her tone was light but when she reached for another handful of berries, Aksel caught her fingers.

He folded her hand into his. "Revna."

At the seriousness of his tone, she looked away.

"Look at me." When she didn't, he squeezed her hand. "Look at me."

Revna blinked before turning her blue eyes to his. He knew she wouldn't want to hear what he had to say, her clenched jaw was evidence enough of that. But it needed to be said.

"Ye picked up the staff instead of yer dagger."

"He attacked us; ye couldna even stand."

"Ye weren't trying to defend yerself. Ye wanted him to suffer."

Revna tried to pull her hand away, but he held tight, anchoring her to himself. "Dunna run from me. Ye ken 'tis true."

"What does it matter? If ye had seen Isa…she has so many scars." She swallowed hard and closed her eyes, taking a deep breath before continuing. "Ye'd say he deserved every blow."

"But ye dinna ken that until later. Ye werena trying to stop him from hurting Isa or me. Ye were bent on destroying him. I saw the fury take over, saw it control ye, and fer the first time, I…well, I was scared of ye."

She scoffed and rolled her eyes, but he pulled her closer until her knees touched his. He lowered his voice, protecting her from listening ears.

"I ken that makes ye angry. I ken ye think yer so terrifying, but I was never afraid, not even all the times ye held yer knife to my throat. Not until today. Ye were ready to destroy that man and yerself."

"Ye stayed wi' me. I could've hurt ye." Her eyes held his, trapping him in her pale gaze. "Why dinna ye run?"

"Because I..." He hesitated, unsure of the right words. There was something lingering on the edge of his lips, but he wasn't ready to release it. "Because ye wouldna have left me."

He thought she might have stopped breathing, so he rubbed his thumb across the back of her hand until he saw her chest rise again. The flavor of a plan simmered amongst his thoughts and, in a flash of inspiration, he switched to his native language.

"I also know what it is to have a thirst that is never quenched, no matter how much you pour down your throat or how many times you try to drown it."

Revna's breath hitched, her eyes silvering but not shedding tears. He pressed her hand to his chest, flattening her fingers so she could feel the beat of his heart against her palm. When her eyes flicked to the others, he tilted his head, drawing her back to him.

"I know what it feels like to have that need, that ache, burning inside of you and to know that if you give into it, everything will feel better. The hurt goes away, even if just for a moment. But it always comes back, does it not? Thirstier and angrier than before."

"What am I supposed to do?" Her answer was a whisper, and it was in his language, confirming a suspicion he had since Kaupang.

"Fight the thirst instead of the enemy."

"I have to defend myself and my friends."

"I know. I know, just..." He drew in a deep breath and looked to the clear black sky peeking between thick leaf-shaped shadows. "Fight me."

"You?"

"Yes. I know you will not hurt me, so just use me to sate that thirst. I am a worthy opponent, am I not?"

"Debatable."

He laughed, groaning again at his mistake. "And try to use your words first. How about that?"

"My words," she huffed, amused.

"Yes, Little Bird." He released her hand then, chucking her chin with his finger. "Your words. I know you have plenty, and I am certain if you try, they can be more deadly than your blade."

She only shook her head.

"And now I know that you can cut a Norseman in his own tongue." When Revna shot a glance his way, he let a lazy grin stretch across his face. "Did you not notice how you were speaking my language just now?" When Revna opened her mouth to respond, he aimed a finger at her. "You did in Kaupang too, so I know it is not that you have just learned. You knew all along, did you not?"

Revna huffed again, lifting a shoulder.

"You are quite the performer. You seemed so very frustrated when we first met and I was explaining my father's records to you. You could travel with the skalds." He drummed his fingers on the toe of her boot, looking up at her from under his lashes. "Why did you hide it?"

She dragged in a long breath before pushing herself to her feet. "'Tis a basic rule of warfare to keep yer most valuable weapons a secret from yer enemy, Prince. Best let them think ye less armed than ye are."

His heart jumped, and he felt the tug of a wicked grin spreading across his lips. "What other weapons are ye hiding?"

She only winked before taking their empty, berry-stained tray to be refilled. When Aksel finally dragged himself to his feet, Ethni beckoned him to the seat where Isa had been. As he lowered himself to the ground with a groan, he couldn't miss Revna's subtle mumble about him "whining like a bairn."

He flinched when Ethni's cold hands pressed against his skin, prodding his wound and applying a thick layer of herbs.

He watched Isa as Ethni worked. She was quiet and seemingly frail, but there was something under the surface. Maybe Revna's trick of hiding her deadliest weapons was one Isa knew as well. He could only imagine the horrors she had endured if Revna was struck wordless by the sight of her scars and bruises. And those were just the visible ones. If it was true that she never screamed...shame swept through him, forcing his eyes to the ground. This woman, barely more than a girl, could endure such terror and pain without making a sound, and he still couldn't even make it through a day without daydreaming about the taste of mead.

"Isa," Ethni spoke in the Norse tongue as she worked on Aksel. "Will you tell us of your settlement? What is it like?"

Isa jumped as Conall came behind her, a fur wrap in his hands. Despite the warmth of summer nights, Aksel noticed Isa hadn't stopped shivering.

"I am sorry," she said when she realized what he was doing. Her face flushed and she pressed her hand to her chest as if she needed to feel her heartbeat and said again, "Sorry."

He took a step back, glancing at Ethni as though asking if he should proceed or walk away. If anyone knew how to care for the heart of a woman who'd been so abused, it was Conall.

He gently explained what he was doing and waited until Isa nodded before placing the wrap over her curled-in shoulders, being careful not to touch her.

Isa's grateful smile was genuine, and she turned her face slightly to the side, inhaling the clean scent of the wrap. He wondered how long she'd been captive, how long it had been since she was warm, or clean, or fed. Or safe.

"Volfsby is a small settlement but is blessed with abundance. Endless green fields with rich soil for grain. A white river, plentiful with fish, deep and wide enough for longboats to reach the sea. There are gray cliffs overlooking the water, home to long veins of silver. And woods are teeming with game and ancient mounds surrounding the farms for protection."

"It sounds lovely." Alpia lingered next to Isa until Isa lifted the edge of her wrap, inviting her in.

"I know that now."

"It was not always so?" Alpia asked.

Isa looked at the girl and turned her eyes to the fire, her gaze seeming to get lost in the flames. "Not when my cousin was the shieldmaiden. It was colorless and dying. Things changed when Astrid came, but..." Isa shook her head.

Revna appeared on the other side of the fire, its orange glow casting long shadows across her cheeks and under her eyes. "Astrid never spoke of a sister."

Revna's eyes darted to his. Now that he knew her secret understanding of the Viking tongue, he assumed she knew there was no use hiding it. He let one side of his mouth curl in a silent declaration of victory at drawing out one of her many secrets.

"If you have not seen Astrid in many winters, she would not have mentioned me." Isa kept her eyes on the flames. "I was born after she disappeared from our shores."

"You say that she knows of you now?" Revna moved her arms, as if to cross them over her chest, but seemed to think better of it and kept them at her side. Her tone was gentle, voice unusually soft as if she knew Isa had endured enough hardness to last a lifetime.

She cut her eyes to Aksel again, giving him a second of her narrowed gaze. It was a look that said, *Stop watching me.* He couldn't help the broader smile that tugged at his lips, but he looked down at the ground in front of him.

"My sister would want to tell the story herself, but she did come back to our lands." Isa finally tore her eyes away from the fire when Revna moved, crossing the distance between them to crouch before her.

"Astrid is here?" Revna paled.

Aksel kept his head low, but raised his eyes, watching Revna's face. Was that fear in his little bird's eyes?

Isa shook her head. "It was three winters past, and Volfsby is a free settlement again because of her. The color has returned."

"But she is safe? Astrid lives?" Revna was as still as death as she perched on the balls of her feet before Isa.

"Yes." Isa blinked then, a single tear streaking down her cheek.

"And the queen of the Vestlands. Did she speak of her?"

"She was also well."

The tension rolled off of Revna as if she had breathed it out of her lungs. She twisted, sitting on the ground to stare into the fire as Isa did. Aksel lobbed his gaze between them. There was something so similar in their empty stares. It looked like a shield behind their eyes that kept their hearts from letting in whatever pain haunted them.

"Some men returned to Volfsby. They had been away for longer than I had been alive and saw more of the world than I ever will." Isa's voice was so soft, Aksel had to lean closer to hear. "They told us of the God above all other gods. The one called Christ."

Ethni's hands found Aksel's shoulders, their weight holding him there, as if she were demanding that he truly listen to what Isa would say next.

"They said that this Christ offered a gift called eternity."

Revna's head snapped up, her eyes locked on Isa who didn't seem to notice. She only kept her gaze on the fire.

"A place better than Valhalla. A place where there is no pain, no tears, no death. They said that all I had to do to receive eternity was to believe in the one true God and make Him the One I served. That He would forgive my wrongs without demanding payment and He would hear me when I called. He would make me into something new."

Ethni's hands squeezed slightly, but Aksel was already listening. Everyone was listening. As the flames held her, Isa's words held them each in a trance. The earth was still; even the night sounds ceased.

"I did believe. I did." Isa broke her stare from the fire then, eyes brimming with tears as she looked at each one of their faces. When she met Aksel's eyes, his chest grew tight.

"My mother only wanted to protect me. I never understood how much she had shielded me from all those years my cousin ruled. I wanted to be like those men. To see the world. When she said I would one day be the new shieldmaiden, I...I..." Isa shook her head again.

Ethni spoke softly from behind Aksel. "Isa, you do not have to—"

"No. I need to. I have kept it for so long." She inhaled a fortifying breath. "I was young. I wanted all the things eternity promised now. One night, I took what I thought to be mine from her wealth and left. I went to Kaupang and then to Oslo when I thought she might come looking for me. *He* found me instead." Tears poured freely from her eyes, and Alpia leaned in close, wrapping her arms around Isa from under the blanket they shared. "He was supposed to be dead."

"I knew I had done wrong. I knew I had broken trust with The Christ. T-t...The man who took me said it was my fault. That I deserved what he was doing to me, and I started to believe him. I wondered if the God above all gods felt the same—if He would still hear me. I just kept calling out to Him. Hoping."

"Then when I was in that clearing today, I begged for death. I had no belief left. I thought He was like the other gods after all. He had abandoned me."

From behind him, Aksel heard Ethni softly sob, and he covered the hand she left on his shoulder with his. His heart was racing at Isa's story—one that sounded so much like Ethni's.

"But He is not like the other gods." Isa's voice broke, cracked open and raw with emotion. "Because even though I ran from my home and turned against my family, He heard the screams I could not voice. And He let you hear them too. He sent you to find me. To save me."

No one spoke. No one moved. Aksel let his eyes leave Isa for a moment. They landed on the place where Revna had been. She was gone.

He searched the trees knowing he wouldn't see her. Some deep, desperate part of him hoped that she had heard the whole of Isa's story. He knew it was meant for her as well as for him.

When Conall came behind Ethni, Aksel slowly pushed himself up and went in search of Revna. The moon was hidden behind billowing clouds, shrouding the forest in an endless darkness.

If she didn't want to be found, he had no hope, not until dawn.

He pursed his lips, sending a soft trilling whistle into the air. When its echo faded, he waited. Silence. He whistled again and waited.

"Come now, Little Bird," he said to himself. "Where are you perched?"

Finally, a matching whistle reached him, and he followed the sound until he found her on the lowest branch of a thick redwood, tucked against the trunk. If she'd been higher, even with the quick acting relief from Ethni's herbs, he wouldn't have attempted to join her. But he was able to carefully swing his leg over the low branch until he was straddling it and faced her. Revna's legs were drawn up to her chest, her chin resting on hands she'd placed on her knees.

"Why did ye run away?"

She didn't lift her head. "I have never enjoyed fairy tales."

"I dunna think she was making that up."

Revna only shrugged. Aksel scooted closer, careful with his movements so as to not agitate his wound. He let his legs dangle on either side of her and curled his hands around her ankles.

"What will ye do?" he asked. When she lifted her head to look at him, he clarified. "Wi' Isa."

"I'll do what Astrid would want me to do." She laid her head back down on her hands, staring into the blackness of the forest. "I'll take her sister home."

18

REVNA

"They said the bonnie prince was dead." A voice, like bubbling water over rocks, sang a haunting lullaby. "Found his bones in his home. *Charred and burned. Charred and burned.*"

Every nerve in Revna's body fired off in painful bursts as she watched a shadow hover over Aksel, slipping bonelessly from one side of him to the other while he lay motionless.

"How much the father must have grieved. In sorrow, the mother's heart did cleave." Teeth clacked in the black night, snapping like the jowls of a wolf before devouring its prey. "When the raven came to claim, their brave and bonnie bairn."

The shadow swirled around Aksel's arm, lifting it away from his body. It dragged its formless nose across his skin as if he were some delicious meal. Then it brushed up against his face with the caress of a lover, but Aksel turned away, repulsed, his eyes finding Revna's in desperation.

Help me. Save me. But it wasn't Aksel's voice she heard next.

The shadow sang again. "Alas, what is this we hear? The Chieftain's son? So close...so near..."

Aksel jerked as his arm was wrenched at an unnatural angle; the tang of a blade sounded in the pitch black.

"How shall we share the news? Which part of him should we choose?" The shadow slithered over Aksel's body, touching his hair, running its greedy shape over his face, stroking a smoky hand down his chest. "A nose, an ear, mayhap an eye? What will his father recognize?"

Aksel's jaw was clenched, his body shaking with the strain of trying to break free of the shadow's invisible bonds.

Then the shadow took solid shape and turned mismatched eyes on Revna, where she was buried to her neck in the grime and sludge of wet ground. Unable to move. Unable to speak. All she could do was watch and scream.

The shadow man's skin was gray, and the gaping slash low on his throat moved when he talked, taunting her. She closed her eyes, not wanting to see. But she could hear him laughing at her helplessness as bile rose in her throat. The sound of his voice came from all around—not from the mouth that was pulled back into a too-wide grin with rows of sharpened yellow teeth. Even behind her closed lids, the image was there.

The shadow slithered up beside her, his eerie rhyme now ended. His next words were a menacing threat that left a thick, bitter taste in her own mouth.

"I held the girl for a full winter, trying to pry the screams from her worthless mouth. You took her from me. Stole my prize."

Aksel jerked again. His scream sent shards of ice up Revna's spine and twisted her stomach into a tangled knot as she kicked and clawed at her muddy prison. "Now I have another to play with. How long will he last?"

"How long, Revna...Revna...Revna..."

"Revna."

Charred and Burned. Charred and Burned.

Hands were on her arms, shaking her.

She shot up, gasping for breath, the blade she kept strapped to

231

her thigh clutched tightly in her fingers. She was no longer trapped in the muck, but she could feel its slimy residue on her skin, taste the bitter earth on her tongue. She launched herself at her attacker, easily pinning him to the ground as she brought down her blade.

"Revna. Stop." A hand wrapped around her wrist, halting her drive.

She blinked, still struggling to catch her breath. Rune was beneath her. She straddled his hips, her hand at his throat, her full weight behind the push of the knife. His eyes were wide and fixed on the dagger, now poised an inch from his chest. She was killing him again. Revna stared at the blade before bringing her eyes back to his. No. Not Rune. It was Aksel, and he was afraid.

Of her.

Again.

The bite of that realization was sharper than that of any monster's teeth from her dreams.

The knife dropped to the ground with a thud and she pushed herself off him, frantically scanning her clothes, turning her palms and examining her arms. They were clean—no muck, no mud.

Aksel sat up, and she ignored how he tensed when she lunged for him again. Her hands roamed over his arms, feeling his bones to ensure they were intact. They moved up to his neck, coming to rest on the sides of his face. She was breathless, every nerve in her body on fire, and her eyes stung with salt water.

"Yer not hurt." The words were strained, pushed out with air she didn't have in her lungs.

Without removing her hands from his face, she swiveled her gaze over the clearing, counting the mounds of sleeping bodies. Since they'd stumbled upon Isa three weeks prior, their numbers had grown by seven as they worked their way back to Volfsby.

She frantically searched the ground around her until she spotted her satchel. She grabbed it with one hand to her chest, as if someone would try and steal it. Her other hand she kept on Aksel, needing to feel his warmth, needing to know he was safe. He pushed himself to sit up, not complaining at how her fingers clutched his skin.

"It was a dream." Aksel swallowed hard, as if his throat was too dry, and lowered his head until his forehead met hers, sliding his fingers through the hair at the nape of her neck. "Just a nightmare."

Just a nightmare.

Charred and burned. Charred and burned.

Aksel curved his other arm around her waist, moving to pull her to his chest. The last three nights she'd shied away when he'd done the same. Tonight, exhaustion won. Her body was so spent, she might have accepted that comfort had her stomach not revolted. She launched herself to her feet, darting for the privacy of the night-cloaked forest.

"Do ye want to talk about it?" He was waiting with a water skin at the edge of the clearing when she returned.

"Nay."

He wouldn't press, just like he hadn't the last three nights, but even if he did, she couldn't tell him about her dreams. He'd been encouraging her to use words instead of fists and blades, but there were no words for the terror that seized her in those evil nightmares. No way to explain the utter helplessness of not knowing if Isa's attacker, the man who recognized Aksel, was alive or dead.

Aksel swore the man wouldn't be able to share what he knew, but as long as he was alive, he was a threat.

They'd taken care to keep as far from Kaupang as possible, but tomorrow they'd be within a day's ride of the settlement. It was either get that close or take two extra weeks to cross a set of treacherous mountains. She had it in her mind to put Aksel on Sgail's back and send him toward those spiked hills for no other reason than to ensure he was never found.

But when she'd suggested as much, he only laughed, as if she were the funniest jokester he'd ever met.

Draining the skin of its last drop, she followed him back to the camp. They passed Conall at the edge of the clearing. He didn't ask why they were both awake, he only nodded and patted the back of the man whose place he took on watch.

The brush of Aksel's warm hand down her arm had her mindlessly trailing him to their sleeping mats.

While Revna was trying to return Isa to her settlement as quickly as possible, Isa was just as ardently attempting to delay that homecoming. She'd insisted Revna keep up her work of finding her people along the way and even requested to remain behind in one settlement alone, reasoning that she would only slow them down.

She knew the grueling pace she'd set was hard on the women and children, many weakened from years of enslavement. Even Aksel struggled to keep up. But she could feel the nip of danger at her heels. The closing in of something terrible, as if it was right behind her, breathing down her neck and dragging sharp nails the length of her spine.

The benefit of their long days traveling was that her midnight thrashing and Aksel's near slaughter weren't witnessed by anyone. They all slept through it. No one made a sound except for Alpia with her occasional rattling cough.

The downside, other than their exhaustion, was something that was also worrying Revna into sleeplessness. Alpia's illness worsened with each day. They'd had to stop more and more frequently for her to rest and for Ethni to brew an herb tea that Alpia consumed under obvious duress, claiming it tasted like the underside of a horse's hoof.

"I have to send them home." Revna settled onto her mat, adjusting her hands to make a pillow under her cheek. "When we get to Volfsby. I'm putting Ethni, Alpia, and Conall on a boat. I dunna care the cost or what they say."

Aksel lay on his own mat, facing her, their hands almost touching. They had done so every night since Kaupang when he sacrificed his body for her people. "They willna want to go wi'out ye."

"It was wrong to allow them to stay this long." She let her eyes search his, wanting to know if he felt the same. If he did, he didn't let it show. "Every day is another chance they could get caught."

"They will say the same fer ye."

She rolled onto her back, wiggling to shift the small pebbles that pressed into her back. At least the late summer nights were pleasant, but fall was not long in coming. A cool breeze kissed her cheeks, soothing the heat that had seeped into her skin from the long days of traveling.

"'Tis different for me."

"I dunna see how." There was amusement in his voice and she jerked her head, spearing him with a narrowed glare.

"Ye ken exactly how, I'm—"

"A violent little bird?"

"Best ye not forget it." She tsked at his teasing, turning her head to stare at the onyx blanket of stars. "I could still—"

"Kill me before the morn. I ken, I ken."

"I could." Her answer was softer.

The ability was there, but the rage was sated. Mostly. She had taken Aksel up on his offer, and every second they weren't traveling, she was sparring with him. He was surprisingly able.

She hadn't burned a stable or a longhouse in months, and her dagger had remained safely sheathed for weeks. Except for tonight.

Aksel's deep voice lowered even more as he answered, "I ken."

She would never hurt Aksel, but if it came to unlocking that dark rage that dwelled within her against an enemy—if it meant destroying herself so her friends would live, she would do it. She would breach the defense she'd so carefully constructed. The one that Aksel had started with his lofty talk of making wrong things right without starting battles.

She turned her head, meeting his eyes until both of them looked away. What was growing between them was something new, something strong. Something that scared her even more than her nightmares.

Her hand found the outline of her list, tucked into the pouch of her vest. It was slowly filling with marks next to names, those that were rescued or mourned. There were far too many who would never return. After nearly twenty years, Revna wasn't surprised, but she was no less grieved.

She didn't strike through their names, though. Ethni had shown her how to ink a tiny cross shape next to their names with a bit of berry juice on the tip of her dagger.

Because *An T-aon* knew their names before they were born, she'd said. They were not forgotten. Ethni said her God would share in their grief.

"What are ye thinking, Little Bird?" Aksel drawled from beside her, his voice deep with exhaustion.

"Ye should go wi' them."

Despite his obvious sleepiness, Aksel pushed up on his side, supporting his head on his palm. "What?"

They'd never really discussed what would happen when she was done. If there was such a time. He had to go with Ethni. Cyrene would welcome him when she found out how much he'd given. She'd welcome him even if he'd given nothing. The queen was a pair of open arms, and Revna the one who would deliver the lost souls into them.

As she let her eyes drift from one star to the next, her mission felt as endless as the sky. Even when all the Picts were accounted for, there was still something else. Some missing piece that she couldn't name. It wasn't even the nameless sister she searched for; it was beyond that, and the emptiness ached in her chest. She never imagined there would be an end—never saw herself back home or growing old. But that didn't mean her friends had to risk their lives forever. That Aksel couldn't find peace.

"They'll need ye to make sure they get home safely."

"Are ye trying to get rid of me?"

"Well, ye are a constant source of aggravation." She let her head roll to the side again, working her lips to control the smile that tugged as she faced him. "And I tire of yer incessant whining."

Despite his still healing injury, Aksel's hands were around her arms in a blink, rolling her until he hovered over her. But the tip of her dagger was also touching his chin, the pressure forcing him to raise his head to avoid getting stuck. His mouth ticked half a heartbeat before she wound her leg around his, using the weight of her body to flip them both.

Stifling laughter, they wrestled until he pinned her on her back again, using his full weight to keep her still. When she tried the same move as before, he shifted his hips slightly, countering her every move.

"I am not as slow as I appear, Little Bird." As if to prove his point, he raised his arm to block her jab and the blade she'd stealthily aimed for his neck again. The dagger skittered across the dirt. "Now what will ye do?"

"I have another," she breathed, grinning wickedly as he grunted against the sting in his side.

There was a daring challenge in his eyes, and she couldn't help that her eyes darted to his lips. Her heart stilled at the thought of what those lips might feel like pressed against her own. The smile she found there faded, and the hint of a flame lit his pale eyes when she dragged her gaze back up.

He stared at her for a long moment, his grip on her waist and wrist softening. But at the tilt of his head, the look in his eyes shifted to something else entirely.

She felt that same tug on her insides as when Cyrene used to focus her emerald eyes on her. As if the queen could see into the very depths of her soul and withdraw whatever hidden truth Revna was keeping secret. Alpia coughed, making Revna jump. His grip loosened instantly when she pushed against his chest. She settled on her mat, and he rolled onto his back, resting his folded hands on his chest.

"I will go when ye go," he said.

"Ye ken I willna leave until—"

"I ken until ye've completed yer list." His tone had lightened, as if he'd gotten a sudden burst of energy. "So, we finish the list. We find yer people. Then we go."

"Ye'd go to my homeland?"

He was quiet for a moment before lifting a shoulder. "I dunna ken what else the ghost of the Chieftain's son would do. I think it would be a grand adventure to see the shores of...what's it called?"

"Tràigh."

"Tràigh." He repeated the word with near perfect pronunciation.

Ethni had taught him far more than language. Aksel often said his perspective changed within two days of his encounter with the raven, but she knew that compassion had been there long before. He'd just been waiting for someone to draw it to the surface.

"Aye, I'd quite like to see this Tràigh."

So simple. It always was with him. He always had a plan. But so did she. A plan she'd been working out since Isa's abductor—Isa still wouldn't speak his name—had discovered who Aksel was.

Chieftain Tollak's power was weakened, his rule teetering on the verge of collapse. The thirst for power, the glory of overthrowing such an empire, would drive men to do foolish things. Things like kidnap the Chieftain's son and send pieces of him to his family until the Chieftain stepped down. Or until Tollak hunted down Aksel himself.

Revna turned her head. Aksel's eyes were closed. His breaths deep. Her skin chilled from the memory of her nightmare—a vision of him screaming in pain. Heat raced up her spine, nearly charing her veins. Her hand crept to the grip of the knife she'd sheathed at her thigh. The need to wield it was almost uncontrollable, even though the monster wasn't real.

"I can feel ye boiling from over here." Aksel didn't open his eyes, but there was a tug at the corner of his mouth. "The night is much too hot fer that extra heat. Go to sleep."

If only it were that easy. Her heart sped up so fast, she was tempted to get up and stalk through the woods until she found some beast to fight, just to release some of the building fury. Her fists clenched and her mouth watered with the need to feel the bite of bone against her knuckles. It didn't help that the lion-shaped mark on her chest pulsed with warning against such actions, making her even more on edge.

That mark called to her. It seemed to sing her name—her true name—the one she might have received had her mother lived to bestow it. It guided her away from wrath and darkness, toward peace and light. But her heart—her wretched heart—still beat the rhythm of rage and vengeance. There was no escape. She could burn the mark off her skin, but how could one live without a heart?

She tried to take a deep breath. Tried to dampen the emotions, to push them away, but they lived off her blood and wouldn't be silenced. The anguish was building, swelling to a wave that would drown her. It was fueled by all the things that were wrong and needed to be righted. Her people sold. Her mother's life ended too soon. Her sister stolen. Families separated. Children neglected. Isa so horribly abused. Ethni violated. Alpia forced into slavery just because of her birth. Conall beaten for claiming them. It was all wrong, and her jaw began to ache from how hard she clenched her teeth. She was seconds away from flying from the ground and exploding with angst.

A warm hand settling over hers made her jump. Aksel's giant palm nearly swallowed hers. Then, mat and all, she was dragged across the small space between them, his heavy arm draping over her middle, curling her back against his chest.

They'd all slept in such cramped quarters, it wasn't unusual for her to wake with an arm or leg draped over her; usually his or Alpia's. Sometimes Alpia's whole body would be tangled with hers, especially on mornings when the frost coated their hair and froze the breath in their lungs. But it was summer, and this was the first time he'd intentionally wrapped her in the vice of his arms.

"What are ye doing?" she whispered, stunned to stone. He'd never held her so near, and she battled between wanting to wriggle in even closer and needing to fling his arm off of her so she could dive straight into the closest stream.

"I canna sleep wi' yer thrashing and worry that ye'll slaughter the entire camp in yer sleep."

She snorted at the accusation, but already, the weight of his arms pushed her racing thoughts down, quelling the turmoil enough that she could draw a full breath. Her limbs relaxed, her muscles grew looser as he squeezed her tighter.

"Just be still." He gently tapped his forehead against the back of her head. "Breathe."

She fixed her eyes on the night sky, wondering about what Isa had said. About the God above all gods who heard her cries even when she didn't let them escape her lips. Wondering if there were listening ears behind all those twinkling lights. Wondering if they would hear her if she called. Wondering...

"Yer thinking much too loudly, Little Bird. Please have mercy on me and let me sleep." He grunted when her elbow connected with his ribs, but his breathing quickly turned deep and ragged again.

How could he simply turn off the churning thoughts in his mind? Sometimes, she wondered if he even had any.

Are ye there? Is it... Am I allowed to speak to ye even if I dunna ken if I believe ye exist? Revna sighed, realizing Aksel's fingers had woven through hers, anchoring her to him—to something solid and real. *Are ye more than a fairy tale?*

Brigid, Cyrene, and Astrid told so many stories. Even though she rarely listened, she knew why. It was to keep the darkness at bay. Those stories were tiny brilliant spots in an otherwise colorless existence. They were hope.

She'd avoided them as much as possible after Brigid's last story, told when she was eight.

"I'm going to tell ye a story, lass."

They'd stood at the edge of the woods. The rounded top of a stone tower peeked over a rolling hillside. At her side, Brigid's voice, the voice of the storyteller, was low and soft.

"A story which is only yers to hear. A story that will make ye hate me and hate the world, but it's one ye must ken and one ye must learn to overcome. All our lives depend on it. 'Tis the story of the lost princesses."

Brigid's story had sent her racing across the field, ready to tear that tower down with her bare hands. And though Cyrene would later tell some other story about how Brigid was lost to the sea, Revna knew it wasn't true. She knew that after the storyteller caught her in that field and sent her storming back into the shadows, the tower soldiers had come. She knew Brigid had fallen.

But what Brigid didn't understand is that Revna had always lived in the shadows. On the outer edge of whatever circle everyone else created to protect themselves and each other. She protected them too, from the darkness. When others were afraid to venture into that blackness, Revna wasn't. For her friends. She would do it and stare down any monster or beast that waited there.

She craned her neck to gaze at Aksel's beautiful, peaceful profile, the image of him blurred by tears. She ached to do as he had done and pull him into her arms. To keep him for herself, but that was the desire of her selfish heart. She pulled his hand to her face, pressing her lips to his knuckles, and she swore to herself that even if the darkness swallowed her whole, she would shove him out of its rancid mouth before it closed its ugly yellow teeth around her.

The darkness cannot have him, she told the sky before brushing a tear from her cheek. *I dunna care the cost.*

19

REVNA

Ethni was stoking the fire for the morning meal when Revna perched beside her.

"I need yer help." Revna kept her voice low, her eyes on Aksel's still-sleeping form.

Ethni looked at him before nodding. Without a word, she wiped her hands on her apron and followed Revna from the clearing.

"The encounter wi' Isa's attacker was worrisome. If word gets out that the son of Kaupang's Chieftain is alive and roaming the countryside, people will hunt fer him. Mayhap even the Chieftain himself."

"I've thought the same. I ken Aksel thinks the Chieftain willna search fer him, but Tollak thinks only of himself. He might be so angry he would hunt down Aksel fer vengeance alone." Ethni wiped wisps of her auburn hair from her face. "But what can we do other than be more careful?"

"First, we need to get these people home. We have the coin fer passage."

Ethni nodded but a question lingered in her eyes.

"Isa is certain her mother will grant them passage on one of their

242

boats." Revna waited a beat before continuing. "I want ye, Alpia, and Conall to go too. And Aksel."

She squared her shoulders, prepared for Ethni's argument.

"Then yer ready to end yer search?"

That was not the response she'd expected, and it took Revna a full breath to reply. "Nay. I will stay. But 'tis time fer ye to go. Aksel too. He will never be safe here. I ken he willna go unless ye do."

Ethni looked as if that was the answer she expected. "He willna want to leave ye."

"That's why I need yer help. Is there any way ye can convince him?" Revna relaxed her stance, crossing her arms and stepping closer to Ethni.

Ethni's blue eyes danced back and forth between Revna's. She opened and closed her mouth twice.

"I ken ye care fer him, Ethni. Ye love him like he's kin. Can ye make him go where he's safe?"

Ethni's eyes went to the ground. She closed them and dragged in a long breath before her shoulders finally relaxed. The woman carried far more years in her eyes than she'd lived. It was easy to forget she was only a few winters older than Aksel.

"Aye." Ethni's hands traveled to her neck, following the wave of red that creeped up from the top of her tunic. "I think I can."

"Do it as soon as we reach Volfsby. I dunna intend to linger there." Revna looked over her shoulder, watching the distant shapes of her people starting to rise in the early morning light. "'Tis too close to Kaupang, and 'tis time ye go home."

Ethni's hand on her arm drew her attention. "Ye can go home too, Revna." There was such sadness in her tone, Revna had to swallow hard against the tightness that threatened to close her throat. "Come wi' us."

When Revna turned, Ethni's hand dropped to her side.

"I canna." She lifted her hand to the place over her heart where the torn and nearly illegible parchment rested. "There are still too many who are lost."

When she turned back, Ethni lowered her eyes and nodded, reluctantly accepting Revna's decision. Revna started for the clearing, but Ethni touched her arm again.

"What I will tell Aksel...it will hurt him." Ethni turned blazing blue eyes on Revna. "Are ye sure ye want me to do this? Are ye certain ye dunna wish him to stay wi' ye? 'Tis what he wants."

Revna almost asked Ethni what this shocking news was, but her mind offered up images from her nightmares that vanquished any curiosity.

It didn't matter how hurtful Ethni's announcement was. They were just words. Aksel could heal from words. What he couldn't heal from was being sliced to pieces.

Of all the dangers facing them, Aksel was the deadliest. Not because of what he would do, but because of what Revna would. Because the thought of him in danger, the thought of losing him, pushed her too close to an edge beyond which there was no return.

It wasn't only his life at stake. Word traveled slowly across the land, but it still traveled. Her time was better spent chasing names on her list than outrunning greedy men who would hunt Aksel. The Vestlands were the safest place for him.

Ethni had wanted her to be a leader, so she would lead. But she didn't understand why the vision of his face growing smaller as he sailed away left her with a twisting pain in her stomach.

She touched her vest again, tracing the outline of the parchment. Her fingers drifted upward to the place where the lion-shaped mark darkened her honey-brown skin. She knew it was a mistake, some battle scar that coincidentally looked identical to Cyrene's birthmark.

She did not share blood with Cyrene; she couldn't be of her lineage. Even if she was, Revna was not like the queen. She wasn't noble and honest and good, which was why when Ethni asked if Revna was willing to break Aksel's heart to save his life, she answered, "Aye, I'm certain."

20

AKSEL

Isa's palpable tension and Alpia's worsening cough kept everyone on edge. Revna had been storming through the woods for the last half day at a break-neck speed while Isa seemed to be doing everything she could to slow them down.

Revna was a rare bird in more ways than one. Behind that seemingly indestructible wall of violence and success-at-all-costs exterior, there was a well of compassion and patience. She would wait to get what she wanted, but returning Isa to her home seemed strangely urgent. It was as if the answer to whatever was wearing on Revna lay in Volfsby.

And there was definitely something wearing on her. She was keeping it from him, but he could see her unraveling. Everyone was unraveling. Even Ethni wore the worry over her daughter's strained breathing as a scratchy and irritating drape across her shoulders, her tone curt and harsh when Isa asked to rest yet again.

Aksel decided he would have to do something drastic before Ethni and his little bird exploded and rained down searing shards of frustration on them all.

Since Kaupang, she'd opened up to the people they rescued. He knew it was unnatural for her—yet another battle she fought daily. Whatever was plaguing her since they'd rescued Isa seemed to draw her back inside of herself, and he found himself facing that same powerlessness he'd felt in Kaupang when the settlers would come to him with problems he knew how to solve but was unable to.

The freed Picts in their envoy were so grateful for what Revna had done for them, they'd accept any amount of swearing and unfettered raging she could unleash, but she would hate herself for it. That was not something he could stomach, not when he'd seen an actual smile on her stoic face.

Before that morning at the creek, he wasn't sure it was an expression Revna could even make, but since, he had come to the conclusion there was no limit to the lengths he would go to see it again. He'd also realized a craving for that bright smile had taken the place of his longing for the taste of mead. It had been days since he'd even thought about having a drink.

He'd aimed to talk to Isa, but Conall beat him to it, approaching slowly when she hung her head, shoulders curled in. He didn't get within arm's reach of her, seeming to understand her need to have the space to escape if she felt threatened. Aksel waited, feeling uneasy about eavesdropping, but finding himself unable to move away.

"Isa," Conall spoke softly, waiting for her to lift wide eyes. "Why do you linger?"

"Alpia is not well; she cannot travel at such a pace." Isa's answer came quickly, as if she'd prepared for such questioning.

Conall had traveled astride Sgail with Alpia in his arms for the last few days, so the pace did not affect her.

"Answer me truthfully." Conall's tone was firm, but not threatening. "Is there danger for you in Volfsby?"

Isa's eyes shot to his and she shook her head, "No. Never."

"If your concern is for Alpia, the best thing for her is to reach a place where she can rest and see a healer."

"I know, and I know that I am slowing everyone down. I asked them to leave me behind, and they would not." Isa's voice grew in panic and Aksel nearly stepped in, but the lift of Conall's hand seemed to quiet her. "It would be better if you all went on without me."

"If that is truly what you want, I will fight for you." Conall's soft response had Aksel tensing from his hiding place. What was he doing? They couldn't leave Isa behind. "I will stay with you until you are ready to return home."

Isa was silent for a moment. "You would do that?"

"I would," Conall answered with more certainty than Aksel had ever felt about his own decisions.

She seemed to consider his offer as she stared out over the endless length of sparse trees before them. "I have thought of nothing but returning home since the moment I was taken."

"But now that you are almost there, all of your fears of what you will face are trapping you as much as your captor."

Isa's chin quivered, her eyes instantly watering as she nodded in agreement.

"Alpia might not be my blood, but she is my child." He looked over Isa's shoulder at Alpia, who was weaving clovers into a dainty crown while she rested against Ethni. "There is nothing she could ever do that would keep me from welcoming her home should she wander."

"But, I—"

"Nothing, Isa." Conall's tone was firm again, but still gentle. He kept his hands locked behind his back, and Aksel thought it might have been to keep from gathering Isa in his arms. "Even if she had done some terrible thing. Whatever consequences came of it, I would stand by her side while she bore them. No parent is perfect, but a good parent loves their child, no matter the distance, no matter how much time passes. It never dims. Is your mother a good parent?"

Isa's fingers brushed her lips, tugging at the bottom one as she looked up at Conall, tears streaming down her cheeks. "Yes. She is."

"Do you think your mother will turn you away?"

"No," Isa sobbed then, presenting empty hands to Conall. "She will not, that is why I cannot face her. I do not deserve her forgiveness and love."

Aksel held his breath, desperate to hear what Conall would say to Isa's claim. While Isa had certainly not deserved the hell she'd endured, even if she had made youthful and impulsive mistakes, he knew well the feeling of unworthiness.

"If you know the one true God, then you also know we do not receive love and forgiveness because we deserve them but because they are a gift we are in desperate need of. Even if you never left home, that would still be true. It is God's goodness that makes you worthy, not your own. It is God's grace that covers your sin and sets you free. You believe that, do you not?"

Isa sniffed, pressing the back of her hand against her lips as she covered another sob and croaked, "I do."

"Then do not let your captor keep you in chains any longer."

Isa's chin shot up, tears still flowing. Her gaze locked with Conall's as he nodded, adding weight to his challenge.

Aksel waited to move until they had gone, but when he rounded the tree he'd been hiding behind, he came face to face with Conall.

"Do you trust me so little that you needed to supervise a simple conversation?" Conall's arms came up to cross over his chest.

"No." Aksel's eyes suddenly found the earth at his feet irresistibly fascinating. When Conall didn't budge, he finally met the man's eyes again. "I am sorry for all that you have endured at my people's hands, Conall. You are a good man."

Conall only blinked, his lips parted but not releasing words.

"A better man than any I have known." Aksel pressed his own lips together, knowing Conall would understand the unforgivable insult Aksel had just uttered against his own father. A tightness filled Aksel's throat, seeping into his chest so he had to flee the clearing.

"Aksel." Conall's call paused Aksel's escape. He looked over his shoulder at Conall. "So are you."

He aimed for a trickling stream they'd just passed, diving his hands into the frigid waters and splashing his burning face until he didn't feel as if he would burst into flames. *So are you.*

Aksel slammed his fists against his thighs. He wished Conall hadn't said those words. He wished the man would have torn him to shreds instead. It was what he deserved. *We do not receive love and forgiveness because we deserve them but because they are a gift we are in desperate need of.* Everything in his heart was a swirling, complicated mess. It was easier to endure Conall's hatred than his undeserved respect. Everything he thought to be true about his people's gods and his future was upended. Isa spoke of a God who hears and helps. Conall spoke of unearned forgiveness. The Norse gods offered none of those things and demanded more than any man could give.

His failure in what his people deemed success had already sealed Aksel's fate after death. Now there was a small, flickering flame in the darkness, and Aksel didn't know if he should save himself the pain of disappointment by snuffing it out or spend his last breath fanning it to life.

"We are leaving." Revna's sharp tone startled him, but he didn't turn. She didn't need to see him in such a state. He couldn't even explain what was wrong with him. "Isa is hurrying us along now. She also says we dunna have to hide; her mother will keep us safe."

Revna paused, and he could feel her mulling over her next words. "There's a river port in Volfsby, large enough to carry a boat to sea."

He wondered how long she'd known about the port. It would explain her urgency. She'd already expressed her concern over the size of their group and keeping them hidden and safe as they traveled. But Revna had faced those same challenges all along, and it had never driven her to the level of anxiety that consumed her now. He'd drag it out of her when they got to Volfsby—he just needed to pull himself together and get on his blasted feet.

Aksel cleared his throat. "I'll be along in a moment."

She didn't reply, but he knew she was still there. His chest still felt as though his lungs had been stretched like the skin of a drum, and he squeezed his eyes closed.

"Are ye well?" Revna's always hoarse voice was soft, edged with concern.

He wanted to ask her the same when she didn't chide him for crying like a bairn.

"Aye." He couldn't think of a reason, even a false one, to explain his current circumstance, so he left it at that.

There was no sound but the distant snap of twig, which he knew she'd allowed him to hear. The thought of her smoldering and gruff amongst all the antsy Picts while she waited had him scrubbing his face once more before hurrying to join them.

Revna had already loaded Conall and Alpia on Sgail's back and was leading the way, with Isa by her side, when he caught up. It might have been the first time she hadn't waited for him. She didn't seek him out amongst the group either. Even when he'd worked his way forward, staying just five steps behind, she never turned. She allowed him a brief breakdown; he could do the same for her. The journey had been hard on all of them, and her nightmares, though she wouldn't describe them, had been getting more and more intense. The growing circles under her eyes were evidence enough of that.

As they neared Volfsby, they were spotted by a woman carrying a loaded basket. She slowed. When her eyes narrowed on Isa, the basket was no longer in her arms but on the ground, potatoes and onions rolling down the slight hill between them. She abandoned her bounty and sprinted over the hill in the opposite direction.

"Should we worry?" Revna asked Isa.

"That was Dagmar." Isa's answer was bland, as if she'd merely commented on the weather. "She is a member of my mother's household. Móðir will know I have returned."

Conall, at the urging of Alpia, nudged Sgail forward, coming to Isa's side.

"You are home, Isa." Alpia's sweet, weary-eyed face brightened.

"I am home." Isa nodded and took the first step before the group followed.

They had barely cleared the hill when a commotion from the small settlement below had Revna reaching for the blades tucked under her vest and Aksel inching closer to Ethni. An older woman walked beside Dagmar, urgently questioning her while waving her arms. When Dagmar lifted her hand, pointing at their group, the other woman stopped and grabbed Dagmar's sleeve, her mouth dropping open.

Isa froze, taking a step back as if she meant to bolt into the woods from where they came. But the woman was running, sprinting with all her strength toward them. Revna slunk back at her approach, her knees bent, arms lax at her sides. A warrior, ready to defend. But the woman did not attack, she didn't even seem to notice anyone else. She only barreled into Isa with an embrace that almost took both of them to the ground.

"My dóttir!" she cried, tears streaming down her face, which was turned to the sky. Prayers of thanksgiving to the same God Isa spoke of poured from her lips. "My dóttir has returned."

Isa was an unmoving statue under her mother's forceful embrace until the woman took her face in her hands and kissed her cheeks, her forehead, her hair. Then she went limp in her mother's arms, as if those kisses had turned her bones to mush. And Isa wept.

THE SERVANT ISA had called Dagmar searched their faces, landing on Revna's. "You have returned the Shieldmaiden's dóttir, you are to be Randi Helgedóttir's most-honored guests."

Aksel jolted a bit at the news that Isa's mother was the Shield-maiden of Volfsby. Would she know his father? He scanned Randi's face, though it was half-hidden over Isa's shoulder. He didn't recognize her and prayed she didn't know who he was either.

"Come," Dagmar urged them toward the settlement. "There is food and a place for you to rest."

Hours later, they were fed, washed, and rested, but he'd not seen Revna since they were greeted on the dirt path leading into the settlement. He did learn that Alpia was being seen by their healer, a woman said to be well versed in herbs and remedies.

When he was led into their great hall, it appeared every settler in Volfsby had come for the celebration. His nose had him seeking out the source of the most delicious smell that, though he'd just eaten, made his greedy stomach rumble again. The settlers stood between long trestle tables that filled the entire space, benches edging their sides.

Wooden trenchers piled high with roasted meats lined the centers. Between those were cauldrons of savory-smelling stews and platters of roasted vegetables. Towers of fruits and nuts dotted the ends of the tables and smiling servants circled the room, filling mugs with a dark red drink he could tell was a heady fruit wine.

There were seats enough for all of them, even Revna's freed countrymen. Aksel found himself marveling at how this particular Shieldmaiden didn't balk at allowing slaves, even freed ones, at her table as if they were equals. He suspected Isa had left out a great deal in her brief mention of the sister that had lived most of her life in Revna's homeland.

Something had happened in Volfsby. He knew it couldn't be true, but it seemed the sun shined brighter and the air blew warmer here. There was a feeling of peace that he'd not experienced in any other settlement.

"You are Aksel Tollaksen?"

He turned sharply at the mention of his full name and felt his muscles tense when he saw it was the Shieldmaiden who'd spoken it.

She smiled, reading his strained expression as she offered him a fruit he'd never seen before. It was a light orange color, jacketed with a soft, thin, slightly furry skin. "You have nothing to fear from me. Isa told me of your part in her rescue and what you suffered to free her from our former Chieftain. If you wish your presence to remain unknown, it shall be so."

When his eyes darted between her and the fruit, she forced it into his hand, explaining. "It is a peach. A delicacy from the southern lands."

"Thank you." He bobbed his head and turned the fruit in his fingers, words feeling thick in his mouth. "That man was your former Chieftain?"

"Yes, unfortunately." Randi let loose a long breath, biting into her own peach and wiping its juice from her chin with the back of her hand. "Isa has not spoken his name, but from the description I was given, I know it was him. I have many regrets for my weaknesses in the past, the greatest of which is allowing Astrid to fear her mother instead of running to her. That was what led to all our troubles."

When she noticed that Aksel clearly didn't understand, she went on. "After losing my family, I allowed my niece and her husband to take control of Volfsby. Even when I saw how they were abusing the power, I did nothing to stop them. It wasn't until Astrid returned that I found my courage. My second biggest regret is not hunting Torsten to the ends of the earth instead of letting him flee like a coward. We were told he was dead, or I might have done just that."

"There is still time." Aksel felt his mouth tick up at the side and sunk his teeth into the foreign fruit. Surprised at its sweetness, he drew it away from his mouth, smiling at the way his bite and small dark spots on its surface resembled a screaming mouth on a pained face. "I would be willing to join that hunt."

"I will keep that in mind." Randi's brow arched, but her smile faded. "I have some...things here in Volfsby that need my attention, or I would be scouring the lands for him now."

"If it brings you any comfort, he was not left with a voice with which to boast of his crimes, and after Revna was finished with him, I doubt very much he will ever be able to fully straighten his fingers. Or freely breathe from his nose."

"Perhaps it speaks poorly of me, but that brings me quite a bit of comfort."

Aksel gazed down at the Shieldmaiden, finding himself in the company of a kindred spirit.

"You seem to have more than made up for any weaknesses of the past, Shieldmaiden. Your settlement is thriving, and its people appear to be happy." Aksel scanned the room, believing his observations to be true.

"Yes, well, maybe it is not how we begin our journey so much as how we finish." Randi accepted a mug of sweet wine from one of the servers who passed, leaving the pit of her peach on the tray.

"Come." She motioned toward the table where Isa and the others were already seated, leading him toward the space next to Revna.

Revna stiffened as he approached, and he nearly veered off course, his cowardice drawing him away from where he was clearly not wanted. But Randi's hand touched his elbow, urging him onward.

When they were seated, Aksel felt utterly humbled to witness Randi give thanks to the God above all gods before their feast. He met Ethni's eyes across the table, finding them wide and brimming with tears. When he asked her an unspoken question, she nodded in reply.

These settlers worshiped the same God. The one she called *An T-aon*. Was that the difference he felt? Was it His peace that bathed the land in that light and warmth?

Halfway through the meal, Isa sagged against her mother and Randi left to escort her to their longhouse.

"Isa needed to rest but insisted I return." Randi slid back into her place at the head of the table near the end of the meal. "She told me you came across the sea from the same land where my other dóttir lives?" Randi's question had Revna straightening in her chair.

She'd been silent during the meal, barely acknowledging Aksel's presence.

"Yes." Revna dropped the piece of bread she'd been tearing into bits. "But I do not understand how she came to be here."

Randi offered the same reassuring smile she'd given Aksel and took a drink from her mug before relaxing against the back of her chair.

"It was the same thing I suspect brought you to our shores." Randi eyed Revna in a way few had courage to, assessing instead of fearing her.

Revna's hand slipped beneath the table into her lap. He didn't have to see to know her small hand was seeking the comfort of her dagger.

"I suspect you have come to right a wrong." If Randi knew Revna was armed and on alert, she didn't show it. "I would like to help you."

"What do you mean?" Revna asked, her shoulders still raised and tense.

"I would like to offer my longboats to give you safe passage across the sea. They are small—our port is not large enough for a cargo vessel—but they are sturdy, and my men are more than capable of making the journey."

Revna opened her mouth and closed it again, clearly fighting for a response. Aksel only watched. For the first time all evening, Revna turned and looked at him.

At the sight of her too-blue eyes, something released in his chest. He realized he hadn't taken a fulfilling breath since she'd left him at the stream in the woods that morning. He didn't understand the sadness there. They'd known of the ports; Isa had already suggested her mother would aid them in their mission. Wasn't this what she wanted? An ally in the Northlands?

She held him captive with her stare for three heartbeats before turning to Randi and placing both hands on the table, no weapons in sight. "I accept your offer, Randi Helgedóttir. The kingdom of Tràigh is indebted to you for your kindness."

21

REVNA

"My dóttir was lost and you returned her to me. I expect the mothers of all lost children would give their last breath to have the same blessing."

Minutes later, Revna's chest burned from the breath she'd been holding. She felt the weight of the dagger on her lap, even after she'd discreetly returned it to its sheath.

The people of Volfsby were entirely different than any others she'd come across in the Northlands, and at first she thought Randi's generosity might be a trick. Some sort of scheme to make them feel at ease before they were set upon and the freed slaves dragged back to their cruel masters. But Randi's eyes were sincere and her words flavored with truth. And she was Astrid's kin.

"Return these people to their home, Revna." Randi's voice drew her back from the edge of a swirling vortex of confusion. "I know that is what you came to do." Randi nodded, holding Revna's gaze for a moment before she returned to her food. She kept her eyes on her plate when Randi spoke again. "You will not find danger here. Not amongst these people. They were all captives once and know what it means to be freed—some in more ways than one."

Revna didn't quite understand what she meant, but she looked down the length of the table. Randi was right. There were no hints of animosity from the settlers who had mixed themselves in with their group. They didn't look down on the freed slaves; instead, easy conversation, smiles, and occasional laughter existed.

"What happened here?" Aksel finally spoke, his voice hoarse and words awkward. "How is Volfsby so different?"

Randi glanced up at him once as she poked at the remaining chunks of buttered potatoes on her plate, a wry smile tugging at her lips. "I am happy to tell you." She glanced at Ethni. "But I suspect you already know."

Revna followed Aksel's and Randi's gazes to Ethni. Ethni nodded at him, as if answering an unspoken question as she'd done several times during the night. They were having some deep, silent conversation, and it made Revna squirm in her seat. He seemed to be on the verge of some great understanding that was still far out of Revna's reach.

Could it be true? Could the God of Brigid's and Cyrene's stories be real? Did He truly help Isa in her distress and Ethni in hers? Was He a God who cared for both Vikings and slaves? Was He capable of taking sworn enemies such as Norsemen and Picts and making them friends?

Revna forced herself to remain at the table when every instinct told her to run at the discomfort and confusion. She could feel the shadows hiding in the corners, desperate to reach her, but there was too much light. It seeped into any space where that darkness might hide. She'd never felt so exposed.

As soon as the people rose from the benches, clasping hands to dance and raising voices in song, she slipped from the suffocating hall, seeking the openness of a crisp night sky.

Aksel found her on the river bank inspecting the boats Randi mentioned.

"Going somewhere?"

She turned, brows raised at his question. He tugged at the satchel on her back. Her hands drifted along the straps, tightening them as she answered with a shrug before turning back to the boat.

"This is certainly an interesting place." He stepped to her side, running his hand along the smoothed bow of the longboat.

She didn't answer. What was there to say? Tomorrow morning, he would board that very boat, and she would watch him sail away. Since she'd mentioned her plan to Ethni, she'd found herself avoiding him. If these were their last minutes together, she should spend them telling him all the things she would never get to say.

It was he who spoke first. "I could see myself in a place like this. It is peaceful here."

She cast a look to the sky. If there was a God up there somewhere, she certainly needed assistance now. Aksel was waiting for a response, but she couldn't form a single word. If she let even one slip, it would lead to her changing her mind and telling Ethni not to convince him to leave.

It would lead to him by her side as she scoured the rest of the Northlands.

Charred and burned. Charred and burned. It would lead to her nightmares coming true and Aksel being ripped from her life. Stolen from this earth. She could stand any manner of heartbreak but that. If she never found her sister, or if she discovered the worst had happened and her twin didn't survive the journey across the sea, Revna could accept that. She could go on. Mayhap it made her the worst sort of creature. But she could not continue living in a world where Aksel didn't exist.

Since she was eight winters, she'd ached for the sister she never knew. But knowing Aksel and his friendship made the choice before her unbearable.

He'd dropped into her life, a drunk mess of a man, and turned all her plans on end. He'd been surprising her ever since, taking every expectation and shattering it with his strong hands. He was good.

Too good for her to let him be destroyed simply because she couldn't breathe when he wasn't near. Revna dragged in a breath to prove to herself she was being overly dramatic. This was the plan and she would stick to it.

She turned toward the settlement, taking three steps before he was in front of her, blocking her way.

"Why are you not speaking to me?" He was using the Norse tongue, trying to worm his way in and force her to talk. "Have I offended you somehow?"

Ethni was certain her news would be enough to convince Aksel to leave with them. But what if it wasn't? What if he refused? Images from Revna's nightmares seized hold of her, coating her thoughts with horrors that turned her stomach sour.

He had to go. He had to live.

"I have more important things to worry about than yer feelings, *Prince*. If ye haven't noticed, we are only a few days away from Kaupang, and I've got a passel of stolen slaves."

He winced but countered when she moved to step past him.

"They will sail in the morning. All will be well." His hands were on his hips, but his fingers twitched as if he were fighting the temptation to touch her.

It would be over if he did. He got past her defenses when they first met; she wouldn't let herself forget the most important rule again. *Never let them get their hands on ye.* Either in violence or in tenderness. Revna added the second part herself. He'd touched her a thousand times, but this was a battle, and his friendship was the one weapon she couldn't defeat. She stepped back, out of his reach.

"Why are you afraid of me?"

She scoffed, letting loose flames of fury she'd kept at bay for months. They licked at the edges of her heart, tentative—as if uncertain she wouldn't slam the door shut again. When she didn't, when she fanned them with a slow breath through pursed lips, they raced along her veins, lighting every nerve.

She refused to speak in his language. "I am only afraid ye'll get in my way."

"Get in your way? How have I ever gotten in your way?" His brows furrowed, a hint of his own anger flaring behind his eyes.

"How have ye not? Instead of coming wi' us when we found Isa, ye went back. Yer message cost us valuable time. We could have been caught and killed that very night."

"How could—"

"And what about yer sister? How do I ken she didn't tell yer father everything? Ye forced my hand, and the truth could be chasing us even now, destroying everything we have worked to build."

"She would not."

"And the fact that yer even here at all." Revna hated the words as they poured out of her mouth, burning her lips like poison. She hated the look on his face and the pain she was about to inflict upon him. But she would do whatever it took to get him on that boat. She would let the darkness devour her whole if it kept him breathing.

"What is that supposed to mean?"

"Yer only here because it would have cost me too much time to bury ye when I found ye, drunk and rambling, outside the mead hall."

That was too far. *Take it back. Take it all back.* The voice in her mind, the one that sounded like her, pleaded and begged her to stop. She didn't let her mind wander to the mark on her chest—the one threatening to sear a hole in her tunic from its heat.

"That was cruel, Little Bird." His hands traveled to his chest, scrubbing over his scar as if it too burned beneath his clothes. He stepped back, moving toward the settlement. "You obviously do not want me around tonight. I will talk to you tomorrow after they sail."

He still spoke in his native tongue and she in hers. What she was doing, what she was about to do—it would ensure they never found a common language again.

"There willna be an after." Her announcement stopped his retreat. "Either go wi' them or go back to Kaupang. Go wherever ye want, but yer not going wi' me."

"Revna." Her name blew through his lips as a plea.

It cracked her heart in half, and she felt the pain through every bone. She nearly dropped to her knees under the agony, but she would stand. For Aksel. She would endure it.

She ripped the tattered parchment from her vest and shook it. "I have thought of nothing but these names from the moment I found this list. Twelve winters I have held it. Twelve winters it has been wi' me, and I have done nothing but make plans to find these people. Ye willna take that from me."

"How can you say that? I bled for them too."

"After how long, Aksel?" It should have been a shock how easily the hurtful words rolled off her tongue, but it wasn't. It was simple to step back into the waiting arms of the shadows. "Ye lived wi' Ethni almost yer entire life. She cared fer ye like she was yer own kin, and ye did nothing to free her. Ye might have been a child when she came, but ye've had power and influence for years and still ye did nothing."

He stepped back again, but she kept firing, hitting him dead center again and again, her aim flawless.

"Ye want to help me now to ease yer guilt and shame, and once ye feel better, ye'll leave. But I canna stop." She slammed her closed fist against her chest, a thud shuttering across her bones. "I will never stop until I find them all. I have left everything and everyone I ever cared about fer them."

"I did too," he roared back, straightening himself. "I left my sister behind."

"I have a sister too, and there has been no one to speak for her. Ever."

"You..." He blinked, shaking his head. "You have a sister?"

She didn't mean to say that.

"Is she the infant you ask about?"

No. She had to turn this around. "It doesna matter. I will not risk my chance to find her because of ye."

"I will help you."

End it. She had to end it now.

"Are ye deaf?" she screamed, holding back the tears that threatened to give away her lies. "Ye only slow me down. Ye get in my way."

His lips opened, but no words came out.

"Ye dunna belong wi' me." And then the final death blow. "I' dunna want ye, Aksel. I have never wanted ye."

The words carved their way from her mouth, slicing like blades across her tongue, and she felt if she spat, there would be blood on the ground.

"Ye were a means to an end."

Aksel stumbled backwards, as if she'd sunk a real blade in his gut. But she had. Rune's face, wearing a twin expression of shock and pain, flashed in her mind.

There would be no wound to bandage, but she'd sliced so deep she surely nicked a vein. Deeper than even his father or Torsten had. If she'd ever sought redemption, it might have been possible before this night. But no more. Of all the horrid things she'd done—the lies, the fighting, the scheming and tricks—this would be a trophy she could place beside the one she earned with Rune's death. She was the true queen of darkness, death, and ruin.

"Go wi' Ethni, Aksel. Go wi' someone who wants ye around."

Somehow, her feet carried her up the riverbank. They carried her through a grove of trees where she stopped briefly to empty her stomach. It did little to rid her of the putrid churning of her gut, and with each step away from him, her chest grew tighter. Mayhap she wasn't being dramatic, because she knew in her now-empty insides that her lungs would open if she turned and raced back to him.

But leaving meant he would live, and, however painful, that knowledge allowed her to continue to Randi's longhouse, where she found Ethni tending to Alpia.

"What's happened?" Ethni rose, reading the look on Revna's face. "Where's Aksel?"

"Go to him now, Ethni." Revna spoke, but her voice didn't sound like her own. It was as dead as the grass in winter. "He is at the river. Make him get on that boat."

"What have ye done, Revna?" Ethni's eyes searched hers, but she would find nothing.

There was nothing left. Revna had left her soul on the shore at Aksel's feet.

"What I had to."

22

AKSEL

Something happened. Something must have happened. She couldn't have meant it. Aksel wrapped his arms around his middle, trying to hold himself together when Revna had just ruthlessly gutted him.

He was afraid to let go; his insides might spill out onto the rocky shores. He didn't know how long he stayed bent and forcing himself to breathe.

"Aksel?"

At first he heard Revna's voice and spun, hoping she'd come back to say she hadn't meant a word. He didn't care about her reasons; he would forgive her anything if she said it wasn't true. But it wasn't Revna. It was Ethni.

She took one look at him and rushed forward. "Oh, Aksel."

His knees screamed against the slice of small stones on the shore, and Ethni followed him down, cradling his head against her chest.

"Did she send you?" He couldn't speak in Ethni's tongue. He couldn't bring himself to reach across that divide again and hope for a life where this night had never happened. Did Revna regret what she'd said? Did she send Ethni to bring him back?

"Revna returned, and I saw you were gone."

No. She didn't regret it.

"She has a sister." He didn't know why that was the first thing that came to his mind, but the fact that she'd kept it secret almost hurt more than anything else she'd said.

"I ken." Ethni ran her hand over his face, his hair, soothing him as she'd done when he was a boy. "A twin."

Gods, he wanted to claw that knowledge from his brain. Another little bird with her same blood had been stolen from its nest and carted off over the sea. He'd heard her ask every person they'd found about a babe and none knew the answer. Every time, she looked as if she had died a little inside.

"Their mother was a Pict who married the king of Tràigh. When the twins were days old, she was murdered by the king. We all thought they'd been thrown into the sea, but they were saved. Secretly taken in by the Picts. But the king—Revna's father—blamed the Picts for his wife's death. In revenge, he killed the Pictish queen and many of her people. He sold the rest of us to the Norsemen, and wi' us his own daughter. Revna's twin sister."

"What happened to Revna?"

"The Pictish princess, just a girl herself, managed to escape to the dark woods with some of our people. Revna was among them."

He'd said once that they were the same, but their similarities ended with having a wretched father. Revna was right. She'd spent her life planning to save the people her father enslaved. People she'd never even met. He'd given up under hardship. He'd become a drunken, pathetic nothing.

He straightened so quickly it startled Ethni.

"I am sorry, Ethni." He took her by the arms. "I should have done more to help you."

"Aksel," she sighed.

He shut his eyes against the tenderness he saw there. He couldn't stand it. "No. I was a boy when you came, but when I became a man, I could have saved you and Alpia from so much pain and I did not. I am a wretch, and I cannot—will not—ask you to forgive me."

Conall had said that forgiveness wasn't given because one deserved it but because they needed it. He was in desperate, dire need but still could not ask it of Ethni.

Though he still gripped her upper arms, he felt her hand move to touch his cheek. "Ye have to let it go. There was nothing you could have done, and we canna change the past."

Eira had said almost the same thing. He released her and opened his eyes, seeing a flicker of something dark behind their ocean blue.

"I ken ye dunna realize it, but ye did do something fer me. Ye saved me in ways ye'll never understand."

He shook his head. She was only trying to ease his pain, but it was making it worse.

"Aksel, if ye'd of tried to free me, what would ye have done? Put me and Alpia on a boat back to our homeland? Stolen away wi' us? Wander the Norselands wi'out a home or means like an outlawer? What of Conall? He would have been all alone. He suffered, but he needed us as much as we needed him. Ye dinna have the power to save us, not until now, and the moment ye were given the opportunity, ye took it."

His emotions were wrecking his concentration, guilt and shame and hurt swirling in his mind with no end of the storm in sight. *You are too.*

Conall's earlier words rang in his ears like a clanging bell. Perhaps he was better than his father, but still...

"I am not enough," he finished his thought aloud. "She wants me to go." His words were lifeless, falling flat as soon as they left his lips. "She does not want me."

The second he said it, it became as real as the ground beneath him. She did not want him. Like his mother. Like his father.

"I'm sorry." Ethni rested her cheek on the top of his head. She didn't try to comfort him or say it wasn't true and that Revna was simply upset. That she'd come around. That he should stay and fight it out with her. She only repeated, "I'm so sorry."

Aksel let his eyes close. He let the agony consume him; there was no use fighting it. Ethni held him as he breathed, his body shuddering as wave upon painful wave tore through him. She bore it silently, just as she'd always done, until he settled, feeling more like a pathetic crawling creature than a man.

"I want ye."

Her voice was so small, he nearly thought it a whisper of the wind. But he lifted his head, looking up at her tear-filled eyes.

"Come wi' me. Come wi' us—wi' me and Alpia and Conall. We want ye. We have always wanted ye."

"I love you for that." He tried to make his lips form a smile, but they would not. Instead, he pushed himself up, brushing his knuckles across her cheek to clear an escaped tear. "You have always been there for me. Loved me as your own."

"Then come." She took his hand in both of hers. "Come wi' us."

"I do not belong in your world. I am a Norseman. It was a dream to think it would ever work with Revna." He shook his head, thinking of how foolish he must have sounded, telling Revna of what an adventure it would be to go to her homeland. She was right. He was an idiot.

"Ye do belong. And it can work. Think of Randi's daughter. She is Norse and serves as the queen's captain. Ye'll be welcome too."

He blew out a soft breath and offered her a half smile. "You have been so good to me, Ethni. But I cannot go. I am not the same as Randi's daughter. As you."

"Aye," she said, her eyes filling with tears again. "Aye, ye are Aksel, more than ye ken."

He started to argue again, but something in her eyes silenced him. When she lowered her head, staring at the hands that were wringing in her lap, he felt a strange sort of panic begin to swirl in his stomach.

"What do you mean?"

Ethni pushed her lips together as tears streamed past her mouth, dripping from her chin.

"Ethni?" He'd never been so harsh, but he was on the verge of crumbling, and her tears were not those of a woman who simply loved a little Viking boy as her own.

"Ye ar'na Aksel." Her voice broke when she spoke.

"What?" His tone was less rough, but still sharp.

Ethni dragged in a breath, wiped her face with her sleeve, and raised her eyes to his. "The Chieftain did have a son called Aksel. When he was but six winters, he grew very ill. Too ill to recover." Ethni's hands shook, and she curled them into fists. "I ken this because I was...I was taken into the Chieftain's household while he was dying. I watched him take his last breath. He was..." Ethni drew in a shaking breath. "He was so very small."

"What are you saying?" Her story made sense, but it didn't. He'd been sick, but he was clearly alive.

"The Chieftain and his wife were so distraught, I thought..." She clenched her fists until her knuckles turned white. "I thought if I could help them in their grief, they might..." She turned red, watery eyes to him. "I was so young, just a lass, and I was so afraid. So alone."

He couldn't speak. Couldn't breathe.

"There was a lad on the boat wi' us when we were taken. He was injured and took ill, but not as severe as the Chieftain's son. Not yet. I ken that if he could just see a healer, he might live. And I thought if he was taken into the Chieftain's home, as his son, he wouldna suffer. He would be raised as one of them. Loved. Protected."

"Ethni." Her name was a breath on Aksel's lips. It couldn't be true. It wasn't. Except that as she talked, he could feel the rocking of a boat though he'd never boarded one. He could smell the pungent odor of unwashed bodies, salty sea air, and stale mead.

"I told the Chieftain's wife about the lad, about where I thought he'd been sent and that he looked so very much like their son. I wasna certain, but I thought him to be near the same age."

Aksel pushed himself away from her, crawling backwards to distance himself from the story she told.

"They found ye. And ye lived." Ethni sniffed, straightening then as if the worst part of her confession was over. "Aksel Tollaksen made a recovery, and no one seemed to notice that he came through his illness just a little taller. Tollak's wife kept ye away from anyone fer so long, and 'tis natural fer a lad to grow."

Aksel was quiet for a long minute. "I dunna have memories of this."

It was not a lie. The flashes that filled his mind were so conflicted and filmy, they could not be considered memories.

"I told the Chieftain's wife of an herb that would make yer memory muddled—that would make ye believe whatever past she gave to ye. And I wasna lying; ye burned wi' such a fever, Aksel. I ken that wi'out help, ye wouldna have lived. Ye'd already forgotten yer own name."

"You gave me nightshade?" That Ethni would have given him a poison that could have killed him was the most unbelievable part of her tale.

"I made the mixture. I ken it wouldna kill ye, only make yer mind able to forget the past, to accept yer mother's words."

"But she is not my mother," he snapped.

"Nay." Ethni lowered her head again. "She isna."

He tumbled over the edge of some cliff in his mind, falling and spiraling as Ethni's story viciously ripped the air from his lungs. His mouth was dry, his tongue burning for the sweet relief of mead. He pushed himself to his feet.

"I do not believe you." He kept to the Norse tongue. He was a Viking, not a Pict.

"Do ye remember?" Ethni's voice was soft and patient, the sound of words in the Vestman language stirring something inside of him. "Do ye remember before ye were sick?"

"Of course I do."

"Truly?"

269

He started to say it again, but the memories he'd always assumed were of the Chieftain and his wife never seemed to fit. He never saw their faces; only flashes of feelings and glimpses of color.

"Do ye remember me teaching ye the language of the Picts?"

"Well, no, but—"

"'Tis because I dinna. Ye've always spoken it."

He shook his head. No this was...she taught him. He remembered her telling him to keep it secret.

"Do ye ken why ye always draw that symbol? The one that looks like a lion?"

Aksel's head snapped up then. He'd never asked anyone about that symbol, never known why he always found himself drawing it, finding it in the clouds, tracing it on his skin.

"'Tis the symbol of our people. The queen of the Picts bore the mark of the lion. 'Twas on the crest of her shield."

"It is a mere coincidence."

"Ye ken it isna." Her voice was so sure.

He shook his head. No. This was not right. He couldn't be from her lands. He couldn't have been her kinsman when she was a slave and he was raised with all the wealth and privilege of a Chieftain's son.

"Aksel."

"Why do you call me that?" He stumbled back a few steps, one clear thought soaring through the mist of vapors in his mind. "Is my name on her list?"

"I dunna ken."

"Does she know?"

A single tear raced down Ethni's cheek and she shook her head. "Nay."

"Who am I?" He rasped, pressing his fists to his chest. His voice carried across the river as he shouted, "Who am I, Ethni?"

"I dunna ken."

He drew away when she approached, reaching for him. She didn't look hurt; she simply let her hand fall to her side.

"Yer name doesna matter, ye are one of us. Ye belong wi' us. Ye always have."

He felt his face twist in a grimace of pain. She was lying. She'd lied to him all his life. How could he believe her now?

"Come wi' us. Come home."

He lowered himself until his forehead nearly touched hers, and for the first time he could remember, Ethni looked afraid of him.

"I have no home."

Then it hit him like a strike to the gut that sent him to his knees. Eira.

She was not his sister. He was not her brother. He was nothing and no one. He couldn't be here. He needed—his hands dove into his hair and scratched at his throat. He was thirsty. So he did what he always had done. He got back up.

He left Ethni sobbing on the riverbank. The sound of her cries hacked at whatever goodness he thought he had and revealed it as the putrid refuse it was. His first instinct was to pitch himself into the water and let the current carry him where it wished or simply take him under. But Conall's talk of a God who forgave bobbed to the surface despite his thoughts trying to drown it out.

His feet carried him past the quaint farms of Volfsby. As he neared the woods edging the town, he spotted a lone mare grazing in a small field. It was foolish of the farmer not to stable the animal at night. A wolf might come along and decide to enjoy a late-night meal. Or a thief might decide he needed an easy means of transport away from his miserable life.

There was even a leather harness draped over the post nearest the gate. It was as if the farmer had left it as a gift for him.

"Thank you, farmer," Aksel muttered darkly as he slipped the reins over the animal's head. He ignored the warning in his heart and thoughts of what Randi would think of him stealing from the people who had been so kind and welcoming. He was a nameless ghost, neither living nor dead. Ghosts had no conscience.

The moon was at its peak and the horse's neck frothy with sweat

271

from their gallop when he heard the sound of revelry. Slowing to a walk, he steered the mare toward the noise.

"What is the occasion?" he asked a man who was stumbling from what appeared to be a bustling mead hall.

"A handfasting." The man's words were slurred but understandable. "Quite the feast, much mead!"

Aksel slipped from the horse's back, rubbing his hand along the animal's nose.

The man slung his arm over Aksel's shoulder. "Come, friend. Come celebrate with us."

Aksel looked over his shoulder. Far behind him was a boat that waited to carry him across the sea to a people he didn't know. Revna didn't want him; there was not one person in the Northlands who did. But Ethni did. He could still hear her begging him to come back long after he'd left the riverbank.

Come wi' us, Aksel. Come home.

"Come," the drunk urged again, sloshing his mead over the front of his tunic. "What are you called, friend?"

He nearly gave the name Aksel. That wasn't his name, though. He didn't even know how old he really was.

"I am *Draugr*."

The man laughed, mug raised, raining the amber drink onto Aksel's tunic as well. "A ghost are you? Well, come, spirit. Come and tell me tales of Valhalla."

The man's arm slipped from his shoulder as he ambled toward the mead hall, swinging his arm in invitation. A boat to a new world at his back, a Viking-filled mead hall before him. What he'd told the man was true. He was a ghost.

23

REVNA

Revna stood on the cliffs overlooking the river. It truly was a majestic sight. Walls of gray rock, glistening in the sunshine, formed the cradle for a white-water river that flowed fast and deep. There should have been a smile on her face at the sight and fresh air filling her lungs, but her horrible words from the night before tainted the scene and left her empty.

"Your boat will be ready by midday." Randi came to her side, breaking through her dark memories.

"I will never forget what you have done for us." Revna turned and clasped Randi's forearm, accepting the same from the Shieldmaiden of Volfsby. "Neither will Astrid."

Tears filled Randi's eyes, and she pulled Revna's arm, folding her into a firm embrace before Revna could resist. Not that she would. This was Astrid's mother. She was still letting that shock settle in.

"You saved my daughter. You brought back what I had lost. *That* is what will never be forgotten." She released Revna, holding her at arm's length. "I beg you, though, choose your words carefully when you tell of what happened here. Astrid will feel she must return if she thinks we are in danger."

"I will make sure whoever tells her is guarded with their story."

Randi's brows drew together. "You are not sailing with them?"

"No. There is still much for me to do and someone I must find."

A flush coated Randi's cheeks, and her breaths quickened; Revna felt a tingle shoot up her spine.

"You must come with me now." Randi was already moving. Revna jogged to keep up.

"What is it?"

"I would have told you before, but I assumed you were going with them, so it was no matter." They hurried through the great hall and toward the center of the settlement.

"Must we race across all of Volfsby for this news?"

"There is someone you must see." Randi never slowed her steps. Randi asked several settlers hushed questions, and both she and Revna were out of breath by the time they reached the mead hall where many were still celebrating Isa's return.

Randi marched directly toward a young man nursing a hefty mug of mead.

"Hermood," she said forcefully, making the young man jolt upright. "You are supposed to be taking your rest and preparing to venture out again. That is what your wages are for."

"It has been many winters, Shieldmaiden, and I have yet to find my charge." His eyes were slightly glazed and his words came slower than Revna thought normal.

Randi raised her voice and issued an order that cleared the mead hall within minutes. Hermood started for the door, but Randi caught his arm.

"Consider yourself blessed, Hermood. I have found your charge. Deliver the message my daughter gave you."

Hermood's eyes widened at the sight of Revna.

"I did not think you would believe me if I gave it." Randi looked from Revna to Hermood. "Go on."

He slid from his stool, instantly sober. "You are the raven?"

Revna jerked at his question, stumbling into Randi, who caught her with a firm grip.

"Do not fear," Randi said. "He will not reveal your secret upon pain of death."

Hermood swallowed hard and nodded. Then the young man gave a soft bow.

"May I hear this message?" Revna was nearly climbing out of her skin.

Hermood, as if he were a king's mage about to deliver a royal decree, clutched the edges of his deerskin vest and lifted his chin, puffing out his chest.

"Speak!" Revna wrung her hands together to keep them from doing the same to his neck.

"I apologize. I never thought this day would come." He cleared his throat. "To reach the one you seek the most, you must go back to the beginning." He grinned when he finished speaking, looking between Revna and Randi as if expecting applause.

Revna didn't move. Randi stepped to her side, watching her expression. Hermood was staring, too, until Randi slapped his arm. Three coins in his palm was the payment for his promise that he would go directly to Randi's home without speaking to anyone.

"Does it mean something to you?" Randi asked after she'd ushered Revna outside.

Revna stared in the direction of the cliffs. They were too far away to see, but she knew they were there beyond the farms and forest.

"She is telling me to come home."

Randi's bright eyes searched hers, her brows furrowed again. "So," she said slowly, "you *will* join the voyage?"

The voyage. The longboat bound for Tràigh that would leave in just a few hours. The boat home. With Aksel.

"No." Revna dropped her gaze to the dusty ground at her feet, her hand drifting mindlessly to the little pouch sewn into her vest. "No, I still have things to do here."

"Revna!" A familiar voice and light footsteps snatched Revna from the daze she'd fallen into.

Alpia raced up the path. But there wasn't a smile on her face, and Revna reached for her dagger.

"Alpia, ye should be resting. Yer not well."

"Come," Alpia choked between heavy breaths. "Come quickly."

Revna exchanged a look with Randi before they hurried along behind Alpia. Ethni sat on a lichen covered rock by the edge of the river, several women surrounding her, their hands on her shoulders. Conall arrived a few seconds later, dragged by a young boy from Volfsby.

"What has happened, Ethni?" Conall demanded, worry permeating his tone. At the broken expression on Ethni's face, he softened his tone and sent the boy and other women scurrying away.

He drove his gaze to Revna, as if she had the answer to his question. When she shook her head, he looked to Ethni again. "I must have enjoyed the feast too much. I fell asleep early, and when I woke, you were gone. I've been searching fer ye."

Ethni turned swollen red eyes up. They didn't land on Conall; they centered on Revna, and the accusation there nearly sent her back a step.

"He's gone." Her voice was hoarse, as if she'd been crying for hours.

"Leave us." Revna didn't tear her eyes from Ethni's. When no one moved, she snapped, earning a whimper from Alpia and making Conall's shoulders stiffen. "Leave us."

Ethni nodded to Conall, who scooped Alpia into his arms and lugged her off toward the settlement. Randi followed, softly touching Ethni's shoulder as she passed.

Revna waited until they were out of hearing range before she spoke. "I ken ye blame me, but he will recover. Whatever it was, he
—"

"Will he?" Ethni's sharp tone sliced like ice up Revna's spine. She lowered her head, burying her face in her hands. "I shouldna have done it."

"What did ye do, Ethni?"

Ethni kept her head down for a long time. Long enough that Revna shifted her feet anxiously.

"I told him the truth." Her words were muffled and quiet. Then she lifted her head, her shocking confession as clear as the dawn. "I told him Aksel Tollaksen is dead."

Revna didn't move, didn't breathe, as Ethni shared the heartbreaking story of two little boys. One lost to sickness and one lost because of an evil king. Her father.

He did this to Aksel. To Ethni. To her.

When Ethni finished, Revna swayed on her feet, feeling as though she had been so very wrong to request this of Ethni. To bring this pain on Aksel.

"He will never forgive me." Ethni's words were interrupted by her sobs.

"Ye saved him," Revna said softly.

"I doomed him too."

"What do ye mean?" Revna finally moved, joining Ethni on the rock.

"I thought they would treat him like a son. That the Chieftain's wife would be so happy to have a child that she would—" Ethni shook her head, her voice tight with emotion. "I was only a lass. I dinna understand that ye couldna replace one child wi' another. And he never kent why they were so cold."

"Why would they take him if they dinna want him?"

"They did. They wanted a son. The Chieftain's wife couldna bear any more bairns after Eira. Wi'out a male heir, he wouldna have been as strong a leader. But even though he looked like their son, he wasna. 'Tis why the Chieftain—" Ethni's shaking fist flew to her lips, her knuckles pressed to her teeth. "He never knew why they dinna love him and I couldna tell him. He was just a little boy."

Revna could not stop herself; she wrapped her arms around the trembling woman, holding Ethni together as she broke apart. Her own heart shattered with each of Ethni's sobs, picturing the sad face of a little boy who could never understand what he'd done wrong. And she knew exactly what that felt like, for she'd been just such a lass. He was right. They were the same.

When Ethni had gathered herself together enough to speak, her words were nothing more than strained breaths.

"If Alpia had been a lad, Aksel would have died. The Chieftain would have killed him. I ken it was *An T-aon* that gave me a daughter. Alpia saved Aksel's life and mine."

"After she was born, the Chieftain dinna—"

"Nay. Not again. His wife looked at him wi' such hate, even though I thought it might have been her plan. He never touched me again. I was so afraid he would send us away to someone who wouldna have such reservations or who would simply have us killed. But he dinna. I ken that was *An T-aon* too. He was wi' me. Always wi' me."

There He was again. *An T-aon*. The invisible God in the middle of another story. Reaching out without being seen and saving another life. Revna's fingers found her temples and then the mark on her chest. It was true. She knew it was true, but it was a truth that could not find a place to land inside her mind. It did not fit with what she expected or believed.

"Alpia kens all of this?"

"Only that the Chieftain is her father. I told her so that she would always be careful. That she wouldna trust him or his wife if anything happened to me or if I wasna wi' her. I hated to place that burden on her; I wished fer her to have a childhood free of fear." Ethni's voice broke again, her shoulders shaking with sobs.

"Ethni." Revna tightened her arms and buried her head against Ethni's shoulder, taking intentional breaths through the waves of rage that pulsed through her body. It should not have been. None of this should have been. "I will kill him."

Ethni sat up, breaking Revna's hold. "Nay." She grabbed Revna's shoulders. "Nay, Revna. Ye dunna go back there. I ken the battle ye fight wi' yer anger and yer grief. I see it because I fight it myself. It would have destroyed me if it weren't for *An T-aon*. He took my pain and turned it into something priceless. He gave me Alpia. And Conall. And Aksel. Alpia was allowed to live because Conall claimed her as his own. Because he claimed me even though we barely ken each other. Even though he was but a young man himself."

"Conall is a good man."

"And *An T-aon* is also good. He saw me in my distress, and He sent help. He filled the emptiness and calmed the anger."

"Ye shouldna have been in distress in the first place." Revna spoke through clenched teeth.

"Mayhap so. But I dunna blame *An T-aon*. I blame the king who sold us. I blame the Chieftain who..." Ethni shook her head again. "*An T-aon* is good, and only good things come from Him. He brings light to dark places. Alpia and Conall were my light. And Aksel. Aksel was light."

"I think Eira was a light fer Aksel's darkness, as was Alpia later on. But Eira was first. She was there when he came, but she was just a tiny thing. She would not remember her brother. As much as I tried to love him, to care for him, it wasna enough and he was fading.

"But Eira was a bright little star. She was so soft and small. Aksel didn't remember her as a bairn, but it was as if he'd always had a sister. As if he was born to be a brother. He became her protector. He lived fer Eira's smiles. No matter how many times his father knocked him down, he got back up fer her. Even though I ken he saw the difference in the way the Chieftain and his wife treated her, Aksel only loved her wi' his whole heart. It wasna until she married and went to her husband's home that he fell into the dark again. He forgot how to get up. And then you came and forced him to his feet."

Revna stared at Ethni, the sincerity in the woman's eyes sating some of Revna's rage. Enough that she could breathe and not feel fire peeling up her throat.

"What was his name?"

"He was too sick to speak it." Ethni dropped her hands from Revna's shoulders. "I never kent his name."

Revna felt a wave of disappointment swell and then recede. He was one of the many taken and not recorded. Like her sister. Nameless and forgotten. At least those she found were able to tell her their names. But Aksel...he was still without an identity. He was without a family. Without a home.

"What did he say?"

"He dinna believe me at first." Ethni lowered her head again. "But when I asked him if he could remember before he was sick, he couldna."

Revna straightened, a thought raising her brows. "'Tis how he kent our language."

"Aye. He couldna remember me teaching it to him. And I told him I ken why he drew that strange symbol."

Realization swept through Revna, raising gooseflesh on her arms. "'Tis the symbol of the Picts, of the king and queen before Cyrene."

"The lion. Aye."

"He believed ye then?"

Ethni nodded.

"Where is he?"

"He was so angry. At me. At the world. He left. I dunna ken where he went. I waited, but he dinna return."

He hadn't been in the mead hall when she received the message Astrid had left, and she hadn't passed him on the way. She sighed, casting a look at the rising sun. The boat would be sailing soon. He wouldn't have run off. He would be angry, but he would recover. He would come back. He had to.

"He will never forgive me." Ethni sobbed into her hands. "I lied to him for all these years."

Revna rested her arms on her drawn up knees, lifting her eyes once again to the cloudless sky. This was so very wrong.

"Yer right." At Revna's answer, Ethni choked on a sob. "He willna forgive ye," Revna explained, "because he will realize there is nothing to forgive. Ye were but a lass, and ye saved his life."

"No one ever kent who he really was." Ethni tilted her head. "Not even Conall, not Alpia. I dinna tell anyone. And every day the Chieftain's wife would threaten me. If I wanted to live until the next dawn, I would keep the secret. I would do whatever I was asked. When Alpia was born, she dinna need to threaten me anymore. She only had to look at my daughter."

"I ken what ye suffered, Ethni. Ye could have given up, but ye fought to keep yer family safe and together. Including Aksel, and if he canna see that, he's a fool."

Ethni sobbed again. When Aksel returned, if he had even one harsh word for Ethni, Revna was determined to put him in his place. She knew his father was the worst sort of person: abusive, selfish, heartless. But how could Aksel have not seen how much he was loved by Ethni?

Instead, he let his troubles swallow him. He threw himself into drink and debauchery. Mayhap when he returned, she would throttle him. Revna launched herself off the rock with such speed Ethni sucked in a sharp breath.

"Where are ye going?"

"To find him," Revna growled. "To drag his princely carcass back here and make him listen until he understands."

"He was just a lad. We were all just children." Ethni reached for her, but Revna was already marching for the woods, her sharp eyes searching for any sign of him.

"He's not a lad now." She didn't know if her grumbled response reached Ethni, and she didn't care.

"Revna." Ethni's sharp bark stopped her. Revna didn't turn, having learned when Ethni used that tone that she was about to deliver some truth she wouldn't want to hear. "Aksel turned to drink, but what about ye?"

"What?" She turned then, her brows driven together in frustration.

"I've heard yer story. Were ye not also an abandoned child loved by one who was not yer kin? Did someone not also sacrifice fer ye?"

Revna closed her eyes, pushing back the sting of tears as visions of her queen filled her mind.

"He turned to mead, but ye also have yer vices. Ye and he are the same."

She had thought the same just minutes before, but it was never true.

"Nay," Revna said softly. "He is better than me. That's why he will be on that boat wi' ye today."

At noon, the boat was loaded but Aksel had not returned. Neither had the men sent to search for him, and Revna's own quest was fruitless. Her imagination was running wild with all the horrible things that could have happened. As she paced the shore, Randi was silent and steady at her side. She put aside her compassion for his heartache and decided she most assuredly wanted to throttle him.

"Revna." Conall's hushed voice had her whirling, dagger drawn.

His breathing was heavy, and a slick sheen of sweat coated his forehead. Something in his eyes sent prickles of alarm across her skin.

"I have news."

"What?"

Conall shook his head.

"Speak, Conall." She slammed fisted hands against her legs.

"He went to Illrstaðr. He was seen in their mead hall and then—he was taken."

Revna flipped Rune's dagger between her fingers, hesitating half a second before looking to Randi.

"The boat will not leave without your say," the Shieldmaiden said. "I will send some of my warband with you."

"Take me to Illrstaðr." She marched past Conall and spoke over her shoulder to Randi. "Tell your men to catch up if they can."

"It was said that six men took him." Conall's warning didn't slow her pace. "They're in the woods somewhere."

Revna squeezed her eyes shut for the length of a step. As much as she wanted him safe, she was equally furious. All his talk of using words, of some kind of fantasy world in which she wouldn't have to fight all the days of her life, filtered through her mind. She'd almost believed him.

A sharp pain crept over her ribs, churning her stomach with nausea. She stretched, cracking her neck, before saying, "We will stop by the longhouse fer more weapons and fer Sgail."

She flipped the dagger again. With each step, she let it in: the fury that coated her tongue with bitterness. The burning, consuming rage that dropped a glaze of red across her vision. She rolled her shoulders, completely ignoring the tingling coming from her mark.

"Did ye hear me? Six," Conall said louder.

"Good." She knew the hard, cruel edge in her voice was why Conall whipped his head in her direction. "One fer ye and five fer me."

24

AKSEL

The familiar rhythm pounded in his head. Ancient drums that beat from somewhere out of time. Pulsing from the inside of his brain, pushing, pushing, pushing to get out.

Even from behind his closed lids, he could feel his eyes watering at the bright light of day.

He groaned and moved to throw an arm over his face, but his arms wouldn't move. Something rough bit into the skin of his wrists and a sharp pain snaked up his shoulders.

He groaned again, rolling over to his side to ease the discomfort. He must have been lying on his hands all night. That's why he couldn't move them. He tried again. No. Something was...his hands were bound. Again.

The first sting of panic coated his skin, swirling in his stomach until everything inside came up and coated the ground inches from his face. He pushed himself up on his knees to keep from falling into his mess. Seconds passed before his cheek met the soil again, its musty earthiness only half covering up the reek of his sick. At least he'd managed to avoid diving headfirst into it.

Someone else was there. He could feel their presence, but his

284

head felt as if it were split in half. The pain was too great to risk opening his eyes and letting in light. His thoughts still sloshed around inside his mead-filled mind. He just needed to sleep. A few hours, and he would be fine. The cramps streaking across his stomach would ease and the dirt dry feeling in his mouth would dissolve. Then he could deal with why his hands were tied.

When he woke again, his head was still filled with the pounding of drums. But he was able to rub his fists against his eyes and peel his eyelids open. There was still something scratchy and uncomfortable around his wrists, but he was free to move, hands no longer bound.

"Whe..." The sound came out like a croak and he cleared his throat. "Where am I?'

He heard the soft slush of a blade sliding into the earth next to his head and he closed his eyes again. He didn't know where he was, or how much time had passed, but he knew who was with him.

Everything came rushing back in flickering bursts, assaulting his mind with the terrible decisions he'd made, starting with his first blasted step into that mead hall.

No, it was before that. It started the second Revna took his future in her small hands and tore it to shreds. Then Ethni came with her story and did the same to his past. He was nothing, nobody. With what Ethni told him, he had no identity, and without Revna, he had no purpose.

He'd managed two hours of staring at the mug in front of him before he'd wrapped his hands around it. Another hour before he'd raised it to his lips and tipped it back. Once he'd tasted the sweetness of mead, it was only seconds between the end of one and the start of another.

He'd planned to return and get on that boat like Revna wanted. But once he took his first drink...so sweet. So quick to ease the pain. He shook his head. The memories were muddled, but they were still there. Bloody brawls, boisterous singing, and busty women running their hands through his hair, along his arms and chest.

"At least I pushed them away." He coughed the excuse, his throat still too dry to make intelligible sounds.

The presence moved beside him, that same shushing sound announcing her nearness as she retrieved her blade from the ground.

Beyond the flashes, there were glimpses of faces drawing close. Sweet whispered words in his ear asking who he was, where he came from. He knew better than to answer truthfully. But it wasn't the truth, was it? Not anymore. So he lied. Loosened by mead, traitorous lips claimed he was the ghost of the Chieftain's only son. Then they pounced. Three, maybe four men? Maybe ten? It didn't matter. He tried to tell them that a Chieftain would never pay ransom for a son that wasn't his. That he didn't even exist. They didn't listen.

Their friendly hands became fists that flew into his gut, his cheek. His laughter only fueled their wrath, but the mead had numbed his nerves and his fear. What harm could come to a ghost?

He cackled through the beating, and when the terrified scream of their lookout reached them from the distance, he nearly rolled on the ground with his howls.

"What is that?" his captors had asked each other as they scurried around him with swords drawn.

"Oh, you are in trouble now," he'd chuckled, spitting blood on the ground at their feet. "My Little Bird is coming."

Then there was pain in his arms and a blow to his head that sent everything black.

"I do not suppose an apology would help?"

The presence huffed. When he finally forced his eyes open, the sight of her made him wish he'd been blinded by his attackers. Wish that she'd left him there to die.

Revna. His Little Bird.

She was perched on the lip of an overhanging rock, satchel at her side, legs dangling, toes skimming the ground. Her face was streaked with smudged kohl, black dirt, and dried blood. Her midnight hair was mussed, slick strands pulled from the tight braids along the side of her head. A long red cut along her arm peeked through the torn fabric of her tunic. There was a strip of cloth wrapped tightly around her thigh.

But it was her eyes. The utter emptiness of her sky blue eyes made him turn his face to the earth and press his forehead against the cold, wet ground. If only his heart were still quietly numb instead of trying to claw and scratch its way free from his chest.

He could hear the sound of her dagger flipping in her hands. And he knew it was because she allowed him to hear it. He deserved to hear it.

He remembered something else. Ethni's tears, her fearful expression as he spat harsh words in her face. And Conall. The man who once hated him almost as much as his father. The one who'd claimed Aksel was a better man than the Chieftain. He'd been there, too, fighting to save him.

"Where is Ethni? Conall?"

"Gone." Her always-hoarse voice was even rougher. As if she'd not slept at all. "They're all gone."

Gone on the boat she meant for him to board. He hadn't wanted to go. Now he'd gotten what he wanted. Why did that make him even more miserable?

"What did you have to do?" he asked, although he retained enough of his memories to piece it together. He deserved to hear it all in detail, to suffer the consequences of his actions.

He'd thought little of his indulgence in mead before, but now he realized, fully and completely, how much it didn't affect only him, but everyone he loved.

She sighed, long and sad. Aksel forced himself to look at her. Her eyes were closed, her head swaying as if she could deny that she had to do anything at all. She'd finally reached a place where she didn't thirst for violence, and because of his foolish tantrum, he'd all but held her captive and poured it down her throat.

He was on his knees, crawling because he couldn't walk. Crawling because he didn't deserve to stand. Cut ropes dangled from his wrists as he wrapped his hands around her calves, burying his face against her knees.

Above the stench of sweat and mead that permeated his clothes, the coppery tang of blood filled his nose. The smell of death. Proof of lives she had to take because of him. His mess she had to clean up. Because he'd been too weak to leave that mug on the counter—too weak to turn around and walk out the door. Because he'd walked away from her and Ethni. No, ran away. Like a coward.

All the hurtful words Revna had said suddenly made sense. This was why she wanted him to leave.

He was exactly who she said he was. A hindrance. A distraction. A drunk.

A silent sob shook his body, and he reached up. Staying on his knees, he wrapped his arms around her waist, tugging her to the edge of the stone until his head rested in her lap. If she would bury that dagger in his back, it would feel better than the agony ripping through him then. It would be a sweet mercy if she angled it just right to pierce his heart.

"I'm sorry, Little Bird." His words were nothing. Hardly more than a moaning curl of sound. He did not ask for forgiveness; he did not beg her to give him another chance. There were no chances left. "I'm so sorry."

The top of his head pressed against her stomach and he felt her tense and then shudder. He should let her go. Should scream at her to leave him in his filth and shame.

But he couldn't. He couldn't force his arms to let go. His shoulders trembled, but no tears came. What was broken inside of him was deeper than tears. No amount of weeping could touch it or piece it back together.

An T-aon is the great healer, Aksel. Ethni's words forced their way into his mind, piercing through guilt and shame. *There is nothing so broken He canna repair it.*

He wanted to believe that. With every bit of his shredded, ruined heart, he wanted to. Something held him back. A small voice that sounded so much like Tollak, telling him he wasn't worth mending, he wasn't worth saving. At that moment, he was inclined to believe that voice over Ethni's.

He didn't know how long Revna let him hold her. Long enough for his knees to scream in pain from the rocks beneath them. Long enough for him to hear the sound of her dagger being sheathed. For her small, trembling fingers to weave into his shaggy hair and clench the roots, tugging just enough for him to feel something other than heartache. Long enough for her to press her forehead against the back of his head and for the sound of her ragged breaths to tear down any stones left in the wall keeping his shame from consuming him.

Long enough for him to know that no matter what he did or how deep of a grave he dug for himself, she would not leave him there to die. She would haul him out at whatever cost. Because, unlike him, Revna did not leave her friends behind.

When she finally spoke, whatever pieces of himself that were still intact shattered like thin glass sheets of ice on frozen puddles.

"I know you think I am the champion of some worthy cause, but I am not a good person, Aksel. I'm not good for you. I planned to send you with them to the Vestlands—should have sent you. I had the chance when you were unconscious. But it seems I am even more wretched than I thought, because there has been nothing in my life I could not walk away from. Until you. I could not let you go." Her voice became a whisper. "And now we are both damned for it."

25

REVNA

825 AD : Three months later

The days were long and the nights warm. The sun rose, set, and rose again. Summer gave way to Autumn. Autumn slipped quietly into winter. Revna, Aksel and two of Randi's men traveled across the Northlands, falling into a practiced rhythm of marking buildings, terrifying freemen, and collecting enslaved Picts. It was a race against the coming frost, and Revna knew not to let the fact that the first snow had held much longer than normal fill her with false confidence.

After she'd rescued Aksel, they didn't mention the horrible things she said to him, Ethni's revelation, or his drunken response. She and Aksel had simply returned to Volfsby and said their farewells to Randi, who vowed to continue helping return their people to the Vestlands.

Their number had grown, starting with one chestnut mare Revna named Bonnie. When Aksel attempted to return the horse he'd stolen from the farmer in Volfsby, the man roughly handled the animal as if it were the horse's fault she was taken. Revna whispered a few threats that turned the man's pale skin green, and then she offered her sweetest smile as he handed her the reins.

Now, with nearly ten freed slaves in their group, it was time to return to Volfsby again and send them home. But Revna was resisting. Some irritating tug kept her from going back.

She'd listened to Ethni's warnings, though, and made herself the most welcoming representation of Tràigh she could be. She'd so immersed herself into caring for the ones they rescued, she could almost pretend the distance between her and Aksel didn't exist. That she wasn't about to burst from the need to repair what was broken between them.

When they reached the northern settlement of Trondheim, the first frost came on suddenly, as if it thought it was late for an important event and burst through the door in full force. She'd shivered herself to sleep the night before and found her hair frosted over that morning. It wouldn't be long before their travel was slowed by snow.

It was a Pict called Dugald that brought them all the way to Trondheim in search of his wife. Revna had been hesitant to travel so far with the current mix of freed Picts that followed. Trondheim was said to be the place to which outlawers escaped, and the Picts they'd collected were older and in poor health. The thin stretch of woods surrounding the settlement wouldn't be a safe haven, even with the added protection of Randi's two warriors. None among them were familiar with the region, and someone would have to travel to the settlement to find Dugald's wife.

Gavin and Elgin, Randi's warriors, were the chosen visitors, as they could easily blend in at the market of the small port city. They could inquire about trading weapons for their journey while discreetly slipping a talkative settler a few coins for information and secrecy. Revna paced the edge of the clearing where her little band had set up camp.

There was another reason she'd agreed to visit Trondheim. It was where Rune's family lived. The closer they'd gotten, the more she felt a burden to ensure his parents knew the truth about their son. That he was brave and kind. That he was more of a leader in his young years than the cowardly captain of that journey. That he had been her friend, even if for just a little while.

If they wanted the payment of her life for how Rune had died, she might let them have it. She was weary, and the fight she'd carried in her veins from childhood was waning.

But even with the burning in her chest to deliver that message and her vow to bring home every stolen Pict, something about Trondheim made her skin crawl. She couldn't get her people away quick enough.

When Gavin and Elgin returned, faces drawn, Revna's heart sank.

"Eilidh is gone," Gavin said.

"How can that be?" A broken voice sounded from the row of trees behind her.

Revna turned to see Dugald.

"I know she was taken here. Did they send her somewhere else?" His shoulders slumped and his arms hung limp at his sides, a much different posture than he'd held most of the journey.

Despite his age, he'd been an unstoppable force, determined to find his wife, who'd been taken away from him two winters past. Now, his frantic question had Revna squeezing her eyes closed, preparing herself for the news none of them wanted to hear.

He was supposed to be in the clearing with the others. She was supposed to have time to consider whatever word they returned with and make a plan. But he was here, and there was no time.

"I am sorry." Gavin took a step toward the gray-haired Dugald, but the old man curled away, as if repulsed by Gavin's words.

"No," Dugald begged, the word nearly solidified in the white cloud formed by his breath in the cold air.

"Eilidh succumbed to illness two months ago." Gavin was oddly gentle for his large size, delivering the news with such compassion it was clear he was genuinely broken for Dugald. "Despite the circumstances of how she came to be here, she was beloved by the family, and she was no longer a slave. They were going to help her find you; they were going to try and free you."

"No," Dugald said again, more forcefully.

"She is buried alongside the farmer's oldest child, who also passed."

Dugald sank to his knees. "Two months?"

"I am truly sorry." Gavin lowered his head before looking to Revna and dropping his voice so only she could hear. "It was the message of the Raven. That is what changed their hearts and made them free Eilidh."

His confession stole her breath for a moment. When she'd recovered, she gave him a nod of thanks, squeezing his arm.

"I will be along," she said.

Gavin offered a weak smile and trailed Elgin to the clearing where the rest of their people waited.

Revna joined Dugald on the ground. "I'll take you to her grave if you want."

"Two months," he repeated, his hands curling into fists as they rested on his thighs.

Revna didn't speak. There were no words to ease his pain, but she felt the weight of it. The questions that must have been swirling in his mind. What if they'd arrived sooner? What if he'd fought harder to keep her with him? A thousand different *what ifs* that could have changed the outcome. A thousand things that no longer mattered, because Eilidh was gone.

Revna pressed her hand to her chest. Would it ever get easier? Her list was almost complete. She didn't come to the Northlands for herself; she came to fulfill her vow to bring her people home. But she'd hoped that would be the key to easing the constant ache inside. She'd almost completed her mission, but the hole in her heart was as gaping as ever.

"Two months." Dugald was fuming now, rocking back and forth on his knees as he pounded his fists against his legs.

"Dugald." Revna reached for him but found herself forced onto her backside as Dugald launched himself to his feet. "Dugald?"

He was aimed for Trondheim. She scrambled up and hurried to his side. "Dugald, you cannot go there."

It was as if he didn't hear her, as if she wasn't even there. If he was intent on going, she wasn't strong enough to stop him without hurting him, and if she ran to the clearing for aid, he might reach the settlement before they caught up to him.

It was a risk, but she shouted the name of the person she needed most, "Aksel!"

Hands on Dugald's chest, she pushed against him, failing to slow the hearty Pict despite his age. His anger had given him strength, and he easily flung her aside, landing her on her backside again.

"Aksel," she screamed again, hauling herself up and into Dugald's path. Again and again he roughly tossed her aside until she heard the thundering of footsteps across the cold-hardened ground.

A felled tree broke her fall as Aksel's arms circled Dugald's waist, bringing him to the ground. Gavin and Elgin were on his heels, helping to subdue the grieving man.

"Let me go!" he wailed, arms flying. "I will kill them! They took her from me!"

"Taking their lives will not bring her back, Dugald, but it will cost the rest of us ours," Aksel argued, attempting to keep from hurting Dugald when the man's head crashed into his face, drawing blood from a split lip.

Gavin and Elgin tried to grab Dugald's flailing limbs. Revna watched, stunned that it took three younger, stronger men to subdue a single older one.

She was slow to rise, her arms burning from Dugald's bruising grip and her ribs aching from where they'd met the hard surface of the fallen tree. By the time she limped to Aksel, he had planted his knee in the center of Dugald's back and pushed his full weight into it, keeping the man from rising again.

Dugald's agonized groans seeped into the thick coating of dead leaves on the forest floor, and that sound hurt worse than any of her injuries, nearly sending her to her knees again.

Elgin offered his hand, but she waved him off, too out of breath to speak.

"Gavin," Aksel called as he wiped his mouth on his sleeve, smearing blood across his cheek.

Gavin replaced him, pinning Dugald to the ground, though the old man hadn't moved again—as if, once his body met the forest floor, the fight seeped into the earth. Gavin spoke soft words, soothing Dugald as he wept.

Aksel stood and stepped toward Revna but paused, as if unsure if he should approach.

"You came." Her voice trembled.

"Of course I came. I will always come for you." With pain-soaked words, Aksel grabbed her, crushing her to his chest. She felt his lips against her hair. "I thought...I do not know what I thought. I just had to get to you."

They'd barely touched since Volfsby. Even though they'd not spent more than a few hours apart, there had been an uncrossable chasm carved between them, dug with shovelfuls of regret and shame over their bad decisions. She'd missed him so much, it hurt to look at him.

Now she melted into his embrace. She let his strength envelop her, let the cocoon of his arms hide the tears that escaped. *Two months.* Dugald's words had gutted her. With their success in the last few settlements, she thought the worst was behind them. Until Eilidh. They'd been too late. That knowledge threatened to steal her breath, but Aksel's presence kept her lungs working and her heart beating.

She managed to dry her tears by the time he leaned back to examine her, but his eyes trailed the path they'd taken anyway.

"Are you hurt?" he asked, lifting her chin with a feather-light touch and turning her face to scan for injuries. She fought the urge to close her eyes and savor the feeling of his warm fingers.

"I will be fine." She tugged the cuff of her tunic over her palm and used the fabric to wipe blood from his face. "You?"

"Hardly felt it." He gave her a gentle smile, his thumb grazing her cheek before hooking his fingers around the nape of her neck and drawing her in until his mouth was at her ear. "Gavin says there are two Picts in Trondheim."

Revna pushed back far enough to meet his eyes. He'd spoken so softly, she was the only one who could have heard, and she glanced at Dugald. Gavin was now sitting next to him, his large hand resting on the man's shuddering shoulder.

Two.

There were two more names on her list. The two in Trondheim could be the last ones.

"Go." Aksel nodded in the direction of the settlement. "Take Gavin and Elgin. I will take care of him."

"You are certain?" She looked up at him, searching his deep blue eyes. He knew what names were on her list; since he'd first seen it, he'd studied it almost as much as she had.

"Yes." He brushed his lips across her forehead before moving to sit next to Dugald.

Her fingers danced across her skin where the warmth of his kiss lingered. When he looked at her again, she mouthed a thank you.

"I am sorry." The old man turned puffy eyes on Aksel, staring at the cut on his lip.

Aksel casually nudged him with his shoulder. "Do not think of it. All is well."

Gavin and Elgin moved to flank her. As they headed for Trondheim, she heard Dugald apologize again.

"We can go back to the clearing," he said. "I will not cause any more trouble."

"If you want," Aksel replied, supporting himself with his hands behind him. "But we can also stay here for as long as you need."

Dugald's response was another weak sob. "Thank you."

Before she got too far away to hear, she heard Dugald sniff and inhale a shuddering breath.

"Can...can I tell you about her?" He asked Aksel.

"I would very much like to hear about your wife, my friend."

She looked back to see Aksel's hand on Dugald's shoulder and the old man leaning into his side.

It was nearly midnight and Dugald was sleeping soundly at the clearing by the time Revna, Gavin, and Elgin returned with two women in tow. Aksel stood guard over Dugald still, and Revna did her best to feed the women and make them comfortable for the night. She missed Ethni's natural ability to soothe anxious hearts and care for people. She really was the mother hen Aksel claimed.

Revna's eyes met Aksel's, and she answered his silent question with a nod. All had gone well. Even the side journey he didn't know about.

She'd listened from a hidden place in the shadows as Gavin was welcomed into the home of Rune's father under the guise of a crew mate who had somehow survived that deadly voyage. Rune's mother wept and his father stood silent and proud as Gavin delivered Revna's message. She wished it was their son she was bringing home and not just tales of his courage. But it was all she had to give. That and Rune's beautiful dagger. It was finally returned to his home.

Even now, Revna's hand drifted to her side, to the place where she'd kept the weapon since the moment Rune had put it in her hand. It had always been a reminder to her of what she'd done—of the darkness that resided inside. But as she'd released it to Gavin, who would place it in the weathered hands of Rune's father, it seemed to glow under the rays of the sun. That brightness hinted that it wasn't a symbol of shadowed rage but a beacon drawing her toward the light all along. A reminder not of death and darkness, but of the hope Rune had found.

She looked to the star-speckled sky, her eyes burning with unshed tears. *If there are truly ears to hear, let them find their son again somehow. Mayhap in the eternity where he waits, if there truly is such a place.*

She'd sworn to believe in things she could see, hear, and touch, but for the first time, she wanted to believe the stories Cyrene and Isa told of a God who listened. She wanted Rune to have found his eternity.

When she finally lowered her head, she found Aksel still watching her. He tilted his head, his blue eyes looking deeper than Revna was ready to allow, and she focused her attention on the women she'd retrieved.

The next morning, Revna took the women to a secluded cave by a creek she'd discovered. The water was too frigid for bathing, but they were able to wash their faces and arms and change into clean clothes Randi had loaded into satchels before they left Volfsby. After ensuring they were fed and warm, she left them nestled under a shared fur by the fire.

Dugald's grief had taken a strange turn and sparked a sudden and intense need in him to serve and nurture the others in the group. He bustled about, doling out handfuls of berries, filling water skins, and ensuring everyone was well warmed with furs.

The morning was calm, and Revna didn't rush the people to get ready to move on. Gavin and Elgin had left before dawn to collect whatever offerings had been given to appease the wrath of Odin's ravens. Everyone could rest until they returned.

"They are related," Aksel said from where he leaned against a tree at the edge of the clearing, his arms crossed. "An aunt and niece."

"How do you know?" Revna looked up from reorganizing her satchel to the women, who were huddled so close they appeared as a single fur-covered lump.

"One of the others remembered them from when they were

taken. She said the aunt fought a Viking sailor off of her niece on the journey over. The girl was but four."

A bitter taste coated the inside of Revna's mouth, and she curled her hands around the leather strap of her satchel as she latched it closed. "I cannot imagine what sacrifices they made to stay together. Especially after all this time."

Aksel hadn't spoken in her language since they'd left Volfsby, and she hadn't either except to prove her identity to the ones they rescued.

"I suppose no sacrifice is too great for someone you love." His gaze was heavy, his words thick, and she felt like he meant so much more than what he'd said.

"Aksel." He was light and she refused to smother that with her shadows. She was prepared to tell him to keep his distance, but he pushed off the tree, rubbing his hands together and blowing hot air onto his fingers before he jerked his head toward the woods.

"Come, Little Bird. Let us take a look at your list and see where you think we should head next."

After a short trek through the trees, he climbed atop a gray rock with a sheared top and patted the empty space on his right side.

"Come on," he said again, wiggling his fingers to urge her on. "Get up here."

She sighed, sliding her satchel from her shoulders and laying it on the sun-warmed surface of the rock before scrambling up next to him. He held out his hand, waiting for her to give him the parchment that was so worn the names were barely legible.

"You know what you will see." She gingerly withdrew the parchment, careful of the torn edges and creases that had been folded and unfolded so many times, it was nearly worn in half.

"I want to see it anyway." He leaned over her shoulder, watching as she spread it across her lap. "Do you not want to savor this moment?"

She lifted a shoulder. "It does not feel real."

His hand rested on the surface of the rock behind her, his chest nearly touching her back. His panic-fueled embrace the day before was the closest they'd been since he'd crawled on his knees to wrap his arms around her in the clearing where she and Conall had fought off the six men who had taken him. Six men who were intent on sending bits of him to Kaupang until his father paid a price they demanded. The first one to die had his blade in one hand and Aksel's head braced against his knee, ready to take off his ear. By the time Randi's men arrived, there was only one remaining, and they'd chased him deep into the woods. He'd escaped.

But unlike before, and despite their vile plans, Revna felt no satisfaction in that violent victory. It sickened her, leaving her aching and empty.

Even now, knowing there were two men wandering the country-side who knew who Aksel was, her heart did not pound with the urge to hunt them down. She did not seek out the fight; she didn't want it.

She also wouldn't try to make him leave again. There was no use. They were not as close as they had been, but he was with her, she could breathe, and that was enough.

"Here." He withdrew a small cloth from the pouch he kept at his side and offered it to her.

"What is this?" She turned, finding his face much too close.

"Open it." He lifted his chin, motioning for her to take the parcel.

She did, revealing a small amount of dark berries.

"Do not eat these," he warned, a hint of amusement in his tone.

"I assume they are not blueberries."

"No. Not blueberries."

"What am I to do with them, then?"

He reached into his pouch again and drew out a stubby twig, whittled to a point at the end. "Ink the symbol."

Offering her the quill-like creation, he inched even closer, his breath warm on her neck. She stabbed at the berries with the stick until the sharp point was dripping with dark ink. There were two names without marks on her parchment.

She read them aloud. "Ishbel, and her niece, Cora."

"Cora has a spark, does she not?"

"Yes." Revna felt a proud smile on her lips. "She would have made a fierce warrior."

"Is there not still time?" Aksel leaned to better see her face.

She let her eyes meet his, the distance between them shrinking under the warmth of his blue irises. "I suppose there is."

Placing the ink-laden tip of the stick to her parchment, she drew a small cross shape by each name.

"Rescued," Aksel breathed.

She let herself feel that same relief as she scanned the page. There was not one name that didn't have a mark. Either a single cross shape for those they'd found alive or two for those who had not survived.

Every name had a story.

Every one of her people were found.

Almost.

She blew a gentle breath across the marks, urging the ink to dry. "As soon as Gavin and Egil return, we can trade for more horses and send them back to Volfsby with all our people." She folded the parchment, preparing to place it back in her vest.

"You still do not mean to go?"

She raised a shoulder again, a feeling of heavy sadness prompting her to draw her legs to her chest. He shifted, turning to face her as she rested her chin on her knees and wrapped her arms around her shins.

"Your list is complete." He picked up the purple-stained stick she'd laid next to the linen cloth.

"Your name is not on this list. We have found many others who were not recorded. How many were overlooked? How many are still waiting for someone." She kept her arms around her legs but watched as he absentmindedly marked the symbol they now knew to be a lion on the light gray of the stone.

"Ahh, but we do not know my name." He flicked his eyes up to hers without lifting his chin. "Do you intend to question every slave in the Northlands?"

For some reason, his question sparked a flame of irritation inside of her, and she lifted her head. "What if I do?"

He was calm, unbothered by the cut of her tone. "Then I will go with you." He continued his drawing. "But I do not think that is what you are doing."

"What am I doing then, oh wise Prince?"

"I think yer hiding." He said it in her native language. *His* native language. He normally used the language of the Norse when he was trying to draw out her secrets, but things had changed since Volfsby. Everything had changed.

She only snorted softly. Her secrets would stay hers.

"Ye like to think of yerself as this brave, fearless savior, and ye are doing a good thing, but yer also using them."

His face was dangerously close to meeting her fist.

"Glare at me all ye want, but ye ken it's true. Yer using them as an excuse not to go home and face whatever it is there that scares ye," he said.

She was off the rock and on her feet, her finger aimed at his face. "Nothing scares me but leaving my people to be forgotten."

"What happened in Volfsby?" He crossed his legs, too casual for the slicing words he was throwing at her.

She felt her face twist into a confused grimace and she answered in the same language. "I think ye ken—"

"No, I mean everywhere we've gone, ye've asked about yer sister. After Volfsby, ye stopped."

She stared, her gaze sliding back and forth between his eyes.

"Did ye think I forgot that ye announced, rather dramatically, that ye had a sister?"

"Nay, I..." She let her head fall back as her voice trailed off, staring at the leafless branches of the trees that cut stark, contrasting lines against the cloudless blue sky. Finally, she lowered her chin, aiming her gaze at the toe of her boot. "I received a message left by Isa's sister, Astrid. She said what I need to ken about my sister is back at home. Dunna ye think I would be there if I dinna have more to do here?"

"That's... Revna, that's what ye've been waiting fer. How can ye not go?" He slid off the rock to stand before her, his tone bright. As if he was ready to race for the first vessel that could carry them to the thing Revna had been chasing all this time.

"What if it is nothing?" Her arms snaked protectively around her middle.

He leaned in, his face even with hers. "What if it's everything?"

She only searched his eyes, as if the answer to his question hid there. He tilted his head, capturing her gaze, doing a little searching of his own.

"Is she the thing yer afraid of?"

"Astrid?" She scrunched her brow, confused.

"Nay, yer sister."

"Of course not." She turned away, catching herself about to fold her arms across her chest like a petulant child.

She didn't lie. Her sister wasn't the *only* thing she was afraid of back in the Vestlands.

"What is she called?" Aksel straightened, towering over her.

Revna was silent for a beat. "She doesna have a name. I mean, she dinna when she was taken."

"Mmm," he tilted his head, his demeanor still wholly casual. "I can relate."

Aksel leaned back on the stone, crossing his legs and letting his weight rest on his hands behind him. "I often wonder what my real parents would think of me, whoever they were. Would they be ashamed to call me son when they learned that I lived my life as a Norseman whose father owned and mistreated our people? Do ye wonder what she will think of ye, Revna?"

"Nay." That was a lie. Revna's fingers danced over all the places her blades were hidden. Was he asking for a fight? With the way her nerves were frayed at his invasive questioning, she was willing to oblige. Mayhap she deserved his cruelty after what she'd done to him on the riverbank.

"Do ye wonder what she will say when she finds out about the rage that lives inside of ye? All that ye've done?"

"Stop." Deserved or not, she could draw up enough leftover scraps of rage to give him a taste.

"What if she lived her whole life as a Viking? What if she owned slaves and became as cruel and heartless as Tollak?"

"Stop it!" She backed away, hands trembling.

"No." He pushed himself up and circled around her until she was backed against the rock he'd just abandoned. "We need to have this conversation."

"What do ye want from me, Aksel?" Her hands were balled into fists at her sides. "Are ye trying to hurt me? Is this because of what I said at the river? Do ye want revenge?"

He closed the space between them, placing a hand on the rock on either side of her, caging her in.

"I might want a little revenge, because I am just as broken as ye are." His eyes dipped to her mouth. "At least I am strong enough to admit it instead of marching around a foreign land blaming other people fer my faults and fears."

Her fist was flying, but he caught it. Curse him and his quick reflexes.

He caught her second swing too. Wrists wrapped in his fingers, she was trapped, her heart thundering.

"Yer asking to be stabbed fer real this time, Prince."

He had the nerve to smile. "If ye really meant that, ye'd have gone fer those blades I ken ye have hidden instead of swinging these tiny fists." He squeezed her wrists, taunting her.

He wanted a fight? Fine. With the tension they'd been ignoring for the past three months, they were long overdue. This morning it seemed things were finally healed between them, and now he was intent on tearing her heart to shreds.

In a move he didn't expect, she twisted both hands and her body at the same time, breaking his hold and spinning him around. She used his body as leverage and ran backwards up the rock until she was high enough to jump on his back and lock her arms around his neck.

"Let's see how smart yer mouth is wi'out breath."

Aksel launched himself back against the rock, driving the air from her lungs.

His voice was strained, but he rasped, "All this talk of mouths... are ye fighting or flirting wi' me."

Face flaming, she tightened her hold until he reached behind his back with one arm and grabbed her leg, swinging it to the side and forcing her to cling to him to keep from falling. While she kicked her other leg out, trying to use the rock to push herself back up, he pried her fingers back until she cried out.

Countering with a vicious move, she sunk her teeth into the exposed skin where his shoulder curved into his neck until she tasted blood.

With a grunt, he dropped to his knees, throwing himself to the side and driving that same shoulder into her gut.

"That was a dirty move not fitting an honorable warrior." He was breathless as he kept his weight on her and fought her flailing hands, trying to capture her wrists again.

"I never claimed honor." She slammed her forehead into his face, gritting her teeth at the flash of pain and stars. "Only victory."

Pulling up her knees, she managed to wedge her feet between them, planting her soles against his chest with enough force to create a small space. She walked up his body and kicked her feet over her head in a flip that had her landing in a crouch, facing him.

He shook his head free from the stun of her head slam and his lips peeled back in a wide, bloody grin that reignited her fury. "Are ye ready to admit I'm right about yer fears or does one of us need to break a bone?"

Ticking her head sharply to the side like the raven she was named for, she narrowed her eyes at him. "Now who's flirting?"

When he launched himself at her again, she repeated the limber move, backflipping just out of his reach. He was too quick, though, and his large palm was around her ankle, jerking her feet out from under her before she could land.

She squeezed her eyes closed, anticipating the crash of her head against the hard ground. It never came. Aksel had released her ankle and twisted one arm behind her back with such force she was immobilized and certain he'd left finger-shaped bruises on her skin. But his other hand flew under her head, taking the brunt of the impact between her skull and the ground.

He dropped his full weight on her so she couldn't move. He grunted when he realized he was also rendered helpless by the sharp point of the blade she'd unsheathed and had pressed against the pulsing vein in his neck.

They both gasped for breath. She wheezed under his weight, afraid to fully empty her lungs for fear they'd be crushed too much to allow an inhale.

Hand sliding gently from under her head to the ground next to her, he pushed himself up enough to relieve the pressure on her lungs. She kept her blade against his neck, but though he quit fighting, she didn't feel victorious.

"Revna," he breathed her name, his deep voice sending waves of gooseflesh across her skin. "I will go wi' ye to the ends of the earth. I will hunt down whatever ghosts ye need to find. I will fight whatever monsters come our way, but I would be one myself if I dinna help ye face the dangers wi'in yer own heart."

She opened her mouth to snap a sharp reply, but another voice answered for her.

"Well, what do we have here? A lover's spat?"

Aksel's hand was gone from her waist, and he dragged her to her feet, her blade at the ready. In their arguing, they hadn't noticed someone step from the trees. Eight someones.

26

REVNA

Two of them she recognized. One was the man from the clearing in Illrstaðr, the deserter who escaped, and the other...

"Torsten." It was Aksel that growled the name.

The despicable creature that kidnapped and tortured Isa leaned casually against a tree, cleaning his nails with the tip of a knife. Thanks to Revna, his right eye drooped a little and his nose was slightly off center, but even from that distance, she could see the light and dark of his mismatched eyes. He lifted his chin, the jagged scar across this throat peeking from under his unkempt beard.

There was another familiar face. She could not place him. He definitely knew her; he'd not taken his eyes off her for one second. And he had a raised pink mark on his forehead. A brand. He was an outlawer.

The outlawer narrowed his eyes at Aksel and glanced at the deserter. "Is this our ghost, Svikar?"

The deserter grinned, "Yes, it is."

"And our mysterious raven?" the outlawer asked Torsten.

Torsten's lips peeled back, revealing white rows of teeth behind his sinister smile. He didn't have the chiseled yellow fangs from her nightmares, but he was no less a monster. Revna readied herself, knees bent, arms loose at her sides.

The outlawer spoke again, eyeing Aksel. "Our quiet friend here says you tried to silence him to keep your little secret. You should have known better, son of Tollak." He flicked his eyes to Torsten. "There are more ways than words to send a message, are there not, Tor?"

Torsten released a silent laugh.

"And you," The outlawer narrowed his eyes on Revna. "Always sticking your nose where it does not belong. But it does not matter, does it?" He cocked his head to the side. "You are just as much a curse on your friends as you are on your enemies."

Revna stiffened, her muscles locked in a frozen cage. Who was this man?

"At least I get to be the one to break that curse," he said.

Torsten pushed himself upright, flipping his knife across his crooked fingers before pointing the end at Revna.

"I think Torsten has chosen the raven for himself." Svikar, the deserter, tipped his head back, releasing a cackle that rattled her bones.

Aksel stepped so close to Revna she could feel the heat of his body at her back. All thoughts of their own sparring match disappeared. Whatever battles they needed to have could wait.

"Tell me ye have blades to spare, Little Bird."

"I thought ye said I should use my words." She flipped the one in her hand until she gripped the blade, handing him the handle over her shoulder.

"Talk in your slave language all you want, but we know who waits in your little camp. Once we are finished with you, we will help ourselves to some escaped slaves and maybe take a trip to retrieve a moon-haired princess as well. I am certain she is missing you by now, right, Tor?" Svikar grinned at Torsten. He seemed too confident, as if eight men were more than enough to subdue her and Aksel.

"You will not touch any of them." Revna shifted her weight onto her toes. Somehow, Torsten was able to tell these men about Isa, which meant they knew she was in Volfsby. Revna was nearly vibrating with the need to protect her. For once, the mark on her chest warmed with what seemed like approval.

"Easy," Aksel breathed from behind her.

"If you come without a fight, we will return your stolen slaves to their masters with both of their eyes." Svikar looked to his companions, nodding as if to confirm they agreed to his condition.

"And what happens to us?" Revna asked.

Svikar huffed, the slow tilt of his head giving him a monstrous aura. "Your offenses are great, Raven."

Her gaze moved to the outlawer and then washed over the rest of them. Were all these men she'd offended somehow? Had they found each other by some supernaturally evil force?

The five she didn't recognize snarled and chortled like beasts from where they moved in slow steps until they formed a circle around her and Aksel. They didn't receive much attention from the outlawer, Torsten, and Svikar.

Nothing more than hired thugs. She could handle them with her eyes closed.

Eight. Revna counted again, just to make sure. She did worry about how many she could end before one got to the people at the clearing. If she could stall, Gavin and Egil would return. *Help. We need help.* The prayer slipped out before she could think.

"If it is rewards you seek, the Chieftain has been searching for his son. Have you not heard? He offers a great ransom for his return." Revna tried to keep her voice steady. "But he will want him alive and unharmed."

"Alive and unharmed?" Svikar's mocking tone dragged like talons down her skin. "How much more will he raise his reward when he receives his son's fingers, one at a time."

His friends laughed, inching closer.

"Only unharmed. The message has spread, or maybe you have been slithering under the rocks for too long to have heard it."

"I dunna think those are the words ye should be using." Aksel's voice was strained, his breathing as shallow as hers.

"But truly," Revna continued. "Why waste your time with the Chieftain? He will pay you once and dismiss you, or simply have you killed. But the mark of the raven...."

Torsten halted at that, lifting his hand to stop the others as well.

"People see the mark, and the offering stones are teeming with treasure the very next morning. Who is to say that Odin's wrath will ever be sated?"

"Clever Little Bird," Aksel breathed so quietly, none but Revna could hear.

The men exchanged a glance, and for a moment she thought she might have found a way out with her words. "Let us go. You will never see us again, and you can become the raven. You can live like kings."

Svikar flipped his blade in a wide arc once, snatching it out of the air by the hilt as he waited for Torsten's silent decision. The only answer he gave was a single step forward.

"I think we will take the mark, but—" he tossed his blade again, catching it by the grip. "Just to ensure you do not interfere, we will go ahead and take you too."

The circle tightened. Aksel and Revna moved until they were back to back.

"Aksel, I'm offering every chance at life, but I'm out of words."

"Ye did well, Little Bird. They've chosen violence. Unleash the beast."

"No honor," she whispered.

"Only victory." The words had barely left his lips when she advanced, her hands still empty, aiming for the biggest threat first— the hulking outlawer whose face swam somewhere in her memory but hadn't made it to shore.

He grinned, as if he were honored she chose him first. Torsten and Svikar had chosen her too, the other five nameless goons closing in on Aksel. She'd seen him fight; he could hold his own, at least until Gavin and Egil returned. The people at the clearing would tell them how long she and Aksel had been gone, and they'd come looking for them. They could survive this—they had to.

"I have been waiting for you." The outlawer moved quicker than Torsten and Svikar, loosening something that was strapped to his back with leather straps that criss crossed his broad chest. "What was it he called you?"

She didn't answer, for she'd nearly blocked out any sound but that of her pounding heart. They could call her whatever manner of foul names they wanted; they could insult and swear until their voices ran out. She would remain unbothered. The only thing that mattered was that she and Aksel kept breathing. That the people at the clearing were safe.

"Ah yes. Little Bird, was it not?"

The memory finally slid ashore, and in that split second, Revna's stealthy advance faltered. It was not even as long as it took to blink, but it was long enough for the man to see that his first strike had found its target.

Aksel had called her that, but only in a language this man didn't know. There was only one other person who said those words. And only one living person who could possibly know that. Everything he'd said finally made sense.

"Hello, crew leader." Revna flexed her hands, continuing her march toward the man who'd slain his crew and fled. She let her gaze linger on his brand. "I see your cowardice caught up with you."

That was all any of them were. Cowards. She'd make them flee again before the day was over. No.

They wouldn't live to run this time.

The thing the crew leader had been hiding came into view, and from his sneer, he expected Revna to quiver in fear, especially since he would think her unarmed. She only eyed the battle ax as if it were a twig, wholly unimpressed. He released a razing shout, storming forward with his weapon circling his head. It cleaved the air with a buzz, the blade glinting against the sun.

Revna didn't slow her advance, but just when the axe's blade would have sliced through the top of her skull, she dropped to her knees, sliding across the ground, blades sliding into her hands. Her arms flew out as she ducked between his legs. When she was clear, she raised one knee to stop herself. When she turned her gaze over her shoulder, Torsten and Svikar had stopped too, staring at the back of the crew leader, who swayed on his feet. All of their attackers froze.

The crew leader turned, his face still twisted with rage. He raised his ax again and barked a cough that sent a spray of blood speckling the ground. A red line raced across his split tunic. A momentary look of surprise had his mouth gaping before he dropped to the ground in a lifeless heap.

He thought he would best her, but she'd gutted him in seconds. Just like he'd done to the man from his own crew that she'd been forced to end out of mercy. She only wished it was Rune's dagger that delivered the final justice. Wiping her blades clean on the grass, she stood to face Torsten and the deserter, ticking her chin sharply to the side.

The crew leader was an outlawer, but he might have lived had he not joined this doomed crew. Doomed was exactly what they were.

"You can still run." Her voice was too soft. The mark on her chest pulsed with the demand that she offer one more chance of mercy. As long as they left her friends alone, they could live.

Only Svikar had the good sense to stifle a shiver.

The rest only growled and slung threatening curses at her. Chin lowered, chest heaving, her eyes darted between them, knowing what they would see behind the deceiving paleness of her eyes. Death. Though she no longer reveled in it, it was coming for them.

"No?" She cocked her head to the other side. "Very well then."

The clearing burst into action. Five aimed for Aksel and only two for her. What an insult. Still, she searched the trees for Gavin and Elgin.

The rage was quiet this time as Torsten and Svikar approached. It wasn't a howling wind that pulsed in her ears. It was a gentle breeze that held open welcoming arms. Mayhap it wasn't rage at all. As her body slipped into the ease of battle, she only thought of the two women huddled together by the fire. The way they'd clung to each other, never letting go even as they were rescued. She marveled at the strength that allowed them to endure unspeakable hardships simply for the hope of remaining together.

She'd known them less than a day but knew they'd have held on until death took them both. So would she. For Ishbel and Cora. For Dugald. For all the others who were ready to finally return home. For her sister who might be waiting for her there. For Aksel, who had never known what home could be.

Torsten unsheathed his blade, a silent fury flaming behind his two-colored eyes, and Svikar held a short sword in each hand. They'd positioned her between them, forcing her to swivel her head to keep them in sight.

A glance between them and they rushed her. Revna darted, jabbed, spun, and ducked. She rolled and crawled. Anything to keep their blades from meeting her bones. Torsten's blade caught her arm, but she ignored the sting. She didn't even look to see how deep the cut was. But as she leaped away from another of his advances, Svikar's foot shot out, catching the side of her knee and sending her to the ground.

She landed with a grunt, her fingers slipping on her own blade. Svikar sneered, sprinting the few steps between them, preparing to let his boot do more damage. Revna locked down the muscles of her stomach and drew in her arms in preparation for the blow just before Gavin and Elgin burst from the tree line. Revna held in her cheers.

Their shouts stunned Svikar long enough for Revna to regain the grip on her dagger and send it flying into his thigh.

He roared with pain, saliva shooting through clenched teeth as he jerked the blade from his leg and threw it to the ground. Daring him to approach, she let her remaining dagger dance across her fingers.

A pained grunt from Aksel drew her attention. Two of his attackers were on the ground, rolling from whatever thrashing he'd unleashed. The one he grappled with entangled both his arms while another man pushed himself up from the ground and slipped behind Aksel, blade raised and ready. Gavin and Elgin raced for him, but they were too far, and the other two men had moved to intercept their rescue.

Aksel jerked his opponent nearly off his feet before slamming his body to the ground, spinning at Gavin's shout.

From the ground, Revna rolled, avoiding another swipe of Svikar's foot as she drew her arm back and let her dagger fly.

Aksel's eyes widened at the sight of the man's raised arm and the death coming for him, but he stumbled back as the man released a pained scream and dropped the knife in his hand, Reyna's blade speared through his palm.

Aksel whipped his head in her direction and took a step before Torsten's grimace-twisted face filled her vision. She pushed up on her elbows, scrambling backwards, but he grabbed her legs, roughly dragging her toward him. Her head collided with the hard ground, sending a blast of light across her vision. She worked her legs, kicking to get free, but Torsten only released a breathy laugh.

Svikar stepped over her, one leg on either side of her torso.

"What will you do now without your blades, Raven?" Svikar's voice was haggard, his chest heaving, but he still laughed as he bent, spit dripping on her face.

She flipped to her belly, clawing at the ground as Torsten yanked her legs again, pulling her almost into his lap. When Svikar grabbed her arms and roughly turned her over, instead of trying to push away, she surged toward him. Her fingers latched onto the fabric of his tunic, and she pulled him down with such force that he lost his balance, nearly coming down on top of her.

She brought her face close to his, staring into his wide eyes as her lips peeled back and she spat, "I have another."

Hand still curled around the grip of the blade he never saw, she thrust her arm up, driving the knife straight into Svikar's heart. The shock stalled Torsten for a heartbeat. A heartbeat was all she needed. One perfectly timed moment of weakness, and she was able to pull back one leg and ram it into his gut.

Torsten doubled over, and she dragged herself from under Svikar's dead weight.

Gavin was nearest to her, drops of sweat flying from his shaggy brown hair. He dropped his attacker with a single slice of his blade. Now they were down to five. They could survive this.

"Get to the clearing. Get them out." Revna's order went unheard as blades collided.

She would have to go; she could give the warning to run and hide before coming back to help. They could all still live. The gruesome sound of metal searing through flesh had her spinning.

Gavin was on his knees, wide eyes turned to the sky as another of Torsten's men withdrew his bloodied sword from his chest.

"Gavin!" Revna's scream echoed through the forest.

The gentle warrior fell. Elgin's roar shook the trees as he launched himself at Gavin's killer.

Then she was hit with a force so hard it sent her head flying backward, her mind spinning. Torsten had barreled into her, taking them both to the ground.

He straddled her, knocking another blade from her hand as she swiped at him. Then his backhand to her face stole the air from her lungs.

The coppery tang of blood coated her mouth, and she spat it back in his face, making him flinch. "Is this what you did to Isa?"

Her words were labored, but she said them anyway as she continued to wrestle with him, his weight on her hips keeping her from bucking him off.

"You like to hurt those weaker than you?" She let him think he was stronger; let him think he was winning.

From over his shoulder, she heard Aksel shout her name. Between them, there were two more bodies on the ground next to Gavin's. The forest swallowed her agonized cry at the sight of Elgin's brown eyes fixed on the sky. He'd fallen but taken another of their attackers with him. There were still four including Torsten. Two held Aksel's arms, one still wincing at Revna's dagger wound in his palm. A third drove his knee into Aksel's gut and then a fist into his chin. Torsten moved on top of her, catching her wrists as she went for the blades still stashed on her body.

"You are nothing but a coward!" she screamed as his fingers bit into her flesh, his grip so hard she felt her bones tremble.

Her insults only strengthened Torsten's rage, and he landed another blow to her face with his open palm. The sting seared her cheek, blinding her again for a moment. He was too heavy, his hands too strong as he grasped both her wrists in one palm and raised her arms above her head.

She turned her head, refusing to let him see what was swirling in her mind. She'd made the worst mistake a warrior could. She'd let him get his hands on her.

Cheek pressed against the musky forest floor, her eyes watered but caught a movement in the trees. Slipping quietly from one tree to the next was Cora.

Only four when she was taken, the horrors she'd survived had turned Cora into a lithe young woman with fire in her eyes. Revna recognized the stance—the way she bounced on the balls of her feet. She had a warrior's heart, but she had no weapons.

Revna thrashed until Cora's eyes met hers.

"Nay," she rasped.

Torsten's hands tightened, thinking she was talking to him.

"Get them out. Take the horses. Run." She turned her face to Torsten again, snarling words that sounded like threats in her native tongue. Words she knew Torsten would not understand but Cora would. "I will find ye."

When he struck her again, her vision flashed black. When her sight returned, Cora was gone. Torsten lowered himself until his chest was nearly flush with hers.

"It is my turn now." His words were nothing but rasps—a breath with no voice—but she heard him nonetheless. "My new *stjarna*."

Then his hand moved around her throat.

27

AKSEL

His muscles screamed against the strain, but the two men holding him didn't let go. The one in front—the one blocking his view of Revna—landed another hit to his gut, driving the breath from his lungs.

"Revna," he coughed through a gag.

Torsten had her on her back, straddling her legs, pinning them to the ground. She kicked and twisted, but his hand was locked around her throat and her movements were slowing.

Aksel kept screaming her name until his voice was nothing but a hoarse whisper, as if the wind from his breath could knock Torsten away from her.

Everything was a blur as he twisted his body with a roar. Nearly tearing his shoulder from the socket, he freed one arm. His fist met flesh and bone, he didn't even flinch when the skin of his knuckles split before his arm was captured again.

"Take me. I will do whatever you want, just let her go." Rough hands pinned his arms back, and no matter how he strained and fought and begged, they would not release him. His brain whirled with panic, trying anything to get them to stop. "Please. Let her go. You do not need her. She is worthless."

Revna worked a hand free and landed a blow against Torsten's side with her balled fist. It stunned him, but not long enough. When he raised his arm, Aksel saw the glint of a blade aimed for her chest. Torsten had no voice, but his lips moved, and Aksel's vision went red as he imagined the foul curses Torsten was breathing over Revna.

"No," he roared.

He was no longer begging the attackers. He was begging the God of his people. His true people. A God he barely knew. *He hears me.* Ethni's words exploded in his mind. *He hears me.* She'd said it so many times.

He called out as loud as he could, "*An T-aon*! Please. Hear me."

Torsten's arm fell and Aksel forced himself to keep his eyes open. If this was the end, she would not go alone. Never alone.

But Revna's other arm was free, her fingers curled into claws that dug into Torsten's face, her thumbs pushing against his eyes. His mouth gaped, but no sound came out as blood dripped from where one of his eyes used to be.

Yes! Fight, Little Bird. Live.

Torsten's hands flew to his face, earning her enough reprieve to free her legs. She twisted her body in the same move that had freed her from Aksel's own trap earlier, and Torsten's neck was trapped between her thighs, his body flipped until he was on his stomach. She was alive, but Torsten still had the blade, and he was pulling his arm from beneath him.

Nothing mattered. Not the pain in his side from the blow that cracked his ribs. Not that he was nameless and without family or home. Not that most of his life had been a lie. Not the horridly painful words Revna had said to him on the river at Volfsby. In that moment, all anger melted away under the burn of his need to get to her.

No honor. Only victory.

With a roar that rivaled the lions he'd always drawn, Aksel used the leverage of the two men holding him to lift both feet off the ground. He slammed his boots into the chest of the man in front of him, sending his attacker reeling backwards. The man's head snapped back and met the unforgiving trunk of a tree, and then his body dropped limply to the ground. Aksel's unexpected move had thrown both men holding him off balance, but he caught himself before following them to the ground. To one, he gifted the toe of his boot to the side of his head and to the other a fist to his nose. Blood pouring down his face, the man was still blinking when Aksel's foot met the side of his head too. The man didn't get up. The first had managed to drag himself to his feet, but he was still bent, trying to catch his breath. The top of Aksel's knee met his face, and when it sent him flying upright, Aksel's hammered elbow to his skull had his eyes rolling back in his head.

Aksel didn't wait to make sure he stayed down. He flew to Revna. Torsten was still fighting, but not nearly as vigorously. She had his arm stretched out and twisted at a painful angle, his blade rendered useless. With her legs clamped around his neck, his face was nearly blue, but she was tiring and he was close to wiggling free. Aksel again let his boot finish the job, and Torsten went limp. Aksel wrapped his arm around Revna's waist and crawled away from Torsten, her body curled to his chest.

He looked over his shoulder; Torsten remained still. Breathless, he laid Revna on the ground, grabbed her face gently, and pressed his forehead to hers. She fisted her hands in his shirt.

"Yer alive." His mouth was so dry, the words stuck to his lips.

"I tried to use my words."

"I ken." He swallowed hard, still trying to force air into his lungs. "I ken; ye did good."

"I only killed two."

"They deserved it," he laughed, but when he drew back, her eyes flicked to something over his shoulder.

"Aksel!" The panic in her voice drove him to turn, but her fingers gripped his arm. When he moved to see what it was, her hand tightened, stilling him.

She held his eyes, and in their reflection, he could see a figure dragging itself up from the ground.

"Is this where ye tell me ye have another?" he whispered, praying again to *An T-aon* it was true.

With the hint of a grin, she produced a dagger from somewhere unseen and pressed it into his palm. He matched his breath to hers until she gave him the slightest of nods.

Releasing her, he spun on his knees, using his arm to scoop Torsten's legs from under him. He launched himself over Torsten's sprawled body,

"Stop now and live." The grunted offer was denied as Torsten fought for the blade, bending Aksel's wrist in an attempt to push the weapon back into Aksel's chest.

Using the force of his full weight, Aksel overpowered Torstens's attempts and drove the blade straight down through bone and vein. Aksel hovered, pushing the dagger even further as Torsten jerked beneath him. With his one remaining eye, Torsten met Aksel's unflinching glare.

"You could have lived. But you chose to die. So, this is for Isa." Aksel let his words drip onto Torsten's vile, evil face as he twisted the blade one way. "And this is for Randi." He twisted the blade again, holding it in place until Torsten's chest stopped moving and his fixed gaze was forever unseeing.

Breathless, he jerked Revna's dagger free as he pushed himself up to his knees.

"I admit it," he said, as he scrambled away from Torsten's lifeless body. "I should have let ye end him the first time."

Revna was still on the ground when he reached her, and all semblance of victory faded at the pale sheen that overtook her normally olive-colored skin. He scanned her body, eyes going wide at a dark stain blossoming across the lower part of her vest.

321

"I tried...to use...my words." Something rattled in her chest, and Aksel's hands were tearing at her vest and the tunic underneath.

Blood. There was so much blood. He pressed his hand over the wound on her abdomen. Hot, thick liquid seeped through his fingers.

Her eyes fluttered. A single tear escaped and rolled down her cheek.

"No." He wrapped his free hand around the back of her head, keeping the other on her wound. His blood-coated fingers tangled in her hair. "Revna. No."

"Take them home."

"NO!" Her eyes opened at his roared denial. "You will take them home. You, Revna."

She nodded, but didn't move.

"Tell me what to do." His voice was little more than a broken groan, his throat so tight the breath could barely pass, his voice rising with each word. He slipped back and forth between the Norse and Pictish tongue. "I dunna ken what to do, tell me. Tell me what to do."

A plan. He needed a plan. But his mind was only a storm of panic. He couldn't snatch a single thought from the torrent of swirling desperation. His eyes burned, salt water blurring his vision.

When Revna rescued him from his own stupidity in Illrstaðr, he didn't believe he could truly receive the healing Ethni said her God offered. But as he stared at Revna, watching the life flow out of her with every beat of her heart, he cried out not for himself, but for her.

He didn't know if Ethni's God required sacrifices or ceremonies. If He demanded flowery language or rehearsed songs. Aksel had none of those to offer. He only had his broken, desperate heart, which he would pull from his own chest and gladly hand over if it meant Revna would live.

He pressed his palm harder on her wound as he prayed again, uttering a simple rambling prayer, not knowing what else to say. *Hear me. Please. I dunna ken what to do. What do I do?*

It was Revna who answered, though. He hadn't realized he'd said his prayer out loud.

"S-stop." Revna's rasped reply shot a jolt of hope through his chest.

"I willna stop. I ken it hurts, but ye have to fight."

"S-top the bleeding," she breathed. "Ye idiot."

Her insult was the most wonderful thing he'd ever heard. She was still here. Still fighting. He looked around. Her satchel lay on the rock where they'd been sitting before their argument. A quarrel that felt so meaningless now.

"Do not move." He placed her own hands on her wound and only released her for the seconds it took to race to the stone and snatch the satchel by its strap. Back at her side, he emptied the contents on the ground, grabbing a bit of linen she'd stolen from one of the freemen's longhouses when they'd collected more of her people. It had been delicately embroidered with colorful floss. She'd said Alpia would like it. Now it was pressed to her side, soaked red with her blood.

"I suppose 'tis a good thing we are still working on the thievery."

She coughed a weak laugh. "Not a battle ye can win."

"Fight me. Like I told ye. Ye fight me, Little Bird." He roughly shoved the contents of her satchel back inside the bag and slung it over his shoulder. Then his arms were under her, lifting her body. The men who still breathed were down but not dead. He could take the time to make sure they didn't rise, or he could help Revna.

Revna. Always Revna. He was moving in the next breath.

A plan. He needed a plan. One of the people they'd rescued might know what to do. He aimed for the clearing.

"They're gone," she breathed.

"What?" His steps slowed but didn't stop.

"Cora came...I told her to get them out. They're gone."

He stopped then, his heart sinking in his chest.

"R-river." As if she could hear his thoughts, she groaned from her place in his arms, and he curled her small form against his chest. "The cave."

The river wasn't far, and the cave was safe from beasts. "'Tis a good plan. I ken ye hate it, but yer going to have to let me carry ye, just this once."

"As ye wish," she echoed words he'd said to her once, very near the first time he'd tried to carry her.

"Keep talking to me. What should I do next?"

She didn't answer, and he jostled her in his arms, making sure the linen stayed pressed against her side.

"Wash in the water."

"Very well, ye needed a bath. I dinna want to say anything before, but the smell was getting unbearable."

Revna's head knocked against his chest, the thump a welcome ache. "Yer stench will kill me before his..." Her breath hitched and she wheezed. "...his blade."

"Enough jesting. Save yer words fer something useful." He laid her on the ground inside the mouth of the cave and scooped up water with his hands, cleaning her wound. She jerked against the chill, and he muttered an apology.

She was still bleeding, but he felt a warm flash of relief across his skin when he saw the wound wasn't very deep. He shared his discovery with Revna. Her eyes were closed, but she nodded in acknowledgement, and he found himself thanking Ethni's God.

Using one hand to brush the wild strands of midnight hair from her face, he pressed the linen against the wound again. "What now?"

He had a few ideas, but he needed her to stay awake, to keep talking to him. To prove that she was fighting.

"Herbs." Her hand shot to her side as she sucked in a sharp breath.

"I ken it hurts. I'll fix it, just keep breathing." He looked around the cave with a foolish notion that he'd find those herbs growing in a magical underground garden. "What herbs? What do they look like?"

"My s-satchel."

"They're brown?"

She lifted the hand on her side and smacked his arm, immediately hissing in pain. "In my satchel."

For once he celebrated her violence. "Ye can pummel me all ye want as long as ye keep talking."

Revna's body jerked as if lightning had reached from the heavens and seized her. He was over her, one hand still holding the cloth and the other cupping her cheek.

"Revna."

Her breaths were shallow. Too shallow.

"Revna," he said, more forcefully. "Quit being a bairn and tell me what to do wi' the herbs."

When she didn't answer, his heart clenched so hard in his chest he thought it might have stopped. How he wished Ethni was there. She would know what to do. He felt so very useless—so helpless. His forehead met Revna's, his breath bathing her face with prayers. "Please. I canna lose her. I canna."

"The only bairn here is ye." It was so soft he wasn't sure it was real.

"Yer right." He brushed her hair from her face, over and over, needing to touch her. To feel the warmth of life on her skin. "I'll stop crying if ye tell me what to do."

"Crush them." He drew back just enough to see her lips move. "Make a p-paste."

It took him half a heartbeat to realize what she meant before his shaking fingers closed around the strap of the satchel, jerking it close. After too long of using one hand to fumble with what was inside, he dumped the entire bag out again. Small linen-wrapped bundles spilled across the dirt. There were so many; he didn't know what any of them were.

"Which ones?"

He froze when Revna began to rasp out a haunting song. "Elder, elder, make ye weller. Clove, clove is a trove, and juniper..."

Aksel picked up several, turning them over in the hand he wasn't using to hold the cloth to her side. He had no idea which was which.

"'Tis a lovely song, can ye sing it again?" She didn't answer. "Revna, which ones? I dunna ken..."

Her jaw was slack, tension released from her shoulders. A jolt of panic locked his muscles in place, and for a split second his breaths stopped. Everything stopped. But his eyes grazed her chest, covered by her torn, bloody tunic. It still rose and fell. She was still alive.

He picked up the herbs, repeating her ragged rhyme as he examined each one, lifting them to his nose. Clove was easily distinguished, and the elder he knew to be a berry, so the deep red beads gave it away. But juniper—he had no idea what that looked or smelled like.

Juniper. He examined one bundle after the other. Juniper, juniper. Panic rose again, his pulse slamming against his neck. *Help. I need help.*

From the deep recesses of his mind a woman's voice hummed the rhyme. *Elder, elder, make ye weller. Clove, clove is a trove, and juniper, wi' berry black—three together snatch ye back.*

May the God above all gods bless ye, Ethni. It must have been her.

"'Tis well, Little Bird. Ye'll be well." He removed the cloth from her side long enough to tear a strip from the bottom. She groaned when he lifted her body to wrap it around her, and then again when he tied a tight knot, securing the wadded fabric to her injured side.

"I ken," he whispered, placing his hand on her cheek, patting gently. "I ken it hurts, but ye are the Raven. Freer of slaves. Burner of worlds. Ye dunna care about pain. Ye fight death back until he cowers in his grave." He gripped her chin, not caring about the blood he smeared on her face. It only made her look more like the warrior she was. "I ken ye can hear me. Ye fight. Beat him back. Send him to the deep where he belongs. Ye. Dunna. Give. In. No honor. Only victory."

He snatched the three parcels of herbs and moved to the edge of the river. Using a rounded stone and one smooth one with curved sides, he ground the herbs as he'd seen Ethni do a hundred times, mixing them with a bit of oil from a small glass jar he found amongst Revna's things.

He dipped the small scrap of linen that had been wrapped around the oil in the clear river water and cleaned her wound again. The bleeding had slowed enough that he could apply a thick coat of the paste. She jerked when it first touched her skin, and a soft moan slipped through her lips.

"This is nothing," he reminded her. "Ye are the raven. Yer name alone brings fear into the hearts of Viking warriors and levels entire settlements. There is nothing that can shake ye." He wasn't sure who needed to hear it more, Revna or himself. "Ye will live."

He scooted back against the cave's smoothest wall and hooked his hands under her arms, tugging her with him until her back was against his chest. The ground against the wall was slightly lower than in the middle, leaving their feet elevated like they were cocooned in an earth-shaped hammock. His breathing was heavy when he slid one arm around her, holding her close. With his free hand, he pressed her head over his heart, holding it there.

"Ye hear that?" he whispered into her hair. "As long as my heart beats, yers will too. Ye dunna get to go first, Little Bird. Ye dunna give in."

He listened to her breaths until the last bit of light faded and they were entombed in frigid darkness. They needed a fire, blankets, and food. But he could not leave her; he could not peel his arms from around her even though there was nothing else he could do. He was at the end of himself.

Revna needed healing—she needed help, but so did he. He needed all the things that Ethni's God offered. If he was truly a Vestman from birth, he must have his own knowledge of *An T-aon* buried inside somewhere.

Squeezing his eyes closed, Aksel plundered the depths of his mind for the proof that all Ethni said was true. He needn't search far, for just atop the surface waited confirmation from Isa, Randi, and all the memories of Ethni's constant reminders in his life.

Whether His name be *An T-aon* or the Christ, He was not a god who sat atop a golden throne demanding His creation scratch and claw their way to Him. No. He left His perfect home. He came for His lost children, and He gave His life for those who could never repay that debt—for those who could never earn His love.

Tollak may have been right that Aksel was a broken, unworthy wretch of a man. His best efforts were not enough, and he was utterly rotten and ruined inside. But as Aksel held Revna's unconscious body in his arms, he was emptied of all those efforts, and he knew that how Tollak saw him wasn't his whole story. He could be made new.

In the utter silence, he could almost hear an unearthly voice calling his name, calling him home.

And in the blackness, he spoke again to Ethni's God, for Revna and for himself. *Let her live. Please let her live. I will do anything. I have nothing to give, but I will serve ye all my days. Forgive me. I am so lost, I canna see my way back, but Ethni says ye can lead the way.* He squeezed his eyes closed, pressing his lips to her hair. *We both need yer help. Please let her live. Save her. Save me. Make me new.*

28

REVNA

Pain. The first sensation Revna could name was pain. A deep ache in her side burned every time she inhaled and pulsed with each exhale. Then there was cold. It was all around. Seeping through whatever hard surface was beneath her back, through her clothes and skin, sinking into her bones and whispering across her cheeks. If she could open her eyes, she would surely see her breath in clouds of white.

Slowly, muddled thoughts turned from mist to shadow and shadow to form. Her body was cold, but there was a warm presence at her side, something that brimmed with life. She reached for it. At least, she wanted to reach for it. Her arms were weighted or had simply ceased to function.

She tried to speak, but her throat was burning and raw. A soft groan was all she could manage.

The warm presence beside her shifted. A rope of heat coiled around her, gently curling her closer until she was enveloped in the calming, heated blanket.

A deep, soothing voice spoke softly. Telling her to sleep. To breathe. To live.

So she did.

When her mind flared to life again, the pain was still there, but the ache was not so deep. The cold was gone. She rested against something warm, her head on a pillow that was not soft but not uncomfortable. Then her firm pillow moved along with the presence at her side. The presence that breathed.

Crusted with sleep, it took her a moment to peel her eyelids open. It was dim, but the faint blue light of early morning illuminated her surroundings. A curved rock ceiling was so close above, she'd almost touch it if she raised her hand. The sound of flowing water echoed off its glistening walls and filled the cavern with constant soothing noise.

She flexed her fingers, relieved they obeyed. A thick fur explained the heaviness anchoring her arms. There was also something else—something even weightier—atop the blanket. Something that flexed when she moved.

She let her head slowly turn to the presence at her side, pain shooting through her skull with each inch. But she needed to see. To see him.

Aksel.

His eyes were closed, his breaths deep. Her head rested on his arm, which was stretched under her. His other was the weight across her chest. The fur, a barrier between them, was tucked snuggly around her.

Despite the flames that licked down her throat when she tried to swallow, she smiled, the action cracking her dry lips.

He lived. She lived. Victory.

She closed her eyes, inhaling his familiar scent. When she opened her eyes again, he was watching her, his lips curved into a soft smile.

"There's my Little Bird." His voice was so low, chills raced over her skin despite how warm she was.

He lifted the hand draped over her torso and dragged his fingertips lightly across her face, brushing back strands of hair that

330

curtained her forehead. He slid a hand along her cheek, his fingers curling around her neck just under her ear. When he stroked his thumb along her jaw, chills melted into flame. Then he drew her close, pressing his lips to her forehead.

"I had to leave ye," he said without releasing her. His words were a whispered confession against her heated skin. "Just long enough to get supplies, but it killed me. Every second I was gone. Every second I didn't ken if you would live—it killed me."

His forehead met hers, and she closed her eyes as she knew he had done. They breathed in each other's air.

"I've never been so terrified." His words were soft. Broken.

She wanted to answer but couldn't peel her tongue from the roof of her mouth. Her insides were dried up, blood replaced with sand that gritted in her veins. If she could crawl, she would plunge herself into the stream that taunted her with its promise of clear, crisp water.

Aksel leaned back and smiled down at her, wearing that same reassuring but concerned expression. His gaze fell upon her throat as she attempted to swallow and his brows drew together.

"Ye need water. Can ye sit up?" He lifted her head, freeing the arm under her.

She nodded, wincing at the flames that seared across her middle when her muscles tightened.

"Take it slow. Let me help ye." He pushed himself to sit up, the top of his head nearly brushing the rock ceiling above them.

Carefully, slowly, he lifted her and shifted behind her so that she sat between his legs and leaned against his chest. Air flew through her clenched teeth as she bit back a string of curses.

"Yer not going to stab me, are ye?" Aksel's breath was hot on her neck. "Ye threatened to do such violent things in yer sleep; I need to ken if I should run."

She blew out an amused breath but speared him with a questioning glance as she noticed the tunic she wore was unfamiliar and much too large.

331

"Yers was ruined." Some dark memory had him clenching his jaw, but with a breath, he donned a smirk and winked at her. "Dunna worry—it was dark. I dinna see anything."

Her narrowed glare had him releasing a soft chuckle as he turned her to rest her back against his chest. "I ken, I am a rogue."

His hands moved up and down her arms while she tried to remember how to breathe through the pain in her side. If she could speak, she would have said she noticed he had placed her weapons on the other side of the cavern out of reach. Even in her delirium, her eyes couldn't help seeking them out.

A water skin was against her lips, and she opened her mouth, letting him tip in small sips until she could swallow without wincing.

"Better?" His hands were on her arms again, soothing her.

"Aye," she managed to croak. "I see ye found all my blades."

He had found all of them. Every single hidden one. He stiffened, a soft chuckle blowing against her skin.

"Uh, aye, I was making sure ye werna injured anywhere else."

"Yer right. Ye are a rogue."

"My intentions were wholly pure." His voice dropped to a low, teasing growl.

"Ow," she grunted at the chuckle she couldn't control. "Dunna make me laugh."

"This is where ye'd tell me it was but a scratch and to stop whining like a bairn."

"I dare ye."

"Nay, I value my life too much." He laughed, but curiosity sent her hand to her side, her fingers gingerly roaming over the strips of cloth that encircled her waist. They were snug but not too tight. She could feel the ache of the wound beneath, but she did not burn with fever.

"Aksel?"

"Mmm." Aksel's hands moved from her arms to her head,

brushing back her hair or stroking her jaw, as if he needed to be continuously reminded she was there. That she was alive.

She found herself cherishing each of those touches. She was in the worst pain of her life, hiding in a frozen, damp cavern from a group of men who wanted to slice them both up. She was hungry, tired, lost...but also the safest she'd ever felt.

"Ye were right about something else too," she whispered.

"What?"

"Ye said I was blaming the people here fer my faults and fears."

He shifted then. "Revna, I——"

She wrapped her hand around his forearm, stilling him. "Let me just...get this out."

"Very well." He relaxed, his hands continuing their lazy path up and down her arms.

"I do want to rescue all of my people that I can. That is not a lie, but ye were right that I have been using them to keep me here." She closed her eyes and drew in a deep breath. "And it is because I abandoned my queen."

Aksel's hands stopped for a moment before moving again.

"I left our homeland wi'out explanation and before ensuring she was safe. I was so angry." When Aksel's lips pressed against the back of her head, she forced herself to keep going. "The king showed mercy to the Norsemen who had come to kill and enslave, and I couldna accept his ruling. I intended to let that ship arrive on shore wi' none alive."

"That wasna what happened, was it?" Aksel's words were muffled against her hair.

"Well, it did, but it wasna because of me. That is why one of those men recognized me. He was the reason the crew died." She squirmed at the memory of Rune's amber eyes. "And ye were also right that I am afraid of what my sister will think of me. Of what I will think of her. But I am even more afraid of facing my queen."

Aksel wrapped his arms around her, squeezing slightly, though not enough that it hurt.

"Do ye remember Randi's face when she saw Isa fer the first time?" he asked.

"Aye, how could I forget?"

"Do ye not think yer queen's will look much the same? Dinna ye say she is like kin?"

"The closest thing I have."

He lowered his head until his mouth was by her ear. "Dunna be afraid then, Little Bird. She will forgive ye fer whatever yer faults may be just to have ye in her arms again. Trust me."

Revna felt a smile tugging at her lips as she nestled further into his embrace. "Are ye speaking from experience, Prince?"

"That I am."

All the angst, longing, and fear that had fueled her rage was dulled to nearly nothing under the comfort of Aksel's steady heartbeat. But it wasn't just him. Some other presence was there with her too. The same One that Ethni said would soothe her through terror-filled nights. The same One that let them hear Isa's silent screams. She suspected that presence had a hand in why she was still breathing. There was only one thing on her tongue to say.

"I think I'm ready to go home now."

"Aye?" Aksel's amused response was light, drawing a smile from her lips.

She nodded under the heavy weight of his cheek resting on her head.

"If I'd kent all it would take was nearly dying, I could have done that ages ago. Or is it the fact that all of the Northlands now kens that the Chieftain's son is alive and the raven is naught but a wee little lass?"

"Give me my blades. I think I really will stab ye this time."

"As long as yer breathing, ye can stab me as many times as ye want." He turned his head, pressing his lips to her temple.

She laughed and then groaned at the ache.

"Something happened last night." Aksel wrapped his arms around her.

She settled into his chest again, relishing the warmth. "Other than me getting stabbed?"

"Other than that. Ye fell asleep before——"

She turned her head sharply, looking up at him. "I fell sleep? Warriors dunna 'fall asleep,'"

The corner of his mouth ticked up before the flex of his muscles coaxed her to relax again. "Very well, battle fatigue stole yer consciousness before ye could tell me all the herbs. I dinna ken what to do. So..." He took a deep breath, as if gathering his courage. "So, I prayed to Ethni's God. The one she calls *An T-aon*. I asked for help."

Revna looked up again, meeting the blue eyes that stared down at her. He dragged the back of his hand slowly down her cheek.

"He answered me. It wasna the first time either. That was when I thought Eira was in trouble. Then again when we were fighting those men and I couldna get to ye, but somehow I broke free." He searched her face. "I swear I saw ye die, and I begged Him to let ye live. Somehow, ye did."

Revna's breath rebelled against her lungs, a tightness seizing the muscles in her chest. He held her gaze captive for a heartbeat before letting his head fall back and rest against the rock wall behind him.

"I used to think the stories Ethni would tell me were meant to make me feel better. To give me something to dream about," he said to the ceiling. "But they werena just stories. They were all true."

"I'm beginning to think so too."

He lifted his head, slowly shifting her to the side so she was sitting up, his legs on either side of her and one arm still behind her back. He drew up one leg, letting his free arm rest on his bent knee.

"Aye?" he asked.

"Aye. I just said as much." It was unnatural to be caged like that, trapped between him and the cave wall. Uncomfortable to be so vulnerable. "Pay attention."

His sudden movement had her last words tangling with her tongue and coming out much too slowly. She felt herself catch and hold a breath when he leaned forward to grab the fur behind her, his cheek brushing hers.

"Oh, I am." He'd deepened his voice so much the sound formed an iron ball in the pit of her stomach.

His eyes dipped to her lips, and she tucked the bottom one between her teeth as if to protect it. Heart hammering in her chest, she thought of all the things she'd wanted to say and had been too afraid to voice. But after their run-in with Torsten and his band of evil men, she'd realized she wasn't promised another chance.

"Aksel, I'm sorry fer what I said in Volfsby. I dinna mean it."

He stilled as she spoke, his face inches from hers.

"I was afraid."

"Of me?" His voice was rough, gravelly.

"Of losing ye. I had such horrible dreams. I just wanted to keep ye safe."

He brought the fur up over her shoulder, holding it until she wrapped her hand around the edge, her fingers brushing his.

"I'd prefer all yer future dreams of me to be pleasant."

"They werena *of* ye, just *about* ye. Of someone hurting ye." Her hand made a weak swipe at his side, but he cupped her face, his eyes on hers.

"I wish I ken my name." His voice was soft. "My true name."

She made a face. "'Tis a strange thing to say."

"Since we are sharing secrets." He smiled, giving a half shrug.

"Yer the only one sharing, Prince."

"True. Tell me a secret." When she made another face, he tugged on a strand of her hair. "I saved yer life; I deserve a secret."

"Is this my payment?"

"Nay, yer penance." A smirk formed on his lips.

"And what, pray tell, is my crime?"

He wiggled a bit, most likely maneuvering around the same tiny, sharp rocks that were digging into her legs.

"Tell me a secret, and I will forgive ye fer nearly dying on me."

"Very well." She tipped her head back to search her mind for an adequate story, aware of his eyes trailing the length of her throat. When she finally settled on what she wanted to reveal, she let her chin fall. "Ye ken I have a sister, but I also have a brother."

"A brother?"

"Aye." She nodded. "He's a king actually."

"The king ye spoke of earlier?"

"Aye."

He laughed, sparks lighting behind his blue eyes.

"What's so funny?"

"Ethni told me yer mother was queen, and I guess I never put it together."

Revna furrowed her brows, feeling the tug of a frown on her lips. "Did ye dip into a cask of mead while I was out?"

"Nay, 'tis just...ye've been calling me a prince all this time, when ye are the princess."

"Aye well, call me that again and I *will* stab ye." She nodded toward her daggers and jabbed her fist into his ribs, instantly regretting that quick movement.

"Ooh," he laughed as the air was forced from his lungs. He rubbed his hand across his middle, narrowing his eyes as a half-smile curved one side of his mouth. "So violent."

"I've never denied it." She rolled her eyes, pursing her lips to hide her own smile.

He lifted his chin. "Yer brother, what is he called?"

"Duncan." She hadn't spoken his name in so long. It still felt strange to call him brother when he'd been her enemy for most of her life. He was also now her king. Because of Astrid's message, she knew they'd all sorted out her and Duncan's relationship. "I was angry wi' him fer a long time. I ken now that he is a good man. I could call ye that if ye want; 'tis a strong name."

Aksel tipped his head to the side, his eyes roaming over her face. He'd always been observant, seeing more than she wanted him to see. But the look in his eyes now was different, and she felt as if a

337

thousand birds suddenly took flight in her stomach. "Is that how ye think of me? As a brother?"

She went still until she started shaking.

"Are ye trembling from the cold or something else?" His voice was low again, its rumble racing across the space between them and intensifying her shivers.

"The cold," she answered too quickly, looking anywhere but at his face and pretending to fumble with the fur blanket.

"Look at me."

She could not.

He gently gripped her chin. "Look at me, Little Bird."

He waited, his fingers warm and patient. Ten long thundering heartbeats he waited—until she forced her eyes upward. Those same ten beats pulsed in her ears and raced in her chest.

"I am no one's brother. Certainly not yours."

Something passed over his expression. A flicker of the hurt she knew he'd carried since finding out about his true heritage. It was gone so quickly, Revna thought she might have imagined it. But she didn't imagine that he'd slipped into the Norseman's tongue—a trick he only used when he was trying to pry something out of her. "But you knew that from the moment you stood over me outside the mead hall and said I was not bad...for a Viking."

"I-I said that out loud?" she answered in the same language.

He nodded.

"And you remember?" She raised a brow.

He nodded again. "I told you, I have been paying attention."

"I am impressed, you were quite...unconscious at the time."

"I remember everything." He turned heated eyes on her, his gaze dipping to her mouth before he slid his hand gently around her neck, his thumb resting just over her pulse.

"I remember seeing you for the first time. I thought you were the most beautiful apparition." He drew her closer until his breath caressed her parted lips.

"And now?" She could not reply with more than a whisper.

"Even more beautiful now that I know you are real."

All her sharp retorts abandoned her. She was left with a trapped breath and thundering heart.

"Your heart is racing," he said as his thumb moved across her throat. "Are you afraid, Little Bird?"

"Yes." She released her held breath.

"Do you want to run away from me now?" His lips brushed across hers, the lightest of touches.

"No."

"Good, because I do not mean to let you go. I think I will keep you locked here in my arms for the rest of my days." He kissed one side of her mouth.

"Only if I allow it." Revna's eyes drifted closed.

"Please allow it." He kissed the other side of her mouth.

"As you wish."

She felt his lips pull back into a smile before he closed the remaining space between them and pressed his mouth to hers. He held her there, motionless, for a heartbeat before she reached for him, her fingers diving into his hair, tugging him closer.

She kissed him with a passion that eclipsed any amount of rage she'd ever felt, because she finally found something stronger and more powerful than fury. Love.

She loved Aksel, even if that was not his name. He was her friend through many trials and the rock upon which she leaned. The one who would never leave her behind. He made her desire light instead of darkness; he made her want to be better. He was strong and loyal, compassionate and broken. She loved every jagged piece of him, every weak and human bit. She loved him. And from the way he was kissing her, she thought he might love her too.

When he finally broke their kiss, she was gasping for air.

"Still impressed?" he said against her lips.

"There might be a small part of me that was pleased wi' that performance." Her grin matched his as she ventured back into her native tongue.

He laughed then, a deep hearty sound that echoed through the cavern until it was brought to a sudden halt by her fist to his gut.

"Shh." She wrapped her hand in his tunic and jerked him close, pressing her lips to his again. "Ye'll let the entire Northlands ken where we are."

He chuckled, kissing her back in short bursts, repeating the same words she'd spoken moments before. "As ye wish, princess."

He blocked her jab and pushed himself up to his knees, reaching for a linen-wrapped parcel that he revealed to be flat bread and dried meats. "I was starving, but someone had me trapped wi' her hard head on my arm."

She lifted a brow.

"Pardon, I meant her *bonnie* hard head." He flashed a grin that sent a spark of heat in her belly as he dug into the food.

"Let's get ye better," he said through a mouthful as he handed a portion to her. His brows jumped, and there was a lightness about him Revna had not seen before. "I've never been on a boat before. I mean, not that I remember. I'm quite excited."

"I have." She was lost to her memories until she felt the back of Aksel's fingers stroke her cheek, drawing her back. "But I dinna get to see much. I was hiding the whole time."

"Well." He handed her a handful of dried berries from another parcel, and a slight catch of the light made his eyes sparkle. "It will be something new fer both of us."

29

AKSEL

826 AD: Five weeks later

Revna's hand tightened in his when her boot met the rough planks of the longboat's deck. Even in the weeks it took her to recover and the time it took them to journey back to Volfsby, she hadn't revealed much about her first voyage other than the fact that she hid for the entirety of it. But from the way her fingers kept fluttering to her side—to the place she had always kept an ornate dagger that was now missing—he assumed that journey was more adventurous than she let on. And he assumed, for that weapon to now be missing, more had happened in her visit to Trondheim than a simple rescue.

But she wasn't ready to share that with him, and he wasn't going to push.

The crew of Randi's longboat looked and sounded much like Tollak's—scraggly and grunting. Aksel felt his hand tighten on Revna's, hauling her closer.

"How did ye survive yer first trip? I might need some advice," he bent to whisper in her ear. "This bunch looks surly."

"I poisoned them."

Her answer was so frank he couldn't help the burst of laughter that blew from his lips. "Of course ye did."

Randi and Isa followed them on board, Randi barking orders to the crew to keep to the course. Winter was fully upon them, and both women were bundled in so many furs their shapes were indistinguishable. He hoped beneath all those layers, Isa had put weight back on her bones. The Shieldmaiden's daughter was closely flanked by a quiet but imposing guardian. He was the same man Aksel had seen with her since he and Revna had arrived days before. With what Isa had endured, he was glad to see her protected.

After issuing strict reminders to her crew to seek trade and not plunder, Randi turned to Aksel and Revna.

"Take care of Sgail." Revna grasped Randi's forearms as she delivered her desperate request. "And Bonnie. Do not let her go back to that cruel farmer, I beg you."

"There will never be steeds more loved." Randi offered a gentle smile, and Revna visibly relaxed. "Tell my dóttir that the spark she brought to Volfsby has become a flame and is spreading."

Aksel looked to Revna and back to Randi, who smiled and placed a hand on both their shoulders. "She will know what it means."

She looked at them for a moment longer, as if she could see something they couldn't, and then leaned in and spoke softly. "I heard of Eilidh. Your flame is spreading too."

Aksel thought he might have understood her then. Volfsby's small dock had become a port of freedom, Randi's settlement being one of the few that shunned the practice of capturing their enemies as slaves. And while many might have expressed fear that their farms and markets would suffer at the loss of laborers, Randi's decision proved just the opposite.

Volfsby was thriving, even in the winter months. Her barns and storehouses were well stocked, most of her people happy and at peace. She'd shared that there had recently been a small group of settlers who were causing her some trouble, but she admitted that there would always be those that opposed a new leadership. Now that she'd called back the men who were searching for Torsten, her warband would be one of the strongest in the region.

Though they'd not been able to save Eilidh, because of her they knew the notion of freedom was catching on in more places than Volfsby.

"It can spread farther," Aksel blurted without thinking. When Randi turned, he didn't quite know what else to say except that he'd made a promise to Eira. Even though he wasn't her brother by blood, she still held a place in his heart. "There is a woman called Eira Tollakdóttir in Kaupang. She needs to hear of the hope that thrives here in Volfsby. Can you...would you..."

"She will hear it." Randi's vow loosened something in his chest. "And anyone else she can get to listen."

He thought of Tollak. Was this God powerful enough to soften a heart as hard as his? Aksel had to believe He was.

"Trondheim."

Aksel jerked his head toward Revna, whose expression was solemn. She cleared her throat before speaking again, an edge of uncertainty to her words.

"There is a family in Trondheim that will listen."

Randi nodded as Revna gave a name Aksel hadn't heard before. His little bird glanced only once in his direction as she spoke, the slight lift of her full lips a promise to explain later.

Randi curved her arm around Isa's shoulders. Aksel scanned the face of the Shieldmaiden's daughter. It was fuller than the gaunt, almost ghost-like shape he'd seen when they'd found her. She looked different. Content. It gave him hope that Isa would find joy one day. Randi turned her daughter and aimed them for the shore.

Isa whispered something to her mother before she hurried back and took Revna's hands.

The dark-haired guardian that hadn't drifted more than a few steps from Isa stiffened as she moved. Randi's hand on his sleeve kept him still, though he didn't seem to like it. The one conversation Aksel had with Isa's young guard made him believe he was a man uncertain about many things—but none were Isa. He was more than dedicated to his charge of protecting her.

Isa looked up at Revna, her ice-blue eyes blazing and her moon-white hair whipping in the cold breeze.

"The one true God sent you here. Not only for me but for all the people you have rescued. I know you are fighting what you already know to be true and I want...I need to tell you that there is strength in surrender." Isa closed her eyes for a moment, and then, as if talking to herself, she said, "I know this to be true."

Isa squeezed Revna's hands before taking Aksel's and saying, "God was with you as well. Ethni shared her story with me. He was with you all, offering help even when you did not ask. He will always be there to help. He fills all the empty places."

She looked between them. "This is not the end of your journey. Of any of our journeys."

With a smile, she was gone, having stunned them both into silence.

JUST OVER TWO weeks and several harbor stops later, they stood in that same reverent silence as the shores of Tràigh came into view.

"We can find yer family."

Aksel jolted at Revna's words. It was the first either of them had spoken since land was spotted hours before.

She looked up at him, a quiet desperation in her eyes. "Mayhap they survived and still live amongst the remnant Picts. Do ye remember anything?"

He watched the growing mountain peaks and darkening outline of the shore, trying to decide if it was familiar. "I have flashes some-times. I used to think they were from before I was sick, that they were of Tollak and his wife." He'd stopped referring to her as his mother. "But, I guess that canna be."

"What do ye see?"

"'Tis more a feeling. I felt the strength of a father, the love of a mother. I do think she had red hair though."

Revna blew out a breath, hands rising to rest on her hips. "That is true fer half of the Picts."

Aksel tugged on a lock of her midnight hair. "Not ye."

"Nay. I am different."

"That ye are."

She was different—from anyone he'd ever met and even from the angry, vengeful woman she'd been when she first found him outside the mead hall in Kaupang. She'd always been quiet, but now there was a peace about her. As if much of her roughness had been smoothed.

On their first day at sea, she shared the meaning of her request regarding the family in Trondheim. The tears she shed for her lost friend had dried his throat, and he could only respond by wrapping her in his arms and sending silent prayers of thanksgiving for the young man named Rune who had kept his little bird alive.

He stepped behind her, hands resting easily on her shoulders. A wave of contentment crested over his heart when she shifted her weight and relaxed against him, letting him support her. Beneath her soft sigh, he felt the swell of restlessness she tried to hide.

"Are ye so afraid of sitting still that ye just canna help finding another mission to complete?" He'd dropped his chin to the top of her head, keeping his voice low as he locked his fingers together in front of her.

Revna's mouth popped open as she wrenched her neck to the side, turning an offended look his way. But when he raised a brow, she snapped her lips closed and grumbled under her breath, "Always noticing."

The boat slowed, and the crew shouted orders in preparation to meet land. Aksel's heart began to beat at a furious pace. This land should be familiar, but it felt foreign. Dangerous. Prickles of alarm skated over his skin, fraying his nerves. He tightened his grip on Revna, secretly wanting to tuck her away into the cavern of his embrace.

"Even if we dunna find yer family, Prince, yer part of mine now. Yer not alone anymore." She stared straight ahead, hands fisted at her side, the fiercest thing he'd ever seen.

"Aye, wife, I guess I am."

The events leading up to their simple ceremony on the riverbank two days before they'd left Volfsby played again in his mind, starting with Revna's sudden declaration after the evening meal in Randi's longhouse.

"I want to be yer wife."

Her words had him laughing until he saw the seriousness on her face. He scanned the table, wondering if anyone else had heard or understood, since she'd spoken in the Vestland language.

"Oh, ye will be, Little Bird. Dunna worry." She'd pulled away when he reached for her, swatting at his hand.

"I mean it. Before we sail fer the Vestlands."

He'd sat back in his chair, narrowing his eyes and scanning every inch of her face. Revna was rarely impulsive. She was quick to lash out but not one to make life-changing decisions on a whim. When she described how she came to be in the Northlands, she called it sudden. But the more he learned, the more he understood she'd been planning that endeavor for years.

"Is this because I said I dinna ken what I would do once we arrived?" As much as he'd wanted to bring her before the lawspeaker right then, he had to know the reason.

"Nay. 'Tis because..." When she hesitated, he'd made up his mind to force her to wait to handfast until she'd reunited with her queen. But then she spoke again. "Because ye promised to keep me in yer arms fer the rest of yer life, and I mean to hold ye to that. I want you at my side fer this new journey and all the rest we will ever take. I want...nay, I-I need—"

He leaned forward, silencing her with a chaste kiss. "As ye wish."

When he drew back, he added a nod to confirm his agreement. Then, as if she hadn't already reached into his chest and taken his heart captive, she winked and popped a bit of bread into her mouth, nearly stopping his heartbeats altogether. "Good, because I canna verra well bring home a rogue to meet the queen."

The next morning, Randi was more than happy to oblige their sudden request. With a few of her household acting as witnesses, including the new lawspeaker, the Shieldmaiden of Volfsby wrapped Aksel and Revna's hands in a beaded leather strap and spoke the words that would bind them together for the remainder of their days.

Warmth flooded his veins at the memory of Revna's unwavering gaze and the certainty with which she spoke her vows. At the knowledge that every bit of fierceness inside her beautiful heart now belonged to him. Unable to resist, he slid his fingers into her dark hair and turned her to face him, forcing her onto her tiptoes as he kissed his wife thoroughly.

30

AKSEL

The boat jerked as it reached the shore, and he tightened his grip to keep them both upright.

"Are ye ready fer this?" he said, intently watching her expression.

"Honestly? Nay."

With the thud of the boarding plank striking the wooden dock, he released her, turning her toward her homeland and giving her a soft shove.

"Be brave." He needed to hear those words as much, if not more, than she did. "I am wi' ye."

As expected, the King's guard had the entire crew, including Aksel and Revna, on their knees and held at sword's end before the sound of hooves crested the hill that guarded the kingdom from the shore.

Again, Aksel found it difficult to control his heart, not only because of his own nervousness but now because of the tension rolling off of Revna in surging waves.

"I can feel you boiling from over here, Little Bird." He shot one of Tràigh's guards a sharp look when the tip of his spear jabbed into his side. He didn't fight back though. As long as the guards kept their spears pointed at him and not Revna. He knew these were her people, but the thought of someone threatening her filled him with a foreign sense of violence. He wondered if this was what Revna felt like all the time.

"Taranau," Revna breathed when two horses bearing riders appeared on the shore. "And Cuddie."

"I thought you said the King's name was Duncan." A spear nudged his side again, and Aksel glared at the guard. "I amna resisting; I'm just talking."

Hearing his own language stunned the guard enough that he backed up half a step.

"Not the men, the horses." Revna's answer was light, a spark of joy saturating her last word.

Aksel breathed a laugh. Of course it would be two animals that calmed her racing heart.

"That is my brother and his captain, Eowin."

Revna's eyes traveled beyond the two riders, scanning the hills as if expecting someone else.

"Which is your kin?" The men neared, one with untamed pale-blond curls and the other a giant with dark waves tied back at the neck.

"On the left."

The blond. Aksel secretly sighed in relief; the other one looked rather formidable should there be a problem. At least the king was human-sized and more likely to use reason instead of force.

"What is your business in these lands?" Revna's brother announced, speaking the language of the Norseman with near perfection.

They'd already been asked the same questions at the entrance to the firth and been granted access by the group of guards that lined the cliffs. The mere fact that they'd been able to sail through the winding firth without being speared through by the many archers standing at the ready must have given the king some assurances, but news of their identity wouldn't have yet reached the tower.

Aksel glanced at Revna, who kept her head down, either not ready to face her brother or knowing the rest of the crew needed to be cleared first.

"We have come at the bidding of your ally, Randi Helgedóttir, Shieldmaiden of Volfsby," the chief crewman bellowed in his baritone voice.

This wouldn't have been the first time they'd heard that same greeting. Randi had sent more than one crew to these lands. Duncan had to know she'd met Revna. The king's captain straightened, turning to one of the guards behind him and whispering a message. The guard nodded, and to Aksel's surprise, climbed atop Cuddie. He gathered the reins and steered the animal over the hills at a gallop.

"Rise, Norseman. What message from Volfsby?" Duncan asked, his tone a mix of wary anticipation.

The crew leader obeyed, lifting himself smoothly to his feet. "She has sent gifts for her dóttir and for the Chieftain of this land. She also bid us return that which was lost." The crewman nodded to his boat. "If you will allow it."

Duncan glanced at Eowin, who nodded to the guards. They kept spears at their sides but, in one unified move, stepped back from the crew, allowing them all to stand.

"What is it that was lost?" Duncan stepped forward, searching the faces of the crew for the first time, as if he knew—as if he was waiting.

Aksel cast a sideways glance where Revna had been. She was gone. He nearly panicked when he felt her presence at his back. Was his fearsome, warrior wife hiding behind him? He shook his head and Duncan's eyes landed on him, brows furrowing. The king's eyes were the same color as Revna's, though that was where their similarities ended.

Revna wasn't the only one who was different. Aksel had never thought of it until Ethni finally revealed the truth about his heritage, but there were subtle differences in his appearance than that of the Norsemen. The slightly less pronounced brow and the shape of his jaw. When he was a boy, it wouldn't have been noticeable, but as he grew older, as those differences became more apparent, so did Tollak's disdain.

From the way the king was examining him, he could tell Duncan saw it too. When the crew began moving toward the boat to unload their cargo, Aksel drew in a breath and whispered, "Forgive me, Little Bird."

Before she could react, he stepped aside and Duncan's sky blue eyes jerked to the raven-haired woman standing in Aksel's shadow.

The king's arm shot out, grabbing the sleeve of his captain. Eowin turned gray eyes on Revna too.

Neither moved.

Aksel couldn't read their expressions. It was a strange combination of relief and reservation. Duncan's face seemed to drain of color completely. This was not quite the reunion Aksel had imagined for her, and suddenly he felt very foolish for rushing it. The sharp prickling of his skin returned, and he felt his shoulders tense, ready to sweep her behind him again. Mayhap she was right to fear this reunion.

"Revna?" Duncan finally rasped.

He took a step, but Eowin muttered a soft grunt and Duncan froze again. Distant hoofbeats had every eye turned toward the dunes that bordered the shores.

The captain's steed crested the hill. Aksel recognized its rider simply from her moon-white locks. That had to be Isa's sister, Astrid. Her horse was followed by another—a gray-speckled mare that bore a fire-haired rider. The queen, he assumed.

Revna gasped from behind him.

The queen's horse didn't even slow to a stop before she swung effortlessly from its back and landed with her feet already moving, rich emerald skirts gathered in her hands. Isa's sister was close on her heels.

The queen's boots pounded against the planks as she tore toward them, only slowing when she reached her husband's side.

Astrid walked, her pace nearly as quick as the queen's, with the same desperate focus on Revna. She stopped next to the captain, grasping his arm in a way that caught Aksel's attention. He swiveled his head toward Revna. She was also staring at the way Eowin covered Astrid's hand with his own.

"Revna?" The queen's voice broke whatever spell held Revna and she moved. Just one step.

The king's grip tightened, almost as if unconsciously, around his wife.

"Revna!" Her voice broke, tears streaming down her face.

Her distress loosened the bonds holding Revna back and she raced for the queen. The queen tore free from her husband's grasp and collided with Revna, their arms encircling each other with such force, they both dropped to their knees.

The emotion nearly knocked Aksel off his feet. The sound of the queen's frantic voice as she said Revna's name, over and over, his undoing.

He was bombarded with flashes of memories. Each its own tragedy but none solid enough for him to take hold. But that agony, the complete brokenness in the queen's voice, he knew that sound. He tore his eyes away from the scene, seeking relief from the searing gash it ripped open inside his chest.

He scanned the shore all the way to where gray rock cliffs jutted from the land, reaching like jagged fingers toward the sea.

Somewhere amongst that swirling mess inside his mind, he knew there should have been a quaint nest of roundhouses stretching on tall piers over the water. But there was only black sand and sea-smoothed rocks. This was wrong. All wrong.

The queen's cries quieted, and he looked back to see her hands combing over Revna's hair, her face, her arms, her hands. He was right. The joy on the queen's face rivaled that of Randi when she held her daughter after so long of being parted.

"'Tis ye?" she cried. "'Tis really ye?"

Revna only bowed, much as he had done the morning after she'd rescued him from the men in Illrstaðr. She buried her face in the queen's lap and wrapped her arms around her waist as the queen folded herself over Revna's back. Revna looked so small; he could almost see the girl she must have been when she'd boarded the longboat that brought her to the Northlands so many winters ago.

The queen sat up and tipped her head to the sky, her sobs carrying over the waves of the sea. Aksel blinked away the stinging salt water that welled in his eyes to see his little bird so loved.

The moon-haired captain joined them, slowly lowering herself next to the queen. Revna sat up when Astrid pressed her hand on her back. Their foreheads met, a sacred circle that could not be breached by time or distance. They wrapped their arms around each other, remaining in silence as the crew unloaded Randi's gifts. Baskets of linens, trunks of pottery and blown glass packed in straw, and small casks of beaded jewelry lined the shore.

Once unloaded, Duncan thanked the crew leader, offering to have food and supplies brought down since the Norsemen declined his offer to dine at the tower. Most of the crew opted to lounge on the shore, leaving Aksel and the crew leader on the dock along with a few Norsemen still securing the longboat.

When the crew leader motioned to one of the Norsemen aboard the longboat, he was handed a linen wrapped parcel before calling out, "Astrid Bjorndóttir."

Astrid's head snapped up from where she still knelt with Revna and the queen.

"A gift from your móðir."

Astrid looked to the queen, whose eyes were swollen and red from tears. She touched Astrid's shoulder and nodded. Astrid smoothed her skirts, a strange choice of wardrobe if she were the queen's captain, as Revna had said. As she stood, Aksel noticed the slight swell of her stomach and his eyes snapped to Revna's.

She noticed too, jerking a narrowed glare at Eowin. She shifted, as if she were going to attack him, but the queen's hands were on her arms.

"Nay, my scout." The queen shook her head. "There is much we need to discuss."

Astrid moved slowly toward the crew leader, pivoting her eyes between his and the offering. He laid it in her palms and gave a small nod before boarding his boat.

Astrid unwrapped the parcel, running her hand across what was inside. She lifted an intricately beaded woven belt, letting it drape over her fingers.

"'Tis bonnie," she breathed. Also in the wrapping she lifted folds of linen with detailed patterns woven into the fabric. Astrid's fingers trembled as she ran her hands across the designs. She touched her lips, catching a small sob.

From where he stood, Aksel could see little, but he recognized the shape of a wolf and that of a lion. Eowin was at her side, his hand across the small of her back. The sun peeked out from behind a cloud, bathing the dock in bright light and catching the glint of a brass ring on the giant captain's finger. Eowin was more than the king's captain, then. He was also Astrid's husband. The storms that Revna had described raging between the two captains must have calmed in the winters she'd been away.

"Look," Astrid said softly to her husband.

Eowin gazed at the gift over her shoulder, his arm tenderly circling her waist.

"She wove our story into the linen." A single tear streaked down Astrid's face.

Duncan moved behind the queen, offering his hand to help her stand. She took it and then offered hers to Revna.

Revna found him then, a complicated mix of emotions drawing her brows together. He felt strangely out of place, not knowing what to do next.

"How?" Astrid turned to Revna then. "How did ye come to be in Volfsby? Is my mother well? My sister?"

"There's so much I need to tell ye," Revna said to both of them. "But first there is someone I want ye to meet."

Astrid stepped aside, Eowin at her back, and the queen looked at him. Eyes of liquid emerald locked onto his.

A memory fluttered and swirled in his mind. He took a step forward, drawn to her. As if he knew her.

Her eyes. Her lips. Her nose. Surely if she had been a young princess when he was taken, he must have seen her before.

Revna smiled as she looked from him to the queen. "This is my —"

"Yer Highness!"

A little boy with wild blond curls like the king raced wildly across the deck, slamming into Duncan's leg. A plump older woman with streaks of white powder decorating her cheeks waddled after the boy.

"Oh, Yer Majesty," the woman panted as the king scooped up the child, who looked to be about four. "The prince was helping in the kitchen when he heard of ships in the firth. I couldna stop him."

"'Tis well, Hilde. I'll take him back."

While the king soothed the woman's fears, Aksel's head started to swim. There was such a tug on his spirit. An uncomfortable twisting, like something long buried was being unearthed. He didn't like it. His hand jolted to his side, but he was unarmed.

"Who is this, papa?" The boy pointed to Revna.

The king jostled the boy in his arms, drawing out a laugh from his little mouth. "This is Revna, Beli. My sister. Yer aunt."

He wanted to watch Revna. He needed to note her reaction to this introduction, but his mind could only focus on one thing.

Beli. The boy's name was Beli. Another wave of blurred memories burst inside his head. He blinked them away, forcing himself to draw in deep breaths as his heart began that rebelliously frantic pace again. His feet remained planted on the dock though everything within him demanded he escape.

"And who is that?" Beli pointed to Aksel.

Revna moved to stand next to him. She slipped her hand into his, threading their fingers together. Aksel tore his gaze from the child, centering it back on the queen.

The queen with fiery hair and emerald eyes.

Smoke and screams. The brush of pine needles against his skin. The thunder of hooves over hills. His heart hammered against his bones. Bile rose in his throat and sweat painted his forehead. Revna cast him a wary look before speaking, her words no longer filled with excitement but tight and reserved.

"This is Aksel. Aksel, this is—"

"Cyrene," he breathed.

Cyrene stared, her lips falling open. She took one step, but he backed up, tugging Revna's hand as he moved. Her brows furrowed, and he felt her tense, as if she sensed danger. His eyes darted to each face surrounding him.

He wasn't one inclined to panic or outbursts, but he felt very much like a cornered lion. His heart beat so wildly, he strained to breathe, heat rising up his neck and scorching his face.

Eyes trained on his wife, the king flinched, one arm tightening around his son and the fingers of his other hand curling around the grip of the sword at his side. Aksel tugged at Revna again, urging her behind him. As the king moved, the ring on his smallest finger caught the sun, and Aksel felt a terrible, aching thirst blaze up his throat. He knew that band, those markings. For the first time in half a year, he wanted nothing more than to feel the sweet coating of mead on his tongue.

Head tilted, the queen stepped toward him again, stopping when she was so close he had to lower his chin to meet her eyes. He didn't move, curiosity winning out over this strange wave of terror. She looked up, staring into his eyes. Deeply. Something turned in his stomach, as if she'd reached down his throat and grabbed hold of his heart.

She gasped, her eyes widening. "Beli?"

31

AKSEL

Beli.

That name on Cyrene's lips was a key to some forgotten chest of memories. It had been buried under a fever and pushed further into the corner of his mind by a dose of nightshade. But now it was thrown open without his permission, and he stumbled back a step from the force of vibrant pictures, sounds, smells, and feelings flooding his mind. Torn green flags littering the ground. The clash of metal swords. The metallic smell of death. They all twisted and swirled, landing on the very clear image of a thicket.

Of whimpering bairns. Of soldiers in blood-red capes creeping closer and of an emerald-eyed lass at his side. Of his mother's weak words, echoing in his ears.

Beli, my lion. Ye must guard the queen.

Protect Cyrene.

Cyrene's small arms were wrapped around two bairns, their cries too loud. He whipped his head back to the approaching soldiers. Dark crimson beads dripped from their blades onto the cold ground. They were nearing, but he couldn't hear their footsteps over the sound of his pounding heart.

Everything was confusing. It was all wrong, and he didn't know what to do. Mama would come; her warriors would come.

But he'd been in the roundhouse. He'd torn free from the warrior maiden, Ailbhe, and seen Brigid sobbing. The healer's body was draped over the linen-covered shape on Mama's bed.

Mama was dead. The queen...was dead.

Beli's lungs seized, refusing to allow air to pass. Mama was dead. How could the sun still be shining? Why were trees, though leafless in the cold of winter, still standing?

Why were men from the tower, meant to be their allies and friends, cutting down the Picts with rage twisting their faces into monstrous expressions?

Mama was dead. The thought kept pulsing in his mind. The queen was dead.

No. Beli looked at Cyrene again, her eyes leaking tears down flushed cheeks. The queen was beside him. Mama said so.

Mama called him Cyrene's guardian; she called him a lion. He knew what to do. Guard the queen. Protect Cyrene.

His sister's green eyes, wide with terror, latched onto his. A question that begged to be answered lingered between them. Were these their last breaths?

Fear turned to determination. The pounding heart in his chest began to burn, fire coursing through his small arms, and he inched to the edge of the thicket, dragging the sword one of his mother's guards had tossed at their feet.

Cyrene reached for him, but he was too quick. He'd always been quick. Help was near. He could bring back warriors to save his sister and the other bairns. He could protect the queen.

He ignored her whispered pleas and darted between the trees without the soldiers spotting him. At a crashing sound in the distance, their attention was torn from the thicket where Cyrene and another lad wrangled the bairns.

The clearing where his mother's warriors fought was but a short sprint. He would bring help. He could make it.

After only one step, a snap of a twig seemed to crack and echo like thunder through the forest. He froze. Cyrene wrestled with a bairn, her eyes wide with terror.

He jerked his gaze to the tower soldiers. They'd turned back and were heading for the thicket. For the little ones. For Cyrene.

Run! she mouthed.

He only looked down at the massive sword he'd dragged with him. He curled both of his small fists around its hilt. Mama said he was a lion; Mama told him to protect the queen. And he'd sworn to do it.

He met Cyrene's eyes one last time, feeling his lips curl into a soft smile. *I will protect ye, Cyrene. I will guard the queen.*

With all his strength, he lifted the weapon, drawing the eye of the soldiers from Tràigh.

Their gaze focused on him. He ignored their taunts and laughs as he backed away, leading them farther from the thicket where his sister hid.

Back. Back. Back he stepped, the men matching his steps with their wider strides, closing in quicker than he could escape. From the corner of his eye, he could see Cyrene and another lad, bairns in their arms and on their heels, racing for the darkest part of The Dorcha.

When one of the men broke his locked gaze and Beli thought he might turn and see Cyrene, he felt a flame nearly burst from his chest.

I will protect ye, Cyrene. I will guard the queen. I will save my sister.

Beli used the remaining strength in his limbs and raised his sword as he opened his mouth and released a sound that matched the beast inside of him. Whatever became of him didn't matter. His sister would escape. She would live and she would lead their people as their mother had done.

Live, Cyrene. Live. His feet pounded against dry ground with the rhythm of his words as they carried him toward the men. In those steps, he felt the strength of a thousand men coursing through his blood. Though they laughed at his charge, their smiles turned to sneers when he didn't slow. Even as they raised their own swords, he never blinked. He would swing this warrior blade until it was ripped from his hands. For his sister. For Cyrene. As the first soldier's blade fell, the force knocking him to the ground, he roared his mantra in his mind.

I will protect ye, Cyrene. I will guard the queen!

Mama trusted him. He made a promise, and he would fight until his last breath to keep it. So he got up.

The soldiers spat taunting curses as they pushed him to the ground with a boot to his chest. Again, he got up.

Taking turns, they circled him. One lashed out, a stinging slap from the back of his hand hit Beli's cheek so hard, white flashes blinded him for a moment. He wiped the blood from the corner of his mouth. And he got up.

Their smiles had faded; their demands for him to stay down, to stop fighting, went ignored as, again and again, he got up.

He knew they would eventually tire of playing with him and run their blades through his middle, but he'd decided the moment he picked up the sword that he didn't need to best them. He only needed to give Cyrene time to run. The risk of one glance to make sure his sister had disappeared cost him.

He cried out at the fiery slice of pain that seared his shoulder. One blink, and the men were upon him. Still, he fought, jabbing his blade, kicking, clawing, biting. Roaring. Praying.

As one soldier landed a blow against Beli's head, darkness spotted his vision and he uttered his final words to the crisp blue sky above.

An T-aon, save my sister. Save the queen.

And one last time, he got up.

32

REVNA

Beli?

Why was Cyrene calling Aksel by her dead brother's name? And why was she pulling at his tunic, tugging it off his shoulder? And why was he just standing there? Staring at...

Cyrene's hand flew to her mouth again at the sight of the scar on Aksel's right shoulder. Revna had seen it before. It was just a scar; he had plenty of them. But the way Cyrene stared at that jagged, pink line...something wasn't right.

As her eyes darted to her brother, Revna knew Duncan felt it too, and his hand rested what looked to be casually on his sword. But Revna knew he was feeling anything but relaxed.

"Beli! It canna be. Ye died. I saw ye die." Cyrene was crying again. She was throwing her arms around Aksel and weeping onto his chest. "It canna be."

Duncan hadn't moved again other than to hand his son to Astrid. He kept his arms loose, ready. She didn't blame him; she felt the same nervous confusion.

The guards who had lingered by the end of the dock slowly approached, curious but keeping their distance.

Revna swung her gaze back to Aksel when his hand went limp in hers. His eyes were empty, his body stiff. But for the rise of his chest, he was motionless. Something was definitely wrong. Revna felt her body slide into that familiar ease of battle. Her knees slightly bent, arms loose. Aksel's jaw was clenched, his blue eyes blazing.

"Cyrene," Duncan warned. "I think ye better come here."

Palpable confusion and turmoil swirled between Revna, Aksel, and Cyrene. It stretched beyond their circle, permeating the air until Duncan's face paled. Revna didn't know who to defend, who to fight. A dull heat flared into flames in her chest as Aksel began to tremble.

When Cyrene didn't move, Duncan spoke again, his voice tight but calm. "Cyrene. Step away, my love."

Despite the tender words, it was a kingly order, and one that had Cyrene's arms dropping to her sides, her head snapping toward the king. At the same time, Duncan's men moved forward.

Randi's Norse crew remained on the shore, hands raised in surrender, as more of Duncan's men turned to keep them back.

Even though the king ordered his men to stand down, one soldier —aimed for the queen—roughly shoved Revna aside and she landed with a pained grunt on the splintered surface of the dock. Another guard gripped her arms, attempting to drag her away.

As if time had slowed, Aksel's head turned, his gaze falling on Revna's shocked face. In a blink, whatever confusion swelled in his eyes turned to stone, a mask of fury dropping in place.

She'd only seen that expression once before. When Torsten had her on her back, his blade plunging into her body. When Aksel thought he was watching her die.

Aksel's eyes slowly raised to the guards holding her, his lips peeled back into a snarl.

Whatever hold had been placed on time lifted, and he moved quicker than Revna had ever seen. The men between them were gone, their bodies tumbling to the ground and over the edge of the dock. The guard holding her cried out as Aksel's boot met his chest, and she was instantly released.

Aksel's hands replaced the guard's, jerking her up with such force that her words of protest were swallowed with a gasp. Another guard attempted to move between Aksel, the queen, and Revna, but Aksel's jutting fist launched him from the dock and into the waist deep waters below.

"I left your men breathing this time, *King*," he growled, securing Revna's back to his chest with an arm across her shoulders. "Touch what is mine again and I will not be so lenient."

"Stand down!" Duncan's order had his remaining men halting in place.

At least her brother wasn't an idiot. Though she might have a few harsh words for Aksel if they survived this reunion. Whatever the connection between him and Cyrene, it seemed to be stealing all sense and reason from his mind.

Before she could question him, Revna was spun, deposited behind Aksel. He released her with equal swiftness, turning again to Cyrene before Revna found her footing.

Then Cyrene was in his grasp, his fingers curled around her slender arms, drawing her so close their noses nearly touched. It was as if he needed to see into the very depths of her mind. Her eyes were wide, but there was no sign of pain or fear on her face. He wasn't hurting her.

"I called off my men, now release my queen." Duncan moved then, his voice hard. "I, too, am protective of what is mine."

He only took one step before Aksel whipped Cyrene around, pressing her back to his chest just as he'd done with Revna. One arm created a vice grip across her shoulders, and in the other, he gripped a blade belonging to one of the tossed guards.

He didn't aim that blade at the queen though; it was leveled at Duncan. Even in his confusion, Aksel was a protector. "You will not harm them."

When Revna moved to his side, Aksel countered, shielding her again and dragging Cyrene with him. "Stay behind me, Little Bird," he ordered, his voice low.

"Aksel?" Revna touched his back, but when he tensed, she dropped her hand.

"Behind me, Revna! Please." His request was desperate, his voice trembling. Revna leaned around him enough to see that he'd closed his eyes for the length of one breath, as if it were taking all his strength to remain calm.

The guards and Duncan had drawn their own weapons. The king still held out his hand, holding them back.

That and Cyrene's quiet soothing mantra. "'Tis well. All is well. I am well."

But for the shushing of the waves and the little prince's wails as he was rushed over the hills by one of the king's men, there were no other sounds.

"Who are ye?" Aksel finally growled, his jaw brushing the top of Cyrene's head.

"'Tis me, Beli. Cyrene." She raised her hands, gently clutching his forearm locked across her collarbone. Her voice was steady, calm. "Yer sister."

Duncan sucked in a sharp breath, still not moving.

Revna felt her own uncertainty turn to defense at the sight of her brother's men, their spears aimed at her husband. A familiar red-tinged rage worked its way up her limbs, sending a pounding pulse in her ears. She didn't question how they'd come to this stand-off or what had Aksel's normally rock-solid calmness shattered into panic. She only knew that Aksel felt threatened and afraid, and that unleashed the same protectiveness in her that he'd just expressed.

"Call off yer men, *King*." A growl rolled up from Revna's own throat as she stepped around Aksel.

Eowin and Astrid had moved toward Duncan, weapons at their sides—Eowin a sword and Astrid a dagger from wherever she hid hers amongst her skirts. Eowin narrowed his eyes on Aksel, but Astrid rocked from foot to foot, her gaze darting between Revna and Cyrene as if she didn't know who to fight either.

"Everyone just breathe," Astrid said, her voice tight. Her ice-blue eyes slid to Revna, the next order directed at her. "Stay calm."

Revna's heart slammed against her ribs. What was happening? These were her friends. Her family. They'd seemed happy to see her return, but she wouldn't let them hurt Aksel. He wouldn't let them hurt her either. And apparently, from the way he was holding Cyrene, he felt she was threatened as well.

If she'd known this was what her homecoming would bring, she'd have stayed in the Northlands. With Aksel.

Every moment they'd shared in the last year flashed through her mind. He was hers. The one thing in the world that was all hers. She inched around to his side. No one would touch him.

"Dunna ye remember, Beli?" Cyrene's voice was soft but trembling. She wiggled in his hold until he loosened his grip enough for her to face him.

His fingers slid to her upper arms, keeping her close.

"Aksel." Revna issued her own order, but kept her back to him, shielding him. "Release her."

He blinked, and then lowered his head and shook it, as if trying to work loose some trapped memories or lock them away again. In the instant his attention was distracted, the guards moved, stopping again under Duncan's order when Revna startled them by producing two blades of her own. She stepped forward, a hairsbreadth in front of Aksel, swiveling her head to watch the men and Cyrene.

Cyrene reached up, touching his face. "Our mother was Derelei. She was kind and good and strong. And our father, Bercilak, ye used to beg him to swing ye in his arms and pretend ye had wings."

"Stop." Aksel breathed, head still down.

"I-I saw ye die." Cyrene's voice broke then. "Ye were so brave. Ye saved me. What happened? What happened to ye, Beli?"

"Stop." He trembled, his tone pleading.

Revna watched his grip on Cyrene finally loosen, saw as he gently lowered her until her feet were flat on the ground. She watched as his heart, his beautiful heart, was twisted so savagely it forced his expression into a painful grimace.

Cyrene didn't have a weapon, but somehow the queen was hurting him.

"Cyrene." Revna's warning went unheard as the queen was focused only on Aksel.

She placed her hands on his chest, pressing above his heart. Tears streamed down her face. "Beli, my lion. The bravest and boldest Pict to ever live."

"Cyrene," he whispered.

"Aye," the queen's voice was full of hope. "Tell me ye remember?"

"I remember." Aksel squeezed his eyes closed, and understanding breached the walls of Revna's confusion.

"Nay," she breathed. "Aksel."

She watched as he crumbled. As he broke. His face drained of color, and Duncan lowered his sword a fraction.

But when Aksel opened his eyes, the pain-fueled fury that burned there had the king hunched into a battle stance again. Revna threw her hands out and Cyrene, still held by Aksel, whipped her head to face her husband.

"Duncan." Cyrene's order stopped them, but the king trembled with his own fury.

"I remember everything." Aksel's jaw clenched, his hands shook, his lips pulled back in a viscous sneer.

Revna's fingers circled tighter around her blade, but the enemy was invisible—there was no one for her to fight, no way to save Aksel. She could only watch as his heart was shredded in front of her eyes.

A prayer peeled free from her own bleeding heart. *An T-aon, he's breaking. Help him—help him please. Just get him out of this.*

"Ye are the queen who married the murderer's son? The man who is wearing our mother's ring!" Aksel gritted out the words through his clenched teeth.

Revna forced her eyes to the silver band encircling Duncan's

366

finger. Duncan blanched for an instant before reclaiming his furious glare.

Aksel was trembling, but Cyrene did not cower. The emerald in her eyes flared and she pushed back. She didn't draw the blade Revna knew she had hidden somewhere. Her queen would never be unarmed.

Please dunna let her hurt him.

"Aye," Cyrene said, leaning toward him instead of away. "And when ye stop to listen ye will understand why."

"I've heard the story." He knew the history Revna had told about a mysterious woodland queen who united herself with her enemy to save both their kingdoms. It sounded like an epic of old. Filled with honorable and gallant deeds by royalty who put their people over their hearts. But that was before the queen was his sister, the one by whose side he'd grieved their mother. The one he'd given everything to protect. She watched as memories tumbled and twisted inside him, new and old, real and imagined, but in the center of it all, he was angry. And hurting.

And Revna couldn't stand it.

"I canna bear this, Huntress," Duncan groaned, echoing Revna's pain in his own words. Eowin's hand on his shoulder seemed to be the only thing holding him back.

"Ye will bear it." Cyrene's voice was as stone, unshakable as she ticked her chin to the side and sent her order over her shoulder. "I will speak wi' my brother." Her eyes were locked on Aksel's again in the next blink.

The king roared and threw his hands up to his temples, fists clenched in frustration. He aimed his blade at Revna. "What have ye done, Revna? What curse have ye brought upon these shores?"

Aksel's gaze snapped to Duncan, something animalistic in his expression. His blade was raised again, a low growl rumbling from his chest as he spoke in the Norse language. "You do not speak to her, Duncan Traitorsen."

What have ye done? The voice from dreams that had haunted her

367

for her first years in the Northlands returned, a familiar bitterness coating her mouth. The desire to rage warmed her bones.

No.

They'd come too far. Crossed entire countries. Vast seas. Aksel had clawed his way free from the grip of mead, from the condemning eye of the man who raised him. He'd found freedom, and now he was sliding back into that dark pit again.

Pull him out. Dunna let him fall. Her prayers flowed freely, unhindered by disbelief, for there was no other choice. Only a God who created life with His very breath could heal a hurt this deep. Only the great hero from those stories she'd avoided was powerful enough to save them now.

"Aksel." When Revna spoke his name, her voice was soft, pleading. He slowly swiveled his narrowed eyes to her, head cocked and a disturbing emptiness darkening his eyes.

"There is no Aksel, Little Bird."

Revna had never been afraid of the darkness. It had been her steady companion for many years, a deceitful ally that would cut when she wasn't looking and, in the next turn, promise it was the only one who could heal those very wounds. She did not balk at the shadows swirling around him. She would stand and fight them off because she did not leave her friends behind. Even if she was consumed, she would not leave him alone.

"It does not matter," she spoke softly in the Norse tongue and lowered her weapons, bending slowly to place them on the planks at her feet. Standing straight, she lifted her hand to his arm. "This is a time for words."

Aksel blinked.

A hint of blue returned to his eyes. He started to turn back to Cyrene, but Revna grabbed his chin, her fingers tugging at his beard.

"Look at me."

Revna could see Cyrene from the corner of her eye. The queen was staring at them. At her and Aksel. Her eyes were wide, but she was not afraid.

"Let her go," Revna's whisper had him peeling back his fingers, one at a time, until his hands were hovering over Cyrene's arms. Revna never once released his gaze, though she let go of his face and raised her hands in surrender.

Cyrene didn't run. She stared at them for a heartbeat before slowly backing into Duncan's arms.

Aksel let Duncan's men roughly force him to his knees, even against the queen's desperate protests. He let them strip him of his blades and clap irons on his wrists. But he never let them tear his eyes from Revna's. Not when Cyrene, with tears spilling down her cheeks, was whisked away. Not when the king's burly captain nodded for the guards to get Aksel to his feet. Not when Astrid, stunned silent, hovered by Revna's side. It was not until he was dragged across the dock by the guards that he was forced to look away. But she did not leave him.

33

AKSEL

It took Duncan's men an hour to get Aksel over the dunes and across the hills to the cell below the tower. Every step solidified more memories, leaving him with a pulsing ache behind his eyes. Everything about this land was utterly familiar and distinctly foreign at the same time. His nerves were frayed, his heart racing, and his guts twisting.

He knew if he asked, he would be taken to the comfort of the tower. But he found himself desiring a quiet, lonely place where he could have a moment to think. Even if it was a dark, dank hole in the ground. But either the murderous king's son frequently housed royal prisoners or the queen had a say in the conditions that awaited him. They didn't even keep the irons on, removing them as he was shoved through the door.

The cell was swept, the stone floors damp as if they'd been given a quick scrub. A clean cot bordered one wall, outfitted with a feather-stuffed pillow and stacks of thick blankets. There was even a parchment screen in one corner, shielding what he assumed was an area meant for him to take care of his needs in privacy.

Two chairs and a table were placed near the back wall—as if he'd be entertaining guests. Atop the table, a wooden trencher piled with something savory-smelling was covered with a clean linen. There was even a plate and a spoon, but no knife.

Revna started to follow him in, silencing one guard's protests with a look that had the man visibly shuddering. Aksel was unable to hide a fiendish smirk despite the torrent of emotions still swirling within him.

"She will have to be searched as well," a second guard announced when Revna refused to leave, cutting off Aksel's flash of amusement.

There was a beat of hesitation between the guards, as if they were silently debating.

"I'll do it," the first one said after clearing his throat. He added, as if to assure himself, "She is but a girl."

Fingers curled around the bars, Aksel growled as the guard stepped forward. He'd never felt so possessive of anything in his life, but the thought of that man's hands on his wife blinded him with a rage that rivaled Revna's. The only consolation was that the guard looked utterly terrified, and even more so when Revna gracefully lifted her arms from her sides without protest. The bars shook under the pressure of Aksel's grip, but as the man relieved her of two blades, she met his eyes and winked. He felt one side of his mouth lift to form a wicked half-grin as he could read the words in her eyes.

I have another.

Once released by the guards, Revna stepped inside and let her blue eyes explore every corner. When the door was sealed shut, she aimed for the table and lifted the linen, sniffing at the roasted meat and vegetables. Next to the trencher was a pitcher of fresh water and another of ale, which she promptly retrieved and splashed through the bars onto the stones outside of the cell, forcing the guards to dance quickly backwards.

"What are you doing, Little Bird?"

"We do not need it." She pinned him where he stood, as if she feared he might break loose and lick the sweet ale from the stones.

He couldn't blame her for her worry; he knew he was acting irrationally.

On the docks, he had a momentary thirst for mead to erase the confusion and pain, but as he stared at his wife, at the way she could make grown men—trained warriors in the king's warband—stumble over themselves without a word, he realized she was his only obsession. He'd never get enough of her, even if they lived a thousand years. Eternity. That was how long he needed with this challenging, fearless, terrifying woman.

"I mean, what are you doing in here? You do not belong in this cell." He spoke in the Norse language, not caring to share their conversation with the eavesdropping guards.

"Neither do you." She was already moving again, unfolding linens and quilts to make up the cot.

"Call to your queen; go to her."

"You know I will not." She kept working.

He didn't bother arguing, for he knew that tone. There would be nothing he could say to convince her until she decided for herself. And selfishly, he quite liked being able to breathe, which he found most difficult when she wasn't around.

The chairs were waiting, as was the cot, but Aksel walked to a bare side of the cell, sliding his back down the cold stone walls until he was seated on the ground. Knees drawn up, he rested his elbows on the tops, the heels of his palms pressed against his forehead. Somewhere inside, he knew he should be ashamed of the way he'd acted—how he'd lost control—but everything was too new and raw, and it was all he could do to keep from tearing the walls of this cell apart with his bare hands. He'd never been a violent person, but he'd also never had memories of a whole other life come rushing at him all at once like an attacking army.

Revna moved, but she made no sound, as if she knew he needed the quiet. His mind hadn't stopped reeling from the onslaught of his past. An eon of silence might not be enough for it all to fall into place.

There were a few things he knew for certain. He wasn't a Norse-man. His parents were dead. He had a sister.

He'd already grieved the loss of Eira. He'd accepted it. But to learn he had a sister again. It wasn't a question of if he believed it. He knew it to be true the moment her green eyes had settled fully on his. Her name was Cyrene. Not Eira. Somehow that knowledge felt like something had been taken from him all over again.

The loss and the pain. It became fresh, rubbing the scabs off healing wounds and letting them bleed. He couldn't understand what was wrong with his wretched heart that made him angry about it all or why Cyrene took the brunt of that fury.

Cyrene.

The name felt as natural to him as his own skin. He tried to remember if Revna had ever said her name. If she had, would he have remembered his true past upon hearing it? Would he have returned at all if he'd known his sister had married the son of a murderer? That she'd given him their mother's ring?

Duncan's father sold their people. He sired children only to abandon them. He meant to murder Revna, ending any chance Aksel would have had of knowing this wild, beautiful, dangerous woman. Mayhap that was what turned his confusion and hurt so volatile.

But was he not also the son of such a man? If not by blood, then by chance? At least he was in a cell where he belonged and not ruling a kingdom.

He rubbed the scar on his shoulder, bits of blurred memories standing at attention from the sensation.

No! Beli! Stay wi' me. Stay wi' me, Beli.

He had been prepared to die for her—so that she could live and save their people. She'd done just that. Instead of falling to his knees and embracing her, instead of thanking the God he'd barely started to believe in that they found each other again—he'd hurt her. If not with his hands, with the hatred in his eyes, with the accusations of his words.

In the cave, when he called out to *An T-aon*, he felt different. Felt

373

new. Now he felt as worthless and ruined as Tollak said he was. Perhaps he'd spent too many years under the influence of such a cold, hardened master. Perhaps he'd said the wrong words.

The cot creaked, and he looked up to see Revna stretched atop, her hands folded behind her head.

"Comfortable?" His tone was flat, emotionless.

After wiggling a bit, she found a spot she liked. "Not bad."

"I know you hate my brother," she stared at the ceiling for a moment before turning to look at him. "Why do you not hate me?"

He exhaled an amused breath. He could ask the same. Although, since he'd begun praying to this new God, that hate couldn't find a place to take hold inside. As if his heart had started to smooth and there were no footholds to grip. Perhaps he was changed, if only a little.

"You know why," he said instead.

"His blood is my blood, Aksel."

"You are not the same."

"His father is my father."

Aksel flexed his hands to keep them from forming fists and repeated his answer, every word a punch. "You are not the same."

"How?" She rolled to her side, propping her head up on her palm.

"You were treated as the rest of the Picts. You suffered with them. You crossed the seas to free them. He was raised in the tower as a prince. He was not by your side when you landed on the North shores. He was not with you while you were undoing his father's evils."

"Our father's evils," she corrected.

He didn't have a reply. She simply wasn't the same as Duncan, and it would have been easier to bury himself alive in a shallow grave than to hate her.

She rolled onto her back again, this time resting her laced fingers across her stomach, a soft hum her only answer.

"You disagree?" he asked.

"No. Everything you said is true."

This felt like a trap, but Aksel couldn't help stepping right into the center. "Why does it still feel like you disagree?"

"Just because something is true does not make it so."

He shook his head then let it fall back against the rough stone wall. "Is that supposed to make sense?"

"I just mean that all those things you said are facts, but they are not the only facts."

"He is your brother, I understand why you would defend him."

Revna sat up then, swinging her legs over the side of the cot. "I have known he was my brother since I was eight years old. Our healer was also our storyteller, and she brought me to the edge of the woods, pointed to the tower, and told me of my history."

Though he knew Revna to the very depths of her soul, she had shared very few stories of her life. So when she did, he listened. Aksel let one of his legs drop, keeping the other bent. He lifted his head, giving her his full attention.

"She told me that my father was the king. That he killed my mother and planned to do the same to my sister and me, but we were rescued by one of Derelei's warriors. Her name was Eden."

Eden. He knew that name. Eden was dead. So many were dead because of Duncan's father.

"Brigid told me that Eden separated my sister and I, knowing twin girls with queen Fiona's black hair and the king's blue eyes would be too difficult to hide. Brigid said my sister had died. I believed everything she told me except that. I...I could feel she was alive somewhere, waiting for me."

Revna was quiet, but he sensed she wasn't finished, so he waited.

"I hated Duncan at first too. I thought since he was raised in the tower, he would be the same as our father. That he was just as guilty. I was ready to crush his heart in my bare hands when he convinced Cyrene to marry him. But he was not the villain I thought him to be. So, you see, I knew facts. But it was not the truth."

"I am sorry for what you suffered." Aksel's heart ached for Revna.

For the loss and hurt she'd had to bear when she was only a lass. Just one winter older than he was when he was taken.

Seven. That memory flamed a bit of anger again. Ethni had said she didn't know for sure, but he'd appeared the same age as Tollak's dead child. He wasn't twenty-six; he was twenty-seven. It was just another of the many lies he'd believed all those years.

"That is my story. But Duncan has his own, and just because it is different does not make it any less true for him." Revna looked at her hands, fingers laced together in her lap. "We were all just children, Aksel. All of us. We cannot bear the responsibility for what our parents did. Only for what we do."

They didn't speak again until Revna whispered so quietly he almost didn't hear it, "Do you truly hate him?"

Aksel didn't answer for a long moment; he met Revna's blue eyes before whispering back in honesty, "I do not know."

A commotion from the stairwell had Revna on her feet and his head turned. He imagined it was Cyrene, storming the halls to try to speak with him, but it wasn't Cyrene's voice he heard echoing down the stone hallway.

"Where is he? Let me through, I must see him. Aksel!" Ethni's voice was panicked, and Aksel was on his feet too, his hands gripping the bars of the cell.

"Ye canna be here," a man's voice argued. "We have instructions not to let anyone through."

"Aksel!"

Ethni's screams had him shaking the bars, fury rising in his chest. He slammed his fist against the metal, pain shooting up his forearm. Revna's hands were behind her, doubtless gripping the handle of some weapon she'd kept hidden.

A softer male voice spoke so low, Aksel couldn't hear what he was saying, and then there were hurried footsteps. Ethni appeared around the corner, her arms stretching out before she reached him. She grasped him through the bars, pulling him to her. Her hands roamed his arms and chest, working up to his face.

"I am well, Ethni," he said softly, resting his forehead on the iron bars.

"Why are ye caged?" She turned her ire on the guard who had escorted her. "Why is he caged?"

"'Tis the King's orders." The guard nervously glanced between Ethni and Aksel. When his gaze landed on Revna, his hand shot to his blade, and he backed away from the cell.

"I will take audience wi' the king." Ethni began to pull away but Aksel caught her.

"No, Ethni. Dunna go. Please." His voice was so raw, Ethni seemed to crumble under its softness.

The guard kept his eyes on Revna but spoke to Aksel and Ethni. "The captain says ye have five minutes."

Having to stretch to reach his head, Ethni ran her hand over his hair, pulling his forehead to hers. "Aksel, my Aksel."

With his eyes closed and Ethni's soothing hum in his ears, he could almost forget where he was. He could almost believe that he was still Aksel, unwanted son of Tollak, brother of Eira, heir of Kaupang.

"What happened?" Ethni's question sounded far away, as if it wasn't directed toward him.

He kept his eyes closed, allowing himself the illusion just a little longer. Revna's warmth blossomed beside him, and her voice was low as she shared all that happened after Ethni had sailed for her homeland.

"Oh, Aksel," she said again, embracing him as much as possible through the bars. Then her hands found his face, drawing him back from his dream world. It wasn't any better than this reality, but it was what he'd been prepared to live with.

She scanned his face, taking in his features. He knew what she was doing. She was searching for the boy he'd been. For Beli. The boy she might have seen dancing at a celebration or strolling at his father's side before their world was ripped apart.

"Aye," she said. "I see ye."

He lowered his head. He didn't want her to see, and he certainly didn't want the listening guards to understand, so he spoke in Norse. "I cannot be here. I cannot find my way around this wall surrounding my heart. Was there not another way for our people than for her to bind herself to *him*? How can she walk these halls? Sleep in the room where that monster slept?"

"We all did what we had to do to survive. And we keep doing it." Ethni's voice was no longer tender, but strong, almost chastising, as she joined him in speaking Norse. "You know what I did to keep us alive, to keep you alive. If you do not blame me for that, then you should not blame your queen either."

"But what if he is hurting her? What if she suffers the same fate as Fiona?" His fear had him jerking back, but Ethni's hands were firm, holding him in place.

"I have been here long enough to see how she is loved. How she smiles in his presence. He cares for her deeply; that is most obvious. You can be proud of the bonds that have been formed between our people. Duncan is a good and strong king, and you are brother to a kind and mighty queen."

"I do not understand anything. I prayed to your God. I thought I was changed, forgiven. But my heart has betrayed me. It is still broken. Still angry." His confession was between the two of them, his voice so quiet he was certain not even Revna could hear. But as he continued, his voice grew louder beyond his control. "I am not a Pict. I am not a Viking. I am certainly not the brother to a queen. There is nowhere I belong and I—I do not know what to do. I do not know who I am."

Revna moved then, drawing both his and Ethni's eyes. Her hands replaced Ethni's on the side of his face as she forced his gaze to lock with hers. "You are mine. That is who you are."

She drew his forehead to hers, her fingers threading through his hair as she kept him anchored to her. "Mine," she said again.

Hers. He belonged to Revna. That promise lifted a weight on his chest so he could finally breathe deeply. And he did. Simply breathe, for several long moments.

He felt Ethni's hand on his back as she held him and Revna. "And you are both mine. If you prayed to follow *An T-aon*, then most importantly, you are His."

"Listen to me," Ethni said, squeezing the back of his neck until he lifted his head to meet her eyes. "You listen good, Aksel Tollaksen, Beli, son of Bercilak. You have been struck down and you are aching inside. I know that feeling well. You grieve for the life you have lost, grieve for what you never had. Grieve as long as you need to. But then you get up." Her blue eyes flamed, mercilessly holding hostage his own.

"You hear me? Get up as you have always done. It does not matter if you are called Aksel or Beli. The name does not change who *An T-aon* intends for you to be. If you confessed to Him, if you believed and trusted, He *has* made you into something new. He will give you a whole new name. He brought you home. He restored you to your family. Your feelings will change like the tides, ebbing and flowing. You cannot trust them. You must trust in the God who does not change, who does not fail or falter. You will fall. But you must get up. For all the ones that do not get to come home, for all the ones who do not have anyone waiting for them, you owe it to them to never waste what you have been given."

The guard cleared his throat and Ethni released Aksel, stepping away. There was a frigid void where she'd been, and Aksel had to step away too, watching as Ethni was gently led back to the stairs.

She turned, speaking to him from the bottom step where he could no longer see her. "Do what ye need to do to prove yer not a threat to the crown. Dunna exchange one prison fer another."

He heard the guard urge her along.

"Make sure he has enough to eat." Her voice faded as she climbed the stairs. "He's always hungry."

When it was quiet again, he turned to find Revna at the table. Her elbows propped on its surface, she casually gnawed on a leg of roasted chicken as if she were attending a harvest feast. As if she was oblivious to the fact that Ethni had just exposed all his darkest doubts and deepest fears. As if Revna hadn't laid claim to him and those words weren't holding his fractured heart together.

Just as when he'd been tied to a tree with her impossible knots, shivering and nauseous from a shameful dependency on mead, there was no judgment in her eyes. She simply let him be and gave him the space he needed to survive the next moment.

"It is still warm." Her words were muffled from the bite she'd just taken. Without taking her eyes off him, she pushed her foot out, shoving the empty chair away from the table.

"Is this your way of asking me to join you for dinner, Princess?"

Something whizzed by his head, clattering against the stone wall behind him. He didn't have to turn to know a dagger lay on the floor behind him.

"I warned you that term would get you stabbed. Pay attention."

He dropped heavily into the chair, facing her as he leaned one arm on the table. "You missed, and now you are down a weapon."

"I did not miss," Revna spoke around the large chunk of bread she'd just shoved in her mouth. "And I have another."

He couldn't help the laugh that rumbled from his chest. Only Revna could make a prison cell seem like the most homey place on earth. He intended to continue their battle of wits, but his stomach betrayed him with a loud gargle. She shoved the trencher toward him and he tore off the other leg. While they ate in comfortable silence, he had to admit that whomever Duncan employed in his kitchen was an excellent cook.

WHEN THE SOUND of the doors opening echoed down the stairs again, Aksel was sitting on the cot, his back against the wall and Revna curled up next to him. She was asleep, her head on his lap as he dragged fingers through the few loose strands of her black hair.

At the noise, she groaned and stretched like a lazy barn cat before rising to sit next to him. The salty smell of the sea still clung to her skin, and her cheeks were sun-kissed from their voyage. He almost called out to tell whoever was coming to go away and let her go back to sleep. Whatever they had to say could wait. It wasn't like he and Revna were going anywhere.

"Any guesses who is coming to visit us now?" she asked, her lips forming a sleepy smile.

"I am guessing it is a sibling. Either mine or yours." He rubbed his hand over her back as she straightened her tunic.

A dark shadow passed over her face and it took him a few heartbeats to remember that Revna had two siblings. One of whom she had never met and had sailed across the sea to find only to learn the answers came from where she started. She'd not mentioned her sister, and he wondered if they needed to finish the conversation they'd started before Torsten showed up and almost took her from him forever. No. He never wanted to revisit that memory for as long as he lived.

The sound of footsteps clicked on the stone stairs, but he kept his eyes on Revna. A rogue strand of hair demanded attention. He tucked it behind her ear before resting his hand on her knee and deciding he would let her hide behind whatever fears she wanted as long as she was alive and breathing by his side.

"Ahh," he said when their visitor stepped into sight. "It is to be my turn again."

Cyrene stood in the small hallway outside the cell, hands clasped behind her back, as regal as any queen ever was. He noticed her eyes skipping more than once to his hand on Revna's knee.

"I am surprised your husband allows you into such depraved holes as this," he said.

"It was actually his suggestion. But I am not here for you, Beli." Cyrene lifted a brow as she spoke in the Norse tongue with near perfect accuracy. Her green eyes drifted to Revna, softening at the sight of her friend. "I am here to speak with my scout."

34

REVNA

To reach the one you seek the most, you must go back to the beginning.

Astrid's message had been playing on repeat in her mind since the moment young Hermood spoke it. Her sister. The other half of her heart. She was here.

Aksel hadn't reopened the box that Torsten slammed shut upon his arrival in the clearing, ushering in her subsequent near-death experience. If she didn't already love Aksel, she would have simply for that mercy.

But now Cyrene was here, and from the way the queen was struggling to swallow, she carried news that would choke her to deliver.

Since she was eight winters, one thought never left Revna's mind. One that was stronger than the desire for violence and vengeance against the ones who'd separated her from her sister. A dream of a twin heart reunited with hers, filling in that missing piece that had left her empty and wanting all these years. The calm to her rage.

To reach the one you seek the most, you must go back to the beginning.

The second she'd heard it, she had a flash of hope. A vision of stepping off a boat to not only Cyrene and Astrid but another face, the mirror image of hers.

But no sister was there. That was half the reason Revna hid in the cell with Aksel. Deep inside, she was still afraid. The other half was simply that she wanted to be where he was.

"I want to stay with Aksel." Revna pushed herself up from the cot but stayed close.

"I will not try to talk you into leaving." Cyrene seemed to falter then, a bit of her resolve softening.

She used the Norse tongue as Revna did. Of course she would. If that was what Revna chose, then Cyrene would join her. She had always gone to Revna, sought her out and offered a hand. She was doing it again. And she was doing it while Revna was safely trapped behind bars of iron. A spark of disappointment flared in her chest. She'd never known Cyrene to cower.

"I think it will be good for you to be together." Cyrene nodded toward Aksel.

Suspicion raised the hair on Revna's arms and sent a heavy rock of discomfort into the pit of her stomach. She suddenly wanted Cyrene to leave. She and Aksel could live the rest of their days in that cell, growing old, gray, and wrinkled until they matched the stone walls. But instead, she heard herself asking, "Why?"

Cyrene swallowed, her lips parting. Then something caught the queen's eye from the direction of the stairs where Revna could not see. The breath she released seemed to be one of relief.

Soundlessly, Astrid came to stand by the queen, the two of them engaging in a silent conversation. Revna felt herself inch closer to Aksel, the warmth of his presence keeping her from turning to a pillar of stone where she stood.

Her eyes dipped to Cyrene's fingers, which pinched the edge of Astrid's sleeve. The queen and her captain were as one, united. Revna on the outside. But it would have been so even if there weren't bars between them. It had always been that way. She'd never bonded with another living soul. Until Aksel. She flicked her gaze over her shoulder, meeting his reassuring blue eyes before looking back to Cyrene. He was there. She could breathe.

Astrid shifted a fraction closer as Cyrene took a breath and turned to face her and Aksel. "Revna, there is something you need to know."

"Does it have anything to do with Astrid's cryptic message?"

"You...it worked? Hermood found you?" Astrid's expression brightened.

"When I returned your sister to Volfsby, your messenger was there receiving his yearly wage."

Astrid's smile held for a heartbeat and then faded.

"Wait, what do you mean you returned my sister? Did something happen to Isa?"

"Ethni did not tell you?" Revna glanced back at Aksel who only lifted his shoulders.

"No?" Astrid's face paled and Revna drew in a deep breath.

"Torsten took her." Revna's voice was hard, her chin ticking to the side at the memory of his villainous two colored eyes. At Astrid's gasp, she hastened to explain, "Do not worry. Aksel killed him."

Astrid slid blazing ice blue eyes to Aksel, her jaw tight from the clench of her teeth.

"Thank you." Astrid's hand went to her heart, her voice breaking before she cleared her throat and straightened. "Would it speak ill of me to inquire if his death was painful?"

"Too swift in my opinion," Aksel remained on the cot behind Revna.

"Pity." Astrid's muttered reply was low but drew a soft chuckle from Aksel's chest.

"You are your mother's daughter," he said.

"And Isa?" Revna recognized the strain in Astrid's voice. The captain was nearing an edge that would end in violence should she tumble over. Though from the absence of her blades and the presence of the bronze ring on her finger, she might not still be called captain. From what Revna knew of Astrid, the moon-haired woman would always be a warrior, though, until her final breath.

"I am supposed to tell you that she is well and it was not the most vile, horrific experience of her life."

"Careful, Little Bird," Aksel's soft correction irritated her.

Randi had asked her to shield Astrid from Isa's pain, fearing her daughter would abandon her post in Tràigh and return to Volfsby. But it felt wrong to keep Isa's endurance and bravery a secret. It felt villainous to take Astrid's choice as Isa's had been taken from her. She turned to tell Aksel as much.

"She deserves to know."

He held her gaze and gave a simple nod before sliding forward on the cot, rubbing his hand along the back of her knee.

Revna returned her focused stare to Astrid, who was now trembling with her own suffocating rage.

"I am not supposed to tell you that your sister carries the strength of ten men. Her resilience is unmatched. That she would rather take a beating than give that sick—" The squeeze of Aksel's hand paused her before she unleashed the foulest of terms. "—that sick animal the satisfaction of hearing her scream."

Revna's voice quivered with passion as her mind filled with the power of Isa's story and Torsten's disgusting grin. "He stole what she did not offer, but she bested him. At every turn, she ousted him as the sniveling coward that he was."

It took Astrid four breaths and Cyrene's steady hand on her shoulder to respond.

"You saved her?"

Revna nodded, then tilted her head to Aksel. "We helped."

Astrid's gaze went to the stones at her feet, her shoulders rising with deep breaths and her hands coming around the small swell of her stomach. Revna waited as Astrid clearly worked to calm herself. When she raised her head, her ice-blue eyes were silvered with tears.

"Thank you for helping my sister." Astrid reached out and took Cyrene's hand.

Aksel was drawing swirls on the back of Revna's trouser-clad calf with his fingers when she spoke again.

"You called me back across the sea. What of my sister? Is she here? Does she know who I am?"

Astrid and Cyrene exchanged a look, and Aksel's circles stopped. If Aksel was being held until he was no longer a threat, mayhap that was why her sister hadn't been brought to her.

"If yer afraid I will be a danger, I can assure ye, I am no threat. Do ye need the rest of my weapons? Here. Take them." Revna hoped her use of her native language added credence to her promises, and she whipped her last two blades from their hidden place as further proof. For once, she held nothing back. There was not another, and she didn't care.

She'd never felt so desperate. Not when Aksel had been hurt, not when she was near death herself. She was willing to kneel before Cyrene and beg if the queen would only allow her to see her sister. She'd equally desired and feared this moment for so long, now that it was upon her, she couldn't wrestle her wild emotions into submission. In a voice so meek it didn't sound like hers, she pleaded again, "I am no threat."

"That isna—" Cyrene said softly. "We dunna fear ye."

Astrid tipped her head in silent affirmation and Cyrene pulled her bottom lip through her teeth before continuing.

"Yer sister did come here. We dinna ken who she was until... after." Cyrene squared her shoulders. "She was the spy, Revna. The one who lit the signal fires fer the first Viking longboats and led them through the gates to ransack the village."

If Aksel's hand hadn't grounded her, Revna would have swayed. But Cyrene kept talking, not waiting for the alternating waves of heat and ice that raced over Revna's skin to subside.

"We believe she ken this was her homeland. Mayhap one of our own people told her what the former king had done, and instead of hating the Norsemen, she hated Tràigh. When given the chance to

386

destroy the kingdom that sold her as a slave, she took it." Cyrene's voice softened at the end. "We dunna ken fer certain."

"Why not ask her?" Revna already knew why. She knew why there was an empty gaol cell waiting for them instead of one occupied by a captured spy.

But what if—just what if...

"She's dead." It was Astrid that delivered the end to all Revna's hopes.

No. No, it couldn't be. It was a cruel, horrid lie. It had to be. Her knees didn't give; they carried her a step forward, but Aksel rose as she moved, his hand sliding up her arm. He held her back. He held her up.

"How?" she breathed, her limbs beginning to tremble.

"She was killed while trying to light the signal fires fer the approaching boats when William's army attacked," Astrid finished the story. Almost. "If those fires would have guided them in, we would have all died. Both kingdoms would have been lost."

Every nerve in her body was on fire, every muscle taut. Both Aksel's large hands wrapped around her upper arms. He was the only thing keeping her from erupting right there in the cell—him and the tingling mark on her chest telling her to let him.

"Who killed her?" Her voice sounded strange. It was too low and too hard. She was slipping away from the light, easing back into the waiting arms of the shadows that she'd worked so hard to lock behind doors.

Yet the light beckoned her so warmly, it held tight to her hands even as she let her own grip go lax. The brightness of it was too exposing; it would reveal her every agony, and the shadows promised to hide it all. Muting. Dulling. It was tempting, though she knew what lies those dark shapes truly told.

"Revna, no one kent, we dinna ken." Astrid shook her head, her gaze darting between Revna and Cyrene. "There was no way we could have."

Cyrene kept her emerald green eyes centered on Revna's.

"Who killed my sister?" Her words were deadly calm.

"I did." Cyrene released Astrid's hand, stepping forward. "'Twas my arrow."

Revna didn't move. Didn't breathe. She only squeezed her eyes closed. No. No. No. Not Cyrene. Anyone but Cyrene.

"Revna, I am so——"

"Nay." She kept her eyes closed as she raised a hand that silenced the queen. Her insides were at war, flesh and sinew vying for control. Above it all, a pulsing in her chest, urging her to open her eyes and look upon the queen she'd loved her entire life. To see whatever truth Cyrene would reveal. But questions and pain battered against the inside of her skull, demanding to be released, and Revna knew she was too weak to fight them.

"If I would have kent——" Cyrene began.

"Did you even ken her name?"

Aksel's hands were still on her, a calm, stalwart presence, making slow, steady paths up and down her arms.

"She called herself Vidarra." She heard Cyrene take another step.

"Did you bury her?" Revna finally opened her eyes, and at the sharp tick of her head, Cyrene stopped. Revna felt the moment the sealed door inched open again—the easy rush of rage seeping slowly through the crack. "Or did you toss her on the pile wi' the rest? Did I watch the smoke from her burning body as I left to free *our* people?"

"Revna." Astrid's tone was sharp as she moved in front of Cyrene, but the queen touched her arm, a shake of her head softly ordering her to stand down.

"I buried her. In the cemetery beside her...yer mother," Cyrene spoke frankly, her voice steady.

"And what of yer aim?" Revna's voice was soft too, but much more menacing.

Cyrene only blinked in confusion.

"Is it still true that ye dunna miss yer target?"

Cyrene blinked again, color draining from her face. "'Tis still true."

"And yet ye aimed fer her heart?" Revna was the one who stepped forward then, out of the safety of Aksel's arms. She was using her words as weapons now, and she couldn't find the ability to lower them. "Or did yer arrow land between her eyes?"

"I had no choice, she was going to light the signal fire."

"No choice?" Revna laughed, but there was no amusement in her tone. The pain of having that long-held hope ripped from her hands was so severe, so breath-stealing, she couldn't control the awful words coming from her mouth. She'd never wanted to hurt Cyrene before, and yet, her lips kept moving. "No choice but to kill my sister. Yer husband's sister."

Astrid shifted, taking a warrior's stance. Cyrene held her ground on the other side of the bars.

"I dinna ken she was your sister. I never saw her face."

Somewhere in her mind, her explanation made sense. But even that distant understanding faded at Cyrene's next words.

"Duncan spoke to her."

Air flew from Revna's mouth, as if she'd been punched in the gut, and her back met Aksel's strong chest.

"Yer brother begged her to stop. She dinna listen. And if she kent who she was, then she would have kent who he was too. Still, she did not stop. I watched it happen." Cyrene kept speaking, kept delivering blow after blow, her voice growing stronger with each word. "But Revna, even if we *had* kent who she was, even if I had the chance to speak wi' her myself, if we couldna stop her from lighting those signal fires...I would have made the same choice. There was no other option when it came to the lives of our entire kingdom."

"You ken as well as I do, ye could have stopped her wi'out a kill shot." Revna saw the words she fired hit their target. "Ye chose who ye wanted to choose."

Cyrene winced but remained composed, speaking through her teeth. "I willna say it again. I dinna ken who she was. And aye, I chose our people over everything. I will always choose our people.

That is what *An T-aon* called me to do as queen. And ye chose our people over me as well when ye left."

A voice in Revna's own head sliced through her grief and hit its target too—right in the center of her aching heart. Her hand flew to the mark on her chest, fingers curling in and nails digging into her flesh even through her tunic. *When you asked for help, I was there,* it said. *I am here now. I always have been.*

No. It wasn't right. Wasn't fair. Just like on the longboat, when she embraced a red-visioned rage—the fury that had cost Rune his life—Revna couldn't stop herself. She didn't want help to overcome this anger or to quiet it. She wanted to right the wrong; to make it not have happened. She wanted her sister to live.

Still, the mark pulsed. The voice called to her, and she felt as if she were being ripped in half.

"Ye took her from me," Revna also spoke through her gritted teeth. As much as she tried, she couldn't stop the tremors that rattled her bones. She couldn't stop the words from coming, couldn't stop her heart from racing in two opposite directions. One half of her easily strode toward the door holding back the screaming black shadows of rage and the other desperately clawed and scratched its way toward the light. Toward the peace promised by all that she'd ever heard of *An T-aon*. Everything inside of her was crumbling; it was shattering and shedding jagged shards that cut as they fell.

"I brought them all back. I kept my word. I served the crown my whole life—ye took the only thing I ever wanted. The only thing I ever asked fer."

"I think it's best ye leave now, sister." Aksel's tone was cold, and Revna could feel him trembling as much as she was.

Cyrene's eyes darted to his. *Sister.* He'd called her *sister.* Mayhap it was the only comfort he had to offer Cyrene in that moment.

"I will stay, Revna. I will be here w' ye," Cyrene pleaded, her hand extended, even as Astrid pulled her back a step. "I ken ye hate me now, but I will bear it. I will answer all your questions. I willna leave ye." Her hand curled into a fist over her heart. "I keep my word too."

"Go." Revna hardly recognized her own voice. Aksel had offered what mercy he had, and Revna did the same, for if the cell door had been unlocked, she would have taken the flames that raged inside of her and left the kingdom of Tràigh in a heap of ash.

"Revna, please." Cyrene's voice finally broke.

Revna's fists found her face, pressing hard against her temples. She couldn't bear Cyrene's agony, couldn't stop herself from making it worse, couldn't find the light, couldn't escape the dark—and for the first time, she desperately, maddeningly wanted to. With all that was in her, she wanted the light.

Then she was turned, pressed against a strong chest, and wrapped in arms that would not bend—would not break. Arms that knew what it was to be lost, to have only shadows and darkness as companions. To feel worthless, helpless, and empty.

"She said go." His voice was calm, but his order echoed off the stones of the cell.

"I will not leave her." Cyrene's shuddered breath cleaved the final slice through Revna's heart, snipping easily through whatever thin string had kept her together.

Revna pushed away from Aksel, whirling on the queen. Tears ran freely down Cyrene's cheeks, though her chin was high. Revna was at the bars, her hands clenched so tightly around the metal her knuckles were white.

"Get. Out." Cyrene had to leave before Revna lost all control and said something she could never take back. Revna's voice broke then too, her final order a desperate plea, "Go. Cyrene. Please."

Isa and Ethni both said their God promised help, and she needed it. That memory pulsed with the same rhythm as her mark, as if reminding her that knowledge of *An T-aon* had always been there. She needed it now more than air. She released gasping, silent words from the shredded halves of her broken heart. *Help me.*

Astrid dragged Cyrene toward the stairs.

"Revna." Cyrene forced Astrid to pause at the first step. Tears silvered the rims of her emerald eyes as she captured Revna's own watery gaze. "Thank ye fer bringing them home."

Cyrene gave a last glance at Aksel before following Astrid out of the cell.

When the sound of their steps had faded into nothing, Revna slid down the bars to her knees, her forehead scraping against the metal.

She was dead. Her sister—the heart keeper—was dead. But it was Cyrene's face—the anguish in her eyes—that was a vivid sight behind Revna's closed lids. The flinch and twist of her expression when Revna's words had sliced through her resolve were like a knife to Revna's gut.

She felt sick to her stomach. The whisper of familiar shadows caressed her shoulders, touched her cheek, and crooned her name. But she did not lean into them. She flinched away. *Help me.*

There's darkness all around us, Revna. Her skin dimpled at the chill of the shadow-kissed air and the memory of Brigid's words sending those shadows hissing back. *If we look for it, 'tis there. But there is also light. 'Tis your choice which ye choose to follow."*

It had sounded so simple on Brigid's lips—but the healer didn't consider that darkness had set its eyes upon Revna from the day of her birth and stalked her like prey.

How could she escape when it tracked her and kept closer than her own shadow? When it was determined to wrap its vine-like fingers around her heart and squeeze until there was no goodness left?

From Revna's buried memories, Brigid spoke again. *It only takes the tiniest spark to light the way, and if that spark is present, no amount of darkness can ever overpower it. It canna overcome.*

Revna slammed her fists against the stones as a scream peeled from her throat, slicing as it left. The sound cleaved through the still air, shaking the bars. *Help me find the spark.*

A warm hand rested on her shoulder as she screamed again, pounding the ground. Aksel didn't try to stop her when her hands dove into her hair, pulling strands from her braids. He only sat by her side as her eyes released tears that seared her lids and cut boiling tracks down her face. A still, small voice gently soothed her with a single word. *Surrender.*

For all her raging and fury, for all the times she walked hand in hand with shadows, that bit of hope had been there. The dream that the other half of her heart still walked the earth, that she could be whole. And now there was nothing. No light. No hope. No dream. Only the knowledge that her sister had been just as ruined as she was.

"She was supposed to tell me my name. Who I am. Now, 'tis gone. Everything is gone."

She could never make up for this—for all the terrible, rage-filled things she'd done. Brigid was in her head again, taking her by the hand as she had done so many winters ago, leading her through the dark woods and filling the thick woodland air with wise words.

Forgiveness isna given to those who earn it. If that were so, no one would receive it. It is given to those who need it. And because of the price that was paid, that forgiveness is complete. Ye have to but accept it, Revna.

Aksel moved closer when she pressed her forehead to stones as hard and cold as her heart. That hardness moved into her bones. It crashed against her lungs, sheering them from the muscle and sinew that held them in place and shredding them into useless ragged pieces. For the first time in her life, Revna panicked.

Surrender. It was the answer that would free her breath, but she could only focus on the tightness in her chest.

"I canna—" She curled her arms in, pressing against the lungs that would not open, against the mark that roared so loudly in her mind there was no other sound. "I canna breathe."

Aksel turned her, moving her legs around his waist and pulling her close until her chest pressed against his. His arms enveloped her, holding her like a child. His heart beat for hers. She managed sharp, shallow breaths against the unending pressure on her chest. *Surrender, Revna. Choose life. Accept forgiveness.*

"Look at me."

His fingertips brushed back her hair. His palms cupped her cheeks, firmly holding her head and forcing her eyes to meet his.

"Look at me, my wife. My love. My heart."

She blinked until she could see him through the salty water still pooling in her eyes.

"I ken who ye are. Ye are the Raven. Crosser of seas. Rescuer of captives. I ken it hurts. But ye are the one who does not leave her friends behind. Ye have fought death and won. Now 'tis time to fight the dark. Battle it back. Crawl if ye have to. Find the light. Let it in. No honor. Only victory."

She was held captive by his fiery blue eyes—knitted back together by the words he spoke in her native language. Her lungs opened, and she drew in a full breath.

"I dunna ken what to do," she spoke into his shoulder, her words as broken as his had been when he'd said the same. "Tell me what to do."

"Breathe." Burying his face in her hair, he snaked his arms tighter and held her until her heart beat at a normal pace and her lungs worked on their own.

His whispers heated her skin, and though he spoke too softly for her to hear, she knew he was praying. For her. She lifted her head when she felt him straighten. The back of his fingers grazed her cheeks, brushing away wild black hair that stuck to her wet cheeks.

He tilted his head to the side, scanning her face. "I told ye that I asked Ethni's God fer help when we were fighting Torsten."

She nodded, remembering.

"And when ye tried to die on me."

She nodded again, feeling the slight tug of a smile at her lips.

"And that He answered me."

Aksel's thumb moved along her jaw, his eyes roaming over her face.

"When I thought I would lose ye, I swore to serve Him all my days if He would let ye live."

A small gasp slipped past Revna's lips. "Aksel," she breathed.

"I dunna think He needs my service or my help at all. I am quite certain it is the other way around, but still…"

Revna let her hand explore his face, grazing her fingers over his bearded jaw where the muscles were like stone from how hard he was clenching his teeth.

"I aim to make good on that promise. He let me keep ye. And all that is to say, my own heart's still broken and wretched. I'm still so…" He closed his eyes, shaking his head.

Revna let the pads of her fingers dance over his face, stroking his cheeks and smoothing the lines of his brow. When he opened his eyes again, he let her see all of him. Every dark and shattered part.

"I ken my feelings are misplaced, but I am angry at my sister when I should be taking her in my arms and cherishing the family I have always longed fer. I ken what I am doing to her is wrong, just as I ken losing myself in endless mugs of mead was wrong. But then—before I ken Ethni's God, there was no way out. Now, even though there is brokenness—there is also hope. There is forgiveness. The one true God will help me out of my mess, and I ken…" He lowered his chin until their foreheads touched. He took a deep breath before speaking again. "I ken that if ye ask Him, He will help ye too."

Revna felt her eyes burn again and closed them until the sting eased.

"I did ask," she whispered. "I prayed."

Aksel didn't lift his head, but his fingers flexed where they held her face and she continued, "He answered me, though I dunna ken how."

He'd been helping her. Since she was a bairn and was meant to die but was rescued. Then there was the strange force that powered her muscles during the battle with Duncan's cousin, when her strength should have run out. How she survived the trip across the seas. So many times, she should have died—the wolves, Torsten's blade.

"What keeps ye from believing, Revna?" Aksel's voice was soft, gentle, and not accusing.

"I have lived in the darkness fer so long, I relished its ice and shadows. 'Tis all I've kent. What if I am too far gone to make my way back to the light?"

He lifted his head, leaning forward to kiss the corner of her mouth before sliding back and untangling her legs from his. He stood, offering a hand. She took it, and he lifted her to her feet.

Cupping her cheek, he pulled her up until she was on her toes as he captured her lips with his. Warmth flooded over her skin, thawing the ice that filled all her empty places and replacing it with a solidness that promised to hold against the strongest of forces. He pulled away too soon and rubbed his thumb over her lips, smoothing away her frown.

"Randi said something to me in Volfsby—'tis not how we begin our journey so much as how we finish. I think she is right. Ye may have walked one way thus far, but there is nothing to say ye canna turn around and walk the other way fer the rest of yer life." He slid his hand down her arm, capturing her fingers in his.

He made it sound easy. There were so many things she would have to release. What if she had to walk away from the purpose that had been driving her whole life—making the wrong things right? It felt impossible. But she knew she couldn't remain where she was. Something had to give.

For years, the idea of a sister was the hope she clung to. But Vidarra was never the thing that could fill the empty place inside. She was just as lost as Revna, just as broken. Mayhap more.

And though Aksel had saved her life from Torsten's blade, she still crumbled under the weight of Cyrene's admission. He could stand by her side, he could love her through all the pain. But he could not make her whole.

Bits of the story she'd always walked away from seeped into her mind. There was a Savior within those words. One she had rejected instead of embracing.

Ye have to but accept it, Revna. With Aksel's hand in hers, his open giving heart beating inches away, Revna did accept it. She didn't fully understand, and she didn't know what it meant for the rest of that life Aksel spoke of, but she realized she was never the one who could make the wrong things right. She needed saving just as much as all the ones she'd brought home.

She touched the mark on her chest, pressing her fingers in with such fervor she thought they might bruise her skin.

"Will ye walk wi' me?" She kept her eyes on their hands.

"Always." He wove his fingers through hers, lifting her hand and placing a sweet kiss on her first finger. "Ye ken, though ye are already my wife, I plan to put a band on this finger so I can announce it to the rest of the world."

35

AKSEL

"Ye think it wrong to keep it from them?" Revna asked, stroking the pad of her thumb over the place on Aksel's finger where a band should be.

The sun was setting, the day slipping away, but he was content to remain with Revna in their own private world. He lifted a shoulder as he tugged her toward the table that had been cleared and refilled with fresh water and warm food while she was sleeping. The guards didn't even bother aiming swords at him when they saw the real danger was resting peacefully in his lap.

"I think there are far worse things they need to forgive us fer. Come, Little Bird, all this talk has left me famished."

A soft laugh blew through her lips. "When are ye not famished?"

"I can think of a few occasions." It was his turn to laugh at the blossom of crimson that spread across her cheeks. It was a rare occasion when he could make Revna blush.

"I kent ye were a rogue from the moment I saw ye." She shook her head, joining him in laughter.

"An irresistible rogue, since it was yer request to be handfasted."

"Ye'll never let me forget that, will ye?"

Aksel placed a hand on his heart as if making a pledge. "Not fer as long as I have breath in my lungs." When she opened her mouth, he pressed a finger to her lips. "I ken, I ken. I should be careful or ye'll kill me before the morning."

"Let that be the thing ye never forget, Prince." She pushed up on her toes and pressed a quick kiss to his lips.

Once they finished eating, she told him to cover his ears when she slipped behind the parchment screen. The second she reappeared, he laughed at the yelp she swallowed when he scooped her up.

"I despise being carried like a bairn." She crossed her arms, resembling a petulant child. "Must ye behave like a hulking beast?"

"Some habits are hard to break." He only flexed his biceps, curling her closer as he carried her to the cot. "Besides, as yer beastly husband, 'tis my right to haul ye about wherever I wish."

The cot wasn't big enough for them to both lie down, so he took his usual position, sitting with his back against the wall so she could put her head on his lap. Once again, he trailed his fingers through her hair.

"Ye said Randi's words stayed wi' ye. Isa said something that stuck wi' me too."

"Mmm." He hummed, his eyes feeling heavy.

"She said there is strength in surrender."

"It seems profound statements run in the silver-haired captain's family." His words were sluggish, and he let his eyes drift closed.

"Do ye think that is true? About surrender, I mean?"

Aksel sighed, relishing the softness of her warm skin against his calloused fingers. "I surrendered to ye the first moment I saw ye, Little Bird, and in some ways, I'm completely powerless. But if anyone were to try and harm ye, I ken I could battle the world if it would keep ye safe. I'd beat down death's door to bring ye back should he try to steal ye from me again."

He stroked his thumb across her jaw, smiling to himself. "Not that ye wouldn't have already slaughtered him yerself by the time I got there."

He forced himself to stay awake until her breaths deepened and she relaxed under the rhythm of his hand rubbing up and down her back. Then he was sucked into a deep, dreamless sleep.

When he peeled his eyes open again, he blinked against the light streaming through the small window near the top of one wall. It was morning. Their first night in their homeland was officially spent in prison. He couldn't help the silent chuckle that shook his chest. It somehow seemed so appropriate for the raven and her wayward prince.

Revna was still asleep, and though his back ached from sitting against the hard wall all night, he smiled down at her little form, curled up like a cat in his lap.

The soft sound of a breath snapped his attention to the bars. A man sat in the small hall outside of the cell. Much like Aksel, he was propped up against the stone wall.

"Is there a reason the floor is sticky and smells like ale?" Duncan asked.

Aksel huffed, running his hand over Revna's hair. "What do ye want, King?" He closed his eyes, hoping when he opened them, it would have been a dream and he'd be alone with his wife again.

"Did ye expect me not to come?" Duncan's voice sounded hoarse, as if he'd slept less than Aksel had. "Cyrene believes ye to be honorable, and believe me, I paid fer doubting her. But Revna is still my sister, and I'm not one to leave important things to chance."

Aksel kept his eyes closed but blew out another amused breath. "Ye have been here all night then?"

"Aye. Since dusk."

"It concerns me that *my* sister's husband spends his nights outside prison cells watching captives sleep." Aksel worked his jaw, tempted to ease the king's worry by letting him know that Revna's honor was perfectly cared for by her husband. He decided against it. Duncan could suffer a little longer. Although, he did respect the man for the lengths he would go for his sister's honor. "How is Cyrene?"

"Broken." Duncan's quick, honest reply had Aksel looking to the king.

His blond curls were in wild waves around his face, purple shadows lingering under his eyes. Cyrene wasn't the only broken one.

"I understand yer hatred fer me," Duncan said as his eyes fell closed. "Yer sister felt much the same when she discovered who I was. I believe she struggled with whether or not to have me run through at first. But war was upon us, and we had little time for battles between ourselves if either kingdom was to survive."

"I've heard the story." He'd said the same to Cyrene.

"Ye would rather she'd slit my throat and taken both kingdoms to victory on her own?"

Aksel drew his lips to the side, considering the idea for a moment and the way she'd stood strong on the dock. "She could have."

Cyrene was not the girl she'd been when he'd last seen her in the woods. There had been a hint of the queen she'd turn out to be in those last moments. The woman she'd become was as much a warrior as a queen, and he felt fiercely proud.

"I have no doubt," Duncan said, sincerity darkening his tone. "Mayhap it is my own self-preservation that kept me from giving her the idea."

Revna dragged in a long breath, stirring, but not waking.

"Ye love my sister," Duncan's words were not a question.

"More than my life." That he could easily admit.

"Were ye one she rescued?"

Aksel looked down to where Revna lay in his lap, her blue eyes slowly opening and a soft smile curling her lips.

"Aye."

Revna blinked up at him, water pooling around her lids.

"Ye rescued me too," she whispered.

He lifted his arm, allowing her to sit up next to him.

"Brother." She nodded at Duncan, untying her braids and running her hands through her hair to untangle the knots.

"Are ye well?" Duncan stood but kept his distance, leaning against the wall behind him.

"Aye. Yer accommodations are most acceptable. Lavish, even, considering I've slept on the ground fer the last five winters. And most of my life before that."

Duncan lowered his chin to hide a smile and shook his head at her subtle jab before looking back up at them, his expression schooled into that of a king. Solemn and demanding.

"Now that ye are both awake, I will say this once and only once." Duncan pushed off the wall, taking one step toward them.

"Ye are our family. Our blood. Ye are welcome in our home and amongst our people as long as ye dunna pose a threat to either. If our decisions and failures are ones that ye canna forgive or overcome, I will pay for passage to wherever ye want to go. Ye'll have my blessing and the protection of my kingdom."

He looked to Aksel. "Yer sister has given her life and heart to protect yer people. She is the queen this kingdom deserves and the wife I never will. If ye canna understand that, at least understand why I canna allow her to suffer more than she already has. I have lost a brother; I ken the pain. Cyrene has mourned yer loss once, and I will help her through that grief again if that is what ye decide. But it will be the last time. She would welcome ye home again and again, but she is a better follower of Christ than I. I am too selfish to watch her splay her heart open over and over. I canna bear it. So make yer choice."

Then Duncan shifted his gaze to Revna. "Sister, we have both lost our family. I also understand yer heartache and anger at what became of Vidarra. Ye canna imagine how many times I have replayed that meeting wi' her, driving myself mad, wishing fer it to be different. But what happened canna be changed. And ye werena here to watch the queen grieve. Ye dinna see how it almost destroyed us. Ye dinna see

402

how she raced to the shores every time a ship was spotted, hoping and praying that ye'd be aboard. Ye werena—" Duncan stopped, looking to the floor again as if needing to regain his composure. "Ye werena the one to hold her through all the nights she woke screaming in agony at what she'd had to do. And make no mistake, it had to be done. No one has mourned the loss of *our* sister more than Cyrene."

"What if she could have been saved? Redeemed?" Revna pushed herself up without a fraction of the aggression she'd had the day before. Aksel sensed the moment the night before when Revna's rage had left her, and only grief remained in its place.

The king took another step, his expression softening at his sister's desperate question.

"We have asked ourselves the same. Believe me, we have had years to ask all the questions, which is why I can forgive ye for breaking Cyrene's heart. We broke each other's when our wounds were fresh too."

Aksel watched as Revna's head dropped, her arms folding over her chest as if to protect her still raw heart. Duncan's words were hard to hear, even for Aksel, but he spoke them with compassion.

"I canna give ye the answer other than to say that the Lord is good and He allows his creation to choose their path. Vidarra chose hers. We are all left to grieve that choice."

"All I ever wanted was to see her, just once." Revna stood, slowly, approaching the bars. "I needed to know if she was the missing half of me."

Duncan closed the distance between himself and his sister. He was close enough for her to reach him. Aksel stood too; a flash of worry left him reeling with uncertainty.

At his movement, Revna flicked her eyes to his, her brows furrowing as she undoubtedly read his concern. "I wouldn't harm my own brother." There was a hint of hurt in her voice, drawing him back to the night he'd stood between her and Eira and she'd said much the same. He reminded himself that when she'd woken, there had been a peace that he'd never seen before. Even as she spoke to Duncan now, her voice had lost its hardness.

So he let his expression relax, a half-smile tugging at the corner of his mouth as he teased, "I ken how fond ye are of the blade."

When her mouth popped open, he brushed his hand over his shoulder where a thin scar marred his skin beneath his tunic. Her eyes narrowed, but the hint of a smile played at her lips.

"Ye stabbed yerself, Prince." Revna turned to Duncan, brows raised as she said, "He stabbed himself."

Duncan watched their exchange, an indiscernible look on his face. When Revna's eyes settled on her brother's, she was suddenly serious, looking too small standing before him. Aksel wanted to shield her from whatever he might say next, even if his heart was beating a warning that demanded he allow her to listen.

"I ken what yer looking fer, sister. I searched fer it myself fer so many years, missing a mother I never ken and again when I lost Fiona and my sisters in the same night." Duncan reached through the bars, his hands resting on her shoulders, his eyes glistening with tears. "I got to hold ye once. One time before ye were taken from me. But I loved ye and Vidarra. From the moment I saw yer tiny round faces. Ye...ye were so perfect. So loved by yer mother."

Revna, trembling under her brother's touch, clasped her hands over her mouth as tears raced down her cheeks. Aksel knew Duncan was saying the words she'd always longed to hear and understood with certainty the goodness Cyrene must have seen in him. Duncan wiped Revna's tears with his thumbs before holding her by her shoulders again.

"Even when I went to the Abbey to study the scriptures, a plague took the rest of my family and what I thought was my purpose. It was all stripped away in an instant, and if I hadna the promise of eternity wi' a living Savior at this life's end, I would have perished from despair."

Aksel leaned against the corner where metal met stone,

enthralled by the power of Duncan's words but ready to catch his little bird, who looked like she might crumble at any moment.

Duncan cupped her cheeks, dipping his brow to meet her eyes. "Revna, it is only the Christ who can fulfill—the One ye call *An T-aon*. Only His presence is sufficient to take all our faults, our grief, our anger and turn us from darkness to light. I ken ye feel like ye've lost all hope, but hope has been wi' ye all along. Yer a warrior, but sometimes victory comes wi' surrender."

Revna stared at her brother, her eyes taking in every detail of his face, and Aksel knew she was searching for any hint that he was less than sincere. He found himself hoping she did not find it. He wanted Revna to have a brother who loved her and guided her to the place where she could bask in the light. It was the brother he should be for Cyrene.

And Duncan's words rang so true, he felt something solidify in his own heart. When Revna shattered his heart on the shores in Volfsby, he thought she'd also shattered his purpose. When Ethni told him the truth of his heritage, he thought he'd lost his identity.

He'd spent months thinking if he only knew his true name, all his questions would be answered, but it only led to more questions. More pain.

Revna said he belonged to her, so did Ethni. But he also belonged to the one true God. It wasn't a name that determined his worth, it was *An T-aon*, the one true God, The Christ. It wasn't Revna or any mission that gave him purpose. That was The Christ too. It was all Christ. All his beginnings and his endings and everything in between.

Every answer to every question was Christ.

Aksel was ready to fully embrace that truth, and he desperately wanted Revna to do the same. He didn't want to go where she was not, but he would lead and he would pray that she would follow.

He'd been staring at the floor, still trying to sort through all the memories, old and new, that mixed with the overwhelming need to find Cyrene. When he finally looked up, Duncan's cobalt eyes were fixed on his.

"The choice is yers," he spoke to Aksel but squeezed Revna's arms once before stepping away.

"There is not much of a choice when we are caged, King." He might respect Duncan, but just like Rendel, no matter how good and honorable a man he was, he'd still stolen away his sister and thus deserved a brother-in-law to constantly challenge him.

Duncan aimed for the stairs but stopped, staring at his hands. He turned and placed something on the ground outside of the cell. "This belongs to Beli."

Aksel froze at the round bit of metal peeking at him from beyond the bars. His mother's ring. Her most precious possession and the only gift she had from their father. The ring their mother had then given to him when he was a lad and she was dying.

Duncan walked backwards to the steps, a knowing smile curling his lips.

"The door is open." He nodded to the closed entrance which neither Aksel nor Revna had touched since they'd been ushered in. "It always has been."

36

REVNA

The door is open.

Duncan's words hung in the air long after he'd climbed the steps. She stepped back from the bars but didn't touch the door. Neither did Aksel.

They'd been free to leave the entire time, but neither she nor Aksel had even tried. As if they'd wanted to stay imprisoned. She'd accepted *An T-aon's* forgiveness, but was she willing to let go of her anger and walk in freedom?

Dunna exchange one prison fer another. Ethni's words to Aksel had her backing up another step.

The start to Brigid's last story sounded in her memory as clear as the day she'd heard it.

I'm going to tell ye a story, Revna. A story which is only yers to hear. A story that will make ye hate me and hate the world, but it's one ye must hear and one ye must learn to overcome. All our lives depend on it.

Though her misunderstanding had led to many of their people, including Aksel, coming home, it wasn't the tower king's choices she had to overcome but her own grief. Grief that had disguised itself as

407

anger for so long. Revna finally understood what Brigid meant when she'd said all their lives depended on it. If Revna and Aksel could not make things right with their siblings, the kingdom would suffer.

Cyrene could face all manner of enemies on the battlefield without flinching. She was truly a warrior queen, but losing her brother twice and losing Revna—it would cause her to crumble and Duncan not long after. All the good Revna had done in returning their people would be in vain, for she would tear down the very kingdom she'd sent them home to. Could she give all of herself to *An T-aon* and trust Him to bring true healing to her own heart and her friends?

She turned to Aksel, a thousand questions swirling in her mind.

He stepped forward, his eyes taking in her drawn expression and his knuckles grazing the curve of her jaw. "What is it?"

"I ken the story of the one they call The Christ. I understand God became flesh and was the sinless sacrifice to atone fer all of our trespasses, and I...I believe it. I want to do as ye did and follow Him. I want to be made new, but He was still taken by death. Darkness still won. So I dunna understand how it works, who I'm praying to and how He answers me."

Aksel tilted his head, brows meeting together over his blue eyes. "Did ye never hear the rest of the story?"

She lifted a shoulder, "What more is there when the hero dies?"

He exhaled a soft laugh before looking to the stone ceiling of the cell, shaking his head as if in disbelief before looking back to her. "And ye still believe. That is impressive." He brushed a strand of her hair behind her ear. "His death is not the end."

"Duncan called Him the Living Savior. Did He not die?" Revna searched her memories for stories that proved otherwise.

"He did. But death couldna hold Him." Aksel's eyes sparked, as if lit from within. "Ethni would say ye missed the best part. She used to whisper it to me and have to cover her mouth when she got to the end, she was so overcome."

"Speak then, Prince! What is the end?" Revna grabbed his arms, more riveted than she'd ever been to hear a story. Where Brigid's had felt like an ending, this one was a beginning.

"The end, Little Bird, is that the God made flesh did die, but on the third day, when some women went to His grave, He wasna there."

"Someone stole His body?"

"That's what they thought too, but nay. He stood, alive and speaking to them."

"How?"

Aksel wrapped his arm around her shoulder, curling her into his side. "Can one truly understand the mystery of the God above all others? But I asked Ethni the same. She said that the One called Christ had battled the darkness of death and hell. That He won, and death was forced to release Him to life once again. She said those who believe will also be released into eternal life."

This was the eternity Rune had sought. The place he would be waiting for her. She could see him again.

"No death?"

"No death," Aksel repeated.

"No darkness."

He leaned in, brushing his lips along her cheek. "No darkness."

"I did miss the best part." Revna straightened, the realization sending shots of fire through her veins. "All this time."

"Do ye still believe it to be true?" His gaze was intensely focused on hers. Her eyes dipped to his chest, finding it still. "Do ye believe in Christ, the living God?"

Did she believe it? Now that she knew the real ending? It made sense that the Christ had died, but that He'd risen again?

She'd never believed in fairy tales, only in things she could feel and touch, things that were true and useful. But as she thought through those conditions, she realized that this wasn't a fairy tale— it was just the same as when she sat at the feet of the healer or the smithy. She was learning what was most true, most useful. She'd been inching closer her whole life, gathering the clues, cataloging the hints only to come to this moment where she would state her answer.

And she realized she'd already decided to believe in and surrender to a Savior she thought was dead but somehow still helped her. That was more impossible than believing He was alive. Aksel was waiting, breath held in his lungs.

"Aye," she said. "I do."

The truth of *An T-aon* was not some fairy tale or legend that could not be touched, felt, or seen. She did see it in the intricate design of creation and in all the ways she'd been helped in some unfathomable way. She felt it in the mercy her brother was able to show, in Astrid's strength and courage, and in Cyrene's wisdom and unconditional love.

And, as Aksel's fingers wove through hers, she knew she could touch this love of the one true God as well. A love that put another above itself. A love that would forever lead her away from darkness and into the light. A love that always got back up.

There was only one answer. Yes.

She'd always done what was necessary for those she loved. So did *An T-aon*.

A peace settled inside of her. Its warmth and light were unbreakable threads that slowly stitched together the shredded sinews of her heart. The whisper of a loving voice seemed to tell her that she'd always been His. That He had been waiting to welcome her with open arms, just like Cyrene and Duncan were waiting now. A gentle pulse from her mark served as evidence of that truth.

She turned to Aksel, her hand pressing against her mark and desperation making her heart race. "I dunna want to go wi'out ye."

Aksel pushed off the wall, coming nearly chest-to-chest with her. He gently wove his fingers into her hair, his thumb rubbing her cheek. Then, he slid his arm around her waist, lifting her to her toes as he lowered his head, his lips hovering over hers. The warmth of his breath sent shivers across her skin and something warm pooled in her stomach.

"Ye'll never have to." He closed the distance between them, possessing her mouth with a kiss that held the promise of forever.

She was breathless when he broke away, and a teasing grin stretched her lips as she whispered, "We could wait just a little longer."

Aksel kissed her quickly once more. "I would not object, but I'm certain yer brother has his guards listening quite intently. He sat outside the cell all night to protect yer virtue."

Revna's mouth popped open. "He did what?"

Aksel straightened, crushing her to his chest so closely she had to tip her chin up to see him.

"Aye. Watched us all night. He was sitting right there when I woke." Aksel tipped his head toward a spot outside the cell before lowering his chin and letting his lips graze her jaw. "He was making sure ye werena being ravished by the savage Viking."

"Ahh," Revna turned her head, pressing her ear to his chest to listen to his heart. "I guess rogue-spotting runs in the family."

"A rogue or a bonnie idiot, which am I?"

"Both. Pay attention." She couldn't help the grin that stretched across her mouth at the chuckle that vibrated through his chest.

"Now," he sighed. "Are ye ever going to talk to me about that verra obvious lion-shaped mark yer always trying to scrub off yer skin?" When she lifted her chin, he laughed at the shock she was certain he saw in her eyes. He raised a brow and lowered his voice. "I am yer husband, and I do pay verra, verra close attention."

She buried her flaming face in his chest again. Clearly, more of his memories had returned. As the son of Queen Derelei, he would have known exactly what it meant. "It appeared the day I found out who I truly was. I always thought it was a mistake. I am not blood kin to yer family. Now, I...I dunna ken."

"I remember the stories my mother and her healer used to tell, of legendary warrior women."

"The lionhearts," Revna said.

"The lionhearts," he repeated, his hand stroking her hair. "If ever there was a woman who had the heart of a lion, 'tis ye, Revna, blood or not. Besides, now ye are related, through me."

Had *An T-aon* known she would be Aksel's wife? Revna rolled her eyes at herself. Of course He would have.

"I just canna believe He chose me. Even when I was raging across the Northlands wi' hate in my heart, burning it to the ground, He dinna take this mark away." She let her secret sink into the safe place that was her husband's arms. "I dunna feel worthy to bear it."

"I am beginning to think *An T-aon* chooses the least worthy on purpose. So that there will be no doubt in the end who He truly is."

"Mayhap so." She released an amused breath. "Mayhap He will make something of my unworthiness yet."

Aksel's lips were on her head, his arms drawing her even closer, as if they were truly one body. "I have no doubt He already has...fer both of us."

They stood in silence for several minutes before he loosened his hold and gazed down at her.

"Are ye ready, Little Bird?"

She closed her eyes, and for the first time, there were no shadows waiting for her. Only a bright, flickering flame.

"Aye, Prince. I'm ready."

He slipped his hand in hers and paused only an instant before wrapping his fingers around the bars of the door and tugging. Just as Duncan said, it was unlocked and easily swung open.

Aksel stood over the ring Duncan had left, the tightness in his hand betraying his hesitation. She stooped, snatching it before he had a chance to protest.

"Ye are Aksel, but ye are also Beli. I've heard stories of yer bravery since I was a bairn. Ye are the lion that sacrificed himself fer the queen so she could save yer people. So she could save me. Ye do not fear this ring. Ye do not fear the past. Ye. Dunna. Give. In."

The flames in his eyes threatened to consume her, but she only welcomed that heat after so long in the dark and cold. He crushed his lips to hers, sucking in a breath as she slid the ring onto his smallest finger. Their kiss was pain and healing, agony and bliss. It was the promise that even if they had to claw and scratch and climb, they would forsake the darkness and embrace the light. Together.

EPILOGUE
REVNA

828 AD

"There are three things ye must always remember." Revna scanned the faces of her students, silently ordering them to pay attention. "The first and most important: *Never* let yer enemy get their hands on ye. Odds are, yer attacker will be stronger than ye. He gets his hands on ye, and yer possibility of escape just decreased by more than half. But ye can be quick. Ye can be smart."

She made one pass around the ring where ten women, young and old, gathered, waiting to be trained.

"The second," Revna said before she retrieved a dagger from some hidden place and sent it flying into the center of the painted mark on a straw-stuffed dummy. "Is never let yer enemy ken how armed ye are."

Revna waited until the gasps and murmurs quieted before she spoke again. "Now, it's best to avoid a physical fight if possible. Get

414

out; get to a place where ye have help. A trusted friend or yer kin. Even if ye have to run and hide behind a stranger—'tis better than remaining alone wi' someone intent on harming ye.

"I ken ye'd think a crowd would be best, but ye'd be surprised how blind a large group can be. But if all yer escape plans fail, if ye find yerself in a situation where ye must defend yerself, I'm going to teach ye some moves that will get ye free and, mayhap as a bonus—" Revna felt her lips curve into a wicked grin. "Ensure yer attacker will never make the mistake of hurting ye again, aye?"

Encouraged murmurs from her students accompanied a few soft claps.

"Ye all ken Aksel." Revna found his blue eyes from where he waited on the outside of her training ring and lifted her hand, directing the attention of her students to him. "He will be playing the role of the attacker today."

Aksel, after gently lowering a fire-haired child from his shoulders and peeling another from his leg, stepped past one of the women who formed their circle. His soft smile faded as he stepped behind Revna. He'd learned to keep the delight from dancing in his eyes while sparring with her during these lessons.

Many of the women who came to Revna for help did so in secret. Most with scars and bruises they could not, or would not, explain. But his calm demeanor, his bright smile, and the way even the smallest of village children flocked to him eased much of their wariness.

Duncan was a man who led by example, loving his wife and children as he loved his kingdom. But not all of his subjects followed that example. There was still darkness dwelling amongst them. There were still men whose hands harmed those they were meant to protect.

But there was also the raven. A secret had spread that there was one who could help a voiceless woman, who could teach her to defend herself enough to get away when she needed to, and who would help when running wasn't enough.

Cyrene said Duncan hadn't spoken a word when the healer mentioned the number of men he'd been called to tend to had risen in the last year and the number of women and children decreased. The gaol cell had also been granted a fair share of residents. Before, many sins inside the village of Tràigh had been clouded in shadow, but a bright light had come to Tràigh, and darkness was made to flee.

Duncan easily granted permission when Revna came with a new list of names.

Names needing a different type of rescue. He offered the coin from his coffers for supplies as a new village formed in The Dorcha. A village where those who were unloved, abused, and neglected could find safety and comfort.

And strength. This is what they saw when Revna faced her husband in the cleared space she used for sparring. Even though every woman had met Aksel and knew he could be trusted, the fear was still palpable as he circled Revna like a predator.

But that was what drove Revna to keep teaching, to keep training. These people didn't need to hide from their fears, nor did they need to race into the darkness and let it consume them. The skills they learned didn't need to urge them to their own level of violence. No. This training was meant to preserve life.

It was meant to give them the courage to face fear and darkness head on, with hope, knowing there was an army behind them and the God above all gods before them. Their goal wasn't to unleash vengeance or pain, but to stop it. To break chains and cycles. To spread light in dark places.

"Watch carefully," Revna instructed as she avoided Aksel's attempts to grab her. "I'll be demonstrating my final rule."

Revna ducked under Aksel's arm, twisted away from his hands, and jumped over his jutting leg. She explained her moves, teaching the women to watch for tells to anticipate their attacker's next move.

She was quick, but so was Aksel, and she'd already asked him not to hold back because the men who these women might face wouldn't. When his broad chest slammed into her back, it nearly drove the air from her lungs, but before he could pin her to the ground with his weight, she curled herself into a ball and sent him stumbling over her body as she rolled.

They'd sparred long enough for him to be ready for most of her tricks, and he managed to wrap his fingers around her arms as he attempted to remain upright.

"Almost had me, Little Bird," he muttered as he spun her around, wrapping his arm around her waist. "Are ya losing yer touch?"

Revna grunted as he tossed her over his shoulder and captured both her flailing ankles with one of his large hands. The sounds of fear and disappointment from her students only made her smile where they couldn't see. They assumed the fight was over and she had been bested.

Using her hands, Revna crawled across his body, wrapping herself around his neck like a snake. She lowered her head so her mouth was near his ear and no one could hear. She whispered words meant only for him. Aksel's face flamed red, his steps faltered, and his grip loosened for the split second she needed.

Instead of trying to use her hands on his back to push herself upright, she lurched further over his shoulders, letting the weight of her torso drag him down and throw him off balance. Aksel had no choice but to release her and use his hands to catch himself before he landed flat on his back.

When her legs were free, she flipped, swung one leg over his head, and locked her ankles, trapping his neck between her legs just above her knees.

Using all her strength, she rolled, taking him with her. She landed on her side, forcing Aksel to his stomach. Keeping just enough pressure on his neck for him to stay conscious, she snatched his outstretched arm, bending it backwards. Her other hand slid down to his, also bending it back so that he had to remain motionless or suffer a broken wrist.

With his free hand, he tapped the ground, and a cheer rose from the watching students.

As Revna loosened her hold, she spoke to the crowd. "One tug, and I can dislocate a shoulder or break a wrist. He lives, but so do I. Dunna let this small victory fool ye, though. Ye have but seconds to get free and get away. Take them."

Unhooking her legs, she swung her foot around so that she was able to rise to her knees. She placed her hand on Aksel's back, silently thanking him for his endurance as he pressed his forehead to the ground, breathing heavily.

"Here is the final rule that ye must always remember. Yer enemy might be bigger, stronger, even smarter, but ye are never wi'out hope. There is always a move to be made. Find it. Use it. Bite, kick, scratch if ye have to. It may not be honorable, but when ye need to survive, there is no honor. Only victory."

After their lesson, Revna tossed Aksel a linen towel to wipe the sweat from his face. He perched on the stump of a sawn-off tree, working the arm she'd twisted in a wide arc.

"Did I hurt ye?" She stepped between his knees—close enough to pick a bit of dried leaf from his hair.

"Nay." He dropped his arm and rested his hands on her hips. "Another riveting lesson, Little Bird."

"Ye held yer own fairly well, Prince. Yer getting harder to take down."

"Is that so?" The flames behind his blue eyes held promises that had fire racing up her neck and spreading across her cheeks. She followed his gaze as he stood, towering over her. His lips tugged to one side before he leaned in, those same lips brushing her ear and sending a shiver up her spine. "And what of the promises ye whispered? I ken it was my idea to use yer words, but that was…"

Revna's fingers shot to her mouth, covering a giggle. She shook her head as he raised a brow. "That was fer demonstration purposes only."

"Demonstration purposes," he repeated, eyes narrowed in disappointment. When she nodded, he straightened, hands resting on his hips as he observed her until she fought not to squirm. Finally, he inhaled deeply and brushed his knuckles across her cheek. "Verra well. But I demand a rematch later."

Before she could respond, he sauntered off to help serve the midday meal, tossing a wink over his shoulder.

"Never in my life would I imagine ye blushing, Revna."

Revna jumped at Astrid's presence behind her. Once her heart restarted, she laughed, watching her husband's brilliant smile as he carried a wooden trencher of crusty bread to a table full of women and children. He announced his presence with a joyful greeting to avoid startling them, and a pulse of molten heat burst from Revna's heart. From their utter brokenness, *An T-aon* had gathered the shattered pieces and formed them into something new. Something whole.

"There are a lot of things I never thought I would see," Revna said.

Astrid linked her arm through Revna's, dragging her to a quiet place of their own. Revna basked in the warm rays of sunshine that snuck through an opening in the thick canopy of trees as Astrid gushed about the progress her group had made with longbows.

"Speaking of such things, Alpia is a much stricter instructor than I, and I fear she might even be a better shot." Astrid shook her head in disbelief.

"She struck me as a mighty warrior the minute I laid eyes on her. But young Jarteign is a fine teacher as well."

"Aye," Astrid said. "He shares Aksel's skill wi' the littles."

Astrid's adopted son had grown into quite the scholar, preferring to spend his time at Duncan's side, gleaning from the king's knowledge of scripture. But he also helped some of the younger ones in simple lessons on safety and accuracy.

Revna followed Astrid's pointing finger and smiled, watching Astrid's younger children, Finn and Máiri, giggle as they playfully tackled their brother.

"He is adjusting well?" Revna asked.

"He is quiet." Astrid breathed deeply, her hand drifting absentmindedly over her middle. "But he is so smart, Revna. There is so much more to my little dragon than he lets anyone see."

Revna watched Jarteign as he lifted Astrid's daughter, Máiri, to the sky, his strength evident but not overbearing. When he placed her gently back on the ground, he puffed his chest and gave a quiet roar that sent his siblings scurrying around him in delight. "A mighty dragon, indeed."

A beautiful glow of contentment lit Astrid's pale skin, and Revna nudged her shoulder. "Am I wrong to assume ye are adding to yer own personal warband again?" Revna let her eyes dip to Astrid's slightly swollen middle.

Astrid's lips pulled back into a wicked grin. "What can I say? Wi' Eowin, I fail miserably at the rule to never let them get their hands on ye."

"As it should be." Cyrene's bright voice came from behind them, Taranau clopping along beside her. "Astrid, ye were made fer motherhood."

With the click of her tongue, Cyrene sent Taranau off to nibble a nearby pile of hay and sank to the ground, trapping Revna between her and Astrid.

"Revna, this is..." Cyrene sighed as she scanned the bustling village and lifted her eyes to the canopy of rich green leaves above them. "Incredible. Truly."

"Aye." Astrid leaned around Revna to meet Cyrene's eye. "I couldna see how it would all work when ye suggested it to the king, how we could keep it a secret, but ye did it."

"I had help." Revna shrugged and cast a thankful gaze to the heavens. "I'm just glad Aksel was as excited as I was at the idea of living in The Dorcha instead of the tower or the villages of Tràigh."

"We miss seeing ye as often, but I ken this is where yer heart lies." Cyrene smiled as she nodded toward Aksel. "As for my brother, as long as ye feed him, he would follow ye anywhere...*Little Bird*."

Astrid barked a laugh at Cyrene's use of Aksel's nickname. Revna only gaped, feigning offense.

420

"I amna the only one wi' a man willing to follow wherever I lead." Revna nudged Astrid and then Cyrene.

"'Tis true," Cyrene said, her eyes gleaming. "I thought Eowin to be a mountain of stone, but the man absolutely melts when Astrid flashes even the hint of a smile."

"Hence their endlessly growing brood," Revna quipped, sliding her eyes to Astrid's belly as Cyrene watched. She nodded when the queen's eyes widened and a smile spread across her lips.

"Me?" Astrid gaped at the queen. "Are ye not the one who tamed the fierce king so that he allowed yer sisters to train a secret army in the woods?"

Cyrene merely bowed her head in the queenliest manner. "'Tis true. His Majesty is a wise leader who saw the benefit of well-trained citizens and who understands one of the greatest rules of warfare."

"And what is that?" Astrid asked.

The queen deferred to Revna with a wink. Revna lowered her chin, feeling her gaze darken wickedly.

"Never..." she said, pausing for effect as she produced a dagger from thin air. "Let yer enemy ken how well armed ye are."

About the Author

Carrie Cotten is a writer of Christian fiction, an accidental farm-girl, homeschool mom, and ministry wife. She lives with her husband and four precious cherubs in a small town in North Carolina.

Carrie is a life-long writer, but it wasn't until 2019 she published her first novel, Dreamwalker. The idea for the story was conceived almost a decade before it's completion. It was not originally a novel that included faith elements. During the years, Carrie came to the important realization, that she simply could not separate who she was as a writer from who she was as a follower of Christ. Once she submitted her whole talent, ideas and creativity, allowing the story to become what it was meant to be, words flowed authentically and the manuscript was completed within a few months.

She hopes that her books inspire readers to share their own faith through everything they do. Above all, she strives, through her words, to share the wonderful news of the saving grace of Jesus Christ.

From Carrie,

I've always had a lot of words. As a child, I would talk my mom's ear off about anything and everything. It's a privilege to get to use my words to share the love of Jesus with readers now.

If anything in this trilogy sparked a flame in your heart to know more about the saving grace of Jesus, or if you're at all unsure where you will spend eternity, please don't let another day pass without finding answers.

You can start here. www.carriecotten.com/gospel

More from this Author

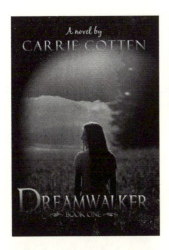
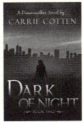
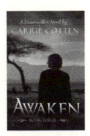

The Dreamwalker series is a speculative fiction trilogy following Andromeda Stone, an ordinary girl with the extraordinary ability to walk in dreams.

The Huntress is a Medieval Christian Fiction series featuring a vibrant cast of strong female warriors, swoon-worthy heroes, and epic faith-filled adventures.